BEAUTIFUL JOE

broadview editions
series editor: L.W. Conolly

"Open thy mouth for the dumb."

Marshall Saunders

Portrait of Margaret Marshall Saunders, from the 1894 edition.

BEAUTIFUL JOE

Margaret Marshall Saunders

edited by Keridiana Chez

broadview editions

Library and Archives Canada Cataloguing in Publication

Saunders, Marshall, 1861-1947, author
  Beautiful Joe / Margaret Marshall Saunders ; edited by Keridiana Chez.

(Broadview editions)
Includes bibliographical references.
ISBN 978-1-55481-173-1 (pbk.)

  1. Dogs—Juvenile fiction. I. Chez, Keridiana, editor II. Title. III. Series:
Broadview editions

PS8487.A867B4 2015   jC813'.4   C2014-907870-6

Broadview Editions

The Broadview Editions series represents the ever-changing canon of literature in English by bringing together texts long regarded as classics with valuable lesser-known works.

Advisory editor for this volume: Juliet Sutcliffe

Broadview Press is an independent, international publishing house, incorporated in 1985.

We welcome comments and suggestions regarding any aspect of our publications— please feel free to contact us at the addresses below or at broadview@broadviewpress.com.

North America
PO Box 1243, Peterborough, Ontario K9J 7H5, Canada
555 Riverwalk Parkway, Tonawanda, NY 14150, USA
Tel: (705) 743-8990; Fax: (705) 743-8353
email: customerservice@broadviewpress.com

UK, Europe, Central Asia, Middle East, Africa, India, and Southeast Asia
Eurospan Group, 3 Henrietta St., London WC2E 8LU, United Kingdom
Tel: 44 (0) 1767 604972; Fax: 44 (0) 1767 601640
email: eurospan@turpin-distribution.com

Australia and New Zealand
Footprint Books
1/6a Prosperity Parade, Warriewood, NSW 2102, Australia
Tel: 61 1300 260 090; Fax: 61 02 9997 3185
email: info@footprint.com.au

www.broadviewpress.com

Broadview Press acknowledges the financial support of the Government of Canada through the Canada Book Fund for our publishing activities.

Typesetting and assembly: True to Type Inc., Claremont, Canada.

PRINTED IN CANADA

Contents

Acknowledgements

I embarked on this project at the suggestion of Richard Kaye, and am very grateful to Carrie Hintz for reading early drafts. Rachel Kravetz and Chong Bretillon also graciously reviewed many versions of the introduction. I would also like to thank Marjorie Mather, Leonard Conolly, and Juliet Sutcliffe at Broadview Press for the care they took in producing this edition.

I am thankful for the indispensable research support provided by Bethany Jost, Archives Coordinator at the Vaughan Memorial Library of Acadia University, for helping me navigate what must be the world's largest collection of Saunders archives. I also received research assistance from Heather Home, Public Services Archivist at Queen's University Archives; Natalya Rattan, Processing Archivist at the Thomas Fisher Rare Book Library of the University of Toronto; Rick Stapleton, librarian at the William Ready Division of Archives and Research Collections of McMaster University; and the librarians at Mount Allison University.

Introduction

If Harriet Beecher Stowe's 1852 *Uncle Tom's Cabin*[1] was the story that ignited the Civil War, then Margaret Marshall Saunders's 1894 *Beautiful Joe* was the book that revolutionized a generation's view of animal welfare. One of the earliest animal viewpoint novels published in the United States,[2] *Beautiful Joe* defined the international movement that changed the way people treated animals.[3]

Yet in spite of her significant contribution to the humane movement, Saunders remains a relatively unknown figure and few have engaged with the text of *Beautiful Joe* as more than a historical artifact. Her life has been chronicled by historians such as Gwendolyn Davies (1995) and Phyllis R. Blakeley (1971). Her writings have been studied as part of theses by Lilian P. Carswell (2004, on the representation of animal subjectivity in North American literature) and Karen E. Sanders (1978, on Saunders's role as an early twentieth-century reformer). *Beautiful Joe* is also included by Elizabeth Waterston as part of Carrie MacMillan's recovery of forgotten Canadian women writers (1993), and in the last decade has enjoyed renewed scholarly interest, as evidenced by discussions in studies by Susan McHugh (2004), Tess Cosslett (2006), Teresa Mangum (2007), and Erica Fudge (2008).

Saunders was born in 1861 in rural Nova Scotia into a warm and loving home of modest means but significant influence. Her parents were Edward Manning Saunders, a prominent Baptist minister, and Maria Kesboro Freeman, daughter of a well-established family. Although in her professional life she signed as Marshall, as a child Saunders was known as Maggie. From grassy

---

1   First serialized in *National Era* from 5 June 1851 to 1 April 1852.

2   Although *Beautiful Joe* is often described as the first animal viewpoint novel published in the US, a dog's "autobiography" had been quietly published in Chicago in 1892: Dr. John Paul Dudley's *Homo et Canis; or, The Autobiography of Old Cato*. A medical treatise masquerading as an autobiography, *Old Cato* seems to not have been widely distributed, and unlike *Beautiful Joe*, uses the dog's voice to argue against the rights and welfare of animals.

3   Many have critiqued the use of the term "animals," favoring instead the designation "non-human animals" or "other animals." For nineteenth-century readers, recognizing human animality was novel, but today the recognition no longer seems to produce a useful feeling of kinship.

plains to concrete lanes, her family moved from the Annapolis Valley to the busy port city of Halifax, a change that made a great impression on the six-year-old Maggie (Saunders, "Story" 42).

Their Halifax home, at the corner of Carleton Street and Spring Garden Road, was dubbed "Noah's Ark" for housing a wide variety of pet animals (Davies, *Education* 7). Maggie's beloved father would help build "rabbit hutches, dog kennels and bird cages—and then disappea[r] into his study to read and prepare his sermon with a favourite setter at his feet" (qtd. in Blakeley 226). Growing up with many pet animals, Maggie grew to value animal companionship. As an adult, she gathered more and more pets, even transforming a large section of her Halifax home into an aviary. By adding a special tunnel from the basement to the screened porch, she was able to provide her birds— almost a hundred in number (Saunders, letter dated 14 March 1904)—with an artificial forest and fresh air. Although her degree of devotion was regarded as a bit eccentric, even in the context of this era's mania for pet-keeping, each year after Christmas local children would help her restock the branches with birds.

A fateful letter, casually written, brought her writing to the notice of a man she called her "hero," Dr. Theodore H. Rand (Waterston 141).[1] Though he suggested that she write about "the beauty of our winter scenery, of the stillness of the woods, the rabbits' track in the snow," she concluded with Rida (Maria, her sister and confidante) that a more "sensational" plotline would be more popular (qtd. in Harkins 179). Rida covered her share of the housework for three weeks while she "scribbled" her first story, "The Blessed Gag of Memory," which was bought by *Frank Leslie's American Magazine* for forty dollars (Blakeley 232). Encouraged by this immediate success, she went on to write more stories for magazines such as *Godey's Lady's Book* and the *Union Signal* before publishing her first novel, *My Spanish Sailor*, at the age of 28. This seafaring romance, though decently reviewed, was not a commercial success. Deflated, Saunders and Rida agreed she should write about what she knew, which was neither romance nor seafaring.

Soon after, Saunders ran across an advertisement from George T. Angell, head of the American Humane Education Society (AHES), seeking a companion novel to Anna Sewell's best-selling autobiography of a horse, *Black Beauty*. In the

---

1 A close friend of her father's, Rand was superintendent of education in Nova Scotia and later chancellor of McMaster University.

summer of 1892, armed with a writing journal, Saunders accompanied her brother to Meaford, where she met an unusual dog: Joe, the dog of William Moore, her brother's future father-in-law. The dog's ears and tail had been cut off by a tenant farmer, and in this wretched state Moore had found him by the roadside. Saunders recognized the pedagogical potential of the story of his suffering. To qualify for the AHES prize, Saunders reset Joe's story in Maine—the state closest to her home province of Nova Scotia. As she describes in a letter dated 19 September 1936 to William A. Deacon, a prominent Canadian literary critic and editor, she Americanized Joe and then "grou[ped her] family pets about him," blending in her own family and her hometown of Halifax (Saunders). Portions of the novel so closely mirror stories described in Angell's *Autobiographical Sketches and Personal Recollections* (1884) that it seems likely that Saunders also read his memoir, as well as his magazine *Our Dumb Animals*, to increase her manuscript's chances of winning. *Beautiful Joe* is, in effect, a quilt of Canadian facts woven with American details.

Black Beauty was itself modeled after Harriet Beecher Stowe's 1852 abolitionist novel, *Uncle Tom's Cabin*. Stowe's novel, an American product, irrevocably shaped abolitionist discourse by its sympathetic portrayal of the long-denied suffering of a population. Sewell wrote her autobiography in this tradition, and the parallels were readily identified by Angell, who marketed *Black Beauty* as "The Uncle Tom's Cabin of the Horse." From the struggle to free enslaved humanity, to the plight of overworked cab horses, to the abused dog, a narrative that effectively emphasized others' capacity for suffering emigrated back and forth across the Atlantic. *Beautiful Joe* set the standard for the genre of the animal autobiography in the US, spearheading the project to distinguish "kindness" from "cruelty."

Beautiful Joe's impact on a generation of international readers is evidenced by its publication statistics: by 1900, the novel sold 625,000 copies in the US, 146,000 copies in the United Kingdom, and 558,000 copies in Canada (Waterston 147). *Beautiful Joe* bears the distinction of being the first book by a Canadian to sell more than a million copies in the author's lifetime (Waterston 137) and has been translated into more than fifteen languages, including Chinese, Japanese, Swedish, Turkish, Esperanto, and Braille (Davies, "Urbanization" 170 and "Regionalism" 148). Along with *Back Beauty*, the novel became part of middle-school curricula across the US and ranked as a favorite among children.

Because of her long-time residence and the fact that most of her work was published in the US, Saunders was claimed by Americans as one of their own. "Confusion has naturally arisen," she wrote, "but I regret it particularly in this case for I am an ardent imperialist" (Saunders, letter dated 14 October 1928). International sojourns were typical of Canadians' literary careers, and Saunders actively courted different national audiences and revised her manuscript to suit their tastes and preferences. Setting this Canadian story in Maine was the first of many manipulations of the novel to access international markets. Her public and private reflections evidence an ambition—and at times, desperation—that reflects the realities of the publishing industry during this period. Canada had a modest literary market and no distinctive literary identity. The economy was depressed, and the few presses that did exist were biased against local literature (Gerson 108). Meanwhile, in the US, publishers and printers proliferated during the latter half of the nineteenth century and welcomed Canadian authors. Saunders was just one of many Canadians who pursued opportunities where they could.[1]

Likely spurred by her first dog story's success as well as her dedication to the humane movement, Saunders went on to publish twenty-five books, ten of which featured animal protagonists and another five which portrayed children's relationships with companion animals.[2] She also used her pen to advocate for playgrounds and to produce reform books for adults, winning a second prize from the AHES for an essay on reducing the rate of crime. Like many women of her station, Saunders dedicated herself to reform causes and participated in and promoted as many as twenty clubs, including the Halifax Local Council of Women, the Playground Association, the Women's Christian Temperance Union, the American Forestry Association, and the Canadian Business and Professional Women's Club. And like many reformers, Saunders's sincere desire to help was at times inconsistent and clouded by middle-class bias (Sanders 3-4).

---

1 Other female Canadian authors who published in the US include Lucy M. Montgomery (author of the best-selling novel *Anne of Green Gables* [Boston: L.C. Page, 1908]), Winnifred Eaton, and Sara Jeannette Duncan (Gerson 108-11). The exodus of Canadian talent was of such a scale that it ignited debate over the nature of Canadian identity. For more on this, see Mount (20-21).

2 For an overview of Saunders's other work, see Waterston.

In the early decades of the twentieth century, *Beautiful Joe* lost favor. Saunders's writing style as well as her subjects, even as they evolved, no longer enticed the public or publishers (Sanders 55). In the early part of the twentieth century, writers like Charles D.G. Roberts and Ernest Thompson Seton developed what is now considered to be Canada's first literary genre, the realistic animal story. In contrast to Saunders's "humanized" animals, the animal story claimed to be a realistic portrayal of animal psychology. (See Appendix E4-E5, pp. 301-04, for excerpts from Roberts and Seton.) This next generation of authors claimed that their fiction was grounded in scientific observation and, as could be expected, favored omniscient narrators over autobiographies and wild animals over domesticated ones. Deeming a work "realistic" to the extent that animal characters were represented as different from humans, and "fake" to the extent that they were represented as similar to humans, the system of valuation these writers subscribed to buttressed the idea that humans and animals were worlds apart. The move towards realism encouraged a more respectful, observation-based treatment, but widened the gap between humans and other animals—a gap that for centuries justified human dominion and the ill-treatment of brute creation. Saunders's characters were far too humanized to be "realistic," and although she considered herself to be of the same "school," the men of that school represented her work as an evolutionary precursor to their own superior work, casting her in the shadows of the past (Norman 29-30). A few letters record how she struggled to remain relevant in this evolving literary landscape; by 1907 she insisted to her publisher that she was working on stories that were "all true," "strictly veracious," "as real as possible," and "convincing" (Norman 20, 29-30, 125). Yet none of her other twenty-four novels sold as well as *Beautiful Joe* (Blakeley 234).[1]

Due to poorly negotiated contracts and continuing copyright issues, royalties for the many editions of Saunders's books petered out to an irregular trickle. Royalties for the many editions of her twenty-five books were few and far between, tapering off to a total of $366.97 in 1941 (Davies, *Education* 12). The aging Saunders supplemented her income by traveling across the US giving talks

---

1 In the 1920s, following *Black Beauty*'s adaptation to film, Saunders entered into negotiations with Universal Film to sell the rights to *Beautiful Joe*, but the film was never produced (Hubman, letters dated 14 December 1922 and 21 February 1923; Saunders, letter dated 24 January 1923; Rice, letter dated 31 July 1923).

on her life's work. The "irresistible quality in her flashing wit and lively humor" (Howard 21) likely made her an engaging speaker, but as her health declined, the lectures were increasingly conducted by her sister. Though celebrated as "Canada's most revered author" in an obituary (Howard 21), the last years of Saunders's life were spent struggling to afford food and keep her Toronto home. Saunders was very ill for the last three years of her life until her death in 1947 at the age of eighty-six.

The Birth of the Humane Movement

Before the nineteenth century, attitudes towards animals were very different. A dog's life was comprised of insult, danger, and want. As veterinary care was scarce and animals' sex lives were less regulated, many would have drowned a "superfluous" animal. Were he to survive to adulthood, he would wander the streets competing with other dogs for scraps. If he were large, he would be used to pull carts loaded with goods; if small, he would be used to run on kitchen treadmills. In the summer, he would flee from the gangs of club-wielding men encouraged to kill strays. Year round, he would evade snatchers who nabbed animals for dog-fighting or scientific experimentation.

Other animals did not fare much better. Malnourished horses bearing excessive weight collapsed, their carcasses littering the streets. Without food or water, sheep were driven for hundreds of miles and cows destined for slaughter were crammed into railroad cars for days. Calves produced "white veal" by being impaled and bled out over the course of a day. A cock would be tethered and greased so that schoolboys, in anticipation of Lent, could pelt it to death. Wild birds had their wings torn off their living bodies to decorate ladies' hats. At country fairs cats would be put in baskets to be shot at, and at protests they would be stuffed into effigies to burn for the sound effect. In bull-baiting, one of many traditions the English brought to America, a bull would be restrained and mutilated (horns sawed off, ears and tail cropped, nose peppered), then attacked by dogs bred and trained for the purpose (hence the name, "bulldog"). Few questioned the ethics of eating animals.[1] From royalty to working poor, fox

---

1 Many would not consider the consumption of animals or their products as cruelty, yet it is an ethical question of equal magnitude: if we ask whether A can whip B, ought we not also ask whether A can kill and eat B? We reflexively presume that killing animals for food is acceptable—an inheritance from nineteenth-century humanitarians.

hunting to cockfights, each station had its own set of practices that impacted millions of animals per year.

This was the grim reality faced by the first animal protection societies: the cadences of every day life depended on the untrammeled exploitation of animals. Before the animal protection movement, only a small minority considered these practices cruel, and keeping an animal solely for companionship was the prerogative of the wealthy.

England is credited as the birthplace of the humane movement, passing the first animal protection law and establishing the first society for the prevention of cruelty to animals in the early 1820s, and the idea of animal welfare quickly gained currency across the Atlantic. Saunders's home province, Nova Scotia, was first to pass anti-cruelty legislation in North America in 1822, and Canada's first animal protection society was established in Montreal in 1869. In the US, less than a year after the Civil War, humanitarians began their crusade for animal welfare. Modeled after the British organization, the American Society for the Prevention of Cruelty to Animals (ASPCA) was founded by Henry Bergh in New York City in 1866. From Boston to Mobile to Los Angeles, humanitarians across the country followed suit. SPCAs intervened in torture, tainted milk, livestock transport, cockfighting, circuses, fur and feather fashions, hunting, pigeon-shooting, and more. A great portion of their work was managing the thousands of stray dogs and cats (most would be "humanely" killed, see Appendix B2, p. 274). They also instituted the first public drinking fountains, ambulances, and low-cost clinics for animals. The first federal statute, the Twenty-Eight Hour Law, was passed in 1873 to mandate rest stops for livestock transported on railroads, and by 1907 every state had anti-cruelty legislation in place.[1]

Why did public opinion shift so dramatically that commonplace behaviors became beyond the pale? Several forces set the stage. Towards the end of the eighteenth century, the English philosopher Jeremy Bentham introduced an alternative argument for animal protection. Instead of focusing on what animals lacked—intelligence, language, the ability to use tools—Bentham emphasized what they shared with humans: the capacity for emotion. Contradicting the French philosopher René Descartes'

---

1 Much of the information on the history of the humane movement in this section of the introduction is provided by Shevelow and Beers. For additional readings on the early history of animal protection, see also Ritvo, Kean, Grier, and Niven.

idea that animals were instinct-driven automatons, Bentham redirected discourse for over a century by asking: "The question is not, Can they *reason?* nor, Can they *talk?* but, Can they *suffer?*" (Wolfe 24). Earlier in the nineteenth century, too, European romanticists and American transcendentalists reengaged nature as a source of study and inspiration (Thomas, Perkins) and abolitionists fostered a sympathy that extended beyond human sufferers (Dolan 7-9). As medical developments improved doctors' ability to relieve pain, it became even less acceptable for any pain to persist unaddressed (Turner). Given these factors, compounded with Darwin's revolutionary argument that humans and other animals were related (*On the Origin of Species*, 1859), animal suffering no longer seemed so irrelevant.

A more immediate concern also contributed to changing attitudes towards animals: humanity's progress became conditional upon animal welfare. As Harriet Ritvo has discussed in her seminal work, *The Animal Estate: The English and Other Creatures in the Victorian Age* (1987), the idea that the course of human evolution proceeded from savagery to civilization shaped much of late nineteenth-century thought. Under this misconception, eradicating cruelty would not only benefit animals, but also further humanity's progress. Seeking to differentiate itself as a class, the urbanite and mostly white bourgeoisie drew new distinctions between what was "civilized" and what was "cruel." The discourse of civilization legitimated projects to "civilize" others—the working class, people of color, barbarians abroad—all in the name of progress.

Yet civilization had its costs. Favoring brain over brawn, many believed, would lead to over-taxed nerves and degenerated bodies, and scientific authorities identified a slew of nervous disorders produced by the civilized condition (Bederman 14-15). This concerned men, whose masculinity was measured by physical prowess, and women, whose reproductive capacity was thought to be endangered by over-thinking. A teleological concept of evolution ranked all humans into racial categories, the white Caucasian as restrained and civilized and the dark-skinned as more passionate and close to the animal (Bederman 22). Under this flawed construct, realignments with the uncivilized— the savage beast, wild nature—would for men counteract the degenerating effects of technological advancement and industrialization. What cruelty would mean, exactly, would be complicated by this contradictory need to both become more civilized by restraining bestial passions and to counter degeneration by indulging bestial passions.

Redefining Kindness: Humane Pet-Keeping

There sits grandfather in his deep chair, gazing at the
embers, dreaming of his childhood; there grandmother opposite with her inseparable knitting, thinking of how she can
make the little ones happy; there father and mother talk of
by-gone days, when they were courting, and there the children play their merry games, the baby rolls on the floor and
Tabby nods in a warm corner, while faithful old dog Tray
watches her with sleepy, yet alert eyes, from the hearth-rug.

This description of a middle-class home, from an 1897 article in
the housekeeping magazine *Family Circle*, shows the centrality of
dogs in the home ("The Home Angel" 17). Even as each family
member goes about their separate activities—daydreaming, knitting, reminiscing, playing, sleeping—they are linked emotionally
by the faithful dog.

Under George T. Angell, the AHES's "heart" education—an
education of sensibilities as opposed to intellect—sought to
change the way young people treated animals. The Bands of
Mercy were Angell's greatest triumph: across the nation, millions
of young people organized to enforce humane ideas and behavior. Children would pledge to "be kind" and to protect animals
and sing songs such as "Don't Rob the Birds, Boys" and "Loving-
Kindness to All" (Eddy 163-64, 99, 36). Teachers were exhorted
to enlist their students and to assign compositions on humane
subjects such as "Acts of Kindness Which I Have Observed" and
"Examples of Animal Intelligence." (See Appendix C, p. 283, for
examples of lesson plans for humane education.) Kindness to
animals became a social activity, and young members were
empowered as heroes combating the "cruel" and "cowardly." And
then, like radiating ripples in a pond, kindness was expected to
reverberate through all levels of society.

In the tradition of "if they only knew," humanitarians argued
that once a child understood that animals could feel pain, he
would change his behavior. But like the adult abuser who derived
pleasure from witnessing or causing harm to animals, the child
who threw rocks at a bird or poked out a cat's eyes would likely
have perceived that animals could feel. Indeed, the animal's
ability to feel and demonstrate pain might have been the source
of entertainment. Humane literature had much more work to do
than to simply show readers that animals could feel.

It became inappropriate ("cruel") for the working class and

poor to keep an animal if they could not emulate bourgeois ways by using their animals primarily for emotional well-being rather than economic gain. In *Beautiful Joe*, the disorder of Jenkins's home is symptomatic of his failure to engage his dogs as intimate companions. Rescued from Jenkins's clutches and into the safety and friendship of the Morris home, Beautiful Joe metaphorically enacts the transformation that the dog as a species underwent, from worthless cur to beloved family member. No longer used to draw heavy carts or run on treadmills, dogs now slept in the house and were trained to perform clever tricks. Completing the family circle, they posed for portraits, wore boots, rode on carriages, and left *cartes de visite* at their neighbors' homes. By 1889, an American writer could claim that "a home without pets is almost as incomplete as one without children" (Potter 38).

Even medical experts exhorted mothers to accept the burden of a household menagerie for the sake of their children (see Appendix D1d, p. 289). As Mrs. Morris explains to Mrs. Montague, her "selfish" sons were cured by the affective economy of pet ownership (p. 76). Once handed birds and rabbits, every boy happily engages himself in the service of others. In this vision, mothers took on a supportive role in humane work: the production of humane men. Laura's duty would also be to direct male interest towards animal protectionism and proactively manage the happiness of her family. (Surpassing expectations, she goes on to devote herself to the happiness of her whole town.)

How were dogs affected by their new role? No more work, and the prospect of a comfortable life—on the surface, this should have been a boon. From literature to art, housekeeping manuals to public monuments, dogs were now extolled as the most disinterested and faithful lovers a human could have. Models of self-sacrifice, dogs would also serve as a moral model in Christian terms—messianic figures. What is particularly remarkable about Joe is not the abuse he suffers, but that he remains faithful to humanity in spite of it. Even the selfish Mrs. Montague is converted into kindness by hearing his story and observing his affectionate obedience: she promptly resolves to visit the poor, be kinder to those she employs, and adopt a dog for her child.

In turn, the dog's sympathy, fidelity, and self-abnegation supported the idea that the dog existed only to shower humans with love. In an early story, Stowe—an unabashed dog lover—describes the dog as "nothing but organized love—love on four feet, encased in fur" (322). Stowe's praise suggests that aside from that love, a dog is "nothing" else; there is no distinct canine identity beyond that of a lover. The animal's attachment was considered instinctual: for another writer, "the dog has *no choice*" but to love "his lord and master" (Miller 221-22). A dog, it was said, would even choose a human over fellow dogs—indeed, over himself. Stories of a dog risking (and often losing) his life to save his endangered master comprise a substantial sub-genre in the nineteenth century's flood of dog literature. Beautiful Joe's devotion to the Morrises peppers the text: a large percentage of the ruminations he shares are declarations of admiration or attachment. Every bruise and cut Joe receives while protecting Laura evidences his value, proving the degree to which he can place human interests above his own. (See Appendix E3, p. 300, for a satirical rendition of this theme.)

This fantasy of the dog's incorruptibility made sense within the binary of selflessness and greed. As the US embraced capitalism, Americans grew anxious, and rightly so, that the race for profits was fostering a fractured society of callous haves and miserable have-nots (Turner 29). The advent of the New Woman— the emancipated woman of the *fin de siècle*, whose life and being no longer revolved solely around her family and home—also threatened to shatter the usefulness of the domestic space as a literal and symbolic haven from public life.[1] The idealized dog offered a satisfying relationship, and no force could "break asunder these voluntary ties or destroy this beloved connection" (Regin 264). Even if the human master went from riches to rags, a dog would stay by his master's side. Honesty, fidelity, and affection were "*stereotyped*" in the nature of dogs by God (Miller 214), and humans hoped to preserve the ability to maintain other relationships by maintaining intimacy with dogs.

Yet *Beautiful Joe* suggests that pet-keeping was not anti-capitalist. Rather, pet-keeping served as training for capitalism. While, as the Reverend Eli Hartness declared in 1872, the dog was "the only animal ... kept out of pure love" (303), that love was designed to prepare boys to enter the marketplace. Psychologists and educational experts argued that keeping a dog was the best way to socialize a boy if he was to grow up "adequately prepared for his life-work" (Marsh 83). Mrs. Morris's pitch to Mrs. Montague about the value of pet-keeping emphasizes that pets create responsibilities that discipline the children into "men of business" (p. 77). Boys practiced manhood by providing for dependents, with pets standing in for their future families:

---

1   For more on the New Woman, see Richardson, Showalter, and Ledger.

mouths to feed, bodies to clothe and house, and minds to break and train. (See Appendix D, p. 287, for readings on pet-keeping culture.)

Monetary investment followed emotional investment, giving rise to the modern pet industry, which further intertwined pet-keeping with the materialism that the "pure love" of a pet was supposed to transcend. Home menageries included dogs, cats, badgers, rabbits, birds, fish, reptiles, and amphibians (Saunders once proclaimed that there was "nothing more lovely than a lapful of little snakes" [Pomeroy 17]). Each of these acquired its own set of accouterments: food, housing, bedding, clothing, manuals, and toys. The dog collar industry rose from five thousand to one million dollars per annum in just ten years; by 1888, one could find dog collars ranging in cost from twenty-five cents to a $250 production of "brilliantly scaled lizard-skin" (Regin 262, 265). Existing breeds were altered to suit the fashions, and most of the breeds we recognize today were created during this period, their price tags reflecting their pedigree. The great paradox of the nineteenth century's cult of the dog, then, was that the dog as a species was worshipped to counteract the negative effects of modernity, but only select dogs were singled out for special treatment based on a scale that was thoroughly intertwined with capitalism.

Redefining Kindness: Humane Rescue

Opponents of animal protectionism represented activists as "sentimental"—weak-willed, ruled by their emotions—thus aligning animal protectionism with feminine irrationality. For a woman to behave in a feminine way was unfortunate but expected, and these ascriptions would bar women (either by legal or social convention) from the right to vote, run for public office, pursue most careers, or own property upon marriage. For a man to act in a flagrantly feminine fashion was to contravene the "natural" law of his sex. A sentimental man's excessive affect was even more offensive when it infringed on the masculine sphere of action (politics, physical labor, public labor, railroads, science).

Even a severe and humorless gentleman such as New York's Henry Bergh could be discredited by the charge of being irrationally sentimental. A critic declared, in a puzzling redefinition of love, that "[t]he true animal lover should be above sentiment" (Berdoe 74). Bergh would seem to have met this requirement: moved by ethical considerations alone, Bergh dedicated his life to protecting creatures whose company he did not like. A friend attested that "never in his life did he see Mr. Bergh lay his hand upon a horse in caress, however slight" and that when touched on the knee by a three-pound dog, his "whole body shrank away, and unmistakable repulsion showed in every feature" ("Henry Bergh as Don Quixote" 76-77). Yet in spite of being untainted by any personal attachment to animals, Bergh was lambasted as a zealot, variously called "Don Quixote," "the ubiquitous biped," "the Moses of the oppressed beasts" (Lossing 847), and the "prince of fanatics" ("Bergh on Pasteur" 217).

Intervening in this characterization of humane men, *Beautiful Joe* challenged the public's understanding of the gendered nature of humane work. Seeking to engage males—the likely perpetrators of animal abuse—*Beautiful Joe* refashioned humaneness into a heroic endeavor. Repurposing the "sanguinary streak" that she believed present "[e]ven in the best of" boys (Saunders, *Paradise* 216), Saunders represented animal protectionism as an opportunity for violence and self-empowerment. When Harry rescues Joe from Jenkins, his actions are quick and powerful. "[S]pringing off," and "hurrying" faster than Jenkins' eye could follow, confronting cruelty "[i]n a trice," with a "fierc[e]" and "angr[y]" manner, and "seiz[ing]" and "pounding ... with all his might," the young Harry overtakes a full-grown adult male (p. 62). His first impulse is not to render first aid to the injured animal—that would be what a girl would do—but to pummel the abuser, suggesting that humaneness granted boys a license to righteous violence.[1]

An anecdote in Angell's memoir illustrates this alternative representation of the humane rescuer, in a tenor that *Beautiful Joe* reflects. Angell describes how "[a] cow run over by an engine in the south part of [Chicago], and both her forefeet cut off, was permitted to lie in a public street twenty-four hours with nobody to care for her; rough men and boys looking at her, some laughing at her, and some poking her with sticks" (George Angell 38). A passive object of sympathy, the helpless female body is lewdly ogled and prodded at by "rough" males. Rescuers, in contrast, were portrayed as able and commanding: in newspapers and periodicals, Bergh was described as "a noticeably tall gentleman" who would "step suddenly" from the curb, "seizing" an abused horse "by the head," and "sternly command[ing]" the abuser to

---

1 Saunders wrote: "As a child, I preferred boys' story books because they had more life, more energy than girls' books" (qtd. in Davies, *Education* 3).

cease and desist (Allen 166-67). The humanitarians responded to accusations of sentimentality not by challenging gendered bifurcation but by abiding by its rules. Like the founders of the ASPCA, Saunders shared in the construction of the masculine rescuer who saves helpless females from barbarous males, a construct that ultimately reaffirmed the opposition's most powerful construct. (See Appendix D1a, p. 287.)

Yet Saunders was torn between her desire to curb cruelty and her admiration for masculine prowess. She critiqued the "civilized" men who eschewed physical labor to "work their brains till they haven't got any more back-bone than a caterpillar" (p. 176), but worried that masculine physicality would find outlet in violence against weaker creatures. The mastery of other beings was gender-appropriate, but to Saunders the objects of that mastery needed redesignation: the humane boy would master the cruel man instead.

Beautiful Joe intertwines the fantasy of speaking animals with facts, leveraging the latter—along with Saunders's insistence in the preface that the stories relayed are true—to support the leap of faith for the former. Erica Fudge considers Beautiful Joe merely "a furry human," an anthropomorphism that "inevitably turns around on itself" by "entirely cancel[ing] out the presence of the pet as animal" (50-51). Yet the question of animal autobiography is complicated by the fact that even though Joe is humanized, he aspires to represent a dog's point of view—a viewpoint that boys could read as believably canine.

The project of making humane work appropriate for males presented a paradox: if the boy reader identified with both Harry and Joe, he would be positioned as both manly rescuer and emasculated victim. The former would be appealing, the latter repulsive. *Beautiful Joe* responded by partly empowering the abused dog so that the boy reader could sustain sympathetic identification with the victim without fully inhabiting a feminized position. Even though he is at Jenkins's mercy, Joe does not submit. The abused dog, in fact, mirrors his rescuer by taking action to protect himself and the females in his life: avenging his mother with a savage bite, protecting Laura from arson, and saving the household cat Malta from the murderous Spitz. And as the would-be arsonist is none other than his former master, the cruel Jenkins, the novel conflates Joe's act of self-sacrifice with his own revenge. The abused dog might be the victim vis-à-vis the monstrous Jenkins and the heroic Harry, but his victimhood has its limits.

The position of females in the novel reflects how women's role in humane work was marginalized. Most SPCA members were white women, but the presidents and directors were almost exclusively white men (Beers 53). Slotted into auxiliary organizations, women led in important (but less valued and more traditionally feminine) areas, such as establishing the first animal shelters and low-cost animal clinics. Still, women such as Philadelphia's Caroline Earle White encouraged other women to intervene in public cruelty and women continued to work on issues concerning large animals (Beers 56). The humane movement, along with other popular progressive causes of the period (temperance, child welfare, working conditions, etc.), provided opportunities for white, middle-class women to exert increasing amounts of influence (Beers 54), yet the history of the humane movement appears on the surface to be a history of great men: men who gained legitimacy by distancing themselves from the taint of femininity.

In the dynamic of *Beautiful Joe*, females serve as the inspiration to humane work in three ways: as sympathetic victims, as barometers of moral outrage, and as lights in a world of darkness. While showing no reluctance to exact justice himself, Harry is reluctant to "tattle" on Jenkins, but Laura insists they report the crime to the police. Her capacity for sympathy then disqualifies her from engaging directly in animal protection: later, when Harry and Laura discover the cruelties of the Englishman, she appears overwhelmed (p. 206). Unable even to assert her desire to help with any conviction, Laura is relegated to the house, where the males would visit when they "want[ed] cheering up" (p. 209). The supposed callousness that made humaneness difficult for men would be precisely the trait that especially prepared them to undertake the humane work, supported by sympathetic women.

In the 1902 sequel, *Beautiful Joe's Paradise* (see Appendix E1, pp. 297-98), Saunders pushes females further into the background of humane work. Both texts emphasize the importance of male manual labor, but the sequel no longer allows women to serve as its inspiration. The narrator is Sam Emerson, a boy who learns the value of humaneness after traveling to an island where dead animals await their masters. In this nearly all-male paradise, the creatures are "never idle" (Saunders, *Paradise* 112)—making homes, baking cakes and breads, landscaping. There is only one female: a suspicious necromancer cat who would "deceive any one" (Saunders, *Paradise* 108), Pussy is called upon only when "magic" is absolutely necessary, but otherwise excluded from island affairs. This misogynistic turn came likely as Saunders endeavored to increase the opportunities for male involvement in humane work, with the confident assumption that most females would act mercifully to animals.

Redefining Cruelty

Kindness entailed pet-keeping and humane rescue, but what was cruel? As the preceding section suggests, cruelty was not simply a list of forbidden acts. *Beautiful Joe* redefined cruelty as the purposeful infliction of pain, for no appropriate reason, on a creature that was at one's mercy.

Motive was everything. First, to be deemed "cruel," the alleged abuser would have to intend to cause pain, which also entailed that he be aware of the possibility of animal pain. Second, the pain would be unnecessary—i.e., serve no other purpose than pain itself. (Making a coat, a pair of boots, or a dinner would be deemed appropriate purposes.) Third, the alleged victim must be recognized as a worthy object of sympathy. When the kindly Uncle Wood shoots Bruno in the head, he is not considered "cruel," but when the milkman Jenkins kills the puppies, he is. Both willfully kill an animal, but the former (who does so calmly and with reluctance) is "humane" while the latter (who acts in anger and without remorse) is "cruel." "Horse, or man, or dog aren't much good till they learn to obey" (p. 148), says Uncle Wood, and a failure to obey signals the worthlessness that justifies Bruno's disposal. Yet Uncle Wood's words ring shallow: Bruno was fairly good at tracking sheep, but is killed because he disobeys his master's rules, looks rough, and *might* bite someone. The killing takes place behind the cover of a barn after much self-pity on the part of the killer, who can hardly bear to think himself cruel. Instead of empathizing with the condemned animal, he bemoans how he *must* be "cruel." The focus is on the state of Uncle Wood's soul, obscuring Bruno's subjective experience.

What the reader sees is an unsympathetic animal. While he is in fact a helpless victim, Bruno does not adequately perform the part: he fails to submit. In the moments before Bruno's execution, the novel curbs the reader's sympathy by describing him as "snapping and snarling" and full of anger and wickedness (p. 149), an anger that is not attributed to the fact that he is being dragged to his execution.[1] According to the nineteenth-century construct of humaneness, the appropriate subject of sympathy must—like Angell's crippled cow—refrain from aggression against those who are marked as "humane" and "good," even those with murderous intent. The "good" animal proves his goodness by his unshakable faith in his master, his total submission to his master's will, and his willingness to yield even his life.

Humaneness, then, forecloses neither physical violence nor killing animals: only acting with rage, anger, and passion or against a "good" dog, as modeled by Beautiful Joe. The "humane" actor is excused for any pain felt by the animal since the pain was an unintended consequence of a necessary killing. In Roxanne Harde's reading (2009), while Saunders brings human and animal in closer affinity, she ultimately refuses to grant animals an equal subject position to humans.[2]

Retreat to Conservatism

While the tide was shifting for animals in the public eye, resistance from the status quo was powerful. The most virulent and organized opposition to animal protectionism came from the medical community, which defended the practice of experiment-

---

1   This was in fact Saunders's express intention. In a letter dated 14 February 1894, Saunders explained that Bruno was included so she could have "different kinds of dogs" in her story. "Bruno was an ugly one," she said, "who would be ugly under any circumstances. When Mr. Wood took him out to kill him Bruno snarled and snapped not at the gun but out of pure wickedness. If Bruno had gone to his death mildly and gently it would have been a cruel thing to kill him. He was a bad dog and ought to have been put out of the world."

2   Later in life, Saunders was increasingly concerned with the ethical implications of consuming animals and became a vegetarian. Over time, she began finding other uses of animals problematic as well. In 1918, she sent an editor a replacement for a photograph that showed her in a coat presumably made of animal materials, perhaps fur (Coleman, letter dated 15 March 1918). The reply to her letter—from the managing editor of the *National Humane Review*, no less—shows how the mainstream humane movement persisted in believing that the use of animals *per se* was not inhumane: "It is rather hard to be a consistent humanitarian to its logical conclusion.... Personally I rather doubt whether the Creator intended that we should abstain from meat and from the use of animal products" (Coleman, letter dated 15 March 1918).

ing on animals without regard to the pain they caused their living subjects (Beers 122). Drawing on direct excerpts from published accounts by the researchers themselves, the English journalist and suffragist Francis Power Cobbe catalogued how in European and American medical schools and research laboratories men performed "hundreds of experiments in which they ke[pt] animals skinned, with nerves laid bare, irritated with electricity and in every possible way, cut open their living bodies, roast[ed], crucif[ied], boil[ed], subject[ed] them to experiments causing the most excruciating agony in the most sensitive nerves" (6).[1] As domestic animals grew more beloved and protected, the idea of cold, rational men bending over a dog strapped onto an operating table, manipulating its muscles and nerves, became abhorrent. Encouraged by Cobbe, Philadelphia's Caroline White established the American Anti-Vivisection Society in 1883 to argue for oversight and restrictions on the practice. (See Appendix B3a, pp. 277-78.)

Defenders of vivisection accused humanitarians of selfishly indulging their sympathetic feelings. "[L]et us attend to humanity's crying needs," says an 1897 article in *Medical World*, "before spending precious time and energy on dogs and cats" ("Questions for Anti-Vivisectionists" 310). A specialist in nervous disorders even suggested that the new mania for pet-keeping was a form of mental disease. In 1909, Dr. Charles Dana pronounced the discovery of a condition he called "zoophil-psychosis," a morbidly obsessive love and concern for the suffering of animals that affected the weak-minded (i.e., women and feminized men) (383). (See Appendix D1a, pp. 287-88.) Tied to other "nervous disorders" such as neurasthenia, hysteria, and obsessive psychosis, zoophil-psychosis was a transgression of the tacit rule that emotional investment should be restricted to the human species. Yet this argument was perhaps the least sound of the opposition's arsenal, since many animal protectionists were also engaged in projects like abolition, women's suffrage, temperance, pacifism, labor conditions, and child welfare. In fact, Bergh established the New York Society for the Protection of Children in 1875 and Angell was a general humanitarian who engaged in causes ranging from world peace to fire escapes to chairs for shop-girls (George Angell 23, 40, 81).

---

1 Retrospectively, Saunders wished she had included something about vivisection, but thought it was "almost too painful a subject for children" (letter dated 14 February 1894).

Critics also criticized humanitarians for imposing their bourgeois values on the working poor. *Beautiful Joe* makes a direct plea for this section of society in Chapter 22, but defines middle-class values and practices as morally superior. Nor would the voices of the working poor be included in policy-making: annual membership dues for most SPCAs would also have been prohibitively expensive for most working poor and a great proportion of African Americans (Beers 52-53). But the class bias question was more complex. Generosity is a luxury of those who have the money, time, and connections to get organized. A man whose livelihood did not immediately depend on the use of animals was also more likely to feel sympathy for animal suffering than a man who relied on animal labor for survival. Most reformers believed, like the Morrises, in their ability and duty to uplift the ignorant masses.

Ultimately, the controversy over vivisection tested the limits of the new definition of cruelty. The alleged abusers were not, for the most part, taken up with rage when they cut into living dogs, nor aiming to cause pain for their own amusement. These learned men of science could claim altruistic motivations: they exchanged the actual suffering and killing of animals for potential cures for human ailments. Perhaps because it was more likely that women (particularly those financially dependent on charity for medical care) would suffer a similar fate at the hands of doctors,[1] women took the lead in agitating for the abolition of vivisection. Despite the class bias of the humane movement, its discourse easily accommodated these new enemies: while the brutish working man who clubbed an animal was taken up by bestial passions, the scientist's humanity was diminished by his excessive dedication to cold, rational "brain work." But as this new confrontation pitted middle-class women (and animals) against middle-class men (and science), it proved very damaging to the humane movement.

The humane movement would eventually fissure over the issue of using animals in medical research, the mainstream increasingly limiting its scope to dogs and cats while the more radical splintered off into new groups. Yet animal protectionism had become fashionable. By the turn of the century, the transformation of the meaning of a "humane society"—from a society that worked on "the revival of drowning persons through resusci-

---

1 For more on human experimentation, see Lederer, Washington, Hurren, and Lansbury.

tation" to one devoted to kindness and mercy to all living beings—was complete ("humane").

The Evolution of the Text

In its 120-year history, *Beautiful Joe* has been translated, expanded, and abridged. Some revisions were licensed and some not, some were made by Saunders and many by others. The core premise—a dog mutilated, then rescued—survives every edition, but characters, major incidents, and meaningful critiques have fallen in and out over time. These substantial emendations raise questions about textual authority and the nature of the text.

From its incipiency, *Beautiful Joe* was shaped by Saunders's first significant publishing contact at the American Baptist Publication Society (ABPS), Col. Charles H. Banes. Their relationship was initially strained—each inexperienced in the book business, they grew impatient with each other as they blundered through the perplexing issue of Canadian copyright, but grew friendly and personal over the coming years (Langille 3, Saunders, letters dated 23 July 1907 and 31 July 1907). In a 9 April 1894 letter, the ABPS editor advised against revising the text to appease critics, but on 21 April wrote with critical suggestions to rearrange, condense, and revise (Banes). (Saunders later recollected that she had been much relieved when he gave up the plan [letter dated 31 July 1907].) Even as she resisted tampering, she was also "anxious" about sales, and described herself in a 20 March letter as ready to "make any changes that may be desired" by an influential Canadian endorser "that [would] be calculated to extend the influence of the book" (Saunders, letter dated 20 March 1894). Other versions were soon produced to please different readerships: she called one early version the "W.C.T.U. edition" because it incorporated suggestions by members of the prominent Women's Christian Temperance Union (Binderup 53), and in 1896 the ABPS authorized London's Jarrold & Sons to produce a revised school edition (Langille 6, 140). The 1907 edition includes a new chapter, "Black Jim," largely written by a later ABPS contact, then stylized by Saunders to fit in with the rest (Norman 24). (See Appendix F1, pp. 307-12 for the chapter.)

Just as the original Canadian story was set in Maine for sales, the English editions evolved with specific markets in mind. The London firm Gay and Bind (G&B) found plenty of areas for revision. In a 28 February 1894 letter, her liaison John Blaikie described how—in addition to changing the title,[1] removing Americanisms, shortening the work, and lowering the price—G&B suggested that the story be reset in Canada "to bring it under the shadow of the English flag." G&B also pushed for omission of the "cruel Englishman" character. "His nationality does not seem essential to his depravity," G&B maintained, "but if he must be a foreigner you had better make him a Russian General (N.B. This last line is meant for a joke)" (Blaikie, letter dated 28 February 1894). This "joke" expresses a desire to distance Englishness from cruelty, occluding the fact that western nations were jockeying for the distinction of being most humane. Saunders reluctantly conceded, then retracted in a 2 April 1898 letter: "The book is essentially American—no alterations can make it English." Yet while the 1895 Jarrold & Sons edition[2] still refers to that character as "the Englishman," the 1925 Jarrolds Pubs. edition panders to the English market at the expense of her first readership: the "cruel Englishman" becomes a "gentleman" with ties to New York financiers.

G&B had also found the reading experience far too slow. Characterizing Beautiful Joe as a "phon-dog-raph[er]"—a mere "reporter" of others' stories—the London publisher requested radical excisions: entire chapters and most of Joe's musings and conversations with other animals (Blaikie, letter dated 28 February 1894). "It is not necessary," G&B chastised, "to make your story range over the whole Animal Kingdom and it spoils the 'go' of the narrative" (Blaikie, letter dated 28 February 1894). This critique suggests that, for English audiences, depictions of canine feeling would not compensate for a lack of an action-centered plot, or that perhaps they responded negatively to stories where protagonists lead comfortable lives. English texts of abuse and rescue emphasized the abuse segment of the rescue plotline:

---

1 Saunders's advisors pointed out the popularity of Beautiful Jim Key, a real-life horse. Known as the "Equine Millionaire," Beautiful Jim was trained by Dr. William Key, a former slave, and could supposedly read, write, spell, do math, tell time, and more. To avoid confusion, Saunders was advised to change her title to "Handsome Joe" or "From the Dog's Point of View" for the English edition (Blaikie, letters dated 28 February 1894 and 17 February 1894). For more on Beautiful Jim Key, see Mim Eichler Rivas, *Beautiful Jim Key: The Lost History of a Horse and a Man Who Changed the World* (New York: William Morrow, 2005).

2 Saunders seems to have chosen Jarrold over G&B for the first UK printing of the novel.

Sewell's *Black Beauty* and William Gordon Stables's *Sable & White: The Autobiography of a Show Dog*, a dog abduction story published in Britain a year before *Beautiful Joe*, dwell on the abuse suffered by the titular animal for nearly the entire novel. Unlike its English model *Black Beauty*, Saunders's novel also refuses the possibility that Jenkins's abusive character is shaped by structural inequalities that reduce lives to the narrow focus of survival. Saunders's working man, Jenkins, is simply depicted as a man whose idleness directly leads to his cruelty. At the same time, even though both Sewell and Saunders depicted the aristocracy as capable of great cruelty, Sewell credited a noble lineage for Black Beauty's excellent temper. These distinctions intersect with the gender dynamics of each novel: Beautiful Joe's ugliness, traceable to his lack of pedigree, is a crucial element of the masculinized aesthetic that Saunders developed to appeal to boys. No reader could accuse Beautiful Joe of effeminacy. Being a mutt also puts Joe on a lower social scale, associated with more masculinity and less restraint, even as his behavior is otherwise impeccably respectable. Beautiful Joe's impulsivity is celebrated, whereas as Peter Stoneley has argued with respect to Black Beauty and Uncle Tom, that kind of willfulness—coded as passionate, associated with beasts and dark-skinned bodies—was something to be wary of (6). Unlike his progenitors, Beautiful Joe was associated with middle-class whiteness, and for him, passionate virility would be empowering.

Beautiful Joe purposefully ranged over the whole animal kingdom in order to fulfill the purpose of the AHES contest: portraying the "Kind and Cruel Treatment of Domestic Animals and Birds in the Northern States." The contest's purpose, in turn, was to change the way people perceived all animals, in the expectation that it would also transform their treatment. The English publisher's plan would have radically changed *Beautiful Joe* from a pedagogical tool for general humaneness into a one-animal show—the effect of which can be seen in the 1920, 1925, and 1934 editions, where Saunders apparently acceded to significant abridgement.

The novel faced other dangers abroad: its first foreign translation was unlicensed. In 1895, the Swedish firm Fahlcrantz & Co. pirated the novel and refused royalties to Saunders despite her repeated entreaties (Langille 61-66, 75). Worse, this unlicensed translation was done by the woman whom the ABPS had permitted to translate the novel into Norwegian (Langille 54, 57). The ABPS responded by pirating back this Swedish translation to offer by subscription to Swedish readers (Langille 70). Saunders also took risks in publishing a German edition despite being unable to secure copyright, thus exposing that edition to reissue and translation (Langille 6). Later revisions of *Beautiful Joe* record the evolving cultural politics of animal protectionism during the course of the twentieth century. After Saunders's death, *Beautiful Joe*'s gender and class constructs were modernized. In the 1965 edition, humane work no longer requires vigilantism; it is inappropriate for males to take the law into one's hands. Harry's attack on Jenkins is significantly less violent and he no longer threatens to physically harm the man who left his farm animals to starve. The female role no longer focuses on nurturing or providing good cheer, and Laura is treated less condescendingly by the males in her life. Yet after these stereotypically feminine behaviors are omitted, Laura's role is significantly reduced (there is one significant addition, discussed below). In the 1990 edition, a special edition produced by Storytellers Ink for distribution at inner city schools across the country, male violence is even more inappropriate and Laura's place in the narrative is further limited. Across these later editions, the novel also evolved into a fantasy of classlessness as virtually all servants disappear and all unpleasant remarks about "beggars" are omitted.

Sanitizing *Beautiful Joe* further, the 1965 and 1990 editions also excise Saunders's critiques of intemperance. To modern readers far distanced from the history of the Eighteenth Amendment,[1] the movement appears archaic. Yet for the bulk of the nineteenth century temperance was the largest women-led movement, at least until men took control in the early twentieth century (Cordell 4, Beard 53). Saunders, like many progressive middle-class women of the time, supported temperance along with many other causes (Beers 54, Sanders). At a time when Americans consumed significantly more alcohol than today, temperance discourse wielded such great influence on American culture that it led thirty-six states to amend the Constitution for a total ban (Oshinsky).

The amount of cruelty and violence in the novel also significantly decreased over time. By the 1920s, Saunders had toned

---

1 The National Prohibition Act of 1920, also known as the Volstead Act, was enacted as the Eighteenth Amendment to completely ban the manufacture, sale, or transportation of intoxicating liquors. The legal alcohol business was replaced by untaxed moonshiners and bootleggers, many affiliated with violent criminal gangs operating with the aid of corrupt officials. Prohibition had such unintended negative effects that it was repealed by popular demand in 1933 (Oshinsky).

down the violence of the scene where Joe's siblings are murdered, omitting the most graphic sentence, "[s]ome of them he seized by the legs and knocked against the stalls, till their brains were dashed out, others he killed with a fork" (pp. 59-60). The details are elsewhere available, but not at the key moment of trauma. Sensibilities to depictions of violence had changed since the time of *Beautiful Joe*'s original publication, particularly after witnessing the unprecedented horrors of the Great War.

Bruno's execution, which in 1894 drew the boundary between kindness and cruelty, also evolved over the course of the editions. In the 1920 and 1934 editions, details are blurred and deemphasized. In the 1925 edition, Uncle Wood announces his purpose and the chapter ends with the line asserting his moral innocence—the line that expresses how much he "hate[s] to take life" (p. 149). This edition also omits how Joe bears partial witness to the deed and expresses sympathy for Bruno. In contrast, in the 1965 edition, Bruno is given a last-minute reprieve from death: the one addition to Laura's role in this edition is that she discovers that the dog's surliness was caused by the pain of a burrowing wood tick—an awkward moment that is inconsistent with Uncle Wood's usual attentiveness to his animals. (See Appendix F3, p. 313.)

In these posthumous editions, all the blood and most of the animal abuse are erased, reflecting evolving practices in the treatment of animals. Farming, butchering, and the care of farmed animals have become increasingly brutal and hidden from public scrutiny. Were it not for the occasional hidden camera, today's public would have little idea how their food is raised or their winter coats produced.[1] The drastic erasures in the posthumous editions do the most damage to the case of farmed animal welfare.

---

1 Recent legislation and policies attempt to further reduce public scrutiny. Anti-whistleblower ("ag-gag") bills have been proposed in the last two decades to prohibit the recording of images or video of animal farming abuses (Oppel, Carlson, Barclay). The United States Department of Agriculture, which sets federal policy on agriculture, conservation, energy, and food, is also moving to expand a 1998 pilot program that allows factory farms to inspect their own facilities for food safety. This would entail firing about 1,000 federal inspectors even as factories propose to run their kill lines 25 per cent faster, killing as many as 175 birds per minute with only the oversight of a single inspector (Avila, Philpott, Jalonick). If such policies are put in place, American consumers would find more ready meat on their plates—but at what cost? For more discussion, see Michael Carolan, *The Real Cost of Cheap Food* (NY: Earthscan, 2011).

As the tales of other animal characters fall off, not only does the story become narrowly limited to one dog's tale, but that tale is thinned as well. Joe's reflections and meditations are decimated—he little wonders, knows, thinks, remembers—and he no longer exhibits the ability to know others' minds or form meaningful relationships. Whether made for reasons of length or to make the canine representation more realistic, the cuts reduce what used to be a detailed catalogue of the human ill-treatment of animals into a story about a single "bad guy" and a singular dog. The treatment Joe deserves no longer calls forth duties toward the rest of animalkind. Unexpectedly, *Beautiful Joe*'s story becomes more like its original inspiration, *Black Beauty*.

Even though the exploitation of farm animals has worsened since Saunders's death (Francione 184), each ensuing version has omitted more and more of humanity's wrongs against animals from the 1894 edition's encyclopedic catalogue. Perhaps the full-length *Beautiful Joe*—once dubbed part of "the declaration of independence for animals" (Graham 100)—was rejected not because of its perceived artlessness and relatively simple style, but because it would expose contemporary readers to the affective demands of an ethic they no longer wish to invest in. Unlike the "realistic" animal stories of Roberts and Seton, and in spite of its limitations, Saunders's *Beautiful Joe* demands a broad ethical response—and action.

Margaret Marshall Saunders: A Brief Chronology[1]

1861	Born in Milton, Nova Scotia.
1867	Family moves from Berwick to Halifax.
1876	Attends Trafalgar House School in Edinburgh, Scotland.
1877	Studies in Orleans, France.
1878	Returns to Halifax.
1889	Death of her sister, Laura Knowles Saunders, aged 17, on whom "Miss Laura" would be based.
1889-90	Attends Dalhousie College.
1889-93	Begins writing stories for magazines; publishes "A Gag of Blessed Memory" in *American* magazine.
1889	Publishes *My Spanish Sailor* in England.
1893	*Beautiful Joe* wins prize from American Humane Education Society.
1894	*Beautiful Joe: An Autobiography* is published by the American Baptist Publication Society.
1895-97	Lives in Boston.
1895	Publishes *Charles and His Lamb*.
1896	Publishes *For the Other Boy's Sake, and Other Stories*.
1897	Publishes *The House of Armour, Daisy: A Tale*, and *King of the Park*.
1897	Spends summer in rural Acadia.
1898	Spends autumn in Halifax.
1898	Publishes *Rose à Charlitte: An Acadien Romance*.
1898-1900	Travels in the US; lives in California with her sister Rida; attends classes at the University of California.
1899	Publishes *Deficient Saints: A Tale of Maine*.
1900	Returns to Halifax.
1900	Publishes *For His Country, and Grandmother and the Crow* and *Her Sailor: A Love Story*, a revision of her first novel.
1901	Publishes *Tilda Jane: An Orphan in Search of a Home*.
1902	Publishes *Beautiful Joe's Paradise*.

---

1 Most of the information in this chronology is from Sanders.

1902	Travels to Europe with the Moores, her brother's in-laws, who owned the dog on which Beautiful Joe was modeled.
1903	Publishes *The Story of the Gravelys*.
1904-06	Buys and lives on a farm in the Annapolis Valley with her sister Grace, with whom she spends the rest of her life.
1904	Publishes *Nita: The Story of an Irish Setter*.
1905	Publishes *Princess Sukey: The Story of a Pigeon and Her Human Friends*.
1906	Publishes *Alpatock: The Story of an Eskimo Dog*.
1906	Publishes "Essay on Prevention of Crime."
1908-09	Travels to Rochester, New York, and Boston.
1908	Publishes *My Pets: Real Happenings in My Aviary*.
1909	Returns to Halifax; travels to Maine for six months to rest.
1909	Publishes *Tilda Jane's Orphans*.
1910	Publishes *The Girl From Vermont: The Story of a Vacation School Teacher*.
1911	Receives honorary MA from Acadia University.
1913	Publishes *Pussy Black-Face: The Story of a Kitten*.
1914	Halifax house sold; family moves to Toronto.
1916	Publishes *"Boy" the Wandering Dog*.
1919	Travels with sister across the US for material.
1919	Publishes *Golden Dicky: The Story of a Canary and His Friends*.
1920-40	Tours with sister lecturing on "Marshall Saunders, The Famous Canadian Author."
1920	Publishes *Bonne Prince Feltar: The Story of a Pony and His Friends*.
1922	Publishes *Jimmy Gold Coast: The Story of a Monkey and His Friends*.
1927	Publishes *Esther de Warren: The Story of a Mid-Victorian Maiden*.
1934	Receives Commander of the British Empire (CBE), one of Britain's highest civilian honors.
1947	Dies in Toronto.

A Note on the Text

The text reproduced here is the 1894 edition, the first published edition of the novel, issued by the American Baptist Publication Society (ABPS). While small errors, virtually all of punctuation, have been corrected, the text otherwise retains all the original language, spelling, and syntax.

Though a case might be made for using the 1907 edition, which Saunders considered her favorite, the 1894 edition had already sold over half a million copies before 1907 and reprints of the 1894 version continued uninterrupted after its first issue (Norman 63, 31, 16). In fact, the ABPS hoped the 1907 edition would "stimulate" the sale of the 1894 edition and had their "hearts set on selling a million copies of all editions" (Norman 67). In post-1907 sales statistics, no distinction seems to be made between editions. In any case, between the 1894 and 1907 editions there were few changes (for reasons of cost, Saunders was constrained from making too many revisions), excepting the addition of the "Black Jim" chapter, which is included in full in Appendix F1, p. 307. Editions published after 1907, as discussed below, were significantly revised and updated to reflect evolving attitudes towards species, class, and gender.

To show how the later editions represented characters and events differently, the text includes illustrations from the 1894, 1895, 1907, 1922, and 1934 editions.

1893 manuscript
The 1893 manuscript is housed at Acadia University's Esther Clark Wright Archives. Excepting minor details, the 1894 edition was largely faithful to the manuscript.

1895 edition (London: Jarrold & Sons)
This edition is substantively the same as the 1894 original.

1907 edition (Philadelphia: Griffith & Rowland)
For this new "gift" edition, the ABPS prepared new plates with larger type, larger pages, illustrations, and a sturdy binding. Aside from one new chapter, "Black Jim," on a mischievous crow, the 1907 edition has few other revisions. In order to cause the least disruption to typesetting, Saunders was constrained from revising the "too long sentences [and] faults of construction" (qtd. in

Norman 20). The new chapter (see Appendix F1, p. 307) was added at the suggestion of her ABPS contact, Charles M. Roe, who provided the first draft based on his memories of a favorite pet crow (Norman 20).

1920 (New York: Grosset & Dunlap), 1922 (New York: A.L. Burt), 1925 (London: Jarrolds Pubs.), and 1934 (Toronto: McClelland) editions

These editions were at least partially coordinated between these publishers and seem to be based on the 1907 edition. The most significant changes from the 1894 and 1907 editions are that the Englishman becomes an American, and chapters 29-31 (on sheep, oxen, and cows) are omitted. The 1920 edition replaces the original introduction (see Appendix F2, p. 312).

1965 "Modern Abridged Edition" (Racine, Wisconsin: Whitman)

This posthumous edition seems to be based on the 1894 edition, as there is no "Black Jim" chapter. Most of the original chapters are reproduced, but with significant revisions. Bruno is not shot (see Appendix F3, p. 313) and nearly all cruelty and violence (human or animal) is omitted.

1990 edition, "Retold by Quinn Currie" (Storytellers Ink)

Produced as a joint effort by Operation Outreach USA and the American Humane Education Society for distribution in schools across the US, this edition cuts over sixty percent of the original, including much of the cruelty and violence and many significant characters (Davies, *Education* 152). In addition to condensing the remaining chapters, the following chapters are cut: 7 (on Jim), 11 (on goldfish and canaries), 12 (on Malta), 17 (on horses), 18 (on poultry), 19 (on the Band of Mercy), 20 (on animal stories), 21 (on Mr. Maxwell), 23 (on wild animals), 24 (on the rabbit and hen), 25 (on Scamp), 26 (on the miser), 27-28 (on the Englishman). All archaic expressions and constructions are revised and some characters are renamed.

BEAUTIFUL JOE

AN AUTOBIOGRAPHY

By MARSHALL SAUNDERS

Author of " My Spanish Sailor "

WITH AN INTRODUCTION

BY

HEZEKIAH BUTTERWORTH

Of *Youth's Companion*

PHILADELPHIA

CHARLES H. BANES

1420 Chestnut Street

TO

GEORGE THORNDIKE ANGELL,

PRESIDENT OF THE AMERICAN HUMANE EDUCATION SOCIETY,

THE MASSACHUSETTS SOCIETY FOR THE PREVENTION

OF CRUELTY TO ANIMALS, AND THE PARENT

AMERICAN BAND OF MERCY,

19 MILK ST., BOSTON,

THIS BOOK IS RESPECTFULLY DEDICATED

BY THE AUTHOR.

PREFACE

BEAUTIFUL JOE is a real dog, and "Beautiful Joe" is his real name.[1] He belonged during the first part of his life to a cruel master, who mutilated him in the manner described in the story. He was rescued from him, and is now living in a happy home with pleasant surroundings, and enjoys a wide local celebrity.

The character of Laura is drawn from life, and to the smallest detail is truthfully depicted. The Morris family has its counterparts in real life, and nearly all of the incidents of the story are founded on fact.

THE AUTHOR.

---

1 *Beautiful Joe* was one of the earliest animal viewpoint novels published in the US and certainly the most popular. Saunders's insistence on the veracity of her story allows the fiction of the animal "autobiography" to function. In effect, the human amanuensis is nothing more than the medium through which the dog's voice can be heard. The 1907, 1965, and 1990 editions omit this preface.

INTRODUCTION[1]

THE wonderfully successful book, entitled "Black Beauty," came like a living voice out of the animal kingdom. But it spake for the horse, and made other books necessary; it led the way. After the ready welcome that it received, and the good it has accomplished and is doing, it followed naturally that some one should be inspired to write a book to interpret the life of a dog to the humane feeling of the world. Such a story we have in "Beautiful Joe."[2]

The story speaks not for the dog alone, but for the whole animal kingdom. Through it we enter the animal world, and are made to see as animals see, and to feel as animals feel. The sympathetic sight of the author, in this interpretation, is ethically the strong feature of the book.

Such books as this is one of the needs of our progressive system of education. The day-school, the Sunday-school, and all libraries for the young, demand the influence that shall *teach* the reader *how* to live in sympathy with the animal world; how to understand the languages of the creatures that we have long been accustomed to call "dumb," and the sign language of the lower orders of these dependent beings. The church owes it to her mission to preach and to teach the enforcement of the "bird's nest commandment"; the principle recognized by Moses in the

---

1 The various introductions served to align Saunders with the nationality of each particular audience. An introduction from Hezekiah Butterworth, a well-known American writer of books for young boys, would serve Saunders well in the US, but for many of the Canadian and English editions Saunders procured an introduction from Lady Aberdeen, the wife of Canada's governor-general and a prominent philanthropist. In the 1990 edition, a new introduction erroneously claims that the real Joe was from Maine, not Ontario, and that Saunders "learned the story of the dog from American friends" (Amory).

2 In 1890 the president of the American Humane Education Society, George T. Angell, had published the English author Anna Sewell's *Black Beauty* (1877) with the subtitle, *The "Uncle Tom's Cabin" of the Horse,* linking the successful abolitionist movement to animal protectionism. Seeking a companion novel to *Black Beauty,* he advertised for regional stories that would feature both the kind and cruel treatment of animals. By resetting her Canadian story in Maine, Saunders was able to win the prize for a story from the northeastern states.

Hebrew world,[1] and echoed by Cowper in English poetry, and Burns in the "Meadow Mouse," and by our own Longfellow in songs of many keys.[2]

Kindness to the animal kingdom is the first, or a first principle in the growth of true philanthropy. Young Lincoln once waded across a half-frozen river to rescue a dog, and stopped in a walk with a statesman to put back a bird that had fallen out of its nest.[3] Such a heart was trained to be a leader of men, and to be crucified for a cause. The conscience that runs to the call of an animal in distress, is girding itself with power to do manly work in the world.

The story of "Beautiful Joe" awakens an intense interest, and sustains it through a series of vivid incidents and episodes, each of which is a lesson. The story merits the widest circulation, and the universal reading and response accorded to "Black Beauty." To circulate it is to do good; to help the human heart as well as the creatures of quick feelings and simple language.

When, as one of the committee to examine the manuscripts offered for prizes to the Humane Society, I read the story, I felt

---

1   Known as the "least" commandment of Moses, the so-called bird's nest commandment reads: "If a bird's nest chance to be before thee in the way, in any tree or on the ground, with young ones or eggs, thou shalt not take the dam with the young; thou shalt in any wise let the dam go, but the young thou mayest take unto thyself: that it may be well with thee, and that thou mayest prolong thy days" (Deuteronomy 22:6-7). It was commonly invoked in sermons (see, for example, Melvill in 1845 and Cox in 1888) as Biblical justification for animal protection. For more on the bird's nest commandment, see Johnston.

2   In a very useful book, *Romanticism and Animal Rights* (Cambridge: Cambridge UP, 2003), David Perkins credits the English poet William Cowper (1731-1800) as the most influential in inspiring compassion towards animals during the eighteenth century, and in an earlier article (2000) Perkins describes Robert Burns (1759-96) as the poet who wrote about animals with the most sympathy ("Human Mouseness" 3). Though Saunders misnames Burns's 1785 poem, "To a Mouse," she rightly cites it as an exemplar of Burns's compassion. On the other side of the Atlantic, Henry Wadsworth Longfellow (1807-82) was one of the greatest Romantic poets. See Haralson for more on Longfellow's influence on nineteenth-century views.

3   Early biographies of Abraham Lincoln told the apocryphal story of how in 1830, at the age of 21, he waded into an icy river to rescue a drowning dog (Whipple 73-74, Whitlock 36, Elias 39, Wheeler 38-39, McSpadden 46-47).

that the writer had a higher motive than to compete for a prize; that the story was a stream of sympathy that flowed from the heart; that it was genuine; that it only needed a publisher who should be able to command a wide influence, to make its merits known, to give it a strong educational mission.

I am pleased that the manuscript has found such a publisher, and am sure that the issue of the story will honor the Publication Society. In the development of the book, I believe that the humane cause has stood above any speculative thought or interest.[1] The book comes because it is called for; the times demand it. I think that the publishers have a right to ask for a little unselfish service on the part of the public in helping to give it a circulation commensurate with its opportunity, need, and influence.

HEZEKIAH BUTTERWORTH,

(Of the committee of readers of the prize stories
offered to the Humane Society.)

BOSTON, MASS., Dec., 1893.

---

1 While Saunders was undoubtedly dedicated to the humane movement, and would be for the rest of her life, she was also not "above" such vulgar matters as royalties.

CONTENTS

"My name is 'Beautiful Joe'"—*p.* 13.

London: Jarrold & Sons, 1895.

CHAPTER 1

ONLY A CUR

MY name is Beautiful Joe, and I am a brown dog of medium size. I am not called Beautiful Joe because I am a beauty.[1] Mr. Morris, the clergyman, in whose family I have lived for the last twelve years, says that he thinks I must be called Beautiful Joe for the same reason that his grandfather, down South, called a very ugly colored slave-lad Cupid, and his mother Venus.[2]

I do not know what he means by that, but when he says it, people always look at me and smile. I know that I am not beautiful, and I know that I am not a thoroughbred.[3] I am only a cur.

When my mistress went every year to register me and pay my tax, and the man in the office asked what breed I was, she said part fox-terrier and part bull-terrier; but he always put me down a cur. I don't think she liked having him call me a cur; still, I have heard her say that she preferred curs, for they have more character than well-bred dogs. Her father said that she liked ugly dogs for the same reason that a nobleman at the court of a certain king did—namely, that no one else would.

I am an old dog now, and am writing, or rather getting a friend to write, the story of my life. I have seen my mistress laughing and crying over a little book that she says is a story of a horse's life, and sometimes she puts the book down close to my nose to let me see the pictures.

I love my dear mistress; I can say no more than that; I love her better than any one else in the world; and I think it will please her if I write the story of a dog's life. She loves dumb animals, and it always grieves her to see them treated cruelly.

I have heard her say that if all the boys and girls in the world were to rise up and say that there should be no more cruelty to animals, they could put a stop to it. Perhaps it will help a little if

---

1 Joe's ugliness is quickly set up as his defining characteristic, immediately distinguishing him from Sewell's protagonist, Black Beauty, who is a handsome horse of noble lineage.

2 In the sequel, *Beautiful Joe's Paradise* (1902), Saunders depicts a paradise for humans and animals that would be racially and ethnically segregated. (See Appendix E1, p. 297.) In the 1965 and 1990 editions, this problematic analogy is omitted.

3 The 1965 edition omits these two instances of "I know that"; this is one of many examples where this later edition undercuts Joe's capacity to think, know, remember, and relate.

I tell a story. I am fond of boys and girls, and though I have seen many cruel men and women, I have seen few cruel children. I think the more stories there are written about dumb animals, the better it will be for us.

In telling my story, I think I had better begin at the first and come right on to the end. I was born in a stable on the outskirts of a small town in Maine called Fairport. The first thing I remember was lying close to my mother and being very snug and warm. The next thing I remember was being always hungry. I had a number of brothers and sisters—six in all—and my mother never had enough milk for us. She was always half starved herself, so she could not feed us properly.

I am very unwilling to say much about my early life.[1] I have lived so long in a family where there is never a harsh word spoken, and where no one thinks of ill-treating anybody or anything, that it seems almost wrong even to think or speak of such a matter as hurting a poor dumb beast.

The man that owned my mother was a milkman.[2] He kept one horse and three cows, and he had a shaky old cart that he used to put his milk cans in. I don't think there can be a worse man in the world than that milkman. It makes me shudder now to think of him. His name was Jenkins, and I am glad to think that he is getting punished now for his cruelty to poor dumb animals and to human beings. If you think it is wrong that I am glad, you must remember that I am only a dog.

The first notice that he took of me when I was a little puppy, just able to stagger about, was to give me a kick that sent me into a corner of the stable. He used to beat and starve my mother. I have seen him use his heavy whip to punish her till her body was covered with blood.[3] When I got older I asked her why she did

---

1 Joe's refined sensibilities are shown by his reluctance to speak of "ugly" events.

2 In the 1990 edition, Jenkins is an ice-delivery man. In the first decades of the twentieth century, until the advent of modern refrigeration, blocks of ice would keep food fresh. According to the United States Department of Agriculture (USDA), milk was still being delivered as late as 1963; almost thirty percent of Americans had their milk delivered. By 1975, less than seven percent, and by 2005, only about 0.4 percent received milk deliveries (Tahmincioglu). Although home ice delivery does not sound any less archaic to modern readers, the change meant that any discussion of milk tampering and failed inspections was omitted in the 1965 edition.

3 The 1965 edition omits nearly all mention of death and blood. Jess is still beaten, starved, and whipped, but the reference to her bloody body

not run away. She said she did not wish to; but I soon found out that the reason she did not run away, was because she loved Jenkins. Cruel and savage as he was, she yet loved him, and I believe she would have laid down her life for him.

Now that I am old, I know that there are more men in the world like Jenkins. They are not crazy, they are not drunkards; they simply seem to be possessed with a spirit of wickedness. There are well-to-do people, yes, and rich people, who will treat animals, and even little children, with such terrible cruelty, that one cannot even mention the things that they are guilty of.[1]

One reason for Jenkins' cruelty was his idleness. After he went his rounds in the morning with his milk cans, he had nothing to do till late in the afternoon but take care of his stable and yard. If he had kept them neat, and groomed his horse, and cleaned the cows, and dug up the garden, it would have taken up all his time; but he never tidied the place at all, till his yard and stable got so littered up with things he threw down, that he could not make his way about.

His house and stable stood in the middle of a large field, and they were at some distance from the road. Passers-by could not see how untidy the place was. Occasionally, a man came to look at the premises, and see that they were in good order, but Jenkins always knew when to expect him, and had things cleaned up a little.

I used to wish that some of the people that took milk from him would come and look at his cows. In the spring and summer he

---

is omitted. Later, the bodies of Jenkins's starved cows are not described as "lean" or "poor." This likely reflects a change in attitudes towards how much "graphic" violence is appropriate in a children's book. The effect, however, is that violence occurs in the 1965 edition without notable consequence.

1   The 1965 edition completely excises the temperance message that Saunders included as part of her support for the work of the Women's Christian Temperance Union (WCTU). Temperance societies comprised the largest group of activist women. In the early 1870s, small bands of women charged into drug stores and saloons, singing the WCTU "Crusade Hymn" and praying until the sellers of alcohol agreed to stop selling the "poison" drink (Gordon 9). Empowering women to leverage their traditional roles as mothers to "mother" the nation, the temperance movement was a critical factor in mobilizing activism for women's suffrage. By the early twentieth century, however, the temperance movement became dominated by men (Cordell, Heider, Hinkle, Morse).

drove them out to pasture, but during the winter they stood all the time in the dirty, dark stable, where the chinks in the wall were so big that the snow swept through almost in drifts. The ground was always muddy and wet; there was only one small window on the north side, where the sun only shone in for a short time in the afternoon.

They were very unhappy cows, but they stood patiently and never complained, though sometimes I know they must have nearly frozen in the bitter winds that blew through the stable on winter nights. They were lean and poor, and were never in good health. Besides being cold they were fed on very poor food.

Jenkins used to come home nearly every afternoon with a great tub in the back of his cart that was full of what he called "peelings." It was kitchen stuff that he asked the cooks at the different houses where he delivered milk, to save for him. They threw rotten vegetables, fruit parings, and scraps from the table into a tub, and gave them to him at the end of a few days. A sour, nasty mess it always was, and not fit to give any creature.

Sometimes, when he had not many "peelings," he would go to town and get a load of decayed vegetables, that grocers were glad to have him take off their hands.

This food, together with poor hay, made the cows give very poor milk, and Jenkins used to put some white powder in it, to give it "body," as he said.[1]

Once a very sad thing happened about the milk, that no one knew about but Jenkins and his wife. She was a poor, unhappy creature, very frightened at her husband, and not daring to speak much to him. She was not a clean woman, and I never saw a worse-looking house than she kept.

She used to do very queer things, that I know now no housekeeper should do. I have seen her catch up the broom to pound potatoes in the pot. She pounded with the handle, and the broom would fly up and down in the air, dropping dust into the pot

---

1   Food adulteration was a common problem in the nineteenth century. Jenkins's swill milk also prefigures the controversy over food purity that would spike in the early 1900s (Levenstein 41). Although pasteurization—the extended heating of milk to a temperature that is lethal to bacteria—was developed in the 1880s, Americans did not manage large-scale pasteurization until 1914 (Levenstein 130). At that point, many local legislatures passed pasteurization regulations, putting out of business the small milk distributors who could not afford the required equipment (Levenstein 41).

where the potatoes were. Her pan of soft-mixed bread she often left uncovered in the kitchen, and sometimes the hens walked in and sat in it.

The children used to play in mud puddles about the door. It was the youngest of them that sickened with some kind of fever early in the spring, before Jenkins began driving the cows out to pasture. The child was very ill, and Mrs. Jenkins wanted to send for a doctor, but her husband would not let her. They made a bed in the kitchen, close to the stove, and Mrs. Jenkins nursed the child as best she could. She did all her work near by, and I saw her several times wiping the child's face with the cloth that she used for washing her milk pans.

Nobody knew outside the family that the little girl was ill. Jenkins had such a bad name, that none of the neighbors would visit them. By-and-by the child got well, and a week or two later Jenkins came home with quite a frightened face, and told his wife that the husband of one of his customers was very ill with typhoid fever.

After a time the gentleman died, and the cook told Jenkins that the doctor wondered how he could have taken the fever, for there was not a case in town.

There was a widow left with three orphans, and they never knew that they had to blame a dirty, careless milkman, for taking a kind husband and father from them.

CHAPTER 2

THE CRUEL MILKMAN

I HAVE said that Jenkins spent most of his days in idleness. He had to start out very early in the morning, in order to supply his customers with milk for breakfast. Oh, how ugly he used to be, when he came into the stable on cold winter mornings, before the sun was up.

He would hang his lantern on a hook, and get his milking stool, and if the cows did not step aside just to suit him, he would seize a broom or fork, and beat them cruelly.

My mother and I slept on a heap of straw in the corner of the stable, and when she heard his step in the morning she always roused me, so that we could run out-doors as soon as he opened the stable door. He always aimed a kick at us as we passed, but my mother taught me how to dodge him.

After he finished milking, he took the pails of milk up to the house for Mrs. Jenkins to strain and put in the cans, and he came back and harnessed his horse to the cart. His horse was called Toby, and a poor, miserable, broken-down creature he was. He was weak in the knees, and weak in the back, and weak all over, and Jenkins had to beat him all the time, to make him go. He had been a cab horse, and his mouth had been jerked, and twisted, and sawed at, till one would think there could be no feeling left in it; still I have seen him wince and curl up his lip when Jenkins thrust in the frosty bit on a winter's morning.

Poor old Toby! I used to lie on my straw sometimes and wonder he did not cry out with pain.[1] Cold and half starved he always was in the winter time, and often with raw sores on his body that Jenkins would try to hide by putting bits of cloth under the harness. But Toby never murmured, and he never tried to kick and bite, and he minded the least word from Jenkins, and if he swore at him, Toby would start back, or step up quickly, he was so anxious to please him.

After Jenkins put him in the cart, and took in the cans, he set out on his rounds. My mother, whose name was Jess, always went with him. I used to ask her why she followed such a brute of a man, and she would hang her head, and say that sometimes she

---

1 In the 1965 and 1990 editions Joe is less reflective. "I used to ..."
becomes "It's a wonder."

got a bone from the different houses they stopped at. But that was not the whole reason. She liked Jenkins so much, that she wanted to be with him.[1]

I had not her sweet and patient disposition, and I would not go with her. I watched her out of sight, and then ran up to the house to see if Mrs. Jenkins had any scraps for me. I nearly always got something, for she pitied me, and often gave me a kind word or look with the bits of food that she threw to me.

When Jenkins came home, I often coaxed mother to run about and see some of the neighbors' dogs with me. But she never would, and I would not leave her. So, from morning to night we had to sneak about, keeping out of Jenkins' way as much as we could, and yet trying to keep him in sight. He always sauntered about with a pipe in his mouth, and his hands in his pockets, growling first at his wife and children, and then at his dumb creatures.[2]

I have not told what became of my brothers and sisters. One rainy day, when we were eight weeks old, Jenkins, followed by two or three of his ragged, dirty children, came into the stable and looked at us. Then he began to swear because we were so ugly, and said if we had been good-looking, he might have sold some of us. Mother watched him anxiously, and fearing some danger to her puppies, ran and jumped in the middle of us, and looked pleadingly up at him.

It only made him swear the more. He took one pup after another, and right there, before his children and my poor distracted mother, put an end to their lives.[3] Some of them he seized by the legs and knocked against the stalls, till their brains were

---

1 In 1965, the paragraph on Toby's suffering and his slavish devotion is omitted. The 1990 edition also omits Jess's unconditional attachment to her abusive master. These changes blur one of the key themes in the novel: that an animal is superior if, like Joe, he can discriminate when it comes to investing his affections.

2 The 1990 edition omits this paragraph, severing the well-established connection between animal abuse and domestic violence. For more on this link, see Frank R. Ascione and Phil Arkow, *Child Abuse, Domestic Violence, and Animal Abuse: Linking the Circles of Compassion for Prevention and Intervention* (West Lafayette, IN: Purdue UP, 1999).

3 Saunders deleted key lines in the scene ("He took one pup after another....") by the 1920s. In the 1965 edition, their corpses are not mistreated, and in the 1990 edition, Joe's siblings are not a part of the novel.

dashed out, others he killed with a fork. It was very terrible. My mother ran up and down the stable, screaming with pain, and I lay weak and trembling, and expecting every instant that my turn would come next. I don't know why he spared me. I was the only one left.

His children cried, and he sent them out of the stable and went out himself. Mother picked up all the puppies and brought them to our nest in the straw and licked them, and tried to bring them back to life, but it was of no use. They were quite dead. We had them in our corner of the stable for some days, till Jenkins discovered them, and swearing horribly at us, he took his stable fork and threw them out in the yard, and put some earth over them.

My mother never seemed the same after this. She was weak and miserable, and though she was only four years old, she seemed like an old dog. This was on account of the poor food she had been fed on. She could not run after Jenkins, and she lay on our heap of straw, only turning over with her nose the scraps of food I brought her to eat. One day she licked me gently, wagged her tail, and died.

As I sat by her, feeling lonely and miserable, Jenkins came into the stable. I could not bear to look at him. He had killed my mother. There she lay, a little, gaunt, scarred creature, starved and worried to death by him. Her mouth was half open, her eyes were staring. She would never again look kindly at me, or curl up to me at night to keep me warm. Oh, how I hated her murderer! But I sat quietly, even when he went up and turned her over with his foot to see if she was really dead. I think he was a little sorry, for he turned scornfully toward me and said, "she was worth two of you; why didn't you go instead."

Still I kept quiet till he walked up to me and kicked at me. My heart was nearly broken and I could stand no more. I flew at him and gave him a savage bite on the ankle.

"Oho," he said, "so you are going to be a fighter, are you? I'll fix you for that." His face was red and furious. He seized me by the back of the neck and carried me out to the yard where a log lay on the ground. "Bill," he called to one of his children, "bring me the hatchet."

He laid my head on the log and pressed one hand on my strug-gling body. I was now a year old and a full-sized dog. There was a quick, dreadful pain, and he had cut off my ear, not in the way they cut puppies' ears, but close to my head, so close that he cut off some of the skin beyond it. Then he cut off the other ear, and, turning me swiftly round, cut off my tail close to my body.

Then he let me go and stood looking at me as I rolled on the ground and yelped in agony. He was in such a passion that he did not think that people passing by on the road might hear me.

CHAPTER 3

MY KIND DELIVERER AND MISS LAURA

THERE was a young man going by on a bicycle. He heard my screams, and springing off his bicycle, came hurrying up the path, and stood among us before Jenkins caught sight of him.

In the midst of my pain, I heard him say fiercely, "What have you been doing to that dog?"

"I've been cuttin' his ears for fightin', my young gentleman," said Jenkins. "There is no law to prevent that, is there?"[1]

"And there is no law to prevent my giving you a beating," said the young man, angrily. In a trice, he had seized Jenkins by the throat, and was pounding him with all his might. Mrs. Jenkins came and stood at the house door, crying, but making no effort to help her husband.

"Bring me a towel," the young man cried to her, after he had stretched Jenkins, bruised and frightened, on the ground. She snatched off her apron, and ran down with it, and the young man wrapped me in it, and taking me carefully in his arms, walked down the path to the gate. There were some little boys standing there, watching him, their mouths wide open with astonishment. "Sonny," he said to the largest of them, "if you will come behind and carry this dog, I will give you a quarter."

The boy took me, and we set out. I was all smothered up in a cloth, and moaning with pain, but still I looked out occasionally to see which way we were going. We took the road to the town, and stopped in front of a house on Washington Street. The young man leaned his bicycle up against the house, took a quarter from his pocket and put it in the boy's hand, and lifting me gently in his arms, went up a lane leading to the back of the house.

There was a small stable there. He went into it, put me down on the floor, and uncovered my body. Some boys were playing about the stable, and I heard them say in horrified tones, "Oh, Cousin Harry, what is the matter with that dog?"

"Hush," he said. "Don't make a fuss. You, Jack, go down to the kitchen and ask Mary for a basin of warm water and a sponge, and don't let your mother or Laura hear you."

---

1 In the 1990 edition, Jenkins simply says, "It's none of your business." Harry replies: "The abuse of helpless animals is everybody's business," then seizes Jenkins by the collar (not the throat) to shake him (not pound him). Young men are no longer encouraged to mete out justice with their own hands.

A few minutes later, the young man had bathed my bleeding ears and tail, and had rubbed something on them that was cool and pleasant, and had bandaged them firmly with strips of cotton. I felt much better, and was able to look about me.

I was in a small stable, that was evidently not used for a stable, but more for a playroom. There were various kinds of toys scattered about, and a swing and bar, such as boys love to twist about on, in two different corners. In a box against the wall, was a guinea pig looking at me in an interested way. This guinea pig's name was Jeff, and he and I became good friends. A long-haired, French rabbit was hopping about, and a tame white rat was perched on the shoulder of one of the boys, and kept his foothold there, no matter how suddenly the boy moved. There were so many boys, and the stable was so small, that I suppose he was afraid he would get stepped on if he went on the floor. He stared hard at me with his little, red eyes, and never even glanced at a queer-looking, gray cat that was watching me too, from her bed in the back of the vacant horse stall. Out in the sunny yard, some pigeons were pecking at grain, and a spaniel lay asleep in a corner.

I had never seen anything like this before, and my wonder at it almost drove the pain away. Mother and I always chased rats and birds, and once we killed a kitten. While I was puzzling over it, one of the boys cried out, "Here is Laura!"

"Take that rag out of the way," said Mr. Harry, kicking aside the old apron I had been wrapped in, and that was stained with my blood. One of the boys stuffed it into a barrel, and then they all looked toward the house.[1]

A young girl, holding up one hand to shade her eyes from the sun, was coming up the walk that led from the house to the stable. I thought then, that I never had seen such a beautiful girl, and I think so still. She was tall and slender, and had lovely brown eyes and brown hair, and a sweet smile, and just to look at her was enough to make one love her. I stood in the stable door, staring at her with all my might.

"Why, what a funny dog," she said, and stopped short to look at me. Up to this, I had not thought what a queer-looking

---

1 In the 1990 edition, Laura does not descend like a white angel onto the scene and Joe does not fall in love with her at first sight. He is still ashamed of his appearance, but not because he feels unfit for "a pretty young lady like that." She does not smile sweetly at the boys nor do they attempt to hide Joe's injuries from her. Harry, for his part, excuses his reluctance to go to the police by noting that he is "only a visitor."

New York: A.L. Burt, 1922.

sight I must be. Now I twisted round my head, saw the white bandage on my tail, and knowing I was not a fit spectacle for a pretty young lady like that, I slunk into a corner.

"Poor doggie, have I hurt your feelings?" she said, and with a sweet smile at the boys, she passed by them, and came up to the guinea pig's box, behind which I had taken refuge. "What is the matter with your head, good dog?" she said, curiously, as she stooped over me.

"He has a cold in it," said one of the boys with a laugh, "so we put a nightcap on." She drew back, and turned very pale. "Cousin Harry, there are drops of blood on this cotton. Who has hurt this dog?"

"Dear Laura," and the young man coming up, laid his hand on her shoulder, "he got hurt, and I have been bandaging him."

"Who hurt him?"

"I had rather not tell you."

"But I wish to know." Her voice was as gentle as ever, but she spoke so decidedly that the young man was obliged to tell her everything. All the time he was speaking, she kept touching me gently with her fingers. When he had finished his account of rescuing me from Jenkins, she said, quietly:

"You will have the man punished?"

Toronto: McLelland & Stewart, 1934.

"What is the use; that won't stop him from being cruel."

"It will put a check on his cruelty."

"I don't think it would do any good," said the young man, doggedly.

"Cousin Harry!" and the young girl stood up very straight and tall, her brown eyes flashing, and one hand pointing at me; "will you let that pass? That animal has been wronged, it looks to you to right it. The coward who has maimed it for life should be punished. A child has a voice to tell its wrong[1]—a poor, dumb creature must suffer in silence; in bitter, bitter silence. And," eagerly, as the young man tried to interrupt her, "you are doing the man himself an injustice. If he is bad enough to ill-treat his dog, he will ill-treat his wife and children. If he is checked and punished now for his cruelty, he may reform. And even if his wicked heart is not changed, he will be obliged to treat them with outward kindness, through fear of punishment."

The young man looked convinced, and almost as ashamed as if he had been the one to crop my ears. "What do you want me to do?" he said, slowly, and looking sheepishly at the boys who were staring open-mouthed at him and the young girl.

The girl pulled a little watch from her belt. "I want you to report that man immediately. It is now five o'clock. I will go down to the police station with you, if you like."

"Very well," he said, his face brightening, and together they went off to the house.

---

1   In the nineteenth century, animals were commonly referred to as "dumb"—that is, mute. Given our increasing understanding of animal intercommunication, we would no longer describe them as mute, but we remain entrenched in the notion of "voice." One of the contemporary trademarks of the American Society for the Prevention of Cruelty to Animals (ASPCA) is, "We are their voice" ("Orange, the ASPCA's Official Color"). Questions about whether animal minds can be known and spoken for were less of a concern in Saunders's time, when anthropomorphized autobiographies were being published by the dozens in both the US and England: stories by dogs, cats, mice, birds, donkeys, and even a lump of coal. For more on animal autobiography, see DeMello.

CHAPTER 4

THE MORRIS BOYS ADD TO MY NAME

THE boys watched them out of sight, then one of them, whose name I afterward learned was Jack, and who came next to Miss Laura in age, gave a low whistle and said, "Doesn't the old lady come out strong when any one or anything gets abused? I'll never forget the day she found me setting Jim on that black cat of the Wilsons'. She scolded me, and then she cried, till I didn't know where to look. Plague on it, how was I going to know he'd kill the old cat?[1] I only wanted to drive it out of the yard. Come on, let's look at the dog."

They all came and bent over me, as I lay on the floor in my corner. I wasn't much used to boys, and I didn't know how they would treat me. But I soon found by the way they handled me and talked to me, that they knew a good deal about dogs, and were accustomed to treat them kindly. It seemed very strange to have them pat me, and call me "good dog." No one had ever said that to me before to-day.

"He's not much of a beauty, is he?" said one of the boys, whom they called Tom.

"Not by a long shot," said Jack Morris, with a laugh. "Not any nearer the beauty mark than yourself, Tom."

Tom flew at him, and they had a scuffle. The other boys paid no attention to them, but went on looking at me.[2] One of them, a little boy with eyes like Miss Laura's, said, "What did Cousin Harry say the dog's name was?"

"Joe," answered another boy. "The little chap that carried him home, told him."

---

1 The 1965 and 1990 editions omit the Morris's boys' casual remembrance of causing the death of a cat. At the time of Saunders's writing, although cats were also increasingly protected from ill treatment, they were less protected than dogs. For centuries cats were portrayed as deceitful and selfish—and female—while dogs were represented as faithful, devoted, and male. The boys' lack of sympathy for the cat was seen as a natural extension of the notion that each gender had an innate affinity for either cats or dogs.

2 In the original, this impromptu "scuffle" serves as an opportunity for Saunders to drive home the point that "boys will be boys." As part of the sanitization of all violence in the text, the 1990 edition omits this fight.

"We might call him 'Ugly Joe' then," said a lad with a round, fat face, and laughing eyes. I wondered very much who this boy was, and, later on, I found out that he was another of Miss Laura's brothers, and his name was Ned. There seemed to be no end to the Morris boys.

"I don't think Laura would like that," said Jack Morris, suddenly coming up behind him. He was very hot, and was breathing fast, but his manner was as cool as if he had never left the group about me. He had beaten Tom, who was sitting on a box, ruefully surveying a hole in his jacket. "You see," he went on, gaspingly, "if you call him 'Ugly Joe,' her ladyship will say that you are wounding the dear dog's feelings. 'Beautiful Joe,' would be more to her liking."

A shout went up from the boys. I didn't wonder that they laughed. Plain looking, I naturally was; but I must have been hideous in those bandages.

"'Beautiful Joe,' then let it be!" they cried. "Let us go and tell mother, and ask her to give us something for our beauty to eat."[1]

They all trooped out of the stable, and I was very sorry, for when they were with me, I did not mind so much the tingling in my ears, and the terrible pain in my back. They soon brought me some nice food, but I could not touch it, so they went away to their play, and I lay in the box they put me in, trembling with pain, and wishing that the pretty young lady was there, to stroke me with her gentle fingers.

By-and-by it got dark. The boys finished their play, and went into the house, and I saw lights twinkling in the windows. I felt lonely and miserable in this strange place. I would not have gone back to Jenkins' for the world, still it was the only home I had known, and though I felt that I should be happy here, I had not yet gotten used to the change. Then the pain all through my body was dreadful. My head seemed to be on fire, and there were sharp, darting pains up and down my backbone. I did not dare to howl, lest I should make the big dog, Jim, angry. He was sleeping in a kennel, out in the yard.

---

1 The story makes clear that the choice of Joe's name was to please Laura, aligning feminine and masculine with the aesthetic categories of beauty and ugliness respectively. Joe's ability to embody both ugliness and beauty equally well was one way in which Saunders's novel made humaneness more attractive to boys. His duality also reflects the gendering of humane work: Laura does the beautiful things, like nursing Joe, while the boys manage the ugly business of rescue and bloody bandages.

Philadelphia: Griffith & Rowland, 1907.

The stable was very quiet. Up in the loft above, some rabbits that I had heard running about, had now gone to sleep. The guinea pig was nestling in the corner of his box, and the cat and the tame rat had scampered into the house long ago.

At last I could bear the pain no longer. I sat up in my box and looked about me. I felt as if I was going to die, and, though I was very weak, there was something inside me that made me feel as if I wanted to crawl away somewhere out of sight. I slunk out into the yard, and along the stable wall, where there was a thick clump of raspberry bushes. I crept in among them and lay down in the damp earth. I tried to scratch off my bandages, but they were fastened on too firmly, and I could not do it. I thought about my poor mother, and wished she was here to lick my sore ears. Though she was so unhappy herself, she never wanted to see me suffer. If I had not disobeyed her, I would not now be suffering so much pain. She had told me again and again not to snap at Jenkins, for it made him worse.

In the midst of my trouble I heard a soft voice calling, "Joe! Joe!" It was Miss Laura's voice, but I felt as if there were weights on my paws, and I could not go to her.

"Joe! Joe!" she said again. She was going up the walk to the stable, holding up a lighted lamp in her hand. She had on a white dress,[1] and I watched her till she disappeared in the stable. She did not stay long in there. She came out and stood on the gravel. "Joe, Joe, Beautiful Joe, where are you? You are hiding somewhere, but I shall find you." Then she came right to the spot where I was. "Poor doggie," she said, stooping down and patting me. "Are you very miserable, and did you crawl away to die? I have had dogs do that before, but I am not going to let you die, Joe." And she set her lamp on the ground, and took me in her arms.

I was very thin then, not nearly so fat as I am now, still I was quite an armful for her. But she did not seem to find me heavy. She took me right into the house, through the back door, and down a long flight of steps, across a hall, and into a snug kitchen.

"For the land sakes, Miss Laura," said a woman who was bending over a stove,[2] "what have you got there?"

"A poor sick dog, Mary," said Miss Laura seating herself on a chair. "Will you please warm a little milk for him? And have you a box or a basket down here that he can lie in?"

"I guess so," said the woman; "but he's awful dirty; you're not going to let him sleep in the house, are you?"

"Only for to-night. He is very ill. A dreadful thing happened to him, Mary." And Miss Laura went on to tell her how my ears had been cut off.

"Oh, that's the dog the boys were talking about," said the woman. "Poor creature, he's welcome to all I can do for him." She opened a closet door, and brought out a box, and folded a piece of blanket for me to lie on. Then she heated some milk in a saucepan, and poured it in a saucer, and watched me while Miss Laura went upstairs to get a little bottle of something that would make[3] me sleep. They poured a few drops of this medicine into

---

1   The emphasis on Laura's white dress—a traditional female symbol of purity—is taken out in the 1965 and 1990 editions. Later in the 1965 edition, likely reflecting the greater gender-consciousness of the civil rights era, Laura does not offer fingers of milk like a surrogate mother and does not check on Joe. Instead, Joe sleeps soundly through the night.

2   By 1990, household technology had replaced servants in middle-class households. The modern edition replaces her with Mrs. Morris "putting flowers in a big bowl."

3   The change from "make" to "help" in the 1990 edition evidences its preoccupation with sanitizing the text.

Toronto: McClelland & Stewart, 1934.

the milk and offered it to me. I lapped a little, but I could not finish it, even though Miss Laura coaxed me very gently to do so. She dipped her finger in the milk and held it out to me, and though I did not want it, I could not be ungrateful enough to refuse to lick her finger as often as she offered it to me. After the milk was gone, Mary lifted up my box, and carried me into the washroom that was off the kitchen.

I soon fell sound asleep, and could not rouse myself through the night, even though I both smelled and heard some one coming near me several times. The next morning I found out that it was Miss Laura. Whenever there was a sick animal in the house, no matter if it was only the tame rat, she would get up two or three times in the night, to see if there was anything she could do to make it more comfortable.

CHAPTER 5

MY NEW HOME AND A SELFISH LADY

I DON'T believe that a dog could have fallen into a happier home than I did. In a week, thanks to good nursing, good food, and kind words, I was almost well. Mr. Harry washed and dressed my sore ears and tail every day till he went home, and one day, he and the boys gave me a bath out in the stable. They carried out a tub of warm water and stood me in it. I had never been washed before in my life, and it felt very queer.[1] Miss Laura stood by laughing and encouraging me not to mind the streams of water trickling all over me. I couldn't help wondering what Jenkins would have said if he could have seen me in that tub.

That reminds me to say, that two days after I arrived at the Morrises', Jack, followed by all the other boys, came running into the stable. He had a newspaper in his hand, and with a great deal of laughing and joking, read this to me:

"*Fairport Daily News*, June 3d. In the police court this morning, James Jenkins, for cruelly torturing and mutilating a dog, fined ten dollars and costs."[2]

Then he said, "What do you think of that, Joe? Five dollars apiece for your ears and your tail thrown in. That's all they're worth in the eyes of the law. Jenkins has had his fun and you'll go through life worth about three-quarters of a dog. I'd lash rascals like that. Tie them up and flog them till they were scarred and mutilated a little bit themselves. Just wait till I'm president.[3] But there's some more, old fellow. Listen: 'Our reporter visited the house of the above-mentioned Jenkins, and found a most deplorable state of affairs. The house, yard and stable were indescribably filthy. His horse bears the marks of ill-usage, and is in

---

1 "Queer" has taken on connotations of homosexuality in recent decades, so the 1990 edition revised this to "strange." This was, after all, the original sense of the word, which came to serve as a derogatory way to refer to persons who deviated from heterosexual norms.

2 In the 1990 edition, Jenkins is fined one hundred dollars instead of ten, likely to reflect modern penalties and the impact of inflation. This is one example of how the edition purposefully attempts to modernize the text by revising its historical details. Also, although the illustrations of this modern edition portray the Morrises in old-fashioned clothing, they are more reminiscent of the 1920s than the 1890s.

3 Jack's threats of "lashing" and "flogging" animal abusers are omitted in the 1965 and 1990 editions.

an emaciated condition. His cows are plastered up with mud and filth, and are covered with vermin. Where is our health inspector, that he does not exercise a more watchful supervision over establishments of this kind? To allow milk from an unclean place like this to be sold in the town, is endangering the health of its inhabitants. Upon inquiry, it was found that the man Jenkins bears a very bad character. Steps are being taken to have his wife and children removed from him.'"[1]

Jack threw the paper into my box, and he and the other boys gave three cheers for the *Daily News* and then ran away. How glad I was! It did not matter so much for me, for I had escaped him, but now that it had been found out what a cruel man he was, there would be a restraint upon him, and poor Toby and the cows would have a happier time.

I was going to tell about the Morris family. There were Mr. Morris, who was a clergyman and preached in a church in Fairport; Mrs. Morris, his wife; Miss Laura, who was the eldest of the family; then Jack, Ned, Carl, and Willie. I think one reason why they were such a good family was because Mrs. Morris was such a good woman.[2] She loved her husband and children, and did everything she could to make them happy.

Mr. Morris was a very busy man and rarely interfered in household affairs. Mrs. Morris was the one who said what was to be done and what was not to be done. Even then, when I was a young dog, I used to think that she was very wise. There was never any noise or confusion in the house, and though there was a great deal of work to be done, everything went on smoothly and pleasantly, and no one ever got angry and scolded as they did in the Jenkins family.

Mrs. Morris was very particular about money matters. Whenever the boys came to her for money to get such things as candy and ice cream, expensive toys, and other things that boys often crave, she asked them why they wanted them. If it was for some selfish reason, she said, firmly: "No, my children; we are not rich

---

1   As with much of the other violence in the text, the 1965 edition omits this paragraph, with the effect that the milk inspector is not indicted and Jenkins's wife and children are not rescued. In fact, domestic violence is entirely erased. In contrast, the 1990 edition directly proclaims what the 1894 original only alludes to, explicitly identifying Jenkins as a domestic abuser and linking this cruelty to animal abuse.

2   In the 1965 edition Mrs. Morris is, like Laura, relatively less constrained by the traditional feminine role of moral and emotional shepherd of the family; this sentence and the next are omitted.

people, and we must save our money for your education. I cannot buy you foolish things."[1]

If they asked her for money for books or something to make their pet animals more comfortable, or for their outdoor games, she gave it to them willingly. Her ideas about the bringing up of children I cannot explain as clearly as she can herself, so I will give part of a conversation that she had with a lady who was calling on her shortly after I came to Washington Street.

I happened to be in the house at the time. Indeed, I used to spend the greater part of my time in the house. Jack one day looked at me, and exclaimed: "Why does that dog stalk about, first after one and then after another, looking at us with such solemn eyes?"

I wished that I could speak to tell him that I had so long been used to seeing animals kicked about and trodden upon, that I could not get used to the change. It seemed too good to be true. I could scarcely believe that dumb animals had rights; but while it lasted, and human beings were so kind to me, I wanted to be with them all the time. Miss Laura understood. She drew my head up to her lap, and put her face down to me: "You like to be with us, don't you, Joe? Stay in the house as much as you like. Jack doesn't mind, though he speaks so sharply. When you get tired of us go out in the garden and have a romp with Jim."

But I must return to the conversation I referred to. It was one fine June day, and Mrs. Morris was sewing in a rocking-chair by the window. I was beside her, sitting on a hassock, so that I could look out into the street. Dogs love variety and excitement, and like to see what is going on outdoors as well as human beings. A carriage drove up to the door, and a finely dressed lady got out and came up the steps.

Mrs. Morris seemed glad to see her, and called her Mrs. Montague. I was pleased with her, for she had some kind of perfume about her that I liked to smell. So I went and sat on the hearth rug quite near her.

They had a little talk about things I did not understand and then the lady's eyes fell on me. She looked at me through a bit of glass that was hanging by a chain from her neck, and pulled away her beautiful dress lest I should touch it.

I did not care any longer for the perfume, and went away and sat very straight and stiff at Mrs. Morris' feet. The lady's eyes still

---

1   Perhaps reflecting 1960s consumer culture, these specific items become, in the 1965 edition, a vague reference to "selfish things."

followed me.

"I beg your pardon, Mrs. Morris," she said; "but that is a very queer-looking dog you have there."

"Yes," said Mrs. Morris, quietly; "he is not a handsome dog."

"And he is a new one, isn't he?" said Mrs. Montague.

"Yes."

"And that makes—"

"Two dogs, a cat, fifteen or twenty rabbits, a rat, about a dozen canaries, and two dozen goldfish, I don't know how many pigeons, a few bantams, a guinea pig, and—well, I don't think there is anything more."

They both laughed, and Mrs. Montague said: "You have quite a menagerie. My father would never allow one of his children to keep a pet animal. He said it would make his girls rough and noisy to romp about the house with cats, and his boys would look like rowdies if they went about with dogs at their heels."

"I have never found that it made my children more rough to play with their pets," said Mrs. Morris.

"No, I should think not," said the lady, languidly. "Your boys are the most gentlemanly lads in Fairport, and as for Laura, she is a perfect little lady. I like so much to have them come and see Charlie. They wake him up, and yet don't make him naughty."[1]

"They enjoyed their last visit very much," said Mrs. Morris. "By the way, I have heard them talking about getting Charlie a dog."

"Oh!" cried the lady, with a little shudder, "beg them not to. I cannot sanction that. I hate dogs."

"Why do you hate them?" asked Mrs. Morris, gently.

"They are such dirty things; they always smell and have vermin on them."

"A dog," said Mrs. Morris, "is something like a child. If you want it clean and pleasant, you have got to keep it so. This dog's skin is as clean as yours or mine. Hold still, Joe," and she brushed the hair on my back the wrong way, and showed Mrs. Montague how pink and free from dust my skin was.

Mrs. Montague looked at me more kindly, and even held out the tips of her fingers to me. I did not lick them. I only smelled them, and she drew her hand back again.

"You have never been brought in contact with the lower creation as I have," said Mrs. Morris; "just let me tell you, in a few

---

1 In the 1990 edition, the pet's role in producing gender is less explicit; the lines from "I have never ..." to "... make him naughty" are cut.

words, what a help dumb animals have been to me in the up-bringing of my children—my boys, especially. When I was a young married woman, going about the slums of New York with my husband,[1] I used to come home and look at my two babies as they lay in their little cots, and say to him, 'What are we going to do to keep these children from selfishness—the curse of the world?'

"'Get them to do something for somebody outside them-selves,' he always said. And I have tried to act on that principle. Laura is naturally unselfish. With her tiny, baby fingers, she would take food from her own mouth and put it into Jack's, if we did not watch her. I have never had any trouble with her. But the boys were born selfish, tiresomely, disgustingly selfish.[2] They were good boys in many ways. As they grew older, they were respectful, obedient, they were not untidy, and not particularly rough, but their one thought was for themselves—each one for himself, and they used to quarrel with each other in regard to their rights. While we were in New York, we had only a small, back yard. When we came here, I said, 'I am going to try an experi-ment.' We got this house because it had a large garden, and a stable that would do for the boys to play in. Then I got them together, and had a little serious talk. I said I was not pleased with the way in which they were living. They did nothing for any one but themselves from morning to night. If I asked them to do an errand for me, it was done unwillingly. Of course, I knew they had their school for a part of the day, but they had a good deal of leisure time when they might do something for some one else. I asked them if they thought they were going to make real, manly Christian boys at this rate, and they said no. Then I asked them what we should do about it. They all said, 'You tell us mother, and we'll do as you say.' I proposed a series of tasks. Each one to do something for somebody, outside and apart from himself,

---

1 Likely a Mrs. Morris of the 1960s would not be touring slums as well-heeled nineteenth-century Americans did. The liberal-minded middle classes were both fascinated and repulsed by the sordid details of the lives of the working poor. Later, on p. 78, Saunders alludes to Jacob Riis's *How the Other Half Lives* (New York: Charles Scribner's Sons, 1890), the well-illustrated study of New York City tenement life that inspired significant reform in New York City, including the razing of the city's most notorious slum, the Five Points.

2 Recognizing the role of socialization in molding gender-specific traits, in the 1965 edition Laura is not "naturally unselfish," just as the boys were not "born selfish."

every day of his life.[1] They all agreed to this, and told me to allot the tasks. If I could have afforded it, I would have gotten a horse and cow, and had them take charge of them; but I could not do that, so I invested in a pair of rabbits for Jack, a pair of canaries for Carl, pigeons for Ned, and bantams for Willie. I brought these creatures home, put them into their hands, and told them to provide for them. They were delighted with my choice, and it was very amusing to see them scurrying about to provide food and shelter for their pets, and hear their consultations with other boys. The end of it all is, that I am perfectly satisfied with my experiment. My boys, in caring for these dumb creatures, have become unselfish and thoughtful. They had rather go to school without their own breakfast than have the inmates of the stable go hungry. They are getting a humane education, a heart education, added to the intellectual education of their schools.[2] Then it keeps them at home. I used to be worried with the lingering about street corners, the dawdling around with other boys, and the idle, often worse than idle, talk indulged in. Now they have something to do, they are men of business. They are always hammering and pounding at boxes and partitions out there in the stable, or cleaning up, and if they are sent out on an errand, they do it and come right home. I don't mean to say that we have deprived them of liberty. They have their days for baseball, and football, and excursions to the woods, but they have so much to do at home, that they won't go away unless for a specific purpose."

While Mrs. Morris was talking, her visitor leaned forward in her chair, and listened attentively. When she finished, Mrs. Montague said, quietly, "Thank you, I am glad that you told me this. I shall get Charlie a dog."

"I am glad to hear you say that," replied Mrs. Morris. "It will be a good thing for your little boy. I should not wish my boys to be without a good, faithful dog. A child can learn many a lesson from a dog. This one," pointing to me, "might be held up as an example to many a human being. He is patient, quiet, and obedient. My husband says that he reminds him of three words in the Bible—'through much tribulation.'"

---

1   In the 1920, 1934, 1965, and 1990 editions, this sentence was omitted. Perhaps a requirement of daily altruistic service no longer seemed reasonable almost three decades after the novel's first publication.

2   The 1965 edition omits specific reference to humane education. In the twentieth century, pet-keeping was no longer seen as part of a larger project of spreading humane values.

"Why does he say that?" asked Mrs. Montague, curiously.

"Because he came to us from a very unhappy home." And Mrs. Morris went on to tell her friend what she knew of my early days.

When she stopped, Mrs. Montague's face was shocked and pained. "How dreadful to think that there are such creatures as that man Jenkins in the world. And you say that he has a wife and children. Mrs. Morris, tell me plainly, are there many such unhappy homes in Fairport?"[1]

Mrs. Morris hesitated for a minute, then she said, earnestly: "My dear friend, if you could see all the wickedness, and cruelty, and vileness, that is practiced in this little town of ours in one night, you could not rest in your bed."

Mrs. Montague looked dazed. "I did not dream that it was as bad as that," she said. "Are we worse than other towns?"

"No; not worse, but bad enough. Over and over again the saying is true, one half the world does not know how the other half lives. How can all this misery touch you? You live in your lovely house out of the town. When you come in, you drive about, do your shopping, make calls, and go home again. You never visit the poorest streets. The people from them never come to you. You are rich, your people before you were rich, you live in a state of isolation."

"But that is not right," said the lady, in a wailing voice. "I have been thinking about this matter lately. I read a great deal in the papers about the misery of the lower classes, and I think we richer ones ought to do something to help them. Mrs. Morris, what can I do?"

The tears came in Mrs. Morris' eyes. She looked at the little, frail lady, and said, simply: "Dear Mrs. Montague, I think the root of the whole matter lies in this. The Lord made us all one family. We are all brothers and sisters. The lowest woman is your sister and my sister. The man lying in the gutter is our brother. What should we do to help these members of our common family, who are not as well off as we are? We should share our last crust with them. You and I, but for God's grace in placing us in different surroundings, might be in their places. I think it is wicked neglect, criminal neglect in us to ignore this fact."

"It is, it is," said Mrs. Montague, in a despairing voice. "I can't help feeling it. Tell me something I can do to help some one."

---

1 In the 1990 edition, the next seventeen paragraphs where Mrs. Morris reforms Mrs. Montague are omitted.

Mrs. Morris sank back in her chair, her face very sad, and yet with something like pleasure in her eyes as she looked at her caller. "Your washerwoman," she said, "has a drunken husband and a cripple boy. I have often seen her standing over her tub, washing your delicate muslins and laces, and dropping tears into the water."

"I will never send her anything more—she shall not be troubled," said Mrs. Montague, hastily.

Mrs. Morris could not help smiling. "I have not made myself clear. It is not the washing that troubles her; it is her husband who beats her, and her boy who worries her.[1] If you and I take our work from her, she will have that much less money to depend upon, and will suffer in consequence. She is a hard-working and capable woman, and makes a fair living. I would not advise you to give her money, for her husband would find it out, and take it from her. It is sympathy that she wants.[2] If you could visit her occasionally, and show that you are interested in her, by talking or reading to her poor foolish boy or showing him a picture-book, you have no idea how grateful she would be to you, and how it would cheer her on her dreary way."

"I will go to see her to-morrow," said Mrs. Montague. "Can you think of any one else I could visit?"

"A great many," said Mrs. Morris; "but I don't think you had better undertake too much at once. I will give you the addresses of three or four poor families, where an occasional visit would do untold good. That is, it will do them good if you treat them as you do your richer friends. Don't give them too much money, or too many presents, till you find out what they need. Try to feel interested in them. Find out their ways of living, and what they are going to do with their children, and help them to get situations for them if you can. And be sure to remember that poverty does not always take away one's self-respect."

---

1 Since in the 1965 edition all mention of interpersonal violence is toned down, the washerwoman's husband does not "beat" her; he merely "worries" her.

2 In the 1965 edition, this sentence is omitted. The wealthy Mrs. Montague no longer needs to feel sympathy for the have-nots. During the time of Saunders's writing, however, one's feelings towards others (the poor, animals) were the mark of the humane, and benevolent action was assumed to ensue from these kindly feelings. Relatedly, the 1920, 1925, and 1934 editions omit the later suggestion, "Try to feel interested in them."

"I will, I will," said Mrs. Montague, eagerly. "When can you give me these addresses?"

Mrs. Morris smiled again, and, taking a piece of paper and a pencil from her work basket wrote a few lines and handed them to Mrs. Montague.

The lady got up to take her leave. "And in regard to the dog," said Mrs. Morris, following her to the door, "if you decide to allow Charlie to have one, you had better let him come in and have a talk with my boys about it. They seem to know all the dogs that are for sale in the town."

"Thank you, I shall be most happy to do so. He shall have his dog. When can you have him?"

"To-morrow, the next day, any day at all. It makes no difference to me. Let him spend an afternoon and evening with the boys, if you do not object."

"It will give me much pleasure," and the little lady bowed and smiled, and after stooping down to pat me, tripped down the steps, and got into her carriage and drove away.

Mrs. Morris stood looking after her with a beaming face, and I began to think that I should like Mrs. Montague too, if I knew her long enough. Two days later I was quite sure I should, for I had a proof that she really liked me. When her little boy Charlie came to the house, he brought something for me done up in white paper. Mrs. Morris opened it, and there was a handsome, nickel-plated collar, with my name on it—*Beautiful Joe*. Wasn't I pleased! They took off the little shabby leather strap that the boys had given me when I came, and fastened on my new collar, and then Mrs. Morris held me up to a glass to look at myself. I felt so happy. Up to this time I had felt a little ashamed of my cropped ears and docked tail, but now that I had a fine new collar I could hold up my head with any dog.

"Dear old Joe," said Mrs. Morris, pressing my head tightly between her hands. "You did a good thing the other day in helping me to start that little woman out of her selfish way of living."

I did not know about that, but I knew that I felt very grateful to Mrs. Montague for my new collar, and ever afterward, when I met her in the street, I stopped and looked at her. Sometimes she saw me and stopped her carriage to speak to me; but I always wagged my tail, or rather my body, for I had no tail to wag, whenever I saw her, whether she saw me or not.

Her son got a beautiful Irish setter, called "Brisk." He had a silky coat and soft brown eyes, and his young master seemed very fond of him.

CHAPTER 6

THE FOX TERRIER BILLY

WHEN I came to the Morrises, I knew nothing about the proper way of bringing up a puppy. I once heard of a little boy whose sister beat him so much, that he said he was brought up by hand; so I think as Jenkins kicked me so much, I may say that I was brought up by foot.

Shortly after my arrival in my new home, I had a chance of seeing how one should bring up a little puppy.

One day I was sitting beside Miss Laura in the parlor, when the door opened, and Jack came in. One of his hands was laid over the other, and he said to his sister, "Guess what I've got here?"

"A bird," she said.

"No."

"A rat."

"No."

"A mouse."

"No—a pup."

"Oh, Jack," she said, reprovingly; for she thought he was telling a story.

He opened his hands, and there lay the tiniest morsel of a fox terrier puppy that I ever saw. He was white, with black and tan markings. His body was pure white, his tail black, with a dash of tan; his ears black, and his face evenly marked with black and tan. We could not tell the color of his eyes, as they were not open. Later on, they turned out to be a pretty brown. His nose was pale pink, and when he got older, it became jet black.

"Why, Jack!" exclaimed Miss Laura, "his eyes aren't open; why did you take him from his mother?"

"She's dead," said Jack. "Poisoned—left her pups to run about the yard for a little exercise. Some brute had thrown over a piece of poisoned meat, and she ate it. Four of the pups died. This is the only one left. Mr. Robinson says his man doesn't understand raising pups without their mothers, and as he is going away, he wants us to have it, for we always had such luck in nursing sick animals."

Mr. Robinson I knew was a friend of the Morrises, and a gentleman who was fond of fancy stock, and imported a great deal of it from England. If this puppy came from him, it was sure to be a good one.

Miss Laura took the tiny creature, and went upstairs very thoughtfully. I followed her, and watched her get a little basket and line it with cotton wool. She put the puppy in it, and looked at him. Though it was midsummer, and the house seemed very warm to me, the little creature was shivering, and making a low, murmuring noise. She pulled the wool all over him, and put the window down, and set his basket in the sun.

Then she went to the kitchen and got some warm milk. She dipped her finger in it, and offered it to the puppy, but he went nosing about it in a stupid way, and wouldn't touch it. "Too young," Miss Laura said. She got a little piece of muslin, put some bread in it, tied a string round it, and dipped it in the milk. When she put this to the puppy's mouth, he sucked it greedily. He acted as if he was starving, but Miss Laura only let him have a little.

Every few hours for the rest of the day, she gave him some more milk, and I heard the boys say that for many nights she got up once or twice and heated milk over a lamp for him. One night the milk got cold before he took it, and he swelled up and became so ill that Miss Laura had to rouse her mother and get some hot water to plunge him in. That made him well again, and no one seemed to think it was a great deal of trouble to take for a creature that was nothing but a dog.

He fully repaid them for all his care, for he turned out to be one of the prettiest and most lovable dogs that I ever saw. They called him Billy, and the two events of his early life were the opening of his eyes and the swallowing of his muslin rag. The rag did not seem to hurt him; but Miss Laura said that, as he had got so strong and greedy, he must learn to eat like other dogs.

He was very amusing when he was a puppy. He was full of tricks, and he crept about in a mischievous way when one did not know he was near. He was a very small puppy and used to climb inside Miss Laura's Jersey sleeve up to her shoulder when he was six weeks old. One day, when the whole family was in the parlor, Mr. Morris suddenly flung aside his newspaper, and began jumping up and down. Mrs. Morris was very much alarmed, and cried out, "My dear William, what is the matter?"

"There's a rat up my leg," he said, shaking it violently. Just then little Billy fell out on the floor and lay on his back looking up at Mr. Morris with a surprised face. He had felt cold and thought it would be warm inside Mr. Morris' trouser's leg.

However, Billy never did any real mischief, thanks to Miss Laura's training. She began to punish him just as soon as he began to tear and worry things.[1] The first thing he attacked was Mr. Morris' felt hat. The wind blew it down the hall one day, and Billy came along and began to try it with his teeth. I dare say it felt good to them, for a puppy is very like a baby and loves something to bite.[2]

Miss Laura found him, and he rolled his eyes at her quite innocently, not knowing that he was doing wrong. She took the hat away, and pointing from it to him, said, "Bad Billy!" Then she gave him two or three slaps with a bootlace. She never struck a little dog with her hand or a stick. She said clubs were for big dogs and switches for little dogs, if one had to use them. The best way was to scold them, for a good dog feels a severe scolding as much as a whipping.

Billy was very much ashamed of himself. Nothing would induce him even to look at a hat again. But he thought it was no harm to worry other things. He attacked one thing after another, the rugs on the floor, curtains, anything flying or fluttering, and Miss Laura patiently scolded him for each one, till at last it dawned upon him that he must not worry anything but a bone. Then he got to be a very good dog.

There was one thing that Miss Laura was very particular about, and that was to have him fed regularly. We both got three meals a day. We were never allowed to go into the dining room, and while the family was at the table, we lay in the hall outside and watched what was going on.

Dogs take a great interest in what any one gets to eat. It was quite exciting to see the Morrises passing each other different dishes, and to smell the nice, hot food. Billy often wished that he could get up on the table. He said that he would make things fly. When he was growing, he hardly ever got enough to eat. I used to tell him that he would kill himself if he could eat all he wanted to.

As soon as meals were over, Billy and I scampered after Miss Laura to the kitchen. We each had our own plate for food. Mary

---

1   In the 1990 edition, puppy training is gentler. Laura does not "punish him"; rather, she gives "lessons." Instead of "Bad Billy!", she says "No, Skippy." The reference to clubbing and whipping more difficult dogs is cut.

2   The handful of instances in the original where animal behavior is directly compared to human behavior is omitted in the 1990 edition; this sentence is omitted. The omissions widen the gulf between human and animal.

the cook often laughed at Miss Laura, because she would not let her dogs "dish" together. Miss Laura said that if she did, the larger one would get more than his share, and the little one would starve.

It was quite a sight to see Billy eat. He spread his legs apart to steady himself, and gobbled at his food like a duck. When he finished he always looked up for more, and Miss Laura would shake her head and say: "No, Billy; better longing than loathing. I believe that a great many little dogs are killed by over-feeding."

I often heard the Morrises speak of the foolish way in which some people stuffed their pets with food, and either kill them by it or keep them in continual ill health. A case occurred in our neighborhood while Billy was a puppy. Some people, called Dobson, who lived only a few doors from the Morrises, had a fine bay mare and a little colt called Sam. They were very proud of this colt, and Mr. Dobson had promised it to his son James. One day Mr. Dobson asked Mr. Morris to come in and see the colt, and I went too. I watched Mr. Morris while he examined it. It was a pretty little creature, and I did not wonder that they thought so much of it.

When Mr. Morris went home his wife asked him what he thought of it.

"I think," he said, "that it won't live long."

"Why, papa!" exclaimed Jack, who overheard the remark, "it is as fat as a seal."

"It would have a better chance for its life if it were lean and scrawny," said Mr. Morris. "They are over-feeding it, and I told Mr. Dobson so; but he wasn't inclined to believe me."

Now, Mr. Morris had been brought up in the country, and knew a great deal about animals, so I was inclined to think he was right. And sure enough, in a few days, we heard that the colt was dead.

Poor James Dobson felt very badly. A number of the neighbors' boys went into see him, and there he stood gazing at the dead colt, and looking as if he wanted to cry. Jack was there and I was at his heels, and though he said nothing for a time, I knew he was angry with the Dobsons for sacrificing the colt's life. Presently he said, "You won't need to have that colt stuffed now he's dead, Dobson."

"What do you mean? Why do you say that?" asked the boy, peevishly.

"Because you stuffed him while he was alive," said Jack, saucily.

Then we had to run for all we were worth, for the Dobson boy was after us, and as he was a big fellow he would have whipped Jack soundly.

I must not forget to say that Billy was washed regularly—once a week with nice-smelling soaps and once a month with strong-smelling, disagreeable, carbolic soap. He had his own towels and wash cloths, and after being rubbed and scrubbed, he was rolled in a blanket and put by the fire to dry. Miss Laura said that a little dog that has been petted and kept in the house, and has become tender, should never be washed and allowed to run about with a wet coat, unless the weather was very warm, for he would be sure to take cold.

Jim and I were more hardy than Billy, and we took our baths in the sea. Every few days the boys took us down to the shore, and we went swimming with them.

CHAPTER 7

TRAINING A PUPPY

"NED, dear," said Miss Laura one day, "I wish you would train Billy to follow and retrieve. He is four months old now, and I shall soon want to take him out in the street."

"Very well, sister," said mischievous Ned; and catching up a stick, he said, "Come out into the garden, dogs."

Though he was brandishing his stick very fiercely, I was not at all afraid of him; and as for Billy, he loved Ned.

The Morris garden was really not a garden, but a large piece of ground with the grass worn bare in many places, a few trees scattered about, and some raspberry and currant bushes along the fence. A lady who knew that Mr. Morris had not a large salary, said one day when she was looking out of the dining-room window, "My dear Mrs. Morris, why don't you have this garden dug up? You could raise your own vegetables. It would be so much cheaper than buying them."

Mrs. Morris laughed in great amusement. "Think of the hens, and cats, and dogs, and rabbits, and, above all, the boys that I have. What sort of a garden would there be, and do you think it would be fair to take their playground from them?"

The lady said, "No, she did not think it would be fair."

I am sure I don't know what the boys would have done without this strip of ground. Many a frolic and game they had there. In the present case, Ned walked around and around it, with his stick on his shoulder, Billy and I strolling after him. Presently Billy made a dash aside to get a bone. Ned turned around and said firmly, "To heel!"

Billy looked at him innocently, not knowing what he meant. "To heel!" exclaimed Ned again. Billy thought he wanted to play, and putting his head on his paws, he began to bark. Ned laughed; still he kept saying "To heel!" He would not say another word. He knew if he said "Come here," or "Follow," or "Go behind," it would confuse Billy.

Finally, as Ned kept saying the words over and over, and pointing to me, it seemed to dawn upon Billy that he wanted him to follow him. So he came beside me, and together we followed Ned around the garden, again and again.

Ned often looked behind with a pleased face, and I felt so proud to think I was doing well; but suddenly I got dreadfully confused when he turned around and said, "Hie out!"

The Morrises all used the same words in training their dogs, and I had heard Miss Laura say this, but I had forgotten what it meant. "Good Joe," said Ned, turning around and patting me, "you have forgotten. I wonder where Jim is? He would help us."

He put his fingers in his mouth and blew a shrill whistle, and soon Jim came trotting up the lane from the street. He looked at us with his large, intelligent eyes, and wagged his tail slowly, as if to say, "Well, what do you want of me?"

"Come and give me a hand at this training business, old Sobersides," said Ned, with a laugh. "It's too slow to do it alone. Now, young gentlemen, attention! To heel!" He began to march around the garden again, and Jim and I followed closely at his heels, while little Billy, seeing that he could not get us to play with him, came lagging behind.

Soon Ned turned around and said, "Hie out!" Old Jim sprang ahead, and ran off in front as if he was after something. Now I remembered what "hie out" meant. We were to have a lovely race wherever we liked. Little Billy loved this. We ran and scampered hither and thither, and Ned watched us, laughing at our antics.

After tea, he called us out in the garden again, and said he had something else to teach us. He turned up a tub on the wooden platform at the back door, and sat on it, and then called Jim to him.

He took a small leather strap from his pocket. It had a nice, strong smell. We all licked it, and each dog wished to have it. "No, Joe and Billy," said Ned, holding us both by our collars; "you wait a minute. Here, Jim."

Jim watched him very earnestly, and Ned threw the strap half-way across the garden, and said, "Fetch it."

Jim never moved till he heard the words, "Fetch it." Then he ran swiftly, brought the strap, and dropped it in Ned's hand. Ned sent him after it two or three times, then he said to Jim, "Lie down," and turned to me. "Here, Joe, it is your turn."

He threw the strap under the raspberry bushes, then looked at me and said, "Fetch it." I knew quite well what he meant, and ran joyfully after it. I soon found it by the strong smell, but the queerest thing happened when I got it in my mouth. I began to gnaw it and play with it, and when Ned called out, "Fetch it," I dropped it and ran toward him. I was not obstinate, but I was stupid.

Ned pointed to the place where it was, and spread out his empty hands. That helped me, and I ran quickly and got it. He made me get it for him several times. Sometimes I could not find it, and sometimes I dropped it; but he never stirred. He sat still till I brought it to him.

After a while he tried Billy, but it soon got dark, and we could not see, so he took Billy and went into the house.

I stayed out with Jim for a while, and he asked me if I knew why Ned had thrown a strap for us, instead of a bone or something hard.

Of course I did not know, so Jim told me it was on his account. He was a bird dog, and was never allowed to carry anything hard in his mouth, because it would make him hard-mouthed, and he would be apt to bite the birds when he was bringing them back to any person who was shooting with him. He said that he had been so carefully trained that he could even carry three eggs at a time in his mouth.

I said to him, "Jim, how is it that you never go out shooting? I have always heard that you were a dog for that, and yet you never leave home."

He hung his head a little, and said he did not wish to go, and then, for he was an honest dog, he gave me the true reason.

CHAPTER 8

A RUINED DOG

"I WAS a sporting dog," he said, bitterly, "for the first three years of my life. I belonged to a man who keeps a livery stable here in Fairport, and he used to hire me out to shooting parties.

"I was a favorite with all the gentlemen. I was crazy with delight when I saw the guns brought out, and would jump up and bite at them. I loved to chase birds and rabbits, and even now when the pigeons come near me, I tremble all over and have to turn away lest I should seize them. I used often to be in the woods from morning till night. I liked to have a hard search after a bird after it had been shot, and to be praised for bringing it out without biting or injuring it.

"I never got lost, for I am one of those dogs that can always tell where human beings are. I did not smell them. I would be too far away for that, but if my master was standing in some place and I took a long round through the woods, I knew exactly where he was, and could make a short cut back to him without returning in my tracks.

"But I must tell you about my trouble. One Saturday afternoon a party of young men came to get me. They had a dog with them, a cocker spaniel called Bob, but they wanted another. For some reason or other, my master was very unwilling to have me go. However, he at last consented, and they put me in the back of the wagon with Bob and the lunch baskets, and we drove off into the country. This Bob was a happy, merry-looking dog, and as we went along, he told me of the fine time we should have next day. The young men would shoot a little, then they would get out their baskets and have something to eat and drink, and would play cards and go to sleep under the trees, and we would be able to help ourselves to legs and wings of chickens, and anything we liked from the baskets.

"I did not like this at all. I was used to working hard through the week, and I liked to spend my Sundays quietly at home. However, I said nothing.

"That night we slept at a country hotel, and drove the next morning to the banks of a small lake where the young men were told there would be plenty of wild ducks. They were in no hurry to begin their sport. They sat down in the sun on some flat rocks at the water's edge, and said they would have something to drink before setting to work. They got out some of the bottles from the

Toronto: McClelland & Stewart, 1934.

wagon, and began to take long drinks from them. Then they got quarrelsome and mischievous and seemed to forget all about their shooting. One of them proposed to have some fun with the dogs. They tied us both to a tree, and throwing a stick in the water, told us to get it. Of course we struggled and tried to get free, and chafed our necks with the rope.

"After a time one of them began to swear at me, and say that he believed I was gun-shy. He staggered to the wagon and got out his fowling piece, and said he was going to try me.

"He loaded it, went to a little distance, and was going to fire, when the young man who owned Bob said he wasn't going to have his dog's legs shot off, and coming up he unfastened him and took him away. You can imagine my feelings, as I stood there tied to the tree, with that stranger pointing his gun directly at me. He fired close to me, a number of times—over my head and under my body. The earth was cut up all around me. I was terribly frightened, and howled and begged to be freed.

"The other young men, who were sitting laughing at me, thought it such good fun that they got their guns, too. I never wish to spend such a terrible hour again. I was sure they would kill me. I dare say they would have done so, for they were all quite drunk by this time, if something had not happened.

"Poor Bob, who was almost as frightened as I was, and who lay shivering under the wagon, was killed by a shot by his own master, whose hand was the most unsteady of all. He gave one loud howl, kicked convulsively, then turned over on his side, and lay quite still. It sobered them all. They ran up to him, but he was quite dead. They sat for a while quite silent, then they threw the rest of the bottles into the lake, dug a shallow grave for Bob, and putting me in the wagon drove slowly back to town. They were not bad young men. I don't think they meant to hurt me, or to kill Bob. It was the nasty stuff in the bottles that took away their reason.[1]

"I was never the same dog again. I was quite deaf in my right ear, and though I strove against it, I was so terribly afraid of even the sight of a gun that I would run and hide myself whenever one was shown to me. My master was very angry with those young men, and it seemed as if he could not bear the sight of me. One day he took me very kindly and brought me here, and asked Mr. Morris if he did not want a good-natured dog to play with the children.

---

1 All references to the evils of alcohol are cut from the 1965 edition. These "rowdies" are no longer under the influence of alcohol when they shoot the dog. They are altogether more sympathetic: the "stranger" is "thoughtless" and the bullet that kills Bob is a "stray." Instead of being excused by drink, in the 1965 edition they are excused by ignorance: "This brought the men to their senses. They weren't bad young men. I suppose when they were little boys, they tied tin cans to puppies' tails and pulled the wings off butterflies. They probably never realized how cruel they were being."

"I have a happy home here and I love the Morris boys; but I often wish that I could keep from putting my tail between my legs and running home every time I hear the sound of a gun."

"Never mind that, Jim," I said. "You should not fret over a thing for which you are not to blame. I am sure you must be glad for one reason that you have left your old life."

"What is that?" he said.

"On account of the birds. You know Miss Laura thinks it is wrong to kill the pretty creatures that fly about the woods."

"So it is," he said, "unless one kills them at once. I have often felt angry with men for only half killing a bird. I hated to pick up the little, warm body, and see the bright eye looking so reproachfully at me, and feel the flutter of life. We animals, or rather the most of us, kill mercifully. It is only human beings who butcher their prey, and seem, some of them, to rejoice in their agony. I used to be eager to kill birds and rabbits, but I did not want to keep them before me long after they were dead. I often stop in the street and look up at fine ladies' bonnets, and wonder how they can wear little dead birds in such dreadful positions. Some of them have their heads twisted under their wings and over their shoulders, and looking toward their tails, and their eyes are so horrible that I wish I could take those ladies into the woods and let them see how easy and pretty a live bird is, and how unlike the stuffed creatures they wear. Have you ever had a good run in the woods, Joe?"

"No, never," I said.

"Some day I will take you, and now it is late and I must go to bed. Are you going to sleep in the kennel with me, or in the stable?"

"I think I will sleep with you, Jim. Dogs like company, you know, as well as human beings." I curled up in the straw beside him, and soon we were fast asleep.

I have known a good many dogs, but I don't think I ever saw such a good one as Jim. He was gentle and kind, and so sensitive that a hard word hurt him more than a blow. He was a great pet with Mrs. Morris, and as he had been so well trained, he was able to make himself very useful to her.

When she went shopping, he often carried a parcel in his mouth for her. He would never drop it nor leave it anywhere. One day, she dropped her purse without knowing it, and Jim picked it up, and brought it home in his mouth. She did not notice him, for he always walked behind her. When she got to her own door, she missed the purse, and turning around saw it in Jim's mouth.

Another day, a lady gave Jack Morris a canary cage as a present for Carl. He was bringing it home, when one of the little seed boxes fell out. Jim picked it up and carried it a long way, before Jack discovered it.

CHAPTER 9

THE PARROT BELLA

I OFTEN used to hear the Morrises speak about vessels that ran between Fairport and a place called the West Indies, carrying cargoes of lumber and fish, and bringing home molasses, spices, fruit, and other things. On one of these vessels, called the "Mary Jane," was a cabin boy, who was a friend of the Morris boys, and often brought them presents.

One day, after I had been with the Morrises' for some months, this boy arrived at the house with a bunch of green bananas in one hand, and a parrot in the other. The boys were delighted with the parrot, and called their mother to see what a pretty bird she was.

Mrs. Morris seemed very much touched by the boy's thoughtfulness in bringing a present such a long distance to her boys, and thanked him warmly. The cabin boy became very shy, and all he could say was, "Go way!" over and over again, in a very awkward manner.

Mrs. Morris smiled, and left him with the boys. I think that she thought he would be more comfortable with them.

Jack put me up on the table to look at the parrot. The boy held her by a string tied around one of her legs. She was a gray parrot with a few red feathers in her tail, and she had bright eyes, and a very knowing air.

The boy said he had been careful to buy a young one that could not speak, for he knew the Morris boys would not want one chattering foreign gibberish, nor yet one that would swear. He had kept her in his bunk in the ship, and had spent all his leisure time in teaching her to talk. Then he looked at her anxiously, and said, "Show off now, can't ye?"

I didn't know what he meant by all this, until afterward. I had never heard of such a thing as birds talking. I stood on the table staring hard at her, and she stared hard at me. I was just thinking that I would not like to have her sharp little beak fastened in my skin, when I heard some one say, "Beautiful Joe." The voice seemed to come from the room, but I knew all the voices there, and this was one I had never heard before, so I thought I must be mistaken, and it was some one in the hall. I struggled to get away from Jack to run and see who it was. But he held me fast, and laughed with all his might. I looked at the other boys and they were laughing, too. Presently, I heard again, "Beau-ti-ful Joe,

Beau-ti-ful Joe." The sound was close by, and yet it did not come from the cabin boy, for he was all doubled up laughing, his face as red as a beet.

"It's the parrot, Joe!" cried Ned. "Look at her, you gaby." I did look at her, and with her head on one side, and the sauciest air in the world, she was saying: "Beau-ti-ful Joe, Beau-ti-ful Joe!"

I had never heard a bird talk before, and I felt so sheepish that I tried to get down and hide myself under the table. Then she began to laugh at me. "Ha, ha, ha, good dog—sic 'em, boy. Rats, rats! Beau-ti-ful Joe, Beau-ti-ful Joe," she cried, rattling off the words as fast as she could.

I never felt so queer before in my life, and the boys were just roaring with delight at my puzzled face. Then the parrot began calling for Jim: "Where's Jim, where's good old Jim? Poor old dog. Give him a bone."

The boys brought Jim in the parlor, and when he heard her funny, little, cracked voice calling him, he nearly went crazy: "Jimmy, Jimmy, James Augustus!" she said, which was Jim's long name.

He made a dash out of the room, and the boys screamed so that Mr. Morris came down from his study to see what the noise meant. As soon as the parrot saw him, she would not utter another word. The boys told him though what she had been saying, and he seemed much amused to think that the cabin boy should have remembered so many sayings his boys made use of, and taught them to the parrot. "Clever Polly," he said, kindly; "Good Polly."

The cabin boy looked at him shyly, and Jack, who was a very sharp boy, said quickly, "Is not that what you call her, Henry?"

"No," said the boy; "I call her Bell, short for Bellzebub."[1]

"I beg your pardon," said Jack, very politely.

"Bell—short for Bellzebub," repeated the boy. "Ye see, I thought ye'd like a name from the Bible, bein' a minister's sons. I hadn't my Bible with me on this cruise, savin' yer presence, an' I couldn't think of any girls' names out of it, but Eve or Queen of Sheba,[2] an' they didn't seem very fit, so I asked one of me mates, an' he says, for his part he guessed Bellzebub was as pretty a girl's

---

1 The well-educated sons of a clergyman are shocked by the impropriety of naming one's pet after the biblical "prince of demons" (Mark 3:22).

2 According to the Bible, the Queen of Sheba ruled Egypt and Ethiopia. She is known for visiting King Solomon to test his famed wisdom with a series of riddles (Kings 1:10).

name as any, so I guv her that. 'Twould 'a been better to let you name her, but ye see 'twouldn't 'a been handy not to call her somethin', where I was teachin' her every day."

Jack turned away and walked to the window, his face a deep scarlet. I heard him mutter, "Beelzebub, prince of devils," so I suppose the cabin boy had given his bird a bad name.

Mr. Morris looked kindly at the cabin boy "Do you ever call the parrot by her whole name?"

"No, sir," he replied; "I always give her Bell but she calls herself Bella."

"Bella," repeated Mr. Morris, "that is a very pretty name. If you keep her, boys, I think you had better stick to that."

"Yes, father," they all said; and then Mr. Morris started to go back to his study. On the doorsill he paused to ask the cabin boy when his ship sailed. Finding that it was to be in a few days, he took out his pocket-book and wrote something in it. The next day he asked Jack to go to town with him, and when they came home, Jack said that his father had bought an oil-skin coat for Henry Smith, and a handsome Bible, in which they were all to write their names.

After Mr. Morris left the room, the door opened, and Miss Laura came in. She knew nothing about the parrot, and was very much surprised to see it. Seating herself at the table, she held out her hands to it. She was so fond of pets of all kinds, that she never thought of being afraid of them. At the same time, she never laid her hand suddenly on any animal. She held out her fingers and talked gently, so that if it wished to come to her it could. She looked at the parrot as if she loved it, and the queer little thing walked right up and nestled its head against the lace in the front of her dress. "Pretty lady," she said, in a cracked whisper, "give Bella a kiss."

The boys were so pleased with this, and set up such a shout, that their mother came into the room and said they had better take the parrot out to the stable. Bella seemed to enjoy the fun. "Come on, boys," she screamed as Henry Smith lifted her on his finger. "Ha, ha, ha—come on, let's have some fun. Where's the guinea pig? Where's Davy, the rat? Where's pussy? Pussy, pussy, come here. Pussy, pussy, dear, pretty puss."

Her voice was shrill and distinct, and very like the voice of an old woman who came to the house for rags and bones. I followed her out to the stable, and stayed there until she noticed me and screamed out, "Ha, Joe, Beautiful Joe! Where's your tail? Who cut your ears off?"

I don't think it was kind in the cabin boy to teach her this, and I think she knew it teased me, for she said it over and over again, and laughed and chuckled with delight. I left her and did not see her till the next day, when the boys had got a fine, large cage for her.

The place for her cage was by one of the hall windows; but everybody in the house got so fond of her that she was moved about from one room to another.

She hated her cage, and used to put her head close to the bars and plead, "Let Bella out; Bella will be a good girl. Bella won't run away."

After a time the Morrises did let her out, and she kept her word and never tried to get away. Jack put a little handle on her cage door so that she could open and shut it herself, and it was very amusing to hear her say in the morning. "Clear the track, children! Bella's going to take a walk," and see her turn the handle with her claw and come out into the room. She was a very clever bird, and I have never seen any creature but a human being that could reason as she did. She was so petted and talked to that she got to know a great many words, and on one occasion she saved the Morrises from being robbed.

It was in the winter time. The family was having tea in the dining room at the back of the house, and Billy and I were lying in the hall watching what was going on. There was no one in the front of the house. The hall lamp was lighted, and the hall door closed, but not locked. Some sneak thieves, who had been doing a great deal of mischief in Fairport, crept up the steps and into the house, and, opening the door of the hall closet, laid their hands on the boys' winter overcoats.

They thought no one saw them, but they were mistaken. Bella had been having a nap upstairs, and had not come down when the tea bell rang. Now she was hopping down on her way to the dining room, and hearing the slight noise below, stopped and looked through the railing. Any pet creature that lives in a nice family hates a dirty, shabby person. Bella knew that those beggar boys had no business in that closet.

"Bad boys!" she screamed, angrily. "Get out—get out! Here, Joe, Joe, Beautiful Joe. Come quick. Billy, Billy, rats—Hie out, Jim, sic 'em boys. Where's the police. Call the police!"[1]

---

1   The 1920, 1925, and 1934 editions refer to the thieves as "beggar boys" that come to pay a social call, and instead of asking for the police, Bella hollers: "Company's coming! ... Get out the tea. Bring some cake! Quick, quick!" The 1965 and the 1990 editions omit the incident entirely.

Billy and I sprang up and pushed open the door leading to the front hall. The thieves in a terrible fright were just rushing down the front steps. One of them got away, but the other fell, and I caught him by the coat, till Mr. Morris ran and put his hand on his shoulder.

He was a young fellow about Jack's age, but not one-half so manly, and he was sniffling and scolding about "that pesky parrot." Mr. Morris made him come back into the house, and had a talk with him. He found out that he was a poor, ignorant lad, half starved by a drunken father. He and his brother stole clothes, and sent them to his sister in Boston, who sold them and returned part of the money.

Mr. Morris asked him if he would not like to get his living in an honest way, and he said he had tried to, but no one would employ him. Mr. Morris told him to go home and take leave of his father and get his brother and bring him to Washington Street the next day. He told him plainly that if he did not he would send a policeman after him.

The boy begged Mr. Morris not to do that, and early the next morning he appeared with his brother. Mrs. Morris gave them a good breakfast and fitted them out with clothes, and they were sent off in the train to one of her brothers, who was a kind farmer in the country, and who had been telegraphed to that these boys were coming, and wished to be provided with situations where they would have a chance to make honest men of themselves.[1]

---

1 On one hand, the middle classes did sincerely sympathize with the abject living conditions of the poor. On the other hand, the more abject the conditions, the more they stoked fears of a labor uprising (Levenstein 45). The middle class drew lines between the "deserving" and "undeserving"—the young thieves who could still be saved versus Jenkins the irredeemable.

CHAPTER 10

BILLY'S TRAINING CONTINUED

WHEN Billy was five months old, he had his first walk in the street. Miss Laura knew that he had been well trained, so she did not hesitate to take him into the town. She was not the kind of a young lady to go into the street with a dog that would not behave himself, and she was never willing to attract attention to herself by calling out orders to any of her pets.

As soon as we got down the front steps, she said, quietly to Billy, "To heel." It was very hard for little, playful Billy to keep close to her, when he saw so many new and wonderful things about him. He had gotten acquainted with everything in the house and garden, but this outside world was full of things he wanted to look at and smell of, and he was fairly crazy to play with some of the pretty dogs he saw running about. But he did just as he was told.

Soon we came to a shop, and Miss Laura went in to buy some ribbons. She said to me, "Stay out," but Billy she took in with her. I watched them through the glass door, and saw her go to a counter and sit down. Billy stood behind her till she said, "Lie down." Then he curled himself at her feet.

He lay quietly, even when she left him and went to another counter. But he eyed her very anxiously till she came back and said, "Up," to him. Then he sprang up and followed her out to the street.

She stood in the shop door, and looked lovingly down on us as we fawned on her. "Good dogs," she said, softly; "you shall have a present." We went behind her again, and she took us to a shop where we both lay beside the counter. When we heard her ask the clerk for solid rubber balls, we could scarcely keep still. We both knew what "ball" meant.

Taking the parcel in her hand, she came out into the street. She did not do any more shopping, but turned her face toward the sea. She was going to give us a nice walk along the beach, although it was a dark, disagreeable, cloudy day, when most young ladies would have stayed in the house. The Morris children never minded the weather. Even in the pouring rain, the boys would put on rubber boots and coats and go out to play. Miss Laura walked along, the high wind blowing her cloak and dress about, and when we got past the houses, she had a little run with us. We jumped, and frisked, and barked, till we were tired; and then we walked quietly along.

A little distance ahead of us were some boys throwing sticks in the water for two Newfoundland dogs. Suddenly a quarrel sprang up between the dogs. They were both powerful creatures, and fairly matched as regarded size. It was terrible to hear their fierce growling, and to see the way in which they tore at each other's throats. I looked at Miss Laura. If she had said a word, I would have run in and helped the dog that was getting the worst of it. But she told me to keep back, and ran on herself.

The boys were throwing water on the dogs, and pulling their tails, and hurling stones at them, but they could not separate them. Their heads seemed locked together, and they went back and forth over the stones, the boys crowding around them, shouting, and beating, and kicking at them.

"Stand back, boys," said Miss Laura, "I'll stop them." She pulled a little parcel from her purse, bent over the dogs, scattered a powder on their noses, and the next instant the dogs were yards apart, nearly sneezing their heads off.

"I say, Missis, what did you do? What's that stuff? Whew, it's pepper!" the boys exclaimed.

Miss Laura sat down on a flat rock, and looked at them with a very pale face. "Oh, boys," she said, "why did you make those dogs fight? It is so cruel. They were playing happily till you set them on each other. Just see how they have torn their handsome coats, and how the blood is dripping from them."

"'Tain't my fault," said one of the lads, sullenly. "Jim Jones there said his dog could lick my dog, and I said he couldn't—and he couldn't, nuther."

"Yes, he could," cried the other boy; "and if you say he couldn't, I'll smash your head."

The two boys began sidling up to each other with clenched fists, and a third boy, who had a mischievous face, seized the paper that had had the pepper in it, and running up to them shook it in their faces.

There was enough left to put all thoughts of fighting out of their heads. They began to cough, and choke, and splutter, and finally found themselves beside the dogs, where the four of them had a lively time.

The other boys yelled with delight, and pointed their fingers at them. "A sneezing concert. Thank you, gentlemen. *Angcore, angcore!*"[1]

---

1 The children are mispronouncing "encore, encore," which is French for "again, again," and the traditional chant to ask for a performance to be repeated.

Miss Laura laughed too, she could not help it, and even Billy and I curled up our lips. After a while they sobered down, and then finding that the boys hadn't a handkerchief between them, Miss Laura took her own soft one, and dipping it in a spring of fresh water near by, wiped the red eyes of the sneezers.

Their ill humor had gone, and when she turned to leave them, and said, coaxingly, "You won't make those dogs fight any more, will you?" they said, "No, sirree, Bob."

Miss Laura went slowly home, and ever afterward when she met any of those boys, they called her "Miss Pepper."

When we got home we found Willie curled up by the window in the hall, reading a book. He was too fond of reading, and his mother often told him to put away his book and run about with the other boys.[1] This afternoon Miss Laura laid her hand on his shoulder and said, "I was going to give the dogs a little game of ball, but I'm rather tired."

"Gammon and spinach," he replied, shaking off her hand, "you're always tired."

She sat down in a hall chair and looked at him. Then she began to tell him about the dog fight. He was much interested, and the book slipped to the floor. When she finished he said, "You're a daisy every day. Go now and rest yourself." Then snatching the balls from her, he called us and ran down to the basement. But he was not quick enough, though, to escape her arm. She caught him to her and kissed him repeatedly. He was the baby and pet of the family, and he loved her dearly, though he spoke impatiently to her oftener than either of the other boys.

We had a grand game with Willie. Miss Laura had trained us to do all kinds of things with balls—jumping for them, playing hide and seek, and catching them.

Billy could do more things than I could. One thing he did which I thought was very clever. He played ball by himself. He was so crazy about ball play that he could never get enough of it. Miss Laura played all she could with him, but she had to help her mother with the sewing and the housework, and do lessons with her father, for she was only seventeen years old, and had not left off studying. So Billy would take his ball and go off by himself. Sometimes he rolled it over the floor, and sometimes he threw it in the air and pushed it through the staircase railings to the hall

---

1 Saunders placed much emphasis on boys' need for outdoor, physical activity. In this scene, the story of the dog fight seems to masculinize Willie, and his beloved book simply slips out of his hand.

below. He always listened till he heard it drop, then he ran down and brought it back and pushed it through again. He did this till he was tired, and then he brought the ball and laid it at Miss Laura's feet.

We both had been taught a number of tricks. We could sneeze and cough, and be dead dogs, and say our prayers, and stand on our heads, and mount a ladder and say the alphabet—this was the hardest of all, and it took Miss Laura a long time to teach us. We never began till a book was laid before us. Then we stared at it, and Miss Laura said, "Begin, Joe and Billy—say A."

For A, we gave a little squeal. B was louder. C was louder still. We barked for some letters, and growled for others. We always turned a summersault for S. When we got to Z, we gave the book a push and had a frolic around the room.

When any one came in, and Miss Laura had us show off any of our tricks, the remark always was, "What clever dogs. They are not like other dogs."

That was a mistake. Billy and I were not any brighter than many a miserable cur that skulked about the streets of Fairport. It was kindness and patience that did it all. When I was with Jenkins he thought I was a very stupid dog. He would have laughed at the idea of any one teaching me anything. But I was only sullen and obstinate, because I was kicked about so much. If he had been kind to me, I would have done anything for him.

I loved to wait on Miss Laura and Mrs. Morris, and they taught both Billy and me to make ourselves useful about the house. Mrs. Morris didn't like going up and down the three long staircases, and sometimes we just raced up and down, waiting on her.

How often I have heard her go into the hall and say, "Please send me down a clean duster, Laura. Joe, you get it." I would run gayly up the steps, and then would come Billy's turn. "Billy, I have forgotten my keys. Go get them."

After a time we began to know the names of different articles, and where they were kept, and could get them ourselves. On sweeping days we worked very hard, and enjoyed the fun. If Mrs. Morris was too far away to call to Mary for what she wanted, she wrote the name on a piece of paper, and told us to take it to her.

Billy always took the letters from the postman, and carried the morning paper up to Mr. Morris's study, and I always put away the clean clothes. After they were mended, Mrs. Morris folded each article and gave it to me, mentioning the name of the owner, so that I could lay it on his bed. There was no need for her to tell me the names. I knew by the smell. All human beings have a strong smell to a dog, even though they mayn't notice it themselves. Mrs. Morris never knew how she bothered me by giving away Miss Laura's clothes to poor people. Once, I followed her track all through the town, and at last found it was only a pair of her boots on a ragged child in the gutter.

I must say a word about Billy's tail before I close this chapter. It is the custom to cut the ends of fox terrier's tails, but leave their ears untouched. Billy came to Miss Laura so young that his tail had not been cut off, and she would not have it done.

One day Mr. Robinson came in to see him, and he said, "You have made a fine-looking dog of him, but his appearance is ruined by the length of his tail."

"Mr. Robinson," said Mrs. Morris, patting little Billy, who lay on her lap, "don't you think that this little dog has a beautifully proportioned body?"

"Yes, I do," said the gentleman. "His points are all correct, save that one."

"But," she said, "if our Creator made that beautiful little body, don't you think he is wise enough to know what length of tail would be in proportion to it?"

Mr. Robinson would not answer her. He only laughed and said that he thought she and Miss Laura were both "cranks."[1]

---

1 A slang term for an eccentric.

CHAPTER 11

GOLDFISH AND CANARIES

THE Morris boys were all different. Jack was bright and clever, Ned was a wag, Willie was a book-worm, and Carl was a born trader.

He was always exchanging toys and books with his school-mates, and they never got the better of him in a bargain. He said that when he grew up he was going to be a merchant, and he had already begun to carry on a trade in canaries and goldfish. He was very fond of what he called "his yellow pets," yet he never kept a pair of birds or a goldfish, if he had a good offer for them.

He slept alone in a large, sunny room at the top of the house. By his own request, it was barely furnished, and there he raised his canaries and kept his goldfish.

He was not fond of having visitors coming to his room, because, he said, they frightened the canaries. After Mrs. Morris made his bed in the morning, the door was closed, and no one was supposed to go in till he came from school. Once Billy and I followed him upstairs without his knowing it, but as soon as he saw us he sent us down in a great hurry.

One day Bella walked into his room to inspect the canaries. She was quite a spoiled bird by this time, and I heard Carl telling the family afterward that it was as good as a play to see Miss Bella strutting in with her breast stuck out, and her little, conceited air, and hear her say, shrilly, "Good morning, birds, good morning! How do you do, Carl? Glad to see you, boy."

"Well, I'm not glad to see you," he said, decidedly, "and don't you ever come up here again. You'd frighten my canaries to death." And he sent her flying downstairs.

How cross she was! She came shrieking to Miss Laura. "Bella loves birds. Bella wouldn't hurt birds. Carl's a bad boy."

Miss Laura petted and soothed her, telling her to go find Davy, and he would play with her. Bella and the rat were great friends. It was very funny to see them going about the house together. From the very first she had liked him, and coaxed him into her cage, where he soon became quite at home,—so much so that he always slept there. About nine o'clock every evening, if he was not with her, she went all over the house, crying: "Davy! Davy! time to go to bed. Come sleep in Bella's cage."

He was very fond of the nice sweet cakes she got to eat, but she never could get him to eat coffee grounds—the food she liked best.

Miss Laura spoke to Carl about Bella, and told him he had hurt her feelings, so he petted her a little to make up for it. Then his mother told him that she thought he was making a mistake in keeping his canaries so much to themselves. They had become so timid, that when she went into the room they were uneasy till she left it. She told him that petted birds or animals are sociable and like company, unless they are kept by themselves, when they become shy. She advised him to let the other boys go into the room, and occasionally to bring some of his pretty singers downstairs, where all the family could enjoy seeing and hearing them, and where they would get used to other people besides himself.

Carl looked thoughtful, and his mother went on to say that there was no one in the house, not even the cat, that would harm his birds.

"You might even charge admission for a day or two," said Jack, gravely, "and introduce us to them, and make a little money."

Carl was rather annoyed at this, but his mother calmed him by showing him a letter she had just gotten from one of her brothers, asking her to let one of her boys spend his Christmas holidays in the country with him.

"I want you to go, Carl," she said.

He was very much pleased, but looked sober when he thought of his pets. "Laura and I will take care of them," said his mother, "and start the new management of them."

"Very well," said Carl, "I will go then; I've no young ones now, so you will not find them much trouble."

I thought it was a great deal of trouble to take care of them. The first morning after Carl left, Billy, and Bella, and Davy, and I followed Miss Laura upstairs. She made us sit in a row by the door, lest we should startle the canaries. She had a great many things to do. First, the canaries had their baths. They had to get them at the same time every morning. Miss Laura filled the little white dishes with water and put them in the cages, and then came and sat on a stool by the door. Bella, and Billy, and Davy climbed into her lap, and I stood close by her. It was so funny to watch those canaries. They put their heads on one side and looked first at their little baths and then at us. They knew we were strangers. Finally, as we were all very quiet, they got into the water; and what a good time they had, fluttering their wings and splashing, and cleaning themselves so nicely.

Then they got up on their perches and sat in the sun, shaking themselves and picking at their feathers.

Miss Laura cleaned each cage, and gave each bird some mixed rape and canary seed. I heard Carl tell her before he left not to give them much hemp seed, for that was too fattening. He was very careful about their food. During the summer I had often seen him taking up nice green things to them: celery, chickweed, tender cabbage, peaches, apples, pears, bananas; and now at Christmas time, he had green stuff growing in pots on the window ledge.

Besides that he gave them crumbs of coarse bread, crackers, lumps of sugar, cuttle-fish to peck at, and a number of other things. Miss Laura did everything just as he told her; but I think she talked to the birds more than he did. She was very particular about their drinking water, and washed out the little glass cups that held it most carefully.

After the canaries were clean and comfortable, Miss Laura set their cages in the sun, and turned to the goldfish. They were in large glass globes on the window-seat. She took a long-handled tin cup, and dipped out the fish from one into a basin of water. Then she washed the globe thoroughly and put the fish back, and scattered wafers of fish food on the top. The fish came up and snapped at it, and acted as if they were glad to get it. She did each globe and then her work was over for one morning.

She went away for a while, but every few hours through the day she ran up to Carl's room to see how the fish and canaries were getting on. If the room was too chilly she turned on more heat, but she did not keep it too warm, for that would make the birds tender.

After a time the canaries got to know her, and hopped gayly around their cages, and chirped and sang whenever they saw her coming. Then she began to take some of them downstairs, and to let them out of their cages for an hour or two every day. They were very happy little creatures, and chased each other about the room, and flew on Miss Laura's head, and pecked saucily at her face as she sat sewing and watching them. They were not at all afraid of me nor of Billy, and it was quite a sight to see them hopping up to Bella. She looked so large beside them.

One little bird became ill while Carl was away, and Miss Laura had to give it a great deal of attention. She gave it plenty of hemp seed to make it fat, and very often the yolk of a hard boiled egg, and kept a nail in its drinking water, and gave it a few drops of alcohol in its bath every morning to keep it from taking cold. The moment the bird finished taking its bath, Miss Laura took the dish from the cage, for the alcohol made the water poisonous.

Then vermin came on it; and she had to write to Carl to ask him what do. He told her to hang a muslin bag full of sulphur over the swing, so that the bird would dust it down on her feathers. That cured the little thing, and when Carl came home, he found it quite well again.

One day, just after he got back, Mrs. Montague drove up to the house with a canary cage carefully done up in a shawl. She said that a bad-tempered housemaid, in cleaning the cage that morning, had gotten angry with the bird and struck it, breaking its leg. She was very much annoyed with the girl for her cruelty,[1] and had dismissed her, and now she wanted Carl to take her bird and nurse it, as she knew nothing about canaries.

Carl had just come in from school. He threw down his books, took the shawl from the cage and looked in. The poor little canary was sitting in a corner. Its eyes were half shut, one leg hung loose, and it was making faint chirps of distress.

Carl was very much interested in it. He got Mrs. Montague to help him, and together they split matches, tore up strips of muslin, and bandaged the broken leg. He put the little bird back in the cage, and it seemed more comfortable. "I think he will do now," he said to Mrs. Montague, "but hadn't you better leave him with me for a few days?"

She gladly agreed to this and went away, after telling him that the bird's name was Dick.

The next morning at the breakfast table, I heard Carl telling his mother that as soon as he woke up he sprang out of bed and went to see how his canary was. During the night, poor, foolish Dick had picked off the splints from his leg, and now it was as bad as ever. "I shall have to perform a surgical operation," he said.

I did not know what he meant, so I watched him when, after breakfast, he brought the bird down to his mother's room. She held it while he took a pair of sharp scissors, and cut its leg right off a little way above the broken place. Then he put some vaseline on the tiny stump, bound it up, and left Dick in his mother's care. All the morning, as she sat sewing, she watched him to see that he did not pick the bandage away.

When Carl came home, Dick was so much better that he had managed to fly up on his perch, and was eating seeds quite gayly.

---

1 The 1920, 1925, and 1934 editions omit "for her cruelty." This interesting omission could mean that the maid's ill-tempered act was no longer considered a "cruel," intentional infliction of pain.

"Poor Dick!" said Carl, "a leg and a stump!" Dick imitated him in a few little chirps, "A leg and a stump!"

"Why, he is saying it too," exclaimed Carl, and burst out laughing.

Dick seemed cheerful enough, but it was very pitiful to see him dragging his poor little stump around the cage, and resting it against the perch to keep him from falling. When Mrs. Montague came the next day, she could not bear to look at him. "Oh, dear!" she exclaimed, "I cannot take that disfigured bird home."

I could not help thinking how different she was from Miss Laura, who loved any creature all the more for having some blemish about it. "What shall I do?" said Mrs. Montague. "I miss my little bird so much. I shall have to get a new one. Carl, will you sell me one?"

"I will *give* you one, Mrs. Montague," said the boy, eagerly. "I would like to do so." Mrs. Morris looked pleased to hear Carl say this. She used to fear sometimes, that in his love for making money, he would become selfish.

Mrs. Montague was very kind to the Morris family, and Carl seemed quite pleased to do her a favor. He took her up to his room, and let her choose the bird she liked best. She took a handsome, yellow one, called Barry. He was a good singer, and a great favorite of Carl's. The boy put him in the cage, wrapped it up well, for it was a cold, snowy day, and carried it out to Mrs. Montague's sleigh.

She gave him a pleasant smile, and drove away, and Carl ran up the steps into the house. "It's all right, mother," he said, giving Mrs. Morris a hearty, boyish kiss, as she stood waiting for him. "I don't mind letting her have it."

"But you expected to sell that one, didn't you?" she asked.

"Mrs. Smith said maybe she'd take it when she came home from Boston, but I dare say she'd change her mind and get one there."

"How much were you going to ask for him?"

"Well, I wouldn't sell Barry for less than ten dollars, or rather, I wouldn't have sold him," and he ran out to the stable.

Mrs. Morris sat on the hall chair, patting me as I rubbed against her, in rather an absent-minded way. Then she got up and went into her husband's study, and told him what Carl had done.

Mr. Morris seemed very pleased to hear about it, but when his wife asked him to do something to make up the loss to the boy, he said: "I had rather not do that. To encourage a child to do a kind action, and then to reward him for it, is not always a sound principle to go upon."

But Carl did not go without his reward. That evening, Mrs. Montague's coachman brought a note to the house addressed to Mr. Carl Morris. He read it aloud to the family.[1]

MY DEAR CARL: I am charmed with my little bird, and he has whispered to me one of the secrets of your room. You want fifteen dollars very much to buy something for it. I am sure you won't be offended with an old friend for supplying you the means to get this something.

ADA MONTAGUE.

"Just the thing for my stationary tank for the goldfish," exclaimed Carl. "I've wanted it for a long time;—it isn't good to keep them in globes, but how in the world did she find out? I've never told any one."

Mrs. Morris smiled, and said; "Barry must have told her," as she took the money from Carl to put away for him.

Mrs. Montague got to be very fond of her new pet. She took care of him herself, and I have heard her tell Mrs. Morris most wonderful stories about him—stories so wonderful that I should say they were not true if I did not how intelligent dumb creatures get to be under kind treatment.

She only kept him in his cage at night, and when she began looking for him at bedtime to put him there, he always hid himself. She would search a short time, and then sit down, and he always came out of his hiding-place, chirping in a saucy way to make her look at him.

She said that he seemed to take delight in teasing her. Once when he was in the drawing room with her, she was called away to speak to some one at the telephone. When she came back, she found that one of the servants had come into the room and left the door open leading to a veranda. The trees outside were full of yellow birds, and she was in despair, thinking that Barry had flown out with them. She looked out, but could not see him. Then, lest he had not left the room, she got a chair and carried it about, standing on it to examine the walls, and see if Barry was hidden among the pictures and bric-a-brac. But no Barry was there. She at last sank down exhausted on a sofa. She heard a

---

1 In the 1893 manuscript, housed in the Esther Clark Wright Archives at Acadia University, Carl receives a six-volume set on natural history instead of money. The change is more in line with Carl's capitalist inclinations.

wicked, little peep, and looking up, saw Barry sitting on one of the rounds of the chair that she had been carrying about to look for him. He had been there all the time. She was so glad to see him, that she never thought of scolding him.

He was never allowed to fly about the dining room during meals, and the table maid drove him out before she set the table. It always annoyed him, and he perched on the staircase, watching the door through the railings. If it was left open for an instant, he flew in. One evening, before tea, he did this. There was a chocolate cake on the sideboard, and he liked the look of it so much that he began to peck at it. Mrs. Montague happened to come in, and drove him back to the hall.

While she was having tea that evening, with her husband and little boy, Barry flew into the room again. Mrs. Montague told Charlie to send him out, but her husband said, "Wait, he is looking for something."

He was on the sideboard, peering into every dish, and trying to look under the covers. "He is after the chocolate cake," exclaimed Mrs. Montague. "Here, Charlie, put this on the staircase for him."

She cut off a little scrap, and when Charlie took it to the hall, Barry flew after him, and ate it up.

As for poor, little, lame Dick, Carl never sold him, and he became a family pet. His cage hung in the parlor, and from morning till night his cheerful voice was heard, chirping and singing as if he had not a trouble in the world. They took great care of him. He was never allowed to be too hot or too cold. Everybody gave him a cheerful word in passing his cage, and if his singing was too loud, they gave him a little mirror to look at himself in. He loved this mirror, and often stood before it for an hour at a time.

CHAPTER 12

MALTA, THE CAT

THE first time I had a good look at the Morris cat, I thought she was the queerest-looking animal I had ever seen. She was dark gray—just the color of a mouse. Her eyes were a yellowish green, and for the first few days I was at the Morrises' they looked very unkindly at me. Then she got over her dislike, and we became very good friends. She was a beautiful cat, and so gentle and affectionate that the whole family loved her.

She was three years old, and she had come to Fairport in a vessel with some sailors, who had gotten her in a far-away place. Her name was Malta, and she was called a Maltese cat.

I have seen a great many cats, but I never saw one as kind as Malta. Once she had some little kittens and they all died. It almost broke her heart. She cried and cried about the house till it made one feel sad to hear her. Then she ran away to the woods. She came back with a little squirrel in her mouth, and putting it in her basket, she nursed it like a mother, till it grew old enough to run away from her.

She was a very knowing cat, and always came when she was called. Miss Laura used to wear a little silver whistle that she blew when she wanted any of her pets. It was a shrill whistle, and we could hear it a long way from home. I have seen her standing at the back door whistling for Malta, and the pretty creature's head would appear somewhere—always high up, for she was a great climber, and she would come running along the top of the fence, saying, "Meow, meow," in a funny, short way.

Miss Laura would pet her, or give her something to eat, or walk around the garden carrying her on her shoulder. Malta was a most affectionate cat, and if Miss Laura would not let her lick her face, she licked her hair with her little, rough tongue. Often Malta lay by the fire, licking my coat or little Billy's, to show her affection for us.

Mary, the cook, was very fond of cats, and used to keep Malta in the kitchen as much as she could, but nothing would make her stay down there if there was any music going on upstairs. The Morris pets were all fond of music. As soon as Miss Laura sat down to the piano to sing or play, we came from all parts of the house. Malta cried to get upstairs, Davy scampered through the hall, and Bella hurried after him. If I was outdoors I ran in the house; and Jim got on a box and looked through the window.

Davy's place was on Miss Laura's shoulder, his pink nose run in the curls at the back of her neck. I sat under the piano beside Malta and Bella, and we never stirred till the music was over; then we went quietly away.

Malta was a beautiful cat—there was no doubt about it. While I was with Jenkins I thought cats were vermin, like rats, and I chased them every chance I got. Mrs. Jenkins had a cat, a gaunt, long-legged, yellow creature, that ran whenever we looked at it.

Malta had been so kindly treated that she never ran from any one, except from strange dogs. She knew they would be likely to hurt her. If they came upon her suddenly, she faced them, and she was a pretty good fighter when she was put to it. I once saw her having a brush with a big mastiff that lived a few blocks from us, and giving him good fright, which just served him right.

I was shut up in the parlor. Some one had closed the door, and I could not get out. I was watching Malta from the window, as she daintily picked her way across the muddy street. She was such a soft, pretty, amiable-looking cat. She didn't look that way, though, when the mastiff rushed out of the alleyway at her.

She sprang back and glared at him like a little, fierce tiger. Her tail was enormous. Her eyes were like balls of fire, and she was spitting and snarling, as if to say, "If you touch me, I'll tear you to pieces!"

The dog, big as he was, did not dare attack her. He walked around and around, like a great clumsy elephant, and she turned her small body as he turned his, and kept up a dreadful hissing and spitting. Suddenly, I saw a Spitz dog hurrying down the street. He was going to help the mastiff, and Malta would be badly hurt. I had barked, and no one had come to let me out, so I sprang through the window.

Just then there was a change. Malta had seen the second dog, and she knew she must get rid of the mastiff. With an agile bound she sprang on his back, dug her sharp claws in, till he put his tail between his legs and ran up the street, howling with pain. She rode a little way, then sprang off, and ran up the lane to the stable.

I was very angry and wanted to fight something, so I pitched into the Spitz dog. He was a snarly, cross-grained creature, no friend to Jim and me, and he would have been only too glad of a chance to help kill Malta.

I gave him one of the worst beatings he ever had. I don't suppose it was quite right for me to do it, for Miss Laura says dogs should never fight; but he had worried Malta before, and he had no business to do it. She belonged to our family. Jim and I never worried *his* cat. I had been longing to give him a shaking for some time, and now I felt for his throat through his thick hair, and dragged him all around the street. Then I let him go, and he was a civil dog ever afterward.

Malta was very grateful, and licked a little place where the Spitz bit me. I did not get scolded for the broken window. Mary had seen from the kitchen window, and told Mrs. Morris that I had gone to help Malta.

Malta was a very wise cat. She knew quite well that she must not harm the parrot nor the canaries, and she never tried to catch them, even though she was left alone in the room with them.

I have seen her lying in the sun, blinking sleepily, and listening with great pleasure to Dick's singing. Miss Laura even taught her not to hunt the birds outside.

For a long time she had tried to get it into Malta's head, that it was cruel to catch the little sparrows that came about the door, and just after I came, she succeeded in doing so.

Malta was so fond of Miss Laura, that whenever she caught a bird, she came and laid it at her feet. Miss Laura always picked up the little, dead creature, pitied it and stroked it, and scolded Malta till she crept into a corner. Then Miss Laura put the bird on a limb of a tree, and Malta watched her attentively from her corner.

One day Miss Laura stood at the window, looking out into the garden. Malta was lying on the platform, staring at the sparrows that were picking up crumbs from the ground. She trembled, and half rose every few minutes, as if to go after them. Then she lay down again. She was trying very hard not to creep on them. Presently a neighbor's cat came stealing along the fence, keeping one eye on Malta and the other on the sparrows. Malta was so angry! She sprang up and chased her away, and then came back to the platform, where she lay down again and waited for the sparrows to come back. For a long time she stayed there, and never once tried to catch them.

Miss Laura was so pleased. She went to the door, and said, softly, "Come here, Malta."

The cat put up her tail, and, meowing gently, came into the house. Miss Laura took her up in her arms, and going down to the kitchen, asked Mary to give her a saucer of her very sweetest milk for the best cat in the United States of America.

Malta got great praise for this, and I never knew of her catching a bird afterward. She was well fed in the house, and had no need to hurt such harmless creatures.

She was very fond of her home, and never went far away, as Jim and I did. Once, when Willie was going to spend a few weeks with a little friend who lived fifty miles from Fairport, he took it into his head that Malta should go with him. His mother told him that cats did not like to go away from home, but he said he would be good to her, and begged so hard to take her, that at last his mother consented.

He had been a few days in this place, when he wrote home to say that Malta had run away. She had seemed very unhappy, and though he had kept her with him all the time, she had acted as if she wanted to get away.

When the letter was read to Mr. Morris, he said, "Malta is on her way home. Cats have a wonderful cleverness in finding their way to their own dwelling. She will be very tired. Let us go out and meet her."

Willie had gone to this place in a coach. Mr. Morris got a buggy and took Miss Laura and me with him, and we started out. We went slowly along the road. Every little while Miss Laura blew her whistle, and called, "Malta, Malta," and I barked as loudly as I could. Mr. Morris drove for several hours, then we stopped at a house, had dinner, and then set out again. We were going through a thick wood, where there was a pretty straight road, when I saw a small, dark creature away ahead, trotting toward us. It was Malta. I gave a joyful bark, but she did not know me, and plunged into the wood.

I ran in after her, barking and yelping, and Miss Laura blew her whistle as loudly as she could. Soon there was a little gray head peeping at us from the bushes, and Malta bounded out, gave me a look of surprise, and then leaped into the buggy on Miss Laura's lap.

What a happy cat she was! She purred with delight, and licked Miss Laura's gloves over and over again. Then she ate the food they had brought, and went sound asleep. She was very thin, and for several days after getting home she slept most of the time.

Malta did not like dogs, but she was very good to cats. One day, when there was no one about and the garden was very quiet, I saw her go stealing into the stable, and come out again, followed by a sore-eyed, starved-looking cat, that had been deserted by some people that lived in the next street. She led this cat up to her catnip bed, and watched her kindly, while she rolled and rubbed herself in it. Then Malta had a roll in it herself, and they both went back to the stable.

Catnip is a favorite plant with cats, and Miss Laura always kept some of it growing for Malta.

For a long time this sick cat had a home in the stable. Malta carried her food every day, and after a time Miss Laura found out about her, and did what she could to make her well. In time she got to be a strong, sturdy-looking cat, and Miss Laura got a home for her with an invalid lady.

It was nothing new for the Morrises to feed deserted cats. Some summers, Mrs. Morris said that she had a dozen to take care of. Careless and cruel[1] people would go away for the summer, shutting up their houses, and making no provision for the poor cats that had been allowed to sit snugly by the fire all winter. At last, Mrs. Morris got into the habit of putting a little notice in the Fairport paper, asking people who were going away for the summer to provide for their cats during their absence.

---

1   As with the earlier instance where the maid breaks Barry's leg, the 1920, 1925, and 1934 editions omit the description of "cruel," suggestive of a more forgiving attitude regarding the treatment of animals.

MISS LAURA

Philadelphia: Griffith & Rowland, 1907.

CHAPTER 13

THE BEGINNING OF AN ADVENTURE

THE first winter I was at the Morrises', I had an adventure. It was a week before Christmas, and we were having cold frosty weather. Not much snow had fallen, but there was plenty of skating, and the boys were off every day with their skates on a little lake near Fairport.

Jim and I often went with them, and we had great fun scampering over the ice after them, and slipping at every step.

On this Saturday night we had just gotten home. It was quite dark outside, and there was a cold wind blowing, so when we came in the front door, and saw the red light from the big hall stove and the blazing fire in the parlor, they looked very cheerful.

I was quite sorry for Jim that he had to go out to his kennel. However, he said he didn't mind. The boys got a plate of nice, warm meat for him and a bowl of milk, and carried them out, and afterward he went to sleep. Jim's kennel was a very snug one. Being a spaniel, he was not a very large dog, but his kennel was as roomy as if he was a great Dane. He told me that Mr. Morris and the boys made it, and he liked it very much, because it was large enough for him to get up in the night and stretch himself, when he got tired of lying in one position.

It was raised a little from the ground, and it had a thick layer of straw over the floor. Above was a broad shelf, wide enough for him to lie on, and covered with an old catskin sleigh robe. Jim always slept here in cold weather, because it was farther away from the ground.

To return to this December evening. I can remember yet how hungry I was. I could scarcely lie still till Miss Laura finished her tea. Mrs. Morris, knowing that her boys would be very hungry, had Mary broil some beefsteak and roast some potatoes for them; and didn't they smell good!

They ate all the steak and potatoes. It didn't matter to me, for I wouldn't have gotten any if they had been left. Mrs. Morris could not afford to give to the dogs good meat that she had gotten for her children, so she used to get the butcher to send her liver, and bones, and tough meat, and Mary cooked them, and made soup and broth, and mixed porridge with them for us.[1]

---

1 In the very new genre of the pet care manual, regulating the dog's diet
   was deemed to be one of the most important facets of dog (continued)

We never got meat three times a day. Miss Laura said it was all very well to feed hunting dogs on meat, but dogs that are kept about a house get ill if they are fed too well. So we had meat only once a day, and bread and milk, porridge, or dog biscuits, for our other meals.

I made a dreadful noise when I was eating. Ever since Jenkins cut my ears off, I had had trouble in breathing. The flaps had kept the wind and dust from the inside of my ears. Now that they were gone my head was stuffed up all the time. The cold weather made me worse, and sometimes I had such trouble to get my breath that it seemed as if I would choke. If I had opened my mouth, and breathed through it, as I have seen some people doing, I would have been more comfortable, but dogs always like to breathe through their noses.

"You have taken more cold," said Miss Laura, this night, as she put my plate of food on the floor for me. "Finish your meat, and then come and sit by the fire with me. What! do you want more?"

I gave a little bark, so she filled my plate for the second time. Miss Laura never allowed any one to meddle with us when we were eating. One day she found Willie teasing me by snatching at a bone that I was gnawing. "Willie," she said, "what would you do if you were just sitting down to the table feeling very hungry, and just as you began to eat your meat and potatoes, I would come along and snatch the plate from you?"

"I don't know what I'd *do*," he said, laughingly; "but I'd *want* to wallop you."

"Well," she said, "I'm afraid that Joe will 'wallop' you some day if you worry him about his food, for even a gentle dog will

---

care. Although in 1827 meat was considered "more natural" and thought to "increas[e] their strength considerably" (Rydge 242), dog diets actually involved a lot of porridge, with cuts of meat (horseflesh or butcher's discards) as an occasional add-on. Eating meat was "stimulating," as opposed to eating vegetables, which had a "cooling effect" (Glover 4). Particularly if the horsemeat was raw, it would have "a tendency to foster ferocity of disposition." Manuals and periodicals were careful to distinguish that those dogs considered more feminized—pet dogs, toy dogs, lapdogs—should not be fed much meat, and certainly never raw meat. Feminized dogs, those belonging to the domestic sphere, would be distinguished by being fed less well, with dubious arguments ranging from the dangers of disease to the undesirable effect of an over-stimulated pet to an offensive smell.

sometimes snap at any one who disturbs him at his meals; so you had better not try his patience too far."

Willie never teased me after that, and I was very glad, for two or three times I had been tempted to snarl at him.

After I finished my tea, I followed Miss Laura upstairs. She took up a book and sat down in a low chair, and I lay down on the hearth rug beside her.

"Do you know, Joe," she said with a smile, "why you scratch with your paws when you lie down, as if to make yourself a hollow bed, and turn around a great many times before you lie down?"

Of course I did not know, so I only stared at her. "Years and years ago," she went on, gazing down at me, "there weren't any dogs living in people's houses, as you are, Joe. They were all wild creatures running about the woods. They always scratched among the leaves to make a comfortable bed for themselves, and the habit has come down to you, Joe, for you are descended from them."

This sounded very interesting, and I think she was going to tell me some more about my wild forefathers, but just then the rest of the family came in.

I always thought that this was the snuggest time of the day— when the family all sat around the fire—Mrs. Morris sewing, the boys reading or studying, and Mr. Morris with his head buried in a newspaper, and Billy and I on the floor at their feet.

This evening I was feeling very drowsy, and had almost dropped asleep, when Ned gave me a push with his foot. He was a great tease, and he delighted in getting me to make a simpleton of myself. I tried to keep my eyes on the fire, but I could not, and just had to turn and look at him.

He was holding his book up between himself and his mother, and was opening his mouth as wide as he could and throwing back his head, pretending to howl.

For the life of me I could not help giving a loud howl. Mrs. Morris looked up and said, "Bad Joe, keep still."

The boys were all laughing behind their books, for they knew what Ned was doing. Presently he started off again, and I was just beginning another howl that might have made Mrs. Morris send me out of the room, when the door opened, and a young girl called Bessie Drury came in.

She had a cap on and a shawl thrown over her shoulders, and she had just run across the street from her father's house. "Oh, Mrs. Morris," she said, "will you let Laura come over and stay with me to-night? Mamma has just gotten a telegram from

Bangor, saying that her aunt, Mrs. Cole, is very ill, and she wants to see her, and papa is going to take her there by to-night's train, and she is afraid I will be lonely if I don't have Laura."

"Can you not come and spend the night here?" said Mrs. Morris.

"No, thank you; I think mamma would rather have me stay in our house."

"Very well," said Mrs. Morris, "I think Laura would like to go."

"Yes, indeed," said Miss Laura, smiling at her friend. "I will come over in half an hour."

"Thank you so much," said Miss Bessie. And she hurried away.

After she left, Mr. Morris looked up from his paper. "There will be some one in the house besides those two girls?"

"Oh, yes," said Mrs. Morris; "Mrs. Drury has her old nurse, who has been with her for twenty years, and there are two maids besides, and Donald, the coachman, who sleeps over the stable. So they are well protected."

"Very good," said Mr. Morris. And he went back to his paper.

Of course dumb animals do not understand all that they hear spoken of; but I think human beings would be astonished if they knew how much we can gather from their looks and voices. I knew that Mr. Morris did not quite like the idea of having his daughter go to the Drurys' when the master and mistress of the house were away, so I made up my mind that I would go with her.

When she came down stairs with her little satchel on her arm, I got up and stood beside her. "Dear, old Joe," she said, "you must not come."

I pushed myself out the door beside her after she had kissed her mother and father and the boys. "Go back, Joe," she said, firmly.

I had to step back then, but I cried and whined, and she looked at me in astonishment. "I will be back in the morning, Joe," she said, gently; "don't squeal in that way." Then she shut the door and went out.

I felt dreadfully. I walked up and down the floor and ran to the window, and howled without having to look at Ned. Mrs. Morris peered over her glasses at me in utter surprise. "Boys," she said, "did you ever see Joe act in that way before?"

"No, mother," they all said.

Mr. Morris was looking at me very intently. He had always taken more notice of me than any other creature about the house, and I was very fond of him. Now I ran up and put my paws on his knees.

"Mother," he said, turning to his wife, "let the dog go."

"Very well," she said, in a puzzled way. "Jack, just run over with him, and tell Mrs. Drury how he is acting, and that I will be very much obliged if she will let him stay all night with Laura."

Jack sprang up, seized his cap, and raced down the front steps, across the street, through the gate, and up the gravelled walk, where the little stones were all hard and fast in the frost.

The Drurys lived in a large, white house, with trees all around it, and a garden at the back. They were rich people and had a great deal of company. Through the summer I had often seen carriages at the door, and ladies and gentlemen in light clothes walking over the lawn, and sometimes I smelled nice things they were having to eat. They did not keep any dogs, nor pets of any kind, so Jim and I never had an excuse to call there.

Jack and I were soon at the front door, and he rang the bell and gave me in charge of the maid who opened it. The girl listened to his message for Mrs. Drury, then she walked upstairs, smiling and looking at me over her shoulder.

There was a trunk in the upper hall, and an elderly woman was putting things in it. A lady stood watching her, and when she saw me, she gave a little scream, "Oh, nurse! look at that horrid dog! Where did he come from? Put him out, Susan."

I stood quite still, and the girl who had brought me upstairs, gave her Jack's message.

"Certainly, certainly," said the lady, when the maid finished speaking. "If he is one of the Morris dogs, he is sure to be a well-behaved one. Tell the little boy to thank his mamma for letting Laura come over, and say that we will keep the dog with pleasure. Now, nurse, we must hurry; the cab will be here in five minutes."

I walked softly into a front room, and there I found my dear Miss Laura. Miss Bessie was with her, and they were cramming things into a portmanteau. They both ran out to find out how I came there, and just then a gentleman came hurriedly upstairs, and said the cab had come.

There was a scene of great confusion and hurry, but in a few minutes it was all over. The cab had rolled away, and the house was quiet.

"Nurse, you must be tired, you had better go to bed," said Miss Bessie, turning to the elderly woman, as we all stood in the hall. "Susan, will you bring some supper to the dining room, for Miss Morris and me? What will you have, Laura?"

"What are you going to have?" asked Miss Laura, with a smile.

"Hot chocolate and tea biscuits."

"Then I will have the same."

"Bring some cake too, Susan," said Miss Bessie, "and something for the dog. I dare say he would like some of that turkey that was left from dinner."

If I had had any ears I would have pricked them up at this, for I was very fond of fowl, and I never got any at the Morrises', unless it might be a stray bone or two.

What fun we had over our supper! The two girls sat at the big dining table, and sipped their chocolate, and laughed and talked, and I had the skeleton of a whole turkey on a newspaper that Susan spread on the carpet.

I was very careful not to drag it about, and Miss Bessie laughed at me till the tears came in her eyes. "That dog is a gentleman," she said; "see how he holds bones on the paper with his paws, and strips the meat off with his teeth. Oh, Joe, Joe, you are a funny dog! And you are having a funny supper. I have heard of quail on toast, but I never heard of turkey on newspaper."

"Hadn't we better go to bed?" said Miss Laura, when the hall clock struck eleven.

"Yes, I suppose we had," said Miss Bessie. "Where is this animal to sleep?"

"I don't know," said Miss Laura; "he sleeps in the stable at home, or in the kennel with Jim."

"Suppose Susan makes him a nice bed by the kitchen stove?" said Miss Bessie.

Susan made the bed, but I was not willing to sleep in it. I barked so loudly when they shut me up alone, that they had to let me go upstairs with them.

Miss Laura was almost angry with me, but I could not help it. I had come over there to protect her, and I wasn't going to leave her, if I could help it.

Miss Bessie had a handsomely furnished room with a soft carpet on the floor, and pretty curtains at the windows. There were two single beds in it, and the two girls dragged them close together, so that they could talk after they got in bed.

Before Miss Bessie put out the light, she told Miss Laura not to be alarmed if she heard any one walking about in the night, for the nurse was sleeping across the hall from them, and she would probably come in once or twice to see if they were sleeping comfortably.

The two girls talked for a long time, and then they fell asleep. Just before Miss Laura dropped off, she forgave me, and put down her hand for me to lick as I lay on a fur rug close by her bed.[1]

I was very tired, and I had a very soft and pleasant bed, so I soon fell into a heavy sleep. But I waked up at the slightest noise. Once Miss Laura turned in bed, and another time Miss Bessie laughed in her sleep, and again, there were queer crackling noises in the frosty limbs of the trees outside, that made me start up quickly out of my sleep.

There was a big clock in the hall, and every time it struck I waked up. Once, just after it had struck some hour, I jumped up out of a sound nap. I had been dreaming about my early home. Jenkins was after me with a whip, and my limbs were quivering and trembling as if I had been trying to get away from him.[2]

I sprang up and shook myself. Then I took a turn around the room. The two girls were breathing gently; I could scarcely hear them. I walked to the door and looked out into the hall. There was a dim light burning there. The door of the nurse's room stood open. I went quietly to it and looked in. She was breathing heavily and muttering in her sleep.

I went back to my rug and tried to go to sleep, but I could not. Such an uneasy feeling was upon me that I had to keep walking about. I went out into the hall again and stood at the head of the staircase. I thought I would take a walk through the lower hall, and then go to bed again.

The Drurys' carpets were all like velvet, and my paws did not make a rattling on them as they did on the oil cloth at the Morrises'. I crept down the stairs like a cat, and walked along the lower hall, smelling under all the doors, listening as I went. There was no night light burning down here, and it was quite dark, but if there had been any strange person about I would have smelled him.

I was surprised when I got near the farther end of the hall, to see a tiny gleam of light shine for an instant from under the dining-room door. Then it went away again. The dining room was

---

1 In the 1965 edition, this touching instance of human-animal connection is cut.

2 In the 1990 edition, Joe does not have this prophetic dream.

the place to eat. Surely none of the people in the house would be there after the supper we had.

I went and sniffed under the door. There was a smell there; a strong smell like beggars and poor people.[1] It smelled like Jenkins. It *was* Jenkins.

---

1   In the 1965 and 1990 editions, the foul smell is no longer associated with "beggars and poor people."

CHAPTER 14

HOW WE CAUGHT THE BURGLAR

WHAT was the wretch doing in the house with my dear Miss Laura? I thought I would go crazy. I scratched at the door, and barked and yelped. I sprang up on it, and though I was quite a heavy dog by this time, I felt as light as a feather.

It seemed to me that I would go mad if I could not get that door open. Every few seconds I stopped and put my head down to the doorsill to listen. There was a rushing about inside the room, and a chair fell over, and some one seemed to be getting out of the window.

This made me worse than ever. I did not stop to think that I was only a medium-sized dog, and that Jenkins would probably kill me, if he got his hands on me. I was so furious that I thought only of getting hold of him.

In the midst of the noise that I made, there was a screaming and a rushing to and fro upstairs. I ran up and down the hall, and half-way up the steps and back again. I did not want Miss Laura to come down, but how was I to make her understand? There she was, in her white gown, leaning over the railing, and holding back her long hair, her face a picture of surprise and alarm.

"The dog has gone mad," screamed Miss Bessie. "Nurse, pour a pitcher of water on him."

The nurse was more sensible. She ran downstairs, her night-cap flying, and a blanket that she had seized from her bed, trailing behind her. "There are thieves in the house," she shouted at the top of her voice, "and the dog has found it out."

She did not go near the dining-room door, but threw open the front one, crying, "Policeman! Policeman! help, help, thieves, murder!"

Such a screaming as that old woman made! She was worse than I was. I dashed by her, out through the hall door, and away down to the gate, where I heard some one running. I gave a few loud yelps to call Jim, and leaped the gate as the man before me had done.

There was something savage in me that night. I think it must have been the smell of Jenkins. I felt as if I could tear him to pieces. I have never felt so wicked since. I was hunting him, as he had hunted me and my mother, and the thought gave me pleasure.

Old Jim soon caught up with me, and I gave him a push with my nose, to let him know I was glad he had come. We rushed swiftly on, and at the corner caught up with the miserable man who was running away from us.

I gave an angry growl, and jumping up, bit at his leg. He turned around, and though it was not a very bright night, there was light enough for me to see the ugly face of my old master.

He seemed so angry to think that Jim and I dared to snap at him. He caught up a handful of stones, and with some bad words threw them at us. Just then, away in front of us, was a queer whistle, and then another one like it behind us. Jenkins made a strange noise in his throat, and started to run down a side street, away from the direction of the two whistles.

I was afraid that he was going to get away, and though I could not hold him, I kept springing up on him, and once I tripped him up. Oh, how furious he was! He kicked me against the side of a wall, and gave me two or three hard blows with a stick that he caught up, and kept throwing stones at me.

I would not give up, though I could scarcely see him for the blood that was running over my eyes. Old Jim got so angry whenever Jenkins touched me, that he ran up behind and nipped his calves, to make him turn on him.

Soon Jenkins came to a high wall, where he stopped, and with a hurried look behind, began to climb over it. The wall was too high for me to jump. He was going to escape. What should I do? I barked as loudly as I could for some one to come, and then sprang up and held him by the leg as he was getting over.

I had such a grip, that I went over the wall with him, and left Jim on the other side. Jenkins fell on his face in the earth. Then he got up, and with a look of deadly hatred on his face, pounced upon me. If help had not come, I think he would have dashed out my brains against the wall, as he dashed out my poor little brothers' against the horse's stall. But just then there was a running sound. Two men came down the street and sprang upon the wall, just where Jim was leaping up and down and barking in distress.

I saw at once by their uniform and the clubs in their hands, that they were policemen. In one short instant they had hold of Jenkins. He gave up then, but he stood snarling at me like an ugly dog. "If it hadn't been for that cur, I'd never a been caught. Why—," and he staggered back and uttered a bad word, "it's me own dog."

"More shame to you," said one of the policemen, sternly; "what have you been up to at this time of night, to have your own dog and a quiet minister's spaniel dog a chasing you through the street?"

Jenkins began to swear and would not tell them anything. There was a house in the garden, and just at this minute some one opened a window and called out: "Hallo, there, what are you doing?"

"We're catching a thief, sir," said one of the policemen, "leastwise I think that's what he's been up to. Could you throw us down a bit of rope? We've no handcuffs here, and one of us has to go to the lock-up and the other to Washington Street, where there's a woman yelling blue murder; and hurry up, please, sir."

The gentleman threw down a rope, and in two minutes Jenkins' wrists were tied together, and he was walked through the gate, saying bad words as fast as he could to the policeman who was leading him. "Good dogs," said the other policeman to Jim and me. Then he ran up the street and we followed him.

As we hurried along Washington Street, and came near our house, we saw lights gleaming through the darkness, and heard people running to and fro. The nurse's shrieking had alarmed the neighborhood. The Morris boys were all out in the street only half clad and shivering with cold, and the Drurys' coachman, with no hat on, and his hair sticking up all over his head, was running about with a lantern.

The neighbors' houses were all lighted up, and a good many people were hanging out of their windows and opening their doors, and calling to each other to know what all this noise meant.

When the policeman appeared with Jim and me at his heels, quite a crowd gathered around him to hear his part of the story. Jim and I dropped on the ground panting as hard as we could, and with little streams of water running from our tongues. We were both pretty well used up. Jim's back was bleeding in several places from the stones that Jenkins had thrown at him, and I was a mass of bruises.

Presently we were discovered, and then what a fuss was made over us. "Brave dogs! noble dogs!" everybody said, and patted and praised us. We were very proud and happy, and stood up and wagged our tails, at least Jim did, and I wagged what I could. Then they found what a state we were in. Mrs. Morris cried, and catching me up in her arms, ran in the house with me, and Jack followed with old Jim.

We all went into the parlor. There was a good fire there, and Miss Laura and Miss Bessie were sitting over it. They sprang up when they saw us, and right there in the parlor washed our wounds, and made us lie down by the fire.

"You saved our silver, brave Joe," said Miss Bessie; "just wait till my papa and mamma come home, and see what they will say. Well, Jack, what is the latest?" as the Morris boys came trooping into the room.

"The policeman has been questioning your nurse, and examining the dining room, and has gone down to the station to make his report, and do you know what he has found out?" said Jack, excitedly.

"No—what?" asked Miss Bessie.

"Why that villain was going to burn your house."

Miss Bessie gave a little shriek. "Why, what do you mean?"

"Well," said Jack, "they think by what they discovered, that he planned to pack his bag with silver, and carry it off; but just before he did so he would pour oil around the room, and set fire to it, so people would not find out that he had been robbing you."

"Why we might have all been burned to death," said Miss Bessie. "He couldn't burn the dining room without setting fire to the rest of the house."

"Certainly not," said Jack, "that shows what a villain he is."

"Do they know this for certain, Jack?" asked Miss Laura.

"Well, they suppose so; they found some bottles of oil along with the bag he had for the silver."

"How horrible! You darling old Joe, perhaps you saved our lives," and pretty Miss Bessie kissed[1] my ugly, swollen head. I could do nothing but lick her little hand, but always after that I thought a great deal of her.

It is now some years since all this happened, and I might as well tell the end of it: The next day the Drurys came home, and everything was found out about Jenkins. The night they left Fairport he had been hanging about the station. He knew just who were left in the house, for he had once supplied them with milk, and knew all about their family. He had no customers at this time, for after Mr. Harry rescued me, and that piece came out in the paper about him, he found that no one would take milk from him. His wife died, and some kind people put his children in an asylum,[2] and he was obliged to sell Toby and the cows. Instead of

---

1 Towards the end of the nineteenth century, health experts raised concerns about excessive intimacy with animals. Kissing animals was regarded as inappropriate and unhygienic. But it wasn't until the 1965 edition that this was revised to an affectionate pat.

2 In the 1920, 1925, and 1934 editions, the asylum is referred to as a home. In the mid-1850s, as an alternative to incarcerating poor, vagrant

learning a lesson from all this, and leading a better life, he kept sinking lower.

He was, therefore, ready for any kind of mischief that turned up, and when he saw the Drurys going away in the train, he thought he would steal a bag of silver from their sideboard, then set fire to the house, and run away and hide the silver. After a time he would take it to some city and sell it.

He was made to confess all this.[1] Then for his wickedness he was sent to prison for ten years, and I hope he will get to be a better man there, and be one after he comes out.[2]

I was sore and stiff for a long time, and one day Mrs. Drury came over to see me. She did not love dogs as the Morrises did. She tried to, but she could not.

Dogs can see fun in things as well as people can, and I buried my muzzle in the hearth-rug, so that she would not see how I was curling up my lip and smiling at her.

"You—are—a—good—dog," she said, slowly. "You are"—then she stopped, and could not think of anything else to say to me. I got up and stood in front of her, for a well-bred dog should not lie down when a lady speaks to him. I wagged my body a little, and I would gladly have said something to help her out of her difficulty, but I couldn't. If she had stroked me it might have helped her; but she didn't want to touch me, and I knew she didn't want me to touch her, so I just stood looking at her.

"Mrs. Morris," she said, turning from me with a puzzled face, "I don't like animals, and I can't pretend to, for they always find

---

children from urban centers like New York, the Children's Aid Society under Charles Loring Brace championed the practice of placing the children in foster homes (O'Connor). Under his "Emigration Plan," "orphan trains" distributed unwanted city children—approximately 105,000 in all—across the country with families who, in exchange for their labor, promised to raise the children as their own. Limited budgets made it impossible for the Society to track these children's fates after they were thus delivered (O'Connor).

1 The implication that Jenkins is forced to confess would contravene jurisprudence on free and voluntary confessions. Over the twentieth century, this became further cemented. The Supreme Court's ruling in *Miranda v. Arizona* (1966), for example, requires government officials to inform arrested suspects of their various rights prior to interrogation, including their right to not incriminate themselves.

2 The 1893 manuscript was harsher: Jenkins is sentenced to 15 years. If Jenkins is not reformed, Joe says: "I hope he will die before the 15 years are up."

me out; but can't you let that dog know that I shall feel eternally grateful to him for saving not only our property,— for that is a trifle,—but my darling daughter from fright and annoyance, and a possible injury or loss of life?"

"I think he understands," said Mrs. Morris. "He is a very wise dog." And smiling in great amusement, she called me to her and put my paws on her lap. "Look at that lady, Joe. She is pleased with you for driving Jenkins away from her house. You remember Jenkins?"

I barked angrily and limped to the window.

"How intelligent he is," said Mrs. Drury. "My husband has sent to New York for a watch-dog, and he says that from this on our house shall never be without one. Now I must go. Your dog is happy, Mrs. Morris, and I can do nothing for him, except to say that I shall never forget him, and I wish he would come over occasionally to see us. Perhaps when we get our dog he will. I shall tell my cook whenever she sees him to give him something to eat. This is a souvenir for Laura of that dreadful night. I feel under a deep obligation to you, so I am sure you will allow her to accept it." Then she gave Mrs. Morris a little box and went away.

When Miss Laura came in, she opened the box, and found in it a handsome diamond ring. On the inside of it was engraved: "Laura, in memory of December 20th, 18—. From her grateful friend, Bessie."

The diamond was worth hundreds of dollars, and Mrs. Morris told Miss Laura that she had rather she would not wear it then, while she was a young girl. It was not suitable for her, and she knew Mrs. Drury did not expect her to do so. She wished to give her a valuable present, and this would always be worth a great deal of money.

CHAPTER 15

OUR JOURNEY TO RIVERDALE

EVERY other summer, the Morris children were sent to place in the country, so that they could have a change of air, see what country life was like. As there were so many of them, they usually went different ways.

The summer after I came to them, Jack and Carl went to an uncle in Vermont, Miss Laura went to another in New Hampshire, and Ned and Willie went to visit a maiden aunt who lived in the White Mountains.

Mr. and Mrs. Morris stayed at home. Fairport was a lovely place in summer, and many people came there to visit.

The children took some of their pets with them, and the others they left at home for their mother to take care of. She never allowed them to take a pet animal anywhere, unless she knew it would be perfectly welcome. "Don't let your pets be a worry to other people," she often said to them, "or they will dislike them and you too."

Miss Laura went away earlier than the others, for she had run down through the spring, and was pale and thin. One day, early in June, we set out. I say "we," for after my adventure with Jenkins, Miss Laura said that I should never be parted from her. If any one invited her to come and see them, and didn't want me, she would stay at home.

The whole family went to the station to see us off. They put a chain on my collar, and took me to the baggage office, and got two tickets for me. One was tied to my collar, and the other Miss Laura put in her purse. Then I was put in a baggage car, and chained in a corner. I heard Mr. Morris say that as we were only going a short distance, it was not worth while to get an express ticket for me.

There was a dreadful noise and bustle at the station. Whistles were blowing and people were rushing up and down the platform. Some men were tumbling baggage so fast into the car where I was, that I was afraid some of it would fall on me.

For a few minutes Miss Laura stood by the door and looked in, but soon the men had piled up so many boxes and trunks that she could not see me. Then she went away. Mr. Morris asked one of the men to see that I did not get hurt, and I heard some money rattle. Then he went away too.

It was the beginning of June, and the weather had suddenly become very hot. We had a long, cold spring, and not being used to the heat, it seemed very hard to bear.

Before the train started, the doors of the baggage car were closed, and it became quite dark inside. The darkness, and the heat, and the close smell, and the noise, as we went rushing along, made me feel sick and frightened.

I did not dare to lie down, but sat up trembling and wishing that we might soon come to Riverdale Station. But we did not get there for some time, and I was to have a great fright.

I was thinking of all the stories that I knew of animals traveling. In February, the Drurys' Newfoundland watch-dog, Pluto, had arrived from New York, and he told Jim and me that he had a miserable journey.

A gentleman friend of Mr. Drury's had brought him from New York. He saw him chained up in his car, and he went into his Pullman, first tipping the baggage-master handsomely to look after him. Pluto said that the baggage-master had a very red nose, and he was always getting drinks for himself when they stopped at a station, but he never once gave him a drink or anything to eat, from the time they left New York till they got to Fairport. When the train stopped there, and Pluto's chain was unfastened, he sprang out on the platform, and nearly knocked Mr. Drury down. He saw some snow that had sifted through the station roof, and he was so thirsty that he began to lick it up. When the snow was all gone, he jumped up and licked the frost on the windows.

Mr. Drury's friend was so angry. He found the baggage-master, and said to him: "What did you mean, by coming into my car every few hours, to tell me that the dog was fed, and watered, and comfortable? I shall report you."

He went into the office at the station, and complained of the man, and was told that he was a drinking man, and was going to be dismissed.

I was not afraid of suffering like Pluto, because it was only going to take us a few hours to get to Riverdale. I found that we always went slowly before we came in to a station, and one time when we began to slacken speed I thought that surely we must be at our journey's end. However, it was not Riverdale. The car gave a kind of jump, then there was a crashing sound ahead, and we stopped.

I heard men shouting and running up and down, and I wondered what had happened. It was all dark and still in the car, and nobody came in, but the noise kept up outside, and I knew something had gone wrong with the train. Perhaps Miss Laura had got hurt. Something must have happened to her or she would come to me.

I barked and pulled at my chain till my neck was sore, but for a long, long time I was there alone. The men running about outside must have heard me. If ever I hear a man in trouble and crying for help I go to him and see what he wants.

After such a long time that it seemed to me it must be the middle of the night, the door at the end of the car opened, and a man looked in. "This is all through baggage for New York, miss," I heard him say, "they wouldn't put your dog in here."

"Yes, they did—I am sure this is the car," I heard in the voice I knew so well, "and won't you get him out, please? He must be terribly frightened."

The man stooped down and unfastened my chain, grumbling to himself because I had not been put in another car. "Some folks tumble a dog round as if he was a chunk of coal," he said, patting me kindly.

I was nearly wild with delight to get with Miss Laura again, but I had barked so much, and pressed my neck so hard with my collar that my voice was all gone. I fawned on her, and wagged myself about, and opened and shut my mouth, but no sound came out of it.

It made Miss Laura nervous. She tried to laugh and cry at the same time, and then bit her lip hard, and said: "Oh, Joe, don't."

"He's lost his bark, hasn't he?" said the man, looking at me curiously.

"It is a wicked thing to confine an animal in a dark and closed car," said Miss Laura, trying to see her way down the steps through her tears.

The man put out his hand and helped her. "He's not suffered much, miss," he said, "don't you distress yourself. Now if you'd been a brakeman on a Chicago train, as I was a few years ago, and seen the animals run in for the stock yards, you might talk about cruelty. Cars that ought to hold a certain number of pigs, or sheep, or cattle, jammed full with twice as many, and half of 'em thrown out choked and smothered to death. I've seen a man running up and down, raging and swearing because the railway people hadn't let him get in to tend to his pigs on the road."

Miss Laura turned and looked at the man with a very white face. "Is it like that now?" she asked.

"No, no," he said, hastily. "It's better now. They've got new regulations about taking care of the stock, but mind you, miss, the cruelty to animals isn't all done on the railways. There's a great lot of dumb creatures suffering all round everywhere, and if they could speak, 'twould be a hard showing for some other people besides the railway men."

He lifted his cap and hurried down the platform, and Miss Laura, her face very much troubled, picked her way among the bits of coal and wood scattered about the platform, and went into the waiting room of the little station.

She took me up to the filter and let some water run in her hand, and gave it to me to lap. Then she sat down and I leaned my head against her knees, and she stroked my throat gently.

There were some people sitting about the room, and, from their talk, I found out what had taken place. There had been a freight train on a side track at this station, waiting for us to get by. The switchman had carelessly left the switch open after this train went by, and when we came along afterward, our train, instead of running in by the platform, went crashing into the freight train. If we had been going fast, great damage might have been done. As it was, our engine was smashed so badly that it could not take us on; the passengers were frightened; and we were having a tedious time waiting for another engine to come and take us to Riverdale.

After the accident, the trainmen were so busy that Miss Laura could get no one to release me.

While I sat by her, I noticed an old gentleman staring at us. He was such a queer-looking old gentleman. He looked like a poodle. He had bright brown eyes, and a pointed face, and a shock of white hair that he shook every few minutes. He sat with his hands clasped on the top of his cane, and he scarcely took his eyes from Miss Laura's face. Suddenly he jumped up and came and sat down beside her.

"An ugly dog, that," he said, pointing to me.

Most young ladies would have resented this, but Miss Laura only looked amused. "He seems beautiful to me," she said, gently.

"H'm, because he's your dog," said the old man, darting a sharp look at me. "What's the matter with him?"

"This is his first journey by rail, and he's a little frightened."

"No wonder. The Lord only knows the suffering of animals in transportation," said the old gentleman. "My dear young lady, if you could see what I have seen, you'd never eat another bit of meat all the days of your life."

Miss Laura wrinkled her forehead. "I know—I have heard," she faltered. "It must be terrible."

"Terrible—it's awful," said the gentleman. "Think of the cattle on the western plains. Choked with thirst in summer, and starved and frozen in winter. Dehorned and goaded on to trains and steamers. Tossed about and wounded and suffering on voyages. Many of them dying and being thrown into the sea. Others landed sick and frightened. Some of them slaughtered on docks and wharves to keep them from dropping dead in their tracks. What kind of food does their flesh make? It's rank poison. Three of my family have died of cancer. I am a vegetarian."

The strange old gentleman darted from his seat, and began to pace up and down the room. I was very glad he had gone, for Miss Laura hated to hear of cruelty of any kind, and her tears were dropping thick and fast on my brown coat.

The gentleman had spoken very loudly, and every one in the room had listened to what he said. Among them, was a very young man, with a cold, handsome face. He looked as if he was annoyed that the older man should have made Miss Laura cry.

"Don't you think, sir," he said, as the old gentleman passed near him in walking up and down the floor, "that there is a great deal of mock sentiment about this business of taking care of the dumb creation? They were made for us. They've got to suffer and be killed to supply our wants. The cattle and sheep, and other animals would over-run the earth, if we didn't kill them."

"Granted," said the old man, stopping right in front of him. "Granted, young man, if you take out that word suffer. The Lord made the sheep, and the cattle, and the pigs. They are his creatures just as much as we are. We can kill them, but we've no right to make them suffer."

"But we can't help it, sir."

"Yes, we can, my young man. It's a possible thing to raise healthy stock, treat it kindly, kill it mercifully, eat it decently. When men do that I, for one, will cease to be a vegetarian. You're only a boy. You haven't traveled as I have. I've been from one end of this country to the other. Up north, down south, and out west, I've seen sights that made me shudder, and I tell you the Lord will punish this great American nation if it doesn't change its treatment of the dumb animals committed to its care."

The young man looked thoughtful, and did not reply. A very sweet-faced old lady sitting near him answered the old gentleman. I don't think I have ever seen such a fine-looking old lady as she was. Her hair was snowy white, and her face was deeply wrinkled, yet she was tall and stately, and her expression was as pleasing as my dear Miss Laura's.[1]

"I do not think we are a wicked nation," she said, softly. "We are a younger nation than many of the nations of the earth, and I think that many of our sins arise from ignorance and thoughtlessness."

"Yes, madame, yes, madame," said the fiery old gentleman, staring hard at her. "I agree with you there."

She smiled very pleasantly at him and went on. "I too have been a traveler, and I have talked to a great many wise and good people on the subject of the cruel treatment of animals, and I find that many of them have never thought about it. They, themselves, never knowingly ill-treat a dumb creature, and when they are told stories of inhuman conduct, they say in surprise, 'Why, these things surely can't exist!' You see they have never been brought in contact with them. As soon as they learn about them, they begin to agitate and say, 'We must have this thing stopped. Where is the remedy?'"

"And what is it, what is it, madame, in your opinion?" said the old gentleman, pawing the floor with impatience.

"Just the remedy that I would propose for the great evil of intemperance," said the old lady, smiling at him. "Legislation and education. Legislation for the old and hardened, and education for the young and tender. I would tell the schoolboys and schoolgirls that alcohol will destroy the framework of their beautiful

---

1 Scholars generally agree that this character represents Caroline Earle White. The daughter of Quaker abolitionists, White took on the task of establishing the first society for the prevention of cruelty to animals in Pennsylvania. At the same time, two other prominent Philadelphia citizens, S. Morris Waln and M. Richards Muckle, published an advertisement seeking others interested in setting up a society. While gathering petition signatures, White would likely have heard of this advertisement, but they did not contact each other—perhaps to retain the power to set their own agendas (Beers 45). Henry Bergh, the founder of the ASPCA, brought them together, and in 1868 they established the Pennsylvania SPCA (Turner 48). When it came time to assign formal power, Waln was elected president but White held no official position. Because it was considered unseemly for women of her class to be so forward, her husband was elected to the board of managers in her stead (Beers 48). While most of the members of SPCAs were white women, the presidents and directors were almost exclusively white men (Beers 53). White went on to establish the Anti-Vivisection Society in 1883.

bodies, and that cruelty to any of God's living creatures will blight and destroy their innocent young souls."

The young man spoke again. "Don't you think," he said, "that you temperance and humane people lay too much stress upon the education of our youth in all lofty and noble sentiments? The human heart will always be wicked. Your Bible tells you that, doesn't it? You can't educate all the badness out of children."

"We don't expect to do that," said the old lady, turning her pleasant face toward him; "but even if the human heart is desperately wicked, shouldn't that make us much more eager to try to educate, to ennoble, and restrain? However, as far as my experience goes, and I have lived in this wicked world for seventy-five years, I find that the human heart, though wicked and cruel, as you say, has yet some soft and tender spots, and the impressions made upon it in youth are never, never effaced. Do you not remember better than anything else, standing at your mother's knee—the pressure of her hand, her kiss on your forehead?"

By this time our engine had arrived. A whistle was blowing, and nearly every one was rushing from the room, the impatient old gentleman among the first. Miss Laura was hurriedly trying to do up her shawl strap, and I was standing by, wishing that I could help her. The old lady and the young man were the only other people in the room, and we could not help hearing what they said.

"Yes, I do," he said in a thick voice, and his face got very red. "She is dead now—I have no mother."

"Poor boy!" and the old lady laid her hand on his shoulder. They were standing up, and she was taller than he was. "May God bless you. I know you have a kind heart. I have four stalwart boys, and you remind me of the youngest. If you are ever in Washington, come to see me." She gave him some name, and he lifted his hat and looked as if he was astonished to find out who she was. Then he too went away, and she turned to Miss Laura. "Shall I help you, my dear?"

"If you please," said my young mistress. "I can't fasten this strap."

In a few seconds the bundle was done up, and we were joyfully hastening to the train. It was only a few miles to Riverdale, so the conductor let me stay in the car with Miss Laura. She spread her coat out on the seat in front of her, and I sat on it and looked out of the car window as we sped along through a lovely country, all green and fresh in the June sunlight. How light and pleasant this car was—so different from the baggage car. What frightens an animal most of all things, is not to see where it is going, not to know what is going to happen to it. I think that they are very like human beings in this respect.

The lady had taken a seat beside Miss Laura, and as we went along, she too looked out of the window and said in a low voice:

"What is so rare as a day in June,
Then, if ever, come perfect days."

"That is very true," said Miss Laura; "how sad that the autumn must come, and the cold winter."

"No, my dear, not sad. It is but a preparation for another summer."

"Yes, I suppose it is," said Miss Laura. Then she continued a little shyly, as her companion leaned over to stroke my cropped ears. "You seem very fond of animals."

"I am, my dear. I have four horses, two cows, a tame squirrel, three dogs, and a cat."

"You should be a happy woman," said Miss Laura, with a smile.

"I think I am. I must not forget my horned toad, Diego, that I got in California. I keep him in the green-house, and he is very happy catching flies and holding his horny head to be scratched whenever any one comes near."

"I don't see how any one can be unkind to animals," said Miss Laura, thoughtfully.

"Nor I, my dear child. It has always caused me intense pain to witness the torture of dumb animals. Nearly seventy years ago, when I was a little girl walking the streets of Boston, I would tremble and grow faint at the cruelty of drivers to over-loaded horses. I was timid and did not dare speak to them. Very often, I ran home and flung myself in my mother's arms with a burst of tears, and asked her if nothing could be done to help the poor animals. With mistaken, motherly kindness, she tried to put the subject out of my thoughts. I was carefully guarded from seeing or hearing of any instances of cruelty. But the animals went on suffering just the same, and when I became a woman, I saw my cowardice. I agitated the matter among my friends, and told them that our whole dumb creation was groaning together in pain, and would continue to groan, unless merciful human beings were willing to help them. I was able to assist in the formation of several societies for the prevention of cruelty to animals, and they have done good service. Good service not only to the horses and cows, but to the nobler animal, man. I believe that in saying to a cruel man, 'You shall not overwork, torture, mutilate, nor kill your animal, or neglect to provide it with proper food and shelter,' we are making him a little nearer the kingdom of heaven than he was before. For, 'Whatsoever a man soweth, that shall he also reap.' If he sows seeds of unkindness and cruelty to man and beast, no one knows what the blackness of the harvest will be. His poor horse, quivering under a blow, is not the worst sufferer. Oh, if people would only understand that their unkind deeds will recoil upon their own heads with tenfold force—but, my dear child, I am fancying that I am addressing a drawing-room meeting—and here we are at your station. Good-bye; keep your happy face and gentle ways. I hope that we may meet again some day." She pressed Miss Laura's hand, gave me a farewell pat, and the next minute we were outside on the platform, and she was smiling through the window at us.

CHAPTER 16

DINGLEY FARM

"MY dear niece," and a stout, middle-aged woman, with a red, lively face, threw both her arms around Miss Laura. "How glad I am to see you, and this is the dog. Good Joe, I have a bone waiting for you. Here is Uncle John."

A tall, good-looking man stepped up and put out a big hand, in which my mistress' little fingers were quite swallowed up. "I am glad to see you, Laura. Well, Joe, how d'ye do, old boy? I've heard about you."

It made me feel very welcome to have them both notice me, and I was so glad to be out of the train that I frisked for joy around their feet as we went to the wagon. It was a big double one, with an awning over it to shelter it from the sun's rays, and the horses were drawn up in the shade of a spreading tree. They were two powerful black horses, and as they had no blinders on, they could see us coming. Their faces lighted up, and they moved their ears and pawed the ground, and whinnied when Mr. Wood went up to them. They tried to rub their heads against him, and I saw plainly that they loved him. "Steady there, Cleve and Pacer," he said, "now back, back up."

By this time, Mrs. Wood, Miss Laura and I were in the wagon. Then Mr. Wood jumped in, took up the reins, and off we went. How the two black horses did spin along! I sat on the seat beside Mr. Wood, and sniffed in the delicious air, and the lovely smell of flowers and grass. How glad I was to be in the country! What long races I should have in the green fields. I wished that I had another dog to run with me, and wondered very much whether Mr. Wood kept one. I knew I should soon find out, for whenever Miss Laura went to a place she wanted to know what animals there were about.

We drove a little more than a mile along a country road where there were scattered houses. Miss Laura answered questions about her family, and asked questions about Mr. Harry, who was away at college and hadn't got home. I don't think I have said before that Mr. Harry was Mrs. Wood's son. She was a widow with one son when she married Mr. Wood, so that Mr. Harry, though the Morrises called him cousin, was not really their cousin.

I was very glad to hear them say that he was soon coming home, for I had never forgotten that but for him I should never have known Miss Laura, and gotten into my pleasant home.

By-and-by, I heard Miss Laura say: "Uncle John, have you a dog?"

"Yes, Laura," he said; "I have one to-day, but I sha'n't have one to-morrow."

"Oh, uncle, what do you mean?" she asked.

"Well, Laura," he replied, "you know animals are pretty much like people. There are some good ones and some bad ones. Now, this dog is a snarling, cross-grained, cantankerous beast, and when I heard Joe was coming, I said: 'Now we'll have a good dog about the place, and here's an end to the bad one.' So I tied Bruno up, and to-morrow I shall shoot him. Something's got to be done, or he'll be biting some one."

"Uncle," said Miss Laura, "people don't always die when they are bitten by dogs, do they?"

"No, certainly not," replied Mr. Wood. "In my humble opinion there's a great lot of nonsense talked about the poison of a dog's bite and people dying of hydrophobia. Ever since I was born I've had dogs snap at me and stick their teeth in my flesh; and I've never had a symptom of hydrophobia, and never intend to have. I believe half the people that are bitten by dogs frighten themselves into thinking they are fatally poisoned. I was reading the other day about the policemen in a big city in England that have to catch stray dogs, and dogs supposed to be mad, and all kinds of dogs, and they get bitten over and over again, and never think anything about it. But let a lady or a gentleman walking along the street have a dog bite them, and they worry themselves till their blood is in a fever, and they have to hurry across to France to get Pasteur to cure them.[1] They imagine they've got hydrophobia, and they've got it because they imagine it. I believe if I fixed my attention on that right thumb of mine, and thought I had a sore there, and picked at it and worried it, in a short time a sore would come, and I'd be off to the doctor to have it cured. At the same

---

1 Hydrophobia—as rabies was then called—was a serious concern, not necessarily because the number of victims was great, but because the nature of the disease was so terrible. The French scientist Louis Pasteur developed a treatment for rabies in 1885, which required "hurrying" over to France to receive the inoculation within the disease's incubation period. While some applauded Pasteur's development, others remained skeptical. An 1897 article in the *Journal of the American Medical Association* advocated instead for "the utter extinction of the canine race" (Shepard 826). It would be, the doctor reflected, "one of the inevitable results of our advancing civilization" (Shepard 826).

time dogs have no business to bite, and I don't recommend any one to get bitten."

"But, uncle," said Miss Laura, "isn't there such a thing as hydrophobia?"

"Oh, yes; I dare say there is. I believe that a careful examination of the records of death reported in Boston from hydrophobia for the space of thirty-two years, shows that two people actually died from it. Dogs are like all other animals. They're liable to sickness, and they've got to be watched. I think my horses would go mad if I starved them, or over-fed them, or over-worked them, or let them stand in laziness, or kept them dirty, or didn't give them water enough. They'd get some disease, anyway. If a person owns an animal, let him take care of it, and it's all right. If it shows signs of sickness, shut it up and watch it. If the sickness is incurable, kill it.[1] Here's a sure way to prevent hydrophobia. Kill off all ownerless and vicious dogs. If you can't do that, have plenty of water where they can get at it. A dog that has all the water he wants, will never go mad. This dog of mine has not one single thing the matter with him but pure ugliness. Yet, if I let him loose, and he ran through the village with his tongue out, I'll warrant you there'd be a cry of 'mad dog!' However, I'm going to kill him. I've no use for a bad dog. Have plenty of animals, I say, and treat them kindly, but if there's a vicious one among them, put it out of the way, for it is a constant danger to man and beast. It's queer how ugly some people are about their dogs. They'll keep them no matter how they worry other people, and even when they're snatching the bread out of their neighbors' mouths. But I say that is not the fault of the four-legged dog. A human dog is the worst of all. There's a band of sheep-killing dogs here in Riverdale, that their owners can't, or won't, keep out of mischief. Meek-looking fellows some of them are. The owners go to bed at night, and the dogs pretend to go, too; but when the house is quiet and the family asleep, off goes Rover or Fido to worry poor, defenseless creatures that can't defend themselves. Their taste for sheep's blood is like the taste for liquor in men, and the dogs will travel as far to get their fun, as the men will travel for theirs. They've got it in them, and you can't get it out."

"Mr. Windham cured his dog," said Mrs. Wood.

Mr. Wood burst into a hearty laugh. "So he did, so he did. I

---

1   Softening the blow, the 1965 edition revises this from "kill it" to "put it out of its misery." Further, the 1965 Uncle Wood proposes to "not let ownerless, vicious dogs roam the streets" instead of extermination.

must tell Laura about that. Windham is a neighbor of ours, and last summer I kept telling him that his collie was worrying my Shropshires.[1] He wouldn't believe me, but I knew I was right, and one night when Harry was home, he lay in wait for the dog and lassoed him. I tied him up and sent for Windham. You should have seen his face, and the dog's face. He said two words, 'You scoundrel!' and the dog cowered at his feet as if he had been shot. He was a fine dog, but he'd got corrupted by evil companions. Then Windham asked me where my sheep were. I told him in the pasture. He asked me if I still had my old ram Bolton. I said yes, and then he wanted eight or ten feet of rope. I gave it to him, and wondered what on earth he was going to do with it. He tied one end of it to the dog's collar, and holding the other in his hand, set out for the pasture. He asked us to go with him, and when he got there, he told Harry he'd like to see him catch Bolton. There wasn't any need to catch him, he'd come to us like a dog. Harry whistled, and when Bolton came up, Windham fastened the rope's end to his horns, and let him go. The ram was frightened and ran, dragging the dog with him. We let them out of the pasture into an open field, and for a few minutes there was such a racing and chasing over that field as I never saw before. Harry leaned up against the bars and laughed till the tears rolled down his cheeks. Then Bolton got mad, and began to make battle with the dog, pitching into him with his horns. We soon stopped that, for the spirit had all gone out of Dash. Windham unfastened the rope, and told him to get home, and if ever I saw a dog run, that one did. Mrs. Windham set great store by him, and her husband didn't want to kill him. But he said Dash had got to give up his sheep-killing, if he wanted to live. That cured him. He's never worried a sheep from that day to this, and if you offer him a bit of sheep's wool now, he tucks his tail between his legs, and runs for home. Now, I must stop my talk, for we're in sight of the farm. Yonder's our boundary line, and there's the house. You'll see a difference in the trees since you were here before."

---

1   Shropshires are a breed of sheep. Uncle Wood references a serious chal-
lenge faced by American farmers: sheep-killing dogs. Many jurisdictions
had laws allowing the owner of the sheep to kill the offending dog. A reference to "sheep-murder" is made in another popular children's book,
Alfred Ollivant's *Bob, Son of Battle* (New York: Doubleday, 1898). The
offense was not taken lightly: sheep roamed wide spaces, so the farmer
could not monitor the safety of his flock. An 1890 expert on collies quotes
a description of a blood-thirsty collie as "a sheep destroyer, for he goes
about his work more cunningly than any other of his race" (Lee 132).

We had come to a turn in the road where the ground sloped gently upward. We turned in at the gate, and drove between rows of trees up to a long, low, red house, with a veranda all round it. There was a wide lawn in front, and away on our right were the farm buildings. They too, were painted red, and there were some trees by them that Mr. Wood called his windbreak, because they kept the snow from drifting in the winter time.

I thought it was a beautiful place. Miss Laura had been here before, but not for some years, so she too was looking about quite eagerly.

"Welcome to Dingley Farm, Joe," said Mrs. Wood, with her jolly laugh, as she watched me jump from the carriage seat to the ground. "Come in, and I'll introduce you to pussy."

"Aunt Hattie, why is the farm called Dingley Farm?" said Miss Laura, as we went into the house. "It ought to be Wood Farm."

"Dingley is made out of 'dingle,' Laura. You know that pretty hollow back of the pasture? It is what they call a 'dingle.' So this farm was called Dingle Farm till the people around about got saying 'Dingley' instead. I suppose they found it easier. Why, here is Lolo coming to see Joe."

Walking along the wide hall that ran through the house was a large tortoise-shell cat. She had a prettily marked face, and she was waving her large tail like a flag, and mewing kindly to greet her mistress. But when she saw me what a face she made. She flew on the hall table, and putting up her back till it almost lifted her feet from the ground, began to spit at me and bristle with rage.

"Poor Lolo," said Mrs. Wood, going up to her. "Joe is a good dog, and not like Bruno. He won't hurt you."

I wagged myself about a little, and looked kindly at her, but she did nothing but say bad words to me. It was weeks and weeks before I made friends with that cat. She was a young thing, and had known only one dog, and he was a bad one, so she supposed all dogs were like him.

There was a number of rooms opening off the hall, and one of them was the dining room where they had tea. I lay on a rug outside the door and watched them. There was a small table spread with a white cloth, and it had pretty dishes and glassware on it, and a good many different kinds of things to eat. A little French girl, called Adèle, kept coming and going from the kitchen to give them hot cakes, and fried eggs, and hot coffee. As soon as they finished their tea, Mrs. Wood gave me one of the best meals that I ever had in my life.

CHAPTER 17

MR. WOOD AND HIS HORSES

THE morning after we arrived in Riverdale, I was up very early and walking around the house. I slept in the woodshed, and could run outdoors whenever I liked.

The woodshed was at the back of the house and near it was the tool shed. Then there was a carriage house, and a plank walk leading to the barnyard.

I ran up this walk, and looked into the first building I came to. It was the horse stable. A door stood open, and the morning sun was glancing in. There were several horses there, some with their heads toward me, and some with their tails. I saw that instead of being tied up, there were gates outside their stalls, and they could stand in any way they liked.

There was a man moving about at the other end of the stable, and long before he saw me, I knew that it was Mr. Wood. What a nice, clean stable he had! There was always a foul smell coming out of Jenkins's stable, but here the air seemed as pure inside as outside. There was a number of little gratings in the wall to let in the fresh air, and they were so placed that drafts would not blow on the horses. Mr. Wood was going from one horse to another, giving them hay, and talking to them in a cheerful voice. At last he spied me, and cried out, "The top of the morning to you, Joe! You are up early. Don't come too near the horses, good dog," as I walked in beside him; "they might think you are another Bruno, and give you a sly bite or kick. I should have shot him long ago. 'Tis hard to make a good dog suffer for a bad one, but that's the way of the world. Well, old fellow, what do you think of my horse stable? Pretty fair, isn't it?" And Mr. Wood went on talking to me as he fed and groomed his horses, till I soon found out that his chief pride was in them.

I like to have human beings talk to me. Mr. Morris often reads his sermons to me, and Miss Laura tells me secrets that I don't think she would tell to any one else.

I watched Mr. Wood carefully, while he groomed a huge, gray cart-horse, that he called Dutchman. He took a brush in his right hand, and a curry-comb in his left, and he curried and brushed every part of the horse's skin, and afterward wiped him with a cloth. "A good grooming is equal to two quarts of oats, Joe," he said to me.

Then he stooped down and examined the horse's hoofs. "Your shoes are too heavy, Dutchman," he said; "but that pig-headed blacksmith thinks he knows more about horses than I do. 'Don't cut the sole nor the frog,' I say to him. 'Don't pare the hoof so much, and don't rasp it; and fit your shoe to the foot, and not the foot to the shoe,' and he looks as if he wanted to say, 'Mind your own business.' We'll not go to him again. ''Tis hard to teach an old dog new tricks.' I got you to work for me, not to wear out your strength in lifting about his weighty shoes."

Mr. Wood stopped talking for a few minutes, and whistled a tune. Then he began again. "I've made a study of horses, Joe. Over forty years I've studied them, and it's my opinion that the average horse knows more than the average man that drives him. When I think of the stupid fools that are goading patient horses about, beating them and misunderstanding them, and thinking they are only clods of earth with a little life in them, I'd like to take their horses out of the shafts and harness them in, and I'd trot them off at a pace, and slash them, and jerk them, till I guess they'd come out with a little less patience than the animal does.

"Look at this Dutchman—see the size of him. You'd think he hadn't any more nerves than a bit of granite. Yet he's got a skin as sensitive as a girl's. See how he quivers if I run the curry-comb too harshly over him. The idiot I got him from, didn't know what was the matter with him. He'd bought him for a reliable horse, and there he was, kicking and stamping whenever the boy went near him. 'Your boy's got too heavy a hand, Deacon Jones,' said I, when he described the horse's actions to me. 'You may depend upon it, a four-legged creature, unlike a two-legged one, has a reason for everything he does.' 'But he's only a draught horse,' said Deacon Jones. 'Draught horse or no draught horse,' said I, 'you're describing a horse with a tender skin to me, and I don't care if he's as big as an elephant.' Well, the old man grumbled and said he didn't want any thoroughbred airs in his stable, so I bought you, didn't I, Dutchman?" and Mr. Wood stroked him kindly and went to the next stall.

In each stall was a small tank of water with a sliding cover, and I found out afterward that these covers were put on when a horse came in too heated to have a drink. At any other time, he could drink all he liked. Mr. Wood believed in having plenty of pure water for all his animals and they all had their own place to get a drink.

Even I had a little bowl of water in the woodshed, though I could easily have run up to the barnyard when I wanted a drink.

As soon as I came, Mrs. Wood asked Adèle to keep it there for me and when I looked up gratefully at her, she said: "Every animal should have its own feeding place and its own sleeping place, Joe, that is only fair."

The next horses Mr. Wood groomed were the black ones, Cleve and Pacer. Pacer had something wrong with his mouth, and Mr. Wood turned back his lips and examined it carefully. This he was able to do, for there were large windows in the stable and it was as light as Mr. Wood's house was.

"No dark corners here, eh Joe!" said Mr. Wood, as he came out of the stall and passed me to get a bottle from a shelf. "When this stable was built, I said no dirt holes for careless men here. I want the sun to shine in the corners, and I don't want my horses to smell bad smells, for they hate them, and I don't want them starting when they go into the light of day, just because they've been kept in a black hole of a stable, and I've never had a sick horse yet."

He poured something from a bottle into a saucer, and went back to Pacer with it. I followed him and stood outside. Mr. Wood seemed to be washing a sore in the horse's mouth. Pacer winced a little, and Mr. Wood said: "Steady, steady, my beauty; 'twill soon be over."

The horse fixed his intelligent eyes on his master and looked as if he knew that he was trying to do him good.

"Just look at these lips, Joe," said Mr. Wood "delicate and fine like our own, and yet there are brutes that will jerk them as if they were made of iron. I wish the Lord would give horses voices just for one week. I tell you they'd scare some of us. Now, Pacer, that's over. I'm not going to dose you much, for I don't believe in it. If a horse has got a serious trouble, get a good horse doctor, say I. If it's a simple thing, try a simple remedy. There's been many a good horse drugged and dosed to death. Well, Scamp, my beauty, how are you, this morning?"

In the stall next to Pacer, was a small, jet-black mare, with a lean head, slender legs, and a curious restless manner. She was a regular greyhound of a horse, no spare flesh, yet wiry and able to do a great deal of work. She was a wicked-looking little thing, so I thought I had better keep at a safe distance from her heels.

Mr. Wood petted her a great deal and I saw that she was his favorite. "Saucebox," he exclaimed, when she pretended to bite him, "you know if you bite me, I'll bite back again. I think I've conquered you," he said, proudly, as he stroked her glossy neck, "but what a dance you led me. Do you remember how I bought you for a mere song, because you had a bad habit of turning around like a flash in front of anything that frightened you, and bolting off the other way? And how did I cure you, my beauty? Beat you and make you stubborn? Not I. I let you go round and round; I turned you and twisted you, the oftener the better for me, till at last I got it into your pretty head that turning and twisting was addling your brains, and you had better let me be master.

"You've minded me from that day, haven't you? Horse, or man, or dog aren't much good till they learn to obey, and I've thrown you down, and I'll do it again if you bite me, so take care."

Scamp tossed her pretty head, and took little pieces of Mr. Wood's shirt sleeve in her mouth, keeping her cunning brown eye on him as if to see how far she could go. But she did not bite him. I think she loved him, for when he left her she whinnied shrilly, and he had to go back and stroke and caress her.[1]

After that I often used to watch her as she went about the farm. She always seemed to be tugging and striving at her load, and trying to step out fast and do a great deal of work. Mr. Wood was usually driving her. The men didn't like her, and couldn't manage her. She had not been properly broken in.

After Mr. Wood finished his work he went and stood in the doorway. There were six horses altogether: Dutchman, Cleve, Pacer, Scamp, a bay mare called Ruby, and a young horse belonging to Mr. Harry, whose name was Fleetfoot.

"What do you think of them all?" said Mr. Wood, looking down at me. "A pretty fine-looking lot of horses, aren't they? Not

---

1 Mr. Wood's stroke reflects the type of dominance that the philosopher Yi-Fu Tuan argues pervades human-pet relationships, even those that appear affectionate. A "good" animal *must* accept the master's caresses—and with evident pleasure—or be deemed "bad." Can it be a coincidence that in the next pages, Uncle Wood turns his attention to dealing with Bruno, the "bad" dog? In this caress, there are also problematic sexual overtones that link his domination to sexual conquest. In her study, Coral Lansbury finds strong connections between pornographic depictions of "breaking" unruly women and representations of horse-breaking. In these texts, the forced bit in a horse's mouth, along with the birch whips, bondage straps, and knives, make both women and horses into victims in what Lansbury terms "coitus atrox"—sadistic and violent depictions of "breaking in" females. And much like Black Beauty and Ginger have been read as slave figures by critics such as Moira Ferguson, so can Scamp, "wicked-looking" and "jet-black," reference a female slave made to submit to her master.

a thoroughbred there, but worth as much to me as if each had pedigree as long as this plank walk. There's a lot of humbug about this pedigree business in horses. Mine have their manes and tails anyway, and the proper use of their eyes which is more liberty than some thoroughbreds get.

"I'd like to see the man that would persuade me to put blinders or check-reins or any other instrument of torture on my horses. Don't the simpletons know that blinders are the cause of—well, I wouldn't like to say how many of our accidents, Joe, for fear you'd think me extravagant, and the check-rein drags up a horse's head out of its fine natural curve and presses sinews, bones, and joints together, till the horse is well-nigh mad. Ah, Joe, this is a cruel world for man or beast. You're a standing token of that, with your missing ears and tail. And now I've got to go and be cruel, and shoot that dog. He must be disposed of before anyone else is astir. How I hate to take life."

He sauntered down the walk to the tool shed, went in and soon came out leading a large, brown dog by a chain. This was Bruno. He was snapping and snarling and biting at his chain as he went along, though Mr. Wood led him very kindly, and when he saw me he acted as if he could have torn me to pieces. After Mr. Wood took him behind the barn, he came back and got his gun. I ran away so that I would not hear the sound of it, for I could not help feeling sorry for Bruno.[1]

Miss Laura's room was on one side of the house, and in the second story. There was a little balcony outside it, and when I got near I saw that she was standing out on it wrapped in a shawl. Her hair was streaming over her shoulders, and she was looking down into the garden where there were a great many white and yellow flowers in bloom.

I barked, and she looked at me. "Dear old Joe, I will get dressed and come down."

She hurried into her room, and I lay on the veranda till I heard her step. Then I jumped up. She unlocked the front door, and we went for a walk down the lane to the road until we heard the breakfast bell. As soon as we heard it we ran back to the house, and Miss Laura had such an appetite for her breakfast that her aunt said the country had done her good already.

---

1 The 1920, 1925, and 1934 editions omit the veiled description of Bruno's killing. In the 1965 edition, Bruno lives: Laura discovers that a wood tick is the source of Bruno's surliness, and nurses him back to health. (See Appendix F3, p. 313.)

CHAPTER 18

MRS. WOOD'S POULTRY

AFTER breakfast, Mrs. Wood put on a large apron, and going into the kitchen, said: "Have you any scraps for the hens, Adèle? Be sure and not give me anything salty."

The French girl gave her a dish of food, then Mrs. Wood asked Miss Laura to go and see her chickens, and away we went to the poultry house.

On the way we saw Mr. Wood. He was sitting on the step of the tool shed cleaning his gun. "Is the dog dead?" asked Miss Laura.

"Yes," he said.

She sighed and said: "Poor creature, I am sorry he had to be killed. Uncle, what is the most merciful way to kill a dog? Sometimes, when they get old, they should be put out of the way."

"You can shoot them," he said, "or you can poison them. I shot Bruno through his head into his neck. There's a right place to aim at.[1] It's a little to one side of the top of the skull. If you'll remind me I'll show you a circular I have in the house. It tells the proper way to kill animals. The American Humane Education Society in Boston puts it out, and it's a merciful thing.

"You don't know anything about the slaughtering of animals, Laura, and it's well you don't. There's an awful amount of cruelty practised, and practised by some people that think themselves pretty good. I wouldn't have my lambs killed the way my father had his for a kingdom. I'll never forget the first one I saw butchered. I wouldn't feel worse at a hanging now.[2] And that white ox, Hattie—you remember my telling you about him. He had to be killed, and father sent for the butcher. I was only a lad, and I was all of a shudder to have the life of the creature I had known taken from him. The butcher, stupid clown, gave him eight blows before he struck the right place. The ox bellowed, and turned his great black eyes on my father, and I fell in a faint."[3]

---

1 The 1920, 1925, and 1934 editions were updated to reflect the advent of other methods (electric cages) of disposing of unwanted animals. (See Appendix B2, p. 274.) The ensuing instructions for animal euthanasia were also revised, reflecting how the novel was, for decades, not read as simply a fiction but also a detailed instruction manual.

2 The 1925 edition omits this comparison to a hanging, perhaps because it so directly juxtaposes a human death with an animal one.

3 The 1920, 1925, and 1934 editions significantly soften this incident by referring to the eight blows vaguely and omitting this vivid description of the animal's death.

Miss Laura turned away, and Mrs. Wood followed her, saying: "If ever you want to kill a cat, Laura, give it cyanide of potassium. I killed a poor old sick cat for Mrs. Windham the other day. We put half a teaspoonful of pure cyanide of potassium in a long-handled wooden spoon, and dropped it on the cat's tongue, as near the throat as we could. Poor pussy—she died in a few seconds. Do you know, I was reading such a funny thing the other day about giving cats medicine. They hate it, and one can scarcely force it into their mouths on account of their sharp teeth. The way is, to smear it on their sides, and they lick it off. A good idea, isn't it? Here we are at the hen house, or rather one of the hen houses."

"Don't you keep your hens all together?" asked Miss Laura.

"Only in the winter time," said Mrs. Wood, "I divide my flock in the spring. Part of them stay here and part go to the orchard to live in little movable houses that we put about in different places. I feed each flock morning and evening at their own little house. They know they'll get no food even if they come to my house, so they stay at home. And they know they'll get no food between times, so all day long they pick and scratch in the orchard, and destroy so many bugs and insects that it more than pays for the trouble of keeping them there."

"Doesn't this flock want to mix up with the other?" asked Miss Laura, as she stepped into the little wooden house.

"No; they seem to understand. I keep my eye on them for a while at first, and they soon find out that they're not to fly either over the garden fence or the orchard fence. They roam over the farm and pick up what they can get. There's a good deal of sense in hens, if one manages them properly. I love them, because they are such good mothers."

We were in the little wooden house by this time, and I looked around it with surprise. It was better than some of the poor people's houses in Fairport. The walls were white and clean, so were the little ladders that led up to different kinds of roosts, where the fowls sat at night. Some roosts were thin and round, and some were broad and flat. Mrs. Wood said that the broad ones were for a heavy fowl called the Brahma. Every part of the little house was almost as light as it was outdoors, on account of the large windows.

Miss Laura spoke of it. "Why, auntie, I never saw such a light hen house."

Mrs. Wood was diving into a partly shut-in place, where it was not so light, and where the nests were. She straightened herself up, her face redder than ever, and looked at the windows with a pleased smile.

"Yes, there's not a hen house in New Hampshire with such big windows. Whenever I look at them, I think of my mother's hens, and wish that they could have had a place like this. They would have thought themselves in a hen's paradise. When I was a girl we didn't know that hens loved light and heat, and all winter they used to sit in a dark hencoop, and the cold was so bad that their combs would freeze stiff, and the tops of them would drop off. We never thought about it. If we'd had any sense, we might have watched them on a fine day go and sit on the compost heap and sun themselves, and then have concluded that if they liked light and heat outside, they'd like it inside. Poor biddies, they were so cold that they wouldn't lay us any eggs in winter."

"You take a great interest in your poultry, don't you, auntie?" said Miss Laura.

"Yes, indeed, and well I may. I'll show you my brown Leghorn, Jenny, that lay eggs enough in a year to pay for the newspapers I take to keep myself posted in poultry matters. I buy all my own clothes with my hen money, and lately I've started a bank account, for I want to save up enough to start a few stands of bees. Even if I didn't want to be kind to my hens, it would pay me to be so for sake of the profit they yield. Of course they're quite a lot of trouble. Sometimes they get vermin on them, and I have to grease them and dust carbolic acid on them, and try some of my numerous cures. Then I must keep ashes and dust wallows for them and be very particular about my eggs when hens are sitting, and see that the hens come off regularly for food and exercise. Oh, there are a hundred things I have to think of, but I always say to any one that thinks of raising poultry: 'If you are going into the business for the purpose of making money, it pays to take care of them.'"

"There's one thing I notice," said Miss Laura, "and that is that your drinking fountains must be a great deal better than the shallow pans that I have seen some people give their hens water in."

"Dirty things they are," said Mrs. Wood; "I wouldn't use one of them. I don't think there is anything worse for hens than drinking dirty water. My hens must have as clean water as I drink myself, and in winter I heat it for them. If it's poured boiling into the fountains in the morning, it keeps warm till night. Speaking of shallow drinking dishes, I wouldn't use them, even before I ever heard of a drinking fountain. John made me something that we read about. He used to take a powder keg and bore a little hole in the side, about an inch from the top, then fill it with water, and cover with a pan a little larger round than the keg. Then he turned the keg upside down, without taking away the pan. The water ran into the pan only as far as the hole in the keg, and it would have to be used before more would flow in. Now let us go and see my beautiful, bronze turkeys. They don't need any houses, for they roost in the trees the year round."

We found the flock of turkeys, and Miss Laura admired their changeable colors very much. Some of them were very large, and I did not like them, for the gobblers ran at me, and made a dreadful noise in their throats.

Afterward, Mrs. Wood showed us some ducks that she had shut up in a yard. She said that she was feeding them on vegetable food, to give their flesh a pure flavor, and by-and-by she would send them to market and get a high price for them.

Every place she took us to was as clean as possible. "No one can be successful in raising poultry in large numbers," she said, "unless they keep their quarters clean and comfortable."

As yet we had seen no hens, except a few on the nests, and Miss Laura said, "Where are they? I should like to see them."

"They are coming," said Mrs. Wood. "It is just their breakfast time, and they are as punctual as clockwork. They go off early in the morning, to scratch about a little for themselves first."

As she spoke she stepped off the plank walk and looked off towards the fields.

Miss Laura burst out laughing. Away beyond the barns the hens were coming. Seeing Mrs. Wood standing there, they thought they were late, and began to run and fly, jumping over each other's backs, and stretching out their necks, in a state of great excitement. Some of their legs seemed sticking straight out behind. It was very funny to see them.

They were a fine-looking lot of poultry, mostly white, with glossy feathers and bright eyes. They greedily ate the food scattered to them and Mrs. Wood said, "They think I've changed their breakfast time, and to-morrow they'll come a good bit earlier. And yet some people say hens have no sense."

CHAPTER 19

A BAND OF MERCY

New York: A.L. Burt, 1922.

A FEW evenings after we came to Dingley Farm, Mrs. Wood and Miss Laura were sitting out on the veranda, and I was lying at their feet.

"Auntie," said Miss Laura, "What do those letters mean on that silver pin that you wear with that piece of ribbon?"

"You know what the white ribbon means, don't you?" asked Mrs. Wood.

"Yes; that you are a temperance woman, doesn't it?"

"It does; and the star pin means that I am a member of a Band of Mercy. Do you know what a Band of Mercy is?"

"No," said Miss Laura.

"How strange! I should think that you would have several in Fairport. A cripple boy, the son of a Boston artist, started this one here. It has done a great deal of good. There is a meeting tomorrow, and I will take you to it if you like."

It was on Monday that Mrs. Wood had this talk with Miss Laura, and the next afternoon, after all the work was done, they got ready to go to the village.

"May Joe go?" asked Miss Laura.

"Certainly," said Mrs. Wood; "he is such good dog that he won't be any trouble."

I was very glad to hear this, and trotted along by them down the lane to the road. The lane was a very cool and pleasant place. There were tall trees growing on each side, and under them, among the grass, pretty wild flowers were peeping out to look at us as we went by.

Mrs. Wood and Miss Laura talked all the way about the Band of Mercy. Miss Laura was much interested, and said that she would like to start one in Fairport.

"It is a very simple thing," said Mrs. Wood. "All you have to do is to write the pledge at the top of a piece of paper: 'I will try to be kind to all harmless living creatures, and try to protect them from cruel usage,' and get thirty people to sign it. That makes a band.

"I have formed two or three bands by keeping slips of paper ready, and getting people that come to visit me to sign them. I call them 'Corresponding Bands,' for they are too far apart to meet. I send the members 'Band of Mercy' papers, and I get such nice letters from them, telling me of kind things they do for animals.

"A Band of Mercy in a place is a splendid thing. There's the greatest difference in Riverdale since this one was started. A few years ago, when a man beat or raced his horse, and any one interfered, he said: 'This horse is mine; I'll do what I like with him.' Most people thought he was right, but now they're all for the poor horse, and there isn't a man anywhere around who would dare to abuse any animal.

"It's all the children. They're doing a grand work, and I say it's a good thing for them. Since we've studied this subject, it's enough to frighten one to read what is sent us about our American boys and girls. Do you know, Laura, that with all our brag about our schools and colleges, that really are wonderful, we're turning out more criminals than any other civilized country in the world, except Spain and Italy?[1] The cause of it is said to be

1   The editions closely following World War I—1920, 1925, and 1934—do not refer disparagingly to Spain and Italy. At the time *Beautiful Joe* was published, it was common for the English and the Americans to portray themselves as more humane, more civilized, by representing (*continued*)

lack of proper training for the youth of our land. Immigration has something to do with it too. We're thinking too much about educating the mind, and forgetting about the heart and soul. So I say now, while we've got all our future population in our schools, saints and sinners, good people and bad people, let us try to slip in something between the geography, and history, and grammar that will go a little deeper, and touch them so much, that when they are grown up and go out in the world, they will carry with them lessons of love and good will to men.

"A little child is such a tender thing. You can bend it any way you like. Speaking of this heart education of children, as set over against mind education, I see that many school-teachers say that there is nothing better than to give them lessons on kindness to animals. Children who are taught to love and protect dumb creatures, will be kind to their fellow-men when they grow up."

I was very much pleased with this talk between Mrs. Wood and Miss Laura, and kept close to them so that I would not miss a word.

As we went along, houses began to appear here and there, set back from the road among the trees. Soon they got quite close together, and I saw some shops.

This was the village of Riverdale, and nearly all the buildings were along this winding street. The river was away back of the village. We had already driven there several times.

We passed the school on our way. It was a square, white building, standing in the middle of a large yard. Boys and girls, with their arms full of books, were hurrying down the steps and coming into the street. Two quite big boys came behind us, and Mrs. Wood turned around and spoke to them, and asked if they were going to the Band of Mercy.

"Oh, yes, ma'am," said the younger one. "I've got a recitation, don't you remember?"

"Yes, yes; excuse me for forgetting," said Mrs. Wood, with her jolly laugh. "And here are Dolly, and Jennie, and Martha," she went on, as some little girls came running out of a house that we were passing.

---

other countries like Spain, Italy, France, and China as inhumane. Christian missionaries to China were equipped with a highly simplified Chinese translation of *Beautiful Joe*, a copy of which remains with the Esther Clark Wright Archives at Acadia University, Nova Scotia. (For a review of this edition, see Appendix A6, p. 272.)

The little girls joined us and looked so hard at my head and stump of a tail, and my fine collar, that I felt quite shy, and walked with my head against Miss Laura's dress.

She stooped down and patted me, and then I felt as if I didn't care how much they stared. Miss Laura never forgot me. No matter how earnestly she was talking, or playing a game, or doing anything, she always stopped occasionally to give me a word or look, to show that she knew I was near.

Mrs. Wood paused in front of a building on the main street. A great many boys and girls were going in, and we went with them. We found ourselves in a large room, with a platform at one end of it. There were some chairs on this platform and a small table.

A boy stood by this table with his hand on a bell. Presently he rang it, and then every one kept still. Mrs. Wood whispered to Miss Laura that this boy was the president of the band, and the young man with the pale face and curly hair who sat in front of him was Mr. Maxwell, the artist's son, who had formed this Band of Mercy.

The lad who presided had a ringing, pleasant voice. He said they would begin their meeting by singing a hymn. There was an organ near the platform and a young girl played on it, while all the other boys and girls stood up, and sang very sweetly and clearly.

After they had sung the hymn, the president asked for the report of their last meeting.

A little girl, blushing and hanging her head, came forward, and read what was written on a paper that she held in her hand.

The president made some remarks after she had finished, and then every one had to vote. It was just like a meeting of grown people, and I was surprised to see how good those children were. They did not frolic nor laugh, but all seemed sober and listened attentively.

After the voting was over, the president called upon John Turner to give a recitation. This was the boy whom we saw on the way there. He walked up to the platform, made a bow, and said that he had learned two stories for his recitation, out of the paper, "Dumb Animals." One story was about a horse, and the other was about a dog, and he thought that they were two of the best animal stories on record. He would tell the horse story first.

"A man in Missouri had to go to Nebraska to see about some land. He went on horseback, on a horse that he had trained himself, and that came at his whistle like a dog. On getting into Nebraska, he came to a place where there were two roads. One went by a river, and the other went over the hill. The man saw that the travel went over the hill, but thought he'd take the river road. He didn't know that there was a quicksand across it, and that people couldn't use it in spring and summer. There used to be a sign board to tell strangers about it, but it had been taken away. The man got off his horse to let him graze, and walked along till he got so far ahead of the horse that he had to sit down and wait for him. Suddenly he found that he was on a quicksand. His feet had sunk in the sand, and he could not get them out. He threw himself down, and whistled for his horse, and shouted for help, but no one came. He could hear some young people singing out on the river, but they could not hear him. The terrible sand drew him in almost to his shoulders, and he thought he was lost. At that moment the horse came running up, and stood by his master. The man was too low down to get hold of the saddle or bridle, so he took hold of the horse's tail, and told him to go. The horse gave an awful pull, and landed his master on safe ground."

Everybody clapped his hands, and stamped when this story was finished, and called out: "The dog story—The dog story!"

The boy bowed and smiled, and began again. "You all know what a 'round-up' of cattle is, so I need not explain. Once a man down south was going to have one, and he and his boys and friends were talking it over. There was an ugly, black steer in the herd, and they were wondering whether their old yellow dog would be able to manage him. The dog's name was Tige, and he lay and listened wisely to their talk. The next day there was a scene of great confusion. The steer raged and tore about, and would allow no one to come within whip touch of him. Tige, who had always been brave, skulked about for a while, and then, as if he had got up a little spirit, he made a run at the steer. The steer sighted him, gave a bellow, and, lowering his horns, ran at him. Tige turned tail, and the young men that owned him were frantic. They'd been praising him, and thought they were going to have it proven false. Their father called out: 'Don't shoot Tige, till you see where he's running to.' The dog ran right to the cattle pen. The steer was so enraged that he never noticed where he was going, and dashed in after him. Tige leaped the wall, and came back to the gate, barking and yelping for the men to come and shut the steer in. They shut the gate and petted Tige, and bought him a collar with a silver plate."

The boy was loudly cheered, and went to his seat. The president said he would like to have remarks made about these two stories.

Several children put up their hands, and he asked each one to speak in turn. One said that if that man's horse had had a docked tail, his master wouldn't have been able to reach it, and would have perished. Another said that if the man hadn't treated his horse kindly, he never would have come at his whistle, and stood over him to see what he could do to help him. A third child said that the people on the river weren't as quick at hearing the voice of the man in trouble as the horse was.

When this talk was over, the president called for some stories of foreign animals.

Another boy came forward, made his bow, and said, in a short, abrupt voice, "My uncle's name is Henry Worthington. He is an Englishman, and once he was a soldier in India. One day when he was hunting in the Punjab, he saw a mother monkey carrying a little dead baby monkey. Six months after, he was in the same jungle. Saw same monkey still carrying dead baby monkey, all shriveled up. Mother monkey loved her baby monkey, and wouldn't give it up."

The boy went to his seat, and the president, with a queer look in his face, said, "That's a very good story, Ronald—if it is true."

None of the children laughed, but Mrs. Wood's face got like a red poppy, and Miss Laura bit her lip, and Mr. Maxwell buried his head in his arms, his whole frame shaking.

The boy who told the story looked very angry. He jumped up again. "My uncle's a true man, Phil Dodge, and never told a lie in his life."

The president remained standing, his face a deep scarlet, and a tall boy at the back of the room got up and said, "Mr. President, what would be impossible in this climate, might be possible in a hot country like India. Doesn't heat sometimes draw up and preserve things?"

The president's face cleared. "Thank you for the suggestion," he said. "I don't want to hurt anybody's feelings; but you know there is a rule in the band that only true stories are to be told here. We have five more minutes for foreign stories. Has any one else one?"

CHAPTER 20

STORIES ABOUT ANIMALS

A SMALL girl, with twinkling eyes and a merry face, got up, just behind Miss Laura, and made her way to the front. "My dranfadder says," she began, in a piping little voice, "dat when he was a little boy his fadder brought him a little monkey from de West Indies. De naughty boys in de village used to tease de little monkey, and he runned up a tree one day. Dey was drowing stones at him, and a man dat was paintin' de house druv 'em away. De monkey runned down de tree, and shook hands wid de man. My dranfadder saw him," she said, with a shake of her head at the president, as if she was afraid he would doubt her.

There was great laughing and clapping of hands when this little girl took her seat, and she hopped right up again and ran back. "Oh, I fordot," she went on, in her squeaky, little voice, "dat my dranfadder says dat afterward de monkey upset de painter's can of oil, and rolled in it, and den jumped down in my dranfadder's flour barrel."

The president looked very much amused, and said, "We have had some good stories about monkeys, now let us have some more about our home animals. Who can tell us another story about a horse?"

Three or four boys jumped up, but the president said they would take one at a time. The first one was this: A Riverdale boy was walking along the bank of a canal in Hoytville. He saw a boy driving two horses, which were towing a canal boat. The first horse was lazy, and the boy got angry and struck him several times over the head with his whip. The Riverdale boy shouted across to him, begging him not to be so cruel; but the boy paid no attention. Suddenly the horse turned, seized his tormentor by the shoulder, and pushed him into the canal. The water was not deep, and the boy, after floundering about for a few seconds, came out dripping with mud and filth, and sat down on the tow path, and looked at the horse with such a comical expression, that the Riverdale boy had to stuff his handkerchief in his mouth to keep from laughing.

"It is to be hoped that he would learn a lesson," said the president, "and be kinder to his horse in the future. Now, Bernard Howe, your story."

The boy was a brother to the little girl who had told the monkey story, and he, too, had evidently been talking to his grandfather. He told two stories, and Miss Laura listened eagerly, for they were about Fairport.

The boy said that when his grandfather was young, he lived in Fairport, Maine. On a certain day he stood in the market square to see their first stagecoach put together. It had come from Boston in pieces, for there was no one in Fairport that could make one. The coach went away up into the country one day, and came back the next. For a long time no one understood driving the horses properly, and they came in day after day with the blood streaming from them. The whiffle-tree[1] would swing round and hit them, and when their collars were taken off, their necks would be raw and bloody. After a time, the men got to understand how to drive a coach, and the horses did not suffer so much.

The other story was about a team-boat, not a steamboat. More than seventy years ago, they had no steamers running between Fairport and the island opposite where people went for the summer, but they had what they called a team-boat, that is, a boat with machinery to make it go, that could be worked by horses. There were eight horses that went around and around, and made the boat go. One afternoon, two dancing masters, who were wicked fellows, that played the fiddle, and never went to church on Sundays, got on the boat, and sat just where the horses had to pass them as they went around.

Every time the horses went by, they jabbed them with their penknives. The man who was driving the horses at last saw the blood dripping from them, and the dancing masters were found out. Some young men on the boat were so angry that they caught up a rope's end, and gave the dancing masters a lashing, and then threw them into the water and made them swim to the island.

When this boy took a seat, a young girl read some verses that she had clipped from a newspaper:

> "Don't kill the toads, the ugly toads,
>   That hop around your door;
> Each meal the little toad doth eat
>   A hundred bugs or more.
>
> "He sits around with aspect meek,
>   Until the bug hath neared,

---

1   A whiffle-tree, also known as a whipple-tree, is a set of linked bars used to hitch a wagon or plow onto draft animals to evenly distribute the force of the loads they are carrying.

Then shoots he forth his little tongue
      Like lightning double-geared.

"And then he soberly doth wink,
      And shut his ugly mug,
And patiently doth wait until
      There comes another bug."

Mr. Maxwell told a good dog story after this. He said the president need not have any fears as to its truth, for it had happened in his boarding house in the village, and he had seen it himself. Monday, the day before, being wash day, his landlady had put out a large washing. Among the clothes on the line was a gray flannel shirt belonging to her husband. The young dog belonging to the house had pulled the shirt from the line and torn it to pieces. The woman put it aside and told him master would beat him. When the man came home to his dinner, he showed the dog the pieces of the shirt, and gave him a severe whipping. The dog ran away, visited all the clothes lines in the village, till he found a gray shirt very like his master's. He seized it and ran home, laying it at his master's feet, joyfully wagging his tail meanwhile.

Mr. Maxwell's story done, a bright-faced boy called Simon Grey got up and said, "You all know our old gray horse Ned. Last week father sold him to a man in Hoytville, and I went to the station when he was shipped. He was put in a box car. The doors were left a little open to give him air, and were locked in that way. There was a narrow, sliding door, four feet from the floor of the car, and, in some way or other, old Ned pushed this door open, crawled through it, and tumbled out on the ground. When I was coming from school, I saw him walking along the track. He hadn't hurt himself, except for a few cuts. He was glad to see me, and followed me home. He must have gotten off the train when it was going full speed, for he hadn't been seen at any of the stations, and the trainmen were astonished to find the doors locked and the car empty, when they got to Hoytville. Father got the man who bought him to release him from his bargain, for he says if Ned is so fond of Riverdale, he shall stay here."

The president asked the boys and girls to give three cheers for old Ned, and then they had some more singing. After all had taken their seats, he said he would like to know what the members had been doing for animals during the past fortnight.

One girl had kept her brother from shooting two owls that came about their barnyard. She told him that the owls would destroy the rats and mice that bothered him in the barn, but if he hunted them, they would go to the woods.

A boy said that he had persuaded some of his friends who were going fishing, to put their bait worms into a dish of boiling water to kill them before they started, and also to promise him that as soon as they took their fish out of the water, they would kill them by a sharp blow on the back of the head. They were all the more ready to do this, when he told them that their fish would taste better when cooked, if they had been killed as soon as they were taken from the water into the air.

A little girl had gotten her mother to say that she would never again put lobsters into cold water and slowly boil them to death. She had also stopped a man in the street who was carrying a pair of fowls with their heads down, and asked him if he would kindly reverse their position. The man told her that the fowls didn't mind, and she pursed up her small mouth and showed the band how she said to him, "I would prefer the opinion of the hens." Then she said he had laughed at her, and said, "Certainly, little lady," and had gone off carrying them as she wanted him to. She had also reasoned with different boys outside the village who were throwing stones at birds and frogs, and sticking butterflies, and had invited them to come to the Band of Mercy.

This child seemed to have done more than any one else for dumb animals. She had taken around a petition to the village boys, asking them not to search for birds' eggs, and she had even gone into her father's stable, and asked him to hold her up, so that she could look into the horses' mouths to see if their teeth wanted filing or were decayed. When her father laughed at her, she told him that horses often suffer terrible pain from their teeth, and that sometimes a runaway is caused by a metal bit striking against the exposed nerve in the tooth of a horse that has become almost frantic with pain.

She was a very gentle girl, and I think by the way that she spoke that her father loved her dearly, for she told how much trouble he had taken to make some tiny houses for her that she wanted for the wrens that came about their farm. She told him that those little birds are so good at catching insects that they ought to give all their time to it, and not have any worry about making houses. Her father made their homes very small, so that the English sparrows could not get in and crowd them out.

A boy said that he had gotten a pot of paint, and painted in large letters on the fences around his father's farm: "Spare the toads, don't kill the birds. Every bird killed is a loss to the country."

"That reminds me," said the president, "to ask the girls what they have done about the millinery business."

"I have told my mother," said a tall, serious-faced girl, "that I think it is wrong to wear bird feathers, and she has promised to give up wearing any of them except ostrich plumes."

Mrs. Wood asked permission to say a few words just here, and the president said: "Certainly, we are always glad to hear from you."

She went up on the platform, and faced the roomful of children. "Dear boys and girls," she began, "I have had some papers sent me from Boston, giving some facts about the killing of our birds, and I want to state a few of them to you: You all know that nearly every tree and plant that grows swarms with insect life, and that they couldn't grow if the birds didn't eat the insects that would devour their foliage. All day long, the little beaks of the birds are busy. The dear little rose-breasted gross-beak carefully examines the potato plants, and picks off the beetles, the martins destroy weevil, the quail and grouse family eats the chinchbug, the woodpeckers dig the worms from the trees, and many other birds eat the flies and gnats and mosquitoes that torment us so. No flying or crawling creature escapes their sharp little eyes. A great Frenchman says that if it weren't for the birds human beings would perish from the face of the earth. They are doing all this for us, and how are we rewarding them? All over America they are hunted and killed. Five million birds must be caught every year for American women to wear in their hats and bonnets. Just think of it, girls. Isn't it dreadful? Five million innocent, hard-working, beautiful birds killed, that thoughtless girls and women may ornament themselves with their little dead bodies. One million bobolinks have been killed in one month near Philadelphia. Seventy song-birds were sent from one Long Island village to New York milliners.

"In Florida cruel men shoot the mother birds on their nests while they are rearing their young, because their plumage is prettiest at that time. The little ones cry pitifully, and starve to death. Every bird of the rarer kinds that is killed, such as humming birds, orioles and kingfishers, means the death of several others— that is, the young that starve to death, the wounded that fly away to die, and those whose plumage is so torn that it is not fit to put in a fine lady's bonnet. In some cases where birds have gay wings, and the hunters do not wish the rest of the body, they tear off the wings from the living bird, and throw it away to die.

"I am sorry to tell you such painful things, but I think you ought to know them. You will soon be men and women. Do what you can to stop this horrid trade. Our beautiful birds are being taken from us, and the insect pests are increasing. The State of Massachusetts has lost over one hundred thousand dollars because it did not protect its birds. The gypsy moth stripped the trees near Boston, and the State had to pay out all this money, and even then could not get rid of the moths. The birds could have done it better than the State, but they were all gone. My last words to you are, 'Protect the birds.'"[1]

Mrs. Wood went to her seat, and though the boys and girls had listened very attentively, none of them cheered her. Their faces looked sad, and they kept very quiet for a few minutes. I saw one or two little girls wiping their eyes. I think they felt sorry for the birds.

"Has any boy done anything about blinders and check-reins?" asked the president, after a time.

A brown-faced boy stood up. "I had a picnic last Monday," he said; "father let me cut all the blinders off our head-stalls with my penknife."

"How did you get him to consent to that?" asked the president.

"I told him," said the boy, "that I couldn't get to sleep for thinking of him. You know he drives a good deal late at night. I told him that every dark night he came from Sudbury I thought of the deep ditch alongside the road, and wished his horses hadn't blinders on. And every night he comes from the Junction, and has to drive along the river bank where the water has washed away the earth till the wheels of the wagon are within a foot or two of the edge, I wished again that his horses could see each side of them, for I knew they'd have sense enough to keep out of danger if they could see it. Father said that might be very true, and yet his horses had been broken in with blinders, and didn't I think they would be inclined to shy if he took them off; and wouldn't they be frightened to look around and see the wagon wheels so near. I told him that for every accident that happened to a horse without blinders,

---

1   During the second half of the nineteenth century, wearing gaudy, exotic feathers on hats—even the stuffed bodies of whole birds—became the fashion for middle- and upper-class women, a craze for which millions of wild birds were killed. Then as now, the drive for maximum efficiency inspired not only mass killings but also the extinction of many species.

several happened to a horse with them; and then I gave him Mr. Wood's opinion—Mr. Wood out at Dingley Farm. He says that the worst thing against blinders is that a frightened horse never knows when he has passed the thing that scared him. He always thinks it is behind him. The blinders are there and he can't see that he has passed it, and he can't turn his head to have a good look at it. So often he goes tearing madly on; and sometimes lives are lost all on account of a little bit of leather fastened over a beautiful eye that ought to look out full and free at the world. That finished father. He said he'd take off his blinders, and if he had an accident, he'd send the bill for damages to Mr. Wood. But we've had no accident. The horses did act rather queerly at first, and started a little; but they soon got over it, and now they go as steady without blinders as they ever did with them."

The boy sat down, and the president said: "I think it is time that the whole nation threw off this foolishness of half covering their horses' eyes. Just put your hands up to your eyes, members of the band. Half cover them, and see how shut in you will feel; and how curious you will be to know what is going on beside you. Suppose a girl saw a mouse with her eyes half covered, wouldn't she run?"

Everybody laughed, and the president asked some one to tell him who invented blinders.

"An English nobleman," shouted a boy, "who had a wall-eyed horse! He wanted to cover up the defect, and I think it is a great shame that all the American horses have to suffer because that English one had an ugly eye."

"So do I," said the president. "Three groans for blinders, boys."

And the children in the room made three dreadful noises away down in their throats. Then they had another good laugh, and the president became sober again. "Seven more minutes," he said; "this meeting has got to be let out at five sharp."

A tall girl at the back of the room rose, and said: "My little cousin has two stories that she would like to tell the band."

"Very well," said the president, "bring her right along."

The big girl came forward, leading a tiny child that she placed in front of the boys and girls. The child stared up into her cousin's face, turning and twisting her white pinafore through her fingers. Every time the big girl took her pinafore away from her, she picked it up again. "Begin, Nannie," said the big girl, kindly.

"Well, Cousin Eleanor," said the child, "you know Topsy, Graham's pony. Well, Topsy *would* run away, and a big, big man came out to papa and said he would train Topsy. So he drove her every day, and beat her, and beat her, till he was tired, but still Topsy would run away. Then papa said he would not have the poor pony whipped so much, and he took her out a piece of bread every day, and he petted her, and now Topsy is very gentle, and never runs away."

"Tell about Tiger," said the girl.

"Well, Cousin Eleanor," said the child, "you know Tiger, our big dog. He used to be a bad dog, and when Dr. Fairchild drove up to the house he jumped up and bit at him. Dr. Fairchild used to speak kindly to him, and throw out bits of meat, and now when he comes, Tiger follows behind and wags his tail. Now, give me a kiss."

The girl had to give her a kiss, right up there before every one, and what a stamping the boys made. The larger girl blushed and hurried back to her seat, with the child clinging to her hand.

There was one more story, about a brave Newfoundland dog, that saved eight lives by swimming out to a wrecked sailing vessel, and getting a rope by which the men came ashore, and then a lad got up whom they all greeted with cheers, and cries of, "The Poet! the Poet!" I didn't know what they meant, till Mrs. Wood whispered to Miss Laura that he was a boy who made rhymes, and the children had rather hear him speak than any one else in the room.

He had a snub nose and freckles, and I think he was the plainest boy there, but that didn't matter, if the other children loved him. He sauntered up to the front, with his hands behind his back, and a very grand manner.

"The beautiful poetry recited here to-day," he drawled, "put some verses in my mind that I never had till I came here to-day." Every one present cheered wildly, and he began in a sing song voice:

"I am a Band of Mercy boy,
      I would not hurt a fly,
I always speak to dogs and cats,
      When'er I pass them by.

"I always let the birdies sing,
      I never throw a stone,
I always give a hungry dog
      A nice, fat, meaty bone.

"I wouldn't drive a bob-tailed horse,
    Nor hurry up a cow,
I—"

Then he forgot the rest. The boys and girls were so sorry. They called out, "Pig," "Goat," "Calf," "Sheep," "Hens," "Ducks," and all the other animals' names they could think of, but none of them was right, and as the boy had just made up the poetry, no one knew what the next could be. He stood for a long time staring at the ceiling, then he said, "I guess I'll have to give it up."

The children looked dreadfully disappointed. "Perhaps you will remember it by our next meeting," said the president, anxiously.

"Possibly," said the boy, "but probably not. I think it is gone forever." And he went to his seat.

The next thing was to call for new members. Miss Laura got up and said she would like to join their Band of Mercy. I followed her up to the platform, while they pinned a little badge on her, and every one laughed at me. Then they sang, "God Bless our Native Land," and the president told us that we might all go home.

It seemed to me a lovely thing for those children to meet together to talk about kindness to animals. They all had bright and good faces, and many of them stopped to pat me as I came out. One little girl gave me a biscuit from her school bag.

Mrs. Wood waited at the door till Mr. Maxwell came limping out on his crutches. She introduced him to Miss Laura, and asked him if he wouldn't go and take tea with them. He said he would be very happy to do so, and then Mrs. Wood laughed, and asked him if he hadn't better empty his pockets first. She didn't want a little toad jumping over her tea table, as one did the last time he was there.

CHAPTER 21

MR. MAXWELL AND MR. HARRY

MR. MAXWELL wore a coat with loose pockets, and while she was speaking, he rested on his crutches, and began to slap them with his hands. "No; there's nothing here to-day," he said, "I think I emptied my pockets before I went to the meeting."

Just as he said that there was a loud squeal: "Oh, my guinea pig," he exclaimed; "I forgot him," and he pulled out a little spotted creature a few inches long. "Poor Derry, did I hurt you?" and he soothed it very tenderly.

I stood and looked at Mr. Maxwell, for I had never seen any one like him. He had thick curly hair and a white face, and he looked just like a girl. While I was staring at him, something peeped up out of one of his pockets and ran out its tongue at me so fast that I could scarcely see it, and then drew back again. I was thunderstruck. I had never seen such a creature before. It was long and thin like a boy's cane, and of a bright green color like grass, and it had queer shiny eyes. But its tongue was the strangest part of it. It came and went like lightning. I was uneasy about it and began to bark.

"What's the matter, Joe?" said Mrs. Wood, "the pig won't hurt you."

But it wasn't the pig I was afraid of, and I kept on barking. And all the time that strange live thing kept sticking up its head and putting out its tongue at me, and neither of them noticed it.

"It's getting on toward six," said Mrs. Wood, "we must be going home. Come, Mr. Maxwell."

The young man put the guinea pig in his pocket, picked up his crutches, and we started down the sunny village street. He left his guinea pig at his boarding house as he went by, but he said nothing about the other creature, so I knew he did not know it was there.

I was very much taken with Mr. Maxwell. He seemed so bright and happy, in spite of his lameness, which kept him from running about like other young men. He looked a little older than Miss Laura, and one day, a week or two later, when they were sitting on the veranda, I heard him tell her that he was just nineteen. He told her too that his lameness made him love animals. They never laughed at him, or slighted him, or got impatient, because he could not walk quickly. They were always good to him, and he said he loved all animals while he liked very few people.[1]

On this day, as he was limping along, he said to Mrs. Wood: "I am getting more absent-minded every day. Have you heard of my latest escapade?"

"No," she said.

"I am glad," he replied. "I was afraid that it would be all over the village by this time. I went to church last Sunday with my poor guinea pig in my pocket. He hasn't been well, and I was attending to him before church, and put him in there to get warm, and forgot about him. Unfortunately I was late, and the back seats were all full, so I had to sit farther up than I usually do. During the first hymn I happened to strike Piggy against the side of the seat. Such an ear-splitting squeal as he set up. It sounded as if I was murdering him. The people stared and stared, and I had to leave the church, overwhelmed with confusion."

Mrs. Wood and Miss Laura laughed, and then they got talking about other matters that were not interesting to me, so I did not listen. But I kept close to Miss Laura, for I was afraid that green thing might hurt her. I wondered very much what its name was. I don't think I should have feared it so much if I had known what it was.

"There's something the matter with Joe," said Miss Laura, when we got into the lane. "What is it, dear old fellow?" She put down her little hand, and I licked it, and wished so much that I could speak.

Sometimes I wish very much that I had the gift of speech, and then at other times I see how little it would profit me, and how many foolish things I should often say. And I don't believe human beings would love animals as well, if they could speak.

When we reached the house, we got a joyful surprise. There was a trunk standing on the veranda, and as soon as Mrs. Wood saw it, she gave a little shriek: "My dear boy!"

Mr. Harry was there, sure enough, and stepped out through the open door. He took his mother in his arms and kissed her, then he shook hands with Miss Laura and Mr. Maxwell, who

---

1 Opponents of animal welfare reform commonly accused humanitarians of putting the needs of animals over those of humans. (See Appendix D1, p. 287.) As a foil to Harry's masculine approach to humaneness, Maxwell is an ambiguous figure. The charge of sentimentalism would easily attach to this gentle, disabled son of an artist.

seemed to be an old friend of his. They all sat down on the veranda and talked, and I lay at Miss Laura's feet and looked at Mr. Harry. He was such a handsome young man, and had such a noble face. He was older and graver looking than when I saw him last, and he had a light, brown mustache that he did not have when he was in Fairport.

He seemed very fond of his mother and of Miss Laura, and however grave his face might be when he was looking at Mr. Maxwell, it always lighted up when he turned to them. "What dog is that?" he said at last, with a puzzled face, and pointing to me.

"Why, Harry," exclaimed Miss Laura, "don't you know Beautiful Joe, that you rescued from that wretched milkman?"

"Is it possible," he said, "that this well-conditioned creature is the bundle of dirty skin and bones that we nursed in Fairport? Come here, sir. Do you remember me?"

Indeed I did remember him, and I licked his hands and looked up gratefully into his face. "You're almost handsome now," he said, caressing me with a firm, kind hand, "and of a solid build too. You look like a fighter—but I suppose you wouldn't let him fight, even if he wanted to, Laura," and he smiled and glanced at her.

"No," she said; "I don't think I should; but he can fight when the occasion requires it." And she told him about our night with Jenkins.

All the time she was speaking, Mr. Harry held me by the paws, and stroked my body over and over again. When she finished, he put his head down to me, and murmured, "Good dog," and I saw that his eyes were red and shining.

"That's a capital story, we must have it at the Band of Mercy," said Mr. Maxwell. Mrs. Wood had gone to help prepare the tea, so the two young men were alone with Miss Laura. When they had done talking about me, she asked Mr. Harry a number of questions about his college life, and his trip to New York, for he had not been studying all the time that he was away.

"What are you going to do with yourself, Gray, when your college course is ended?" asked Mr. Maxwell.

"I am going to settle right down here," said Mr. Harry.

"What, be a farmer?" asked his friend.

"Yes; why not?"

"Nothing, only I imagined that you would take a profession."

"The professions are overstocked, and we have not farmers enough for the good of the country.[1] There is nothing like farming, to my mind. In no other employment have you a surer living. I do not like the cities. The heat and dust, and crowds of people, and buildings overtopping one another, and the rush of living, take my breath away. Suppose I did go to a city. I would sell out my share of the farm, and have a few thousand dollars. You know I am not an intellectual giant. I would never distinguish myself in any profession. I would be a poor lawyer or doctor, living in a back street all the days of my life, and never watch a tree or flower grow, or tend an animal, or have a drive unless I paid for it. No, thank you. I agree with President Eliot, of Harvard.[2] He says, scarcely one person in ten thousand betters himself permanently by leaving his rural home and settling in a city. If one is a millionaire, city life is agreeable enough, for one can always get away from it; but I am beginning to think that it is a dangerous thing, in more ways than one, to be a millionaire. I believe the safety of the country lies in the hands of the farmers; for they are seldom very poor or very rich.

---

1 Harry passionately critiques a social reality that was becoming more pronounced in the early 1890s: the large migration of the population from farms to cities. At the country's birth, ninety-five per cent of the population lived in rural areas, with small cities at key seaports like New York and Boston (Bender 1101). Linked to the development of the railroad system and westward expansion, urbanization in the US happened rapidly in the decades after 1890 (excepting the South, which stubbornly maintained economic isolation until the Great Depression) (Lloyd 485-86, Bender 1101). City living, at this time, was unenviable—in 1894, three out of five city residents lived in slums ("Urbanization")—but it is unlikely that a more "attractive" farm could have halted the forces of change. By 1920, more of the US population lived in densely packed urban centers than in rural areas (Bender 1101).

2 Saunders refers to Charles William Eliot, Harvard University President from 1869 to 1909, best known today for his two key contributions to American educational reform: replacing set curriculums with an elective system and improving professional education (Hutcheson). According to the Faculty of Arts and Sciences, the new elective system would allow for greater academic freedom, bringing forth "a manly and liberal method of government, appealing to the conscience and reason of the student" ("Special Meeting" 242-43). Eliot did critique "the evils which attend the growth of modern cities and the factory system" (qtd. in Gottlieb 101), and his views were linked to the playground movement that Saunders also supported (Langille 1). For more on the playground movement, see Cavallo.

We stand between the two dangerous classes—the wealthy and the paupers."

"But most farmers lead such a dog's life," said Mr. Maxwell.

"So they do; farming isn't made one-half as attractive as it should be," said Mr. Harry.

Mr. Maxwell smiled. "Attractive farming. Just sketch an outline of that, will you, Gray?"

"In the first place," said Mr. Harry, "I would like to tear out of the heart of the farmer the thing that is as firmly implanted in him as it is in the heart of his city brother—the thing that is doing more to harm our nation than anything else under the sun."

"What is that?" asked Mr. Maxwell, curiously.

"The thirst for gold. The farmer wants to get rich, and he works so hard to do it that he wears himself out soul and body, and the young people around him get so disgusted with that way of getting rich, that they go off to the cities to find out some other way, or at least to enjoy themselves, for I don't think many young people are animated by a desire to heap up money."

Mr. Maxwell looked amused. "There is certainly a great exodus from country places cityward," he said. "What would be your plan for checking it?"

"I would make the farm so pleasant, that you couldn't hire the boys and girls to leave it. I would have them work, and work hard too, but when their work was over, I would let them have some fun. That is what they go to the city for. They want amusement and society, and to get into some kind of a crowd when their work is done. The young men and young women want to get together, as is only natural. Now that could be done in the country. If farmers would be contented with smaller profits and smaller farms, their houses could be nearer together. Their children would have opportunities of social intercourse, there could be societies and clubs, and that would tend to a distribution of literature. A farmer ought to take five or six papers and two or three magazines. He would find it would pay him in the long run, and there ought to be a law made, compelling him to go to the post office once a day."

Mr. Maxwell burst out laughing. "And another to make him mend his roads as well as mend his ways. I tell you Gray, the bad roads would put an end to all these fine schemes of yours. Imagine farmers calling on each other on a dark evening after a spring freshet. I can see them mired and bogged, and the house a mile ahead of them."

"That is true," said Mr. Harry, "the road question is a serious one. Do you know how father and I settle it?"

"No," said Mr. Maxwell.

"We got so tired of the whole business, and the farmers around here spent so much time in discussing the art of road-making, as to whether it should be viewed from the engineering point of view, or the farmers' practical point of view, and whether we would require this number of stump extractors or that number, and how many shovels and crushers and ditchers would be necessary to keep our roads in order, and so on, that we simply withdrew. We keep our own roads in order. Once a year, father gets a gang of men and tackles every section of the road that borders upon our land, and our roads are the best around here. I wish the government would take up this matter of making roads and settle it. If we had good, smooth, country roads, such as they have in some parts of Europe, we would be able to travel comfortably over them all through the year, and our draught animals would last longer, for they would not have to expend so much energy in drawing their loads."

CHAPTER 22

WHAT HAPPENED AT THE TEA TABLE

FROM my station under Miss Laura's chair, I could see that all the time Mr. Harry was speaking, Mr. Maxwell, although he spoke rather as if he was laughing at him, was yet glancing at him admiringly.

When Mr. Harry was silent, he exclaimed, "You are right, you are right, Gray. With your smooth highways, and plenty of schools, and churches, and libraries, and meetings for young people, you would make country life a paradise, and I tell you what you would do, too: you would empty the slums of the cities. It is the slowness and dullness of country life, and not their poverty alone, that keep the poor in dirty lanes and tenement houses. They want stir and amusement, too, poor souls, when their day's work is over. I believe they would come to the country if it were made more pleasant for them."

"That is another question," said Mr. Harry, "a burning question in my mind—the labor and capital one. When I was in New York, Maxwell, I was in a hospital, and saw a number of men who had been day laborers. Some of them were old and feeble, and others were young men, broken down in the prime of life. Their limbs were shrunken and drawn. They had been digging in the earth, and working on high buildings, and confined in dingy basements, and had done all kinds of hard labor for other men. They had given their lives and strength for others, and this was the end of it—to die poor and forsaken. I looked at them, and they reminded me of the martyrs of old. Ground down, living from hand to mouth, separated from their families in many cases—they had had a bitter lot. They had never had a chance to get away from their fate, and had to work till they dropped. I tell you there is something wrong. We don't do enough for the people that slave and toil for us. We should take better care of them, we should not herd them together like cattle, and when we get rich, we should carry them along with us, and give them a part of our gains, for without them we would be as poor as they are."

"Good, Harry—I'm with you there," said a voice behind him, and looking around, we saw Mr. Wood standing in the doorway, gazing down proudly at his step-son.

Mr. Harry smiled, and getting up, said, "Won't you have my chair, sir?"

"No, thank you, your mother wishes us to come to tea. There are muffins, and you know they won't improve with keeping."

They all went to the dining room, and I followed them. On the way, Mr. Wood said, "Right on top of that talk of yours, Harry, I've got to tell you of another person who is going to Boston to live."

"Who is it?" said Mr. Harry.

"Lazy Dan Wilson. I've been to see him this afternoon. You know his wife is sick, and they're half starved. He says he is going to the city, for he hates to chop wood and work, and he thinks maybe he'll get some light job there."

Mr. Harry looked grave, and Mr. Maxwell said, "He will starve, that's what he will do."

"Precisely," said Mr. Wood, spreading out his hard, brown hands, as he sat down at the table. "I don't know why it is, but the present generation has a marvelous way of skimming around any kind of work with their hands. They'll work their brains till they haven't got any more backbone than a caterpillar, but as for manual labor, it's old-timey and out of fashion. I wonder how these farms would ever have been carved out of the backwoods, if the old Puritans had sat down on the rocks with their noses in a lot of books, and tried to figure out just how little work they could do, and yet exist."

"Now, father," said Mrs. Wood, "you are trying to insinuate that the present generation is lazy, and I'm sure it isn't. Look at Harry. He works as hard as you do."

"Isn't that like a woman?" said Mr. Wood, with a good-natured laugh. "The present generation consists of her son, and the past of her husband. I don't think all our young people are lazy, Hattie; but how in creation, unless the Lord rains down a few farmers, are we going to support all our young lawyers and doctors? They say the world is getting healthier and better, but we've got to fight a little more, and raise some more criminals, and we've got to take to eating pies and doughnuts for breakfast again, or some of our young sprouts from the colleges will go a begging."

"You don't mean to undervalue the advantages of a good education, do you, Mr. Wood?" said Mr. Maxwell.

"No, no; look at Harry there. Isn't he pegging away at his studies with my hearty approval? and he's going to be nothing but a plain, common farmer. But he'll be a better one than I've been though, because he's got a trained mind. I found that out when he was a lad going to the village school. He'd lay out his little garden by geometry, and dig his ditches by algebra. Education's a help to any man. What I am trying to get at is this, that in some way or other we're running more to brains and less to hard work than our forefathers did."

Mr. Wood was beating on the table with his forefinger while he talked, and every one was laughing at him. "When you've quite finished speechifying, John," said Mrs. Wood, "perhaps you'll serve the berries and pass the cream and sugar. Do you get yellow cream like this in the village, Mr. Maxwell?"

"No, Mrs. Wood," he said; "ours is a much paler yellow," and then there was a great tinkling of china, and passing of dishes, and talking and laughing, and no one noticed that I was not in my usual place in the hall. I could not get over my dread of the green creature, and I had crept under the table, so that if it came out and frightened Miss Laura, I could jump up and catch it.

When tea was half over, she gave a little cry. I sprang up on her lap, and there, gliding over the table toward her, was the wicked-looking green thing. I stepped on the table, and had it by the middle before it could get to her. My hind legs were in a dish of jelly, and my front ones were in a plate of cake, and I was very uncomfortable. The tail of the green thing hung in a milk pitcher, and its tongue was still going at me, but I held it firmly and stood quite still.

"Drop it, drop it!" cried Miss Laura, in tones of distress, and Mr. Maxwell struck me on the back, so I let the thing go, and stood sheepishly looking about me. Mr. Wood was leaning back in his chair, laughing with all his might, and Mrs. Wood was staring at her untidy table with rather a long face. Miss Laura told me to jump on the floor, and then she helped her aunt to take the spoiled things off the table.

I felt that I had done wrong, so I slunk out into the hall. Mr. Maxwell was sitting on the lounge, tearing his handkerchief in strips and tying them around the creature where my teeth had stuck in. I had been careful not to hurt it much, for I knew it was a pet of his; but he did not know that, and scowled at me, saying: "You rascal, you've hurt my poor snake terribly."

I felt so badly to hear this that I went and stood with my head in a corner. I had almost rather be whipped than scolded. After a while, Mr. Maxwell went back into the room, and they all went on with their tea. I could hear Mr. Wood's loud, cheery voice, "The dog did quite right. A snake is mostly a poisonous creature, and his instinct told him to protect his mistress. Where is he? Joe, Joe!"

I would not move till Miss Laura came and spoke to me. "Dear old dog," she whispered, "you knew the snake was there all the time, didn't you?" Her words made me feel better, and I followed her to the dining room, where Mr. Wood made me sit beside him and eat scraps from his hand all through the meal.

Mr. Maxwell had got over his ill humor, and was chatting in a lively way. "Good Joe," he said, "I was cross to you, and I beg your pardon. It always riles me to have any of my pets injured. You didn't know my poor snake was only after something to eat. Mrs. Wood has pinned him in my pocket so he won't come out again. Do you know where I got that snake, Mrs. Wood?"

"No," she said; "you never told me."

"It was across the river by Blue Ridge," he said. "One day last summer I was out rowing, and, getting very hot, tied my boat in the shade of a big tree. Some village boys were in the woods, and, hearing a great noise, I went to see what it was all about. They were Band of Mercy boys, and finding a country boy beating a snake to death, they were remonstrating with him for his cruelty, telling him that some kinds of snakes were a help to the farmer, and destroyed large numbers of field mice and other vermin. The boy was obstinate. He had found the snake, and he insisted upon his right to kill it, and they were having rather a lively time when I appeared. I persuaded them to make the snake over to me. Apparently it was already dead. Thinking it might revive, I put it on some grass in the bow of the boat. It lay there motionless for a long time, and I picked up my oars and started for home. I had got half-way across the river, when I turned around and saw that the snake was gone. It had just dropped into the water, and was swimming toward the bank we had left. I turned and followed it.

"It swam slowly and with evident pain, lifting its head every few seconds high above the water, to see which way it was going. On reaching the bank it coiled itself up, throwing up blood and water. I took it up carefully, carried it home, and nursed it. It soon got better, and has been a pet of mine ever since."

After tea was over, and Mrs. Wood and Miss Laura had helped Adèle finish the work, they all gathered in the parlor. The day had been quite warm, but now a cool wind had sprung up, and Mr. Wood said that it was blowing up rain.

Mrs. Wood said that she thought a fire would be pleasant; so they lighted the sticks of wood in the open grate, and all sat round the blazing fire.

Mr. Maxwell tried to get me to make friends with the little snake that he held in his hands toward the blaze, and now that I knew that it was harmless I was not afraid of it; but it did not like me, and put out its funny little tongue whenever I looked at it.

By-and-by the rain began to strike against the windows, and Mr. Maxwell said, "This is just the night for a story. Tell us something out of your experience, won't you, Mr. Wood?"

"What shall I tell you?" he said, good-humoredly. He was sitting between his wife and Mr. Harry, and had his hand on Mr. Harry's knee.

"Something about animals," said Mr. Maxwell. "We seem to be on that subject to-day."

"Well," said Mr. Wood, "I'll talk about something that has been running in my head for many a day. There is a good deal of talk nowadays about kindness to domestic animals, but I do not hear much about kindness to wild ones. The same Creator formed them both. I do not see why you should not protect one as well as the other. I have no more right to torture a bear than a cow. Our wild animals around here are getting pretty well killed off, but there are lots in other places. I used to be fond of hunting when I was a boy, but I have got rather disgusted with killing these late years; and unless the wild creatures ran in our streets, I would lift no hand to them. Shall I tell you some of the sport we had when I was a youngster?"

"Yes, yes," they all exclaimed.

CHAPTER 23

TRAPPING WILD ANIMALS

"WELL," Mr. Wood began: "I was brought up, as you all know, in the eastern part of Maine, and we often used to go over into New Brunswick for our sport. Moose were our best game. Did you ever see one, Laura?"

"No, uncle," she said.

"Well, when I was a boy there was no more beautiful sight to me in the world than a moose with his dusky hide, and long legs, and branching antlers, and shoulders standing higher than a horse's. Their legs are so long that they can't eat close to the ground. They browse on the tops of plants, and the tender shoots and leaves of trees. They walk among the thick underbrush, carrying their horns adroitly to prevent their catching in the branches, and they step so well, and aim so true, that you'll scarcely hear a twig fall as they go.[1]

"They're a timid creature except at times. Then they'll attack with hoofs and antlers whatever comes in their way. They hate mosquitoes, and when they're tormented by them it's just as well to be careful about approaching them. Like all other creatures, the Lord has put into them a wonderful amount of sense, and when a female moose has her one or two fawns she goes into the deepest part of the forest, or swims to islands in large lakes, till they are able to look out for themselves.

"Well, we used to like to catch a moose, and we had different ways of doing it. One way was to snare them. We'd make a loop in a rope and hide it on the ground under the dead leaves in one of their paths. This was connected with a young sapling whose top was bent down. When the moose stepped on the loop it would release the sapling, and up it would bound, catching him by the leg. These snares were always set deep in the woods, and we couldn't visit them very often. Sometimes the moose would be there for days, raging and tearing around, and scratching the skin off his legs. That was cruel. I wouldn't catch a moose in that way now for a hundred dollars.

---

1   In a letter dated 19 September 1936, Saunders said that this chapter was "dictated" to her by her father: "We had Indians all about us and he had been much with them for hunting. They liked him because he did not swear, as some of the other white men did."

"Another way was to hunt them on snow-shoes with dogs. In February and March the snow was deep, and would carry men and dogs. Moose don't go together in herds. In the summer they wander about over the forest, and in the autumn they come together in small groups, and select a hundred or two of acres where there is plenty of heavy undergrowth, and to which they usually confine themselves. They do this so that their tracks won't tell their enemies where they are.

"Any of these places where there were several moose we called a moose yard. We went through the woods till we got on to the tracks of some of the animals belonging to it, then the dogs smelled them and went ahead to start them. If I shut my eyes now I can see one of our moose hunts. The moose running and plunging through the snow crust, and occasionally rising up and striking at the dogs that hang on to his bleeding flanks and legs. The hunters' rifles going crack, crack, crack, sometimes killing or wounding dogs as well as moose. That too was cruel.

"Two other ways we had of hunting moose: Calling and stalking. The calling was done in this way: We took a bit of birch bark and rolled it up in the shape of a horn. We took this horn and started out, either on a bright moonlight night, or just at evening, or early in the morning. The man who carried the horn hid himself, and then began to make a lowing sound like a female moose. He had to do it pretty well to deceive them. Away in the distance some moose would hear it, and with answering grunts would start off to come to it. If a young male moose was coming, he'd mind his steps, I can assure you, on account of fear of the old ones; but if it was an old fellow, you'd hear him stepping out bravely and rapping his horns against the trees, and plunging into any water that came in his way. When he got pretty near, he'd stop to listen, and then the caller had to be very careful and put his trumpet down close to the ground, so as to make a lower sound. If the moose felt doubtful he'd turn; if not, he'd come on, and unlucky for him if he did, for he got a warm reception, either from the rifles in our hands as we lay hid near the caller, or from some of the party stationed at a distance.

"In stalking, we crept on them the way a cat creeps on a mouse. In the daytime a moose is usually lying down. We'd find their tracks and places where they'd been nipping off the ends of branches and twigs, and follow them up. They easily take the scent of men, and we'd have to keep well to the leeward. Sometimes we'd come upon them lying down, but, if in walking along, we'd broken a twig, or made the slightest noise, they'd think it was one of their mortal enemies, a bear—creeping on them, and they'd be up and away. Their sense of hearing is very keen, but they're not so quick to see. A fox is like that, too. His eyes aren't equal to his nose.

"Stalking is the most merciful way to kill moose. Then they haven't the fright and suffering of the chase."

"I don't see why they need to be killed at all," said Mrs. Wood. "If I knew that forest back of the mountains was full of wild creatures, I think I'd be glad of it, and not want to hunt them, that is, if they were harmless and beautiful creatures like the deer."

"You're a woman," said Mr. Wood, "and women are more merciful than men. Men want to kill and slay.[1] They're like the Englishman, who said 'What a fine day it is; let's go out and kill something.'"

"Please tell us some more about the dogs that helped you catch the moose, uncle," said Miss Laura. I was sitting up very straight beside her, listening to every word Mr. Wood said, and she was fondling my head.

"Well, Laura, when we camped out on the snow and slept on spruce boughs while we were after the moose, the dogs used to be a great comfort to us. They slept at our feet and kept us warm. Poor brutes, they mostly had a rough time of it. They enjoyed the running and chasing as much as we did, but when it came to broken ribs and sore heads, it was another matter. Then the porcupines bothered them. Our dogs would never learn to let them alone. If they were going through the woods where there were no signs of moose and found a porcupine, they'd kill it. The quills would get in their mouths and necks and chests, and we'd have to gag them and take bullet molds or nippers, or whatever we had, sometimes our jack-knives, and pull out the nasty things. If we got hold of the dogs at once, we could pull out the quills with our fingers. Sometimes the quills worked in, and the dogs would go home and lie by the fire with running sores till they worked out. I've seen quills work right through dogs. Go in on one side and come out on the other."

"Poor brutes," said Mrs. Wood. "I wonder you took them."

---

1 This chapter's inclusion likely stemmed from Saunders's desire to make the story appealing to young boys. It might appear out of character for this humane family to enjoy Uncle Wood's reminiscences of "cruel" practices as part of an evening's story hour, but the depiction of cruelty was thought essential to the emotional education of young readers. (See Appendix D1f, p. 291.)

"We once lost a valuable hound while moose hunting," said Mr. Wood. "The moose struck him with his hoof and the dog was terribly injured, and he lay in the woods for days, till a neighbor of ours, who was looking for timber, found him and brought him home on his shoulders. Wasn't there rejoicing among us boys to see old Lion coming back. We took care of him and he got well again.

"It was good sport to see the dogs when we were hunting a bear with them. Bears are good runners, and when dogs get after them, there is great skirmishing. They nip the bear behind, and when they turn, the dogs run like mad, for a hug from a bear means sure death to a dog. If they got a slap from his paws, over they'd go. Dogs new to the business were often killed by the bears."

"Were there many bears near your home, Mr. Wood?" asked Mr. Maxwell.

"Lots of them. More than we wanted. They used to bother us fearfully about our sheep and cattle. I've often had to get up in the night, and run out to the cattle. The bears would come out of the woods, and jump on to the young heifers and cows, and strike them and beat them down, and the cattle would roar as if the evil one had them. If the cattle were too far away from the house for us to hear them, the bears would worry them till they were dead.

"As for the sheep, they never made any resistance. They'd meekly run in a corner when they saw a bear coming, and huddle together, and he'd strike at them, and scratch them with his claws, and perhaps wound a dozen before he got one firmly. Then he'd seize it in his paws, and walk off on his hind legs over fences and anything else that came in his way, till he came to a nice, retired spot, and there he'd sit down and skin that sheep just like a butcher. He'd gorge himself with the meat, and in the morning we'd find the other sheep that he'd torn, and we'd vow vengeance against that bear. He'd be almost sure to come back for more, so for a while after that we always put the sheep in the barn at nights and set a trap by the remains of the one he had eaten.

"Everybody hated bears, and hadn't much pity for them; still they were only getting their meat as other wild animals do, and we'd no right to set such cruel traps for them as the steel ones. They had a clog attached to them, and had long, sharp teeth. We put them on the ground and strewed leaves over them, and hung up some of the carcass left by the bear near by. When he attempted to get this meat, he would tread on the trap, and the teeth would spring together, and catch him by the leg. They always fought to get free. I once saw a bear that had been making a desperate effort to get away. His leg was broken, the skin and flesh were all torn away, and he was held by the tendons. It was a foreleg that was caught, and he would put his hind feet against the jaws of the trap, and then draw by pressing with his feet, till he would stretch those tendons to their utmost extent.

"I have known them to work away till they really pulled these tendons out of the foot, and got off. It was a great event in our neighborhood when a bear was caught. Whoever caught him blew a horn, and the men and boys came trooping together to see the sight. I've known them to blow that horn on a Sunday morning, and I've seen the men turn their backs on the meeting house to go and see the bear."

"Was there no more merciful way of catching them than by this trap?" asked Miss Laura.

"Oh, yes, by the deadfall[1]—that is by driving heavy sticks into the ground, and making a boxlike place, open on one side, where two logs were so arranged with other heavy logs upon them, that when the bear seized the bait, the upper log fell down and crushed him to death. Another way was to fix a bait in a certain place, with cords tied to it, which cords were fastened to triggers of guns placed at a little distance. When the bear took the bait, the guns went off, and he shot himself.

"Sometimes it took a good many bullets to kill them. I remember one old fellow that we put eleven into, before he keeled over. It was one fall, over on Pike's Hill. The snow had come earlier than usual, and this old bear hadn't got into his den for his winter's sleep. A lot of us started out after him. The hill was covered with beech trees, and he'd been living all the fall on the nuts, till he'd got as fat as butter. We took dogs and worried him, and ran him from one place to another, and shot at him, till at last he dropped. We took his meat home, and had his skin tanned for a sleigh robe.[2]

---

1   Deadfalls involve propping up something heavy, perhaps a large log or rock, with some precariously balanced sticks. The bait would be placed near these sticks, tempting animals to trigger the fall of the heavy object and thus, from Uncle Wood's point of view, "kill themselves."

2   Steel leghold traps came into use in 1823, accelerating the extermination of millions of animals for their fur. When national sources were nearly exhausted, Americans turned abroad. Although humanitarians attempted to organize a boycott, fur was used so extensively that the idea never took off the ground (Beers 82).

"One day I was in the woods, and looking through the trees espied a bear. He was standing up on his hind legs, snuffing in every direction, and just about the time I espied him, he espied me. I had no dog and no gun, so I thought I had better be getting home to my dinner. I was a small boy then, and the bear, probably thinking I'd be a mouthful for him anyway, began to come after me in a leisurely way. I can see myself now going through those woods—hat gone, jacket flying, arms out, eyes rolling over my shoulder every little while to see if the bear was gaining on me. He was a benevolent-looking old fellow, and his face seemed to say, 'Don't hurry, little boy.' He wasn't doing his prettiest, and I soon got away from him, but I made up my mind then, that it was more fun to be the chaser than the chased.

"Another time I was out in our cornfield, and hearing a rustling, looked through the stalks, and saw a brown bear with two cubs. She was slashing down the corn with her paws to get at the ears. She smelled me, and getting frightened, began to run. I had a dog with me this time, and shouted and rapped on the fence, and set him on her. He jumped up and snapped at her flanks, and every few instants she'd turn and give him a cuff, that would send him yards away. I followed her up, and just back of the farm she and her cubs took into a tree. I sent my dog home, and my father and some of the neighbors came. It had gotten dark by this time, so we built a fire under the tree, and watched all night, and told stories to keep each other awake. Toward morning we got sleepy, and the fire burnt low, and didn't that old bear and one cub drop right down among us and start off to the woods. That waked us up. We built up the fire and kept watch, so that the one cub, still in the tree, couldn't get away. Until daylight the mother bear hung around, calling to the cub to come down."

"Did you let it go, uncle?" asked Miss Laura.

"No, my dear, we shot it."

"How cruel!" cried Mrs. Wood.

"Yes, weren't we brutes?" said her husband; "but there was some excuse for us, Hattie. The bears ruined our farms. This kind of hunting that hunts and kills for the mere sake of slaughter is very different from that. I'll tell you what I've no patience with, and that's with these English folks that dress themselves up, and take fine horses and packs of dogs, and tear over the country after one little fox or rabbit. Bah, it's contemptible. Now if they were hunting cruel, man-eating tigers[1] or animals that destroy property, it would be different thing."

---

1 The "man-eating" tiger of India was singled out as a cunning, reprehensible enemy that had to be put in its place. There was also a sense of masculine battle and conquest, of risking one's life in pursuit of the tiger's hide. During this period, Theodore Roosevelt, soon to be President, promoted his new identity as a manly huntsman as a model for all men. Hunting was a key feature of his larger project of imperial expansion and the advancement of white civilization; supposedly, it allowed for a "temporary reversion to the primitive" that would equip white middle-class men with the virility necessary for the hardening of the race (Bederman 182).

CHAPTER 24

THE RABBIT AND THE HEN

"YOU had foxes up in Maine, I suppose, Mr. Wood, hadn't you?" asked Mr. Maxwell.

"Heaps of them. I always want to laugh when I think of our foxes, for they were so cute. Never a fox did I catch in a trap, though I'd set many a one. I'd take the carcass of some creature that had died, a sheep, for instance, and put it in a field near the woods, and the foxes would come and eat it. After they got accustomed to come and eat and no harm befell them, they would be unsuspecting. So just before a snowstorm, I'd take a trap and put it this spot. I'd handle it with gloves, and I'd smoke it, and rub fir boughs on it to take away the human smell, and then the snow would come and cover it up, and yet those foxes would know it was a trap and walk all around it. It's a wonderful thing, that sense of smell in animals, if it is a sense of smell. Joe here has got a good bit of it."

"What kind of traps were they, father?" asked Mr. Harry.

"Cruel ones—steel ones. They'd catch an animal by the leg and sometimes break the bone. The leg would bleed, and below the jaws of the trap it would freeze, there being no circulation of the blood. Those steel traps are an abomination. The people around here use one made on the same principle for catching rats. I wouldn't have them on my place for any money. I believe we've got to give an account for all the unnecessary suffering we put on animals."

"You'll have some to answer for, John, according to your own story," said Mrs. Wood.

"I have suffered already," he said. "Many a night I've lain on my bed and groaned, when I thought of needless cruelties I'd put upon animals when I was a young, unthinking boy—and I was pretty carefully brought up too, according to our light in those days. I often think that if I was cruel, with all the instruction I had to be merciful, what can be expected of the children that get no good teaching at all when they're young."

"Tell us some more about the foxes, Mr. Wood," said Mr. Maxwell.

"Well, we used to have rare sport hunting them with foxhounds. I'd often go off for the day with my hounds. Sometimes in the early morning they'd find a track in the snow. The leader for scent would go back and forth, to find out which way the fox was going. I can see him now. All the time that he ran, now one way and now another on the track of the fox, he was silent, but kept his tail aloft, wagging it as a signal to the hounds behind. He was leader in scent, but he did not like bloody, dangerous fights. By-and-by, he would decide which way the fox had gone. Then his tail still kept high in the air would wag more violently. The rest followed him in single file, going pretty slow, so as to enable us to keep up to them. By-and-by, they would come to a place where the fox was sleeping for the day. As soon as he was disturbed he would leave his bed under some thick fir or spruce branches near the ground. This flung his fresh scent into the air. As soon as the hounds sniffed it, they gave tongue in good earnest. It was a mixed, deep baying, that made the blood quicken in my veins. While in the excitement of first fright, the fox would run fast for a mile or two, till he found it an easy matter to keep out of the way of the hounds. Then he, cunning creature, would begin to bother them. He would mount to the top pole of the worm fence dividing the fields from the woods. He could trot along here quite a distance and then make a long jump into the woods. The hounds would come up, but could not walk the fence, and they would have difficulty in finding where the fox had left it. Then we saw generalship. The hounds scattered in all directions, and made long detours into the woods and fields. As soon as the track was lost, they ceased to bay, but the instant a hound found it again, he bayed to give the signal to the others. All would hurry to the spot, and off they would go baying as they went.

"Then Mr. Fox would try a new trick. He would climb a leaning tree, and then jump to the ground. This trick would soon be found out. Then he'd try another. He would make a circle of a quarter of a mile in circumference. By making a loop in his course, he would come in behind the hounds, and puzzle them between the scent of his first and following tracks. If the snow was deep, the hounds had made a good track for him. Over this he could run easily, and they would have to feel their way along, for after he had gone around the circle a few times, he would jump from the beaten path as far as he could, and make off to other cover in a straight line. Before this was done it was my plan to get near the circle, taking care to approach it on the leeward side. If the fox got a sniff of human scent, he would leave his circle very quickly, and make tracks fast to be out of danger. By the baying of the hounds, the circle in which the race was kept up could be easily known. The last runs to get near enough to shoot had to be done when the hounds' baying came from the side of the circle nearest to me. For then the fox would be on the opposite side farthest away. As soon as I got near enough to see the hounds when they passed, I stopped. When they got on the opposite side, I then kept a bright lookout for the fox. Sometimes when the brush was thick, the sight of him would be indistinct. The shooting had to be quick. As soon as the report of the gun was heard, the hounds ceased to bay, and made for the spot. If the fox was dead, they enjoyed the scent of his blood. If only wounded, they went after him with all speed. Sometimes he was overtaken and killed, and sometimes he got into his burrow in the earth, or in a hollow log, or among the rocks.

"One day, I remember, when I was standing on the outside of the circle, the fox came in sight. I fired. He gave a shrill bark, and came toward me. Then he stopped in the snow and fell dead in his tracks. I was a pretty good shot in those days."

"Poor little fox," said Miss Laura. "I wish you had let him get away."

"Here's one that nearly got away," said Mr. Wood. "One winter's day, I was chasing him with the hounds. There was a crust on the snow, and the fox was light, while the dogs were heavy. They ran along, the fox trotting nimbly on the top of the crust and the dogs breaking through, and every few minutes that fox would stop and sit down to look at the dogs. They were in a fury, and the wickedness of the fox in teasing them, made me laugh so much that I was very unwilling to shoot him."

"You said your steel traps were cruel things, uncle," said Miss Laura. "Why didn't you have a deadfall for the foxes as you had for the bears?"

"They were too cunning to go into deadfalls. There was a better way to catch them, though. Foxes hate water, and never go into it unless they are obliged to, so we used to find a place where a tree had fallen across a river, and made a bridge for them to go back and forth on. Here we set snares, with spring poles that would throw them into the river when they made struggles to get free, and drown them. Did you ever hear of the fox, Laura, that wanted to cross a river, and lay down on the bank pretending that he was dead, and a countryman came along, and, thinking he had a prize, threw him in his boat and rowed across, when the fox got up and ran away?"

"Now, uncle," said Miss Laura, "you're laughing at me. That couldn't be true."

"No, no," said Mr. Wood, chuckling, "but they're mighty cute at pretending they're dead. I once shot one in the morning, carried him a long way on my shoulders, and started to skin him in the afternoon, when he turned around and bit me enough to draw blood. At another time, I dug one out of a hole in the ground. He feigned death. I took him up, and threw him down at some distance, and he jumped up and ran into the woods."

"What other animals did you catch when you were a boy?" asked Mr. Maxwell.

"Oh, a number. Otters and beavers—we caught them in deadfalls and in steel traps. The mink we usually took in deadfalls, smaller, of course, than the ones we used for the bears. The musk-rat we caught in box traps like a mouse trap. The wild-cat we ran down like the *loup cervier*—"

"What kind of an animal is that?" asked Mr. Maxwell.

"It is a lynx, belonging to the cat species. They used to prowl about the country killing hens, geese, and sometimes sheep. They'd fix their tushes in the sheep's neck and suck the blood. They did not think much of the sheep's flesh. We ran them down with dogs. They'd often run up trees, and we'd shoot them. Then there were rabbits that we caught, mostly in snares. For musk-rats, we'd put a parsnip or an apple on the spindle of a box trap. When we snared a rabbit, I always wanted to find it caught around the neck and strangled to death. If they got half through the snare and were caught around the body, or by the hind legs, they'd live for some time, and they'd cry just like a child. I like shooting them better, just because I hated to hear their pitiful cries. It's a bad business this of killing dumb creatures, and the older I get, the more chicken-hearted I am about it."

"Chicken-hearted—I should think you are," said Mrs. Wood. "Do you know, Laura, he won't even kill a fowl for dinner. He gives it to one of the men to do."

"'Blessed are the merciful,'" said Miss Laura, throwing her arm over her uncle's shoulder. "I love you, dear Uncle John, because you are so kind to every living thing."

"I'm going to be kind to you now," said her uncle, "and send you to bed. You look tired."

"Very well," she said, with a smile. Then bidding them all good-night, she went upstairs. Mr. Wood turned to Mr. Maxwell. "You're going to stay all night with us, aren't you?"

"So Mrs. Wood says," replied the young man, with a smile.

"Of course," she said. "I couldn't think of letting you go back to the village on such a night as this. It's raining cats and dogs—but I mustn't say that, or there'll be no getting you to stay. I'll go and prepare your old room next to Harry's." And she bustled away.

The two young men went to the pantry for doughnuts and milk, and Mr. Wood stood gazing down at me. "Good dog," he said; "you look as if you sensed that talk to-night. Come, get a bone, and then away to bed."

He gave me a very large mutton bone, and I held it in my mouth, and watched him opening the woodshed door. I love human beings; and the saddest time of day for me is when I have to be separated from them while they sleep.

"Now, go to bed and rest well, Beautiful Joe," said Mr. Wood, "and if you hear any stranger round the house, run out and bark. Don't be chasing wild animals in your sleep, though. They say a dog is the only animal that dreams. I wonder whether it's true?" Then he went into the house and shut the door.

I had a sheepskin to lie on, and a very good bed it made. I slept soundly for a long time; then I waked up and found that, instead of rain pattering against the roof, and darkness everywhere, it was quite light. The rain was over, and the moon was shining beautifully. I ran to the door and looked out. It was almost as light as day. The moon made it very bright all around the house and farm buildings, and I could look all about and see that there was no one stirring. I took a turn around the yard, and walked around to the side of the house, to glance up at Miss Laura's window. I always did this several times through the night, just to see if she was quite safe. I was on my way back to my bed, when I saw two small, white things moving away down the lane. I stood on the veranda and watched them. When they got nearer, I saw that there was a white rabbit hopping up the road, followed by a white hen.

It seemed to me a very strange thing for these creatures to be out this time of night, and why were they coming to Dingley Farm? This wasn't their home. I ran down on the road and stood in front of them.

Just as soon as the hen saw me, she fluttered in front of the rabbit, and, spreading out her wings, clucked angrily, and acted as if she would peck my eyes out if I came nearer.

I saw that they were harmless creatures, and, remembering my adventure with the snake, I stepped aside. Besides that, I knew by their smell that they had been near Mr. Maxwell, so perhaps they were after him.

They understood quite well that I would not hurt them, and passed by me. The rabbit went ahead again and the hen fell behind. It seemed to me that the hen was sleepy, and didn't like to be out so late at night, and was only following the rabbit because she thought it was her duty.

He was going along in a very queer fashion, putting his nose to the ground, and rising up on his hind legs, and sniffing the air, first on this side and then on the other, and his nose going, going all the time.

He smelled all around the house till he came to Mr. Maxwell's room at the back. It opened on the veranda by a glass door, and the door stood ajar. The rabbit squeezed himself in, and the hen stayed out. She watched for a while, and when he didn't come back, she flew upon the back of a chair that stood near the door, and put her head under her wing.

I went back to my bed, for I knew they would do no harm. Early in the morning, when I was walking around the house, I heard a great shouting and laughing from Mr. Maxwell's room. He and Mr. Harry had just discovered the hen and the rabbit; and Mr. Harry was calling his mother to come and look at them. The rabbit had slept on the foot of the bed.

Mr. Harry was chaffing Mr. Maxwell very much, and was telling him that any one who entertained him was in for a traveling menagerie. They had a great deal of fun over it, and Mr. Maxwell said that he had had that pretty, white hen as a pet for a long time in Boston. Once when she had some little chickens, a frightened rabbit, that was being chased by a dog, ran into the yard. In his terror he got right under the hen's wings, and she sheltered him, and pecked at the dog's eyes, and kept him off till help came. The rabbit belonged to a neighbor's boy, and Mr. Maxwell bought it from him. From the day the hen protected him, she became his friend, and followed him everywhere.

I did not wonder that the rabbit wanted to see his master. There was something about that young man that made dumb animals just delight in him. When Mrs. Wood mentioned this to him he said, "I don't know why they should—I don't do anything to fascinate them."

"You love them," she said, "and they know it. That is the reason."

CHAPTER 25

A HAPPY HORSE

FOR a good while after I went to Dingley Farm I was very shy of the horses, for I was afraid they might kick me, thinking that I was a bad dog like Bruno. However, they all had such good faces, and looked at me so kindly, that I was beginning to get over my fear of them.

Fleetfoot, Mr. Harry's colt, was my favorite, and one afternoon, when Mr. Harry and Miss Laura were going out to see him, I followed them. Fleetfoot was amusing himself by rolling over and over on the grass under a tree, but when he saw Mr. Harry, he gave a shrill whinny, and running to him, began nosing about his pockets.

"Wait a bit," said Mr. Harry, holding him by the forelock. "Let me introduce you to this young lady, Miss Laura Morris. I want you to make her a bow." He gave the colt some sign, and immediately he began to paw the ground and shake his head.

Mr. Harry laughed and went on: "Here is her dog Joe. I want you to like him, too. Come here, Joe." I was not at all afraid, for I knew Mr. Harry would not let him hurt me, so I stood in front of him, and for the first time had a good look at him. They called him the colt, but he was really a full-grown horse, and had already been put to work. He was of a dark chestnut color, and had a well-shaped body and a long, handsome head, and I never saw, in the head of a man or beast, a more beautiful pair of eyes than that colt had—large, full, brown eyes they were that he turned on me almost as a person would. He looked me all over as if to say: "Are you a good dog, and will you treat me kindly, or are you a bad one like Bruno, and will you chase me and snap at my heels and worry me, so that I shall want to kick you?"

I looked at him very earnestly and wagged my body, and lifted myself on my hind legs toward him. He seemed pleased and put down his nose to sniff at me, and then we were friends. Friends, and such good friends, for next to Jim and Billy, I have loved Fleetfoot.

Mr. Harry pulled some lumps of sugar out of his pocket, and giving them to Miss Laura, told her to put them on the palm of her hand and hold it out flat toward Fleetfoot. The colt ate the sugar, and all the time eyed her with his quiet, observing glance, that made her exclaim: "What a wise-looking colt!"

"He is like an old horse," said Mr. Harry, "When he hears a sudden noise, he stops and looks all about him to find an explanation."

"He has been well trained," said Miss Laura.

"I have brought him up carefully," said Mr. Harry. "Really, he has been treated more like a dog than a colt. He follows me about the farm and smells everything I handle, and seems to want to know the reason of things."

"Your mother says," replied Miss Laura, "that she found you both asleep on the lawn one day last summer, and the colt's head was on your arm."

Mr. Harry smiled and threw his arm over the colt's neck. "We've been comrades, haven't we, Fleetfoot? I've been almost ashamed of his devotion. He has followed me to the village, and he always wants to go fishing with me. He's four years old now, so he ought to get over those coltish ways. I've driven him a good deal. We're going out in the buggy this afternoon, will you come?"

"Where are you going?" asked Miss Laura.

"Just for a short drive back of the river, to collect some money for father. I'll be home long before tea time."

"Yes, I should like to go," said Miss Laura "I shall go to the house and get my other hat."

"Come on, Fleetfoot," said Mr. Harry. And he led the way from the pasture, the colt following behind with me. I waited about the veranda, and in a short time Mr. Harry drove up to the front door. The buggy was black and shining, and Fleetfoot had on a silver-mounted harness that made him look very fine. He stood gently switching his long tail to keep the flies away, and with his head turned to see who was going to get into the buggy. I stood by him, and as soon as he saw that Miss Laura and Mr. Harry had seated themselves, he acted as if he wanted to be off. Mr. Harry spoke to him and away he went, I racing down the lane by his side, so happy to think he was my friend. He liked having me beside him, and every few seconds put down his head toward me. Animals can tell each other things without saying a word. When Fleetfoot gave his head a little toss in a certain way, I knew that he wanted to have a race. He had a beautiful even gait, and went very swiftly. Mr. Harry kept speaking to him to check him.

"You don't like him to go too fast, do you?" said Miss Laura.

"No," he returned. "I think we could make a racer of him if we liked, but father and I don't go in for fast horses. There is too much said about fast trotters and race horses. On some of the farms around here, the people have gone mad on breeding fast horses. An old farmer out in the country had a common cart-horse that he suddenly found out had great powers of speed and endurance. He sold him to a speculator for a big price, and it has set everybody wild. If the people who give all their time to it can't raise fast horses I don't see how the farmers can. A fast horse on a farm is ruination to the boys, for it starts them racing and betting. Father says he is going to offer a prize for the fastest walker that can be bred in New Hampshire. That Dutchman of ours, heavy as he is, is a fair walker, and Cleve and Pacer can each walk four and a half miles an hour."

"Why do you lay such stress on their walking fast?" asked Miss Laura.

"Because so much of the farm work must be done at a walk. Ploughing, teaming, and drawing produce to market, and going up and down hills. Even for the cities it is good to have fast walkers. Trotting on city pavements is very hard on the dray horses. If they are allowed to go at a quick walk, their legs will keep strong much longer. It is shameful the way horses are used up in big cities. Our pavements are so bad that cab horses are used up in three years. In many ways we are a great deal better off in this new country than the people in Europe; but we are not in respect of cab horses, for in London and Paris they last for five years. I have seen horses drop down dead in New York just from hard usage. Poor brutes, there is a better time coming for them though. When electricity is more fully developed, we'll see some wonderful changes. As it is, last year in different places, about thirty thousand horses were released from those abominable horse cars, by having electricity introduced on the roads. Well, Fleetfoot, do you want another spin? All right, my boy, go ahead."

Away we went again along a bit of level road. Fleetfoot had no check-rein on his beautiful neck, and when he trotted, he could hold his head in an easy, natural position. With his wonderful eyes and flowing mane and tail, and his glossy, reddish-brown body, I thought that he was the handsomest horse I had ever seen. He loved to go fast, and when Mr. Harry spoke to him to slow up again, he tossed his head with impatience. But he was too sweet-tempered to disobey. In all the years that I have known Fleetfoot, I have never once seen him refuse to do as his master told him.

"You have forgotten your whip, haven't you Harry?" I heard Miss Laura say, as we jogged slowly along, and I ran by the buggy panting and with my tongue hanging out.

"I never use one," said Mr. Harry; "if I saw any man lay one on Fleetfoot, I'd knock him down." His voice was so severe that

I glanced up into the buggy. He looked just as he did the day that he stretched Jenkins on the ground, and gave him a beating.

"I am so glad you don't," said Miss Laura. "You are like the Russians. Many of them control their horses by their voices, and call them such pretty names. But you have to use a whip for some horses, don't you, Cousin Harry?"

"Yes, Laura. There are many vicious horses that can't be controlled otherwise, and then with many horses one requires a whip in case of necessity for urging them forward."

"I suppose Fleetfoot never balks," said Miss Laura.

"No," replied Mr. Harry; "Dutchman sometimes does, and we have two cures for him, both equally good. We take up a forefoot and strike his shoe two or three times with a stone. The operation always interests him greatly, and he usually starts. If he doesn't go for that, we pass a line round his forelegs, at the knee joint, then go in front of him and draw on the line. Father won't let the men use a whip, unless they are driven to it."

"Fleetfoot has had a happy life, hasn't he?" said Miss Laura, looking admiringly at him. "How did he get to like you so much, Harry?"

"I broke him in after a fashion of my own. Father gave him to me, and the first time I saw him on his feet, I went up carefully and put my hand on him. His mother was rather shy of me, for we hadn't had her long, and it made him shy too, so I soon left him. The next time I stroked him; the next time I put my arm around him. Soon he acted like a big dog. I could lead him about by a strap, and I made a little halter and a bridle for him. I didn't see why I shouldn't train him a little while he was young and manageable. I think it is cruel to let colts run till one has to employ severity in mastering them. Of course, I did not let him do much work. Colts are like boys—a boy shouldn't do a man's work, but he had exercise every day, and I trained him to draw a light cart behind him. I used to do all kinds of things to accustom him to unusual sounds. Father talked a good deal to me about Rarey, the great horse tamer, and it put ideas into my head. He said he once saw Rarey come on a stage in Boston with a timid horse that he was going to accustom to a loud noise. First a bugle was blown, then some louder instrument, and so on, till there was a whole brass band going. Rarey reassured the animal, and it was not afraid."

"You like horses better than any other animals, don't you, Harry?" asked Miss Laura.

"I believe I do, though I am very fond of that dog of yours. I think I know more about horses than dogs. Have you noticed

Scamp very much?"

"Oh, yes; I often watched her. She is such an amusing little creature."

"She's the most interesting one we've got, that is, after Fleet-foot. Father got her from a man who couldn't manage her, and she came to us with a legion of bad tricks. Father has taken solid comfort though, in breaking her of them. She is his pet among our stock. I suppose you know that horses, more than any other animals, are creatures of habit. If they do a thing once, they will do it again. When she came to us, she had a trick of biting at a person who gave her oats. She would do it without fail, so father put a little stick under his arm, and every time she would bite, he would give her a rap over the nose. She soon got tired of biting, and gave it up. Sometimes now, you'll see her make a snap at father as if she was going to bite, and then look under his arm to see if the stick is there. He cured some of her tricks in one way, and some in another. One bad one she had, was to start for the stable the minute one of the traces was unfastened when we were unharnessing. She pulled father over once, and another time she ran the shaft of the sulky clean through the barn door. The next time father brought her in, he got ready for her. He twisted the lines around his hands, and the minute she began to bolt, he gave a tremendous jerk, that pulled her back upon her haunches, and shouted, 'Whoa.' It cured her, and she never started again, till he gave her the word. Often now, you'll see her throw her head back when she is being unhitched. He only did it once, yet she remembers. If we'd had the training of Scamp, she'd be a very different animal. It's nearly all in the bringing up of a colt, whether it will turn out vicious or gentle. If any one were to strike Fleetfoot, he would not know what it meant. He has been brought up differently from Scamp.

"She was probably trained by some brutal man who inspired her with distrust of the human species. She never bites an animal, and seems attached to all the other horses. She loves Fleetfoot and Cleve and Pacer. Those three are her favorites."

"I love to go for drives with Cleve and Pacer," said Miss Laura, "they are so steady and good. Uncle says they are the most trusty horses he has. He has told me about the man you had, who said that those two horses knew more than most 'humans.'"

"That was old Davids," said Mr. Harry; "when we had him, he was courting a widow who lived over in Hoytville. About once a fortnight, he'd ask father for one of the horses to go over to see her. He always stayed pretty late, and on the way home he'd tie the reins to the whip-stock and go to sleep, and never wake up till Cleve or Pacer, whichever one he happened to have, would draw up in the barnyard. They would pass any rigs they happened to meet, and turn out a little for a man. If Davids wasn't asleep, he could always tell by the difference in their gait which they were passing. They'd go quickly past a man, and much slower, with more of a turn out, if it was a team. But I dare say father told you this. He has a great stock of horse stories, and I am almost as bad. You will have to cry 'halt,' when we bore you."

"You never do," replied Miss Laura. "I love to talk about animals. I think the best story about Cleve and Pacer is the one that uncle told me last evening. I don't think you were there. It was about stealing the oats."

"Cleve and Pacer never steal," said Mr. Harry. "Don't you mean Scamp? She's the thief."

"No, it was Pacer that stole. He got out of his box, uncle says, and found two bags of oats, and he took one in his teeth and dropped it before Cleve, and ate the other himself, and uncle was so amused that he let them eat a long time, and stood and watched them."

"That *was* a clever trick," said Mr. Harry. "Father must have forgotten to tell me. Those two horses have been mates ever since I can remember, and I believe if they were separated, they'd pine away and die. You have noticed how low the partitions are between the boxes in the horse stable. Father says you wouldn't put a lot of people in separate boxes in a room, where they couldn't see each other, and horses are just as fond of company as we are. Cleve and Pacer are always nosing each other. A horse has a long memory. Father has had horses recognize him, that he has been parted from for twenty years. Speaking of their memories reminds me of another good story about Pacer that I never heard till yesterday, and that I would not talk about to any one but you and mother. Father wouldn't write me about it, for he never will put a line on paper where any one's reputation is concerned."

CHAPTER 26

THE BOX OF MONEY

"THIS story," said Mr. Harry, "is about one of the hired men we had last winter, whose name was Jacobs. He was a cunning fellow, with a hangdog look, and a great cleverness at stealing farm produce from father on the sly, and selling it. Father knew perfectly well what he was doing, and was wondering what would be the best way to deal with him, when one day something happened that brought matters to a climax.

"Father had to go to Sudbury for farming tools, and took Pacer and the cutter. There are two ways of going there—one the Sudbury Road, and the other the old Post Road, which is longer and seldom used. On this occasion father took the Post Road. The snow wasn't deep, and he wanted to inquire after an old man who had been robbed and half frightened to death, a few days before. He was a miserable old creature, known as Miser Jerrold, and he lived alone with his daughter. He had saved a little money that he kept in a box under his bed. When father got near the place, he was astonished to see by Pacer's actions that he had been on this road before, and recently, too. Father is so sharp about horses, that they never do a thing that he doesn't attach a meaning to. So he let the reins hang a little loose, and kept his eye on Pacer. The horse went along the road, and seeing father didn't direct him, turned into the lane leading to the house. There was an old red gate at the end of it, and he stopped in front of it, and waited for father to get out. Then he passed through, and instead of going up to the house, turned around, and stood with his head toward the road.

"Father never said a word, but he was doing a lot of thinking. He went into the house, and found the old man sitting over the fire, rubbing his hands, and half-crying about 'the few poor dollars,' that he said he had had stolen from him. Father had never seen him before, but he knew he had the name of being half silly, and question him as much as he liked, he could make nothing of him. The daughter said that they had gone to bed at dark the night her father was robbed. She slept up stairs, and he down below. About ten o'clock she heard him scream, and running down stairs, she found him sitting up in bed, and the window wide open. He said a man had sprung in upon him, stuffed the bedclothes into his mouth, and dragging his box from under the bed, had made off with it. She ran to the door and looked out, but there was no one to be seen. It was dark, and snowing a little, so no traces of footsteps were to be perceived in the morning.

"Father found that the neighbors were dropping in to bear the old man company, so he drove on to Sudbury, and then returned home. When he got back, he said Jacobs was hanging about the stable in a nervous kind of a way, and said he wanted to speak to him. Father said very good, but put the horse in first. Jacobs unhitched, and father sat on one of the stable benches and watched him till he came lounging along with a straw in his mouth, and said he'd made up his mind to go West, and he'd like to set off at once.

"Father said again, very good, but first he had a little account to settle with him, and he took out of his pocket a paper, where he had jotted down, as far as he could, every quart of oats, and every bag of grain, and every quarter of a dollar of market money that Jacobs had defrauded him of. Father said the fellow turned all the colors of the rainbow, for he thought he had covered up his tracks so cleverly that he would never be found out. Then father said, 'Sit down, Jacobs, for I have got to have a long talk with you.' He had him there about an hour, and when he finished, the fellow was completely broken down. Father told him that there were just two courses in life for a young man to take, and he had gotten on the wrong one. He was a young, smart fellow, and if he turned right around now, there was a chance for him. If he didn't, there was nothing but the State's prison ahead of him, for he needn't think he was going to gull and cheat all the world, and never be found out. Father said he'd give him all the help in his power, if he had his word that he'd try to be an honest man. Then he tore up the paper, and laid there was an end of his indebtedness to him.

"Jacobs is only a young fellow, twenty-three or thereabout, and father says he sobbed like a baby. Then, without looking at him, father gave an account of his afternoon's drive, just as if he was talking to himself. He said that Pacer never to his knowledge had been on that road before, and yet he seemed perfectly familiar with it, and that he stopped and turned already to leave again quickly, instead of going up to the door, and how he looked over his shoulder and started on a run down the lane, the minute father's foot was in the cutter again. In the course of his remarks, father mentioned the fact that on Monday, the evening that the robbery was committed, Jacobs had borrowed Pacer to go to the Junction, but had come in with the horse steaming, and looking as if he had been driven a much longer distance than that. Father said that when he got done, Jacobs had sunk down all in a heap on the stable floor, with his hands over his face. Father left him to have it out with himself, and went to the house.

"The next morning, Jacobs looked just the same as usual, and went about with the other men doing his work, but saying nothing about going West. Late in the afternoon, a farmer going by hailed father, and asked if he'd heard the news. Old Miser Jerrold's box had been left on his door-step some time through the night, and he'd found it in the morning. The money was all there, but the old fellow was so cute that he wouldn't tell any one how much it was. The neighbors had persuaded him to bank it, and he was coming to town the next morning with it, and that night some of them were going to help him mount guard over it. Father told the men at milking time, and he said Jacobs looked as unconscious as possible. However, from that day there was a change in him. He never told father in so many words that he'd resolved to be an honest man, but his actions spoke for him. He had been a kind of sullen, unwilling fellow, but now he turned handy and obliging, and it was a real trial to father to part with him."

Miss Laura was intensely interested in this story. "Where is he now, Cousin Harry?" she asked, eagerly. "What became of him?"

Mr. Harry laughed in such amusement that I stared up at him, and even Fleetfoot turned his head around to see what the joke was. We were going very slowly up a long, steep hill, and in the clear, still air, we could hear every word spoken in the buggy.

"The last part of the story is the best, to my mind," said Mr. Harry, "and as romantic as even a girl could desire. The affair of the stolen box was much talked about along Sudbury way, and Miss Jerrold got to be considered quite a desirable young person among some of the youth near there, though she is a frowsy-headed creature, and not as neat in her personal attire as a young girl should be. Among her suitors was Jacobs. He cut out a black-smith and a painter, and several young farmers, and father said he never in his life had such a time to keep a straight face, as when Jacobs came to him this spring, and said he was going to marry old Miser Jerrold's daughter. He wanted to quit father's employ, and he thanked him in a real manly way for the manner in which he had always treated him. Well, Jacobs left, and mother says that father would sit and speculate about him, as to whether he had fallen in love with Eliza Jerrold, or whether he was deter-mined to regain possession of the box, and was going to do it honestly, or whether he was sorry for having frightened the old man into a greater degree of imbecility, and was marrying the girl so that he could take care of him, or whether it was something else, and so on, and so on. He had a dozen theories, and then mother says he would burst out laughing, and say it was one of the cutest tricks that he had ever heard of.

"In the end, Jacobs got married, and father and mother went to the wedding. Father gave the bridegroom a yoke of oxen, and mother gave the bride a lot of household linen, and I believe they're as happy as the day is long. Jacobs makes his wife comb her hair, and he waits on the old man as if he was his son, and he is improving the farm that was going to rack and ruin, and I hear he is going to build a new house."

"Harry," exclaimed Miss Laura, "can't you take me to see them?"

"Yes, indeed; mother often drives over to take them little things, and we'll go, too, sometime. I'd like to see Jacobs myself, now that he is a decent fellow. Strange to say, though he hadn't the best of character, no one has ever suspected him of the robbery, and he's been cunning enough never to say a word about it. Father says Jacobs is like all the rest of us. There's mixture of good and evil in him, and sometimes one predominates and sometimes the other. But we must get on and not talk here all day. Get up, Fleetfoot."

"Where did you say we were going?" asked Miss Laura, as we crossed the bridge over the river.

"A little way back here in the woods," he replied. "There's an Englishman on a small clearing that he calls Penhollow. Father loaned him some money three years ago, and he won't pay either interest or principal."

"I think I've heard of him," said Miss Laura "Isn't he the man whom the boys call Lord Chesterfield?"

"The same one. He's a queer specimen of a man. Father has always stood up for him. He has a great liking for the English. He says we ought to be as ready to help an Englishman as an American, for we spring from common stock."

"Oh, not Englishmen only," said Miss Laura, warmly; "Chinamen, and Negroes, and everybody. There ought to be a brotherhood of nations, Harry."[1]

---

1 Laura's warm views reflect the growing sentiment that led to the establishment of the American Peace Society and the organization of the first International Peace Congress at the Hague in 1889, wherein the "Great

"Yes, Miss Enthusiasm, I suppose there ought to be," and looking up, I could see that Mr. Harry was gazing admiringly into his cousin's face.

"Please tell me some more about the Englishman," said Miss Laura.

"There isn't much to tell. He lives alone, only coming occasionally to the village for supplies, and though he is poorer than poverty, he despises every soul within a ten-mile radius of him, and looks upon us as no better than an order of thrifty, well-trained lower animals."

"Why is that?" asked Miss Laura, in surprise.

"He is a gentleman, Laura, and we are only common people. My father can't hand a lady in and out of a carriage as Lord Chesterfield can, nor can he make so grand a bow, nor does he put on evening dress for a late dinner, and we never go to the opera nor to the theatre, and know nothing of polite society, nor can we tell exactly whom our great-great-grandfather sprang from. I tell you, there is a gulf between us and that Englishman, wider than the one young Curtius[1] leaped into."

Miss Laura was laughing merrily. "How funny that sounds, Harry. So he despises you," and she glanced at her good-looking cousin, and his handsome buggy and well-kept horse, and then burst into another merry peal of laughter.

Mr. Harry laughed, too. "It does seem absurd. Sometimes when I pass him jogging along to town in his rickety old cart, and look at his pale, cruel face, and know that he is a broken-down gambler and man of the world, and yet considers himself infinitely superior to me—a young man in the prime of life, with a good constitution and happy prospects, it makes me turn away to hide a smile."

By this time we had left the river and the meadows far behind us, and were passing through a thick wood. The road was narrow and very broken, and Fleetfoot was obliged to pick his way care-

---

Powers" agreed to settle disputes through arbitration rather than war (Reinalda 65-71). In the 1920, 1925, and 1934 editions of the novel, however, this conversation was omitted, likely reflecting changing attitudes after World War I.

1 Harry refers to the legend of Marcus Curtius, a Roman who in 362 BCE sacrificed himself for the sake of his people. A giant chasm opened in the middle of Rome's forum, and the gods demanded a great sacrifice in exchange for closing it. Curtius mounted his horse and rode into the gulf, after which the chasm was closed.

fully. "Why does the Englishman live in this out-of-the-way place, if he is so fond of city life?" said Miss Laura.

"I don't know," said Mr. Harry. "Father is afraid that he has committed some misdeed, and is in hiding; but we say nothing about it. We have not seen him for some weeks, and to tell the truth, this trip is as much to see what has become of him, as to make a demand upon him for the money. As he lives alone, he might lie there ill, and no one would know anything about it. The last time that we knew of his coming to the village was to draw quite a sum of money from the bank. It annoyed father, for he said he might take some of it to pay his debts. I think his relatives in England supply him with funds. Here we are at the entrance to the mansion of Penhollow. I must get out and open the gate that will admit us to the winding avenue."

We had arrived in front of some bars which were laid across an opening in the snake fence that ran along one side of the road. I sat down and looked about. It was a strange, lonely place. The trees almost met overhead, and it was very dim and quiet. The sun could only send little straggling beams through the branches. There was a muddy pool of water before the bars that Mr. Harry was letting down, and he got his feet wet in it. "Confound that Englishman," he said, backing out of the water, and wiping his boots on the grass. "He hasn't even gumption enough to throw down a load of stone there. Drive in Laura and I'll put up the bars." Fleetfoot took us through the opening, and then Mr. Harry jumped into the buggy and took up the reins again.

We had to go very slowly up a narrow, rough road. The bushes scratched and scraped against the buggy, and Mr. Harry looked very much annoyed.

"No man liveth to himself," said Miss Laura, softly. "This man's carelessness is giving you trouble. Why doesn't he cut these branches that overhang the road?"

"He can't do it, because his abominable laziness won't let him," said Mr. Harry. "I'd like to be behind him for a week, and I'd make him step a little faster. We have arrived at last, thank goodness."

There was a small grass clearing in the midst of the woods. Chips and bits of wood were littered about, and across the clearing was a roughly-built house of unpainted boards. The front door was propped open by a stick. Some of the panes of glass in the windows were broken, and the whole house had a melancholy dilapidated look. I thought that I had never seen such a sad-looking place.

"It seems as if there was no one about," said Mr. Harry, with a puzzled face. "Barron must be away. Will you hold Fleetfoot, Laura, while I go and see?"

He drew the buggy up near a small log building that had evidently been used for a stable, and I lay down beside it and watched Miss Laura.

CHAPTER 27

A NEGLECTED STABLE

I HAD not been on the ground more than a few seconds, before I turned my eyes from Miss Laura to the log hut. It was deathly quiet, there was not a sound coming from it, but the air was full of queer smells, and I was so uneasy that I could not lie still. There was something the matter with Fleetfoot too. He was pawing the ground and whinnying, and looking, not after Mr. Harry, but toward the log building.

"Joe," said Miss Laura, "what is the matter with you and Fleetfoot? Why don't you stand still? Is there any stranger about?" and she peered out of the buggy.

I knew there was something wrong somewhere, but I didn't know what it was; so I stretched myself up on the step of the buggy, and licked her hand, and barking, to ask her to excuse me, I ran off to the other side of the log hut. There was a door there, but it was closed, and propped firmly up by a plank that I could not move, scratch as hard as I liked. I was determined to get in, so I jumped against the door, and tore and bit at the plank, till Miss Laura came to help me.

"You won't find anything but rats in that ramshackle old place, Beautiful Joe," she said, as she pulled the plank away; "and as you don't hurt them, I don't see what you want to get in for. However, you are a sensible dog, and usually have a reason for having your own way, so I am going to let you have it."

The plank fell down as she spoke, and she pulled open the rough door and looked in. There was no window inside, only the light that streamed through the door, so that for an instant she could see nothing. "Is any one here?" she asked, in her clear, sweet voice. There was no answer except a low, moaning sound. "Why, some poor creature is in trouble, Joe," said Miss Laura, cheerfully. "Let us see what it is," and she stepped inside.

I shall never forget seeing my dear Miss Laura going into that wet and filthy log house, holding up her white dress in her hands, her face a picture of pain and horror. There were two rough stalls in it, and in the first one was tied a cow, with a calf lying beside her. I could never have believed, if I had not seen it with my own eyes, that an animal could get so thin as that cow was. Her backbone rose up high and sharp, her hip bones stuck away out, and all her body seemed shrunken in. There were sores on her sides, and the smell from her stall was terrible. Miss Laura gave one cry of pity, then with a very pale face she dropped her dress, and seizing a little penknife from her pocket, she hacked at the rope that tied the cow to the manger, and cut it so that the cow could lie down. The first thing the poor cow did was to lick her calf, but it was quite dead. I used to think Jenkins's cows were thin enough, but he never had one that looked like this. Her head was like the head of a skeleton, and her eyes had such a famished look, that I turned away, sick at heart, to think that she had suffered so.

When the cow lay down, the moaning noise stopped, for she had been making it. Miss Laura ran outdoors, snatched a handful of grass and took it in to her. The cow ate it gratefully, but slowly, for her strength seemed all gone.

Miss Laura then went into the other stall to see if there was any creature there. There had been a horse. There was now a lean, gaunt-looking animal lying on the ground, that seemed as if he was dead. There was a heavy rope knotted round his neck, and fastened to his empty rack. Miss Laura stepped carefully between his feet, cut the rope and going outside the stall spoke kindly to him. He moved his ears slightly, raised his head, tried to get up, fell back again, tried again, and succeeded in staggering outdoors after Miss Laura, who kept encouraging him, and then he fell down on the grass.

Fleetfoot stared at the miserable-looking creature as if he did not know what it was. The horse had no sores on his body, as the cow had, nor was he quite so lean; but he was the weakest, most distressed-looking animal that I ever saw. The flies settled on him, and Miss Laura had to keep driving them away. He was a white horse, with some kind of pale-colored eyes, and whenever he turned them on Miss Laura, she would look away. She did not cry, as she often did over the sick and suffering animals. This seemed too bad for tears. She just hovered over that poor horse with her face as white as her dress, and an expression of fright in her eyes. Oh, how dirty he was! I would never have imagined that a horse could get in such a condition.

All this had only taken a few minutes, and just after she got the horse out, Mr. Harry appeared. He came out of the house with a slow step, that quickened to a run when he saw Miss Laura. "Laura!" he exclaimed, "what are you doing?" Then he stopped and looked at the horse, not in amazement, but very sorrowfully. "Barron is gone," he said, and crumpling up a piece of paper, he put it in his pocket. "What is to be done to these animals? There is a cow, isn't there?"

He stepped to the door of the log hut, glanced in, and said, quickly: "Do you feel able to drive home?"

"Yes," said Miss Laura.

"Sure?" and he eyed her anxiously.

"Yes, yes," she returned, "what shall I get?"

"Just tell father that Barron has run away and left a starving pig, cow, and horse. There's not a thing to eat here. He'll know what to do. I'll drive you to the road."

Miss Laura got into the buggy and Mr. Harry jumped in after her. He drove her to the road and put down the bars, then he said: "Go straight on. You'll soon be on the open road, and there's nothing to harm you. Joe will look after you. Meanwhile I'll go back to the house and heat some water."

Miss Laura let Fleetfoot go as fast as he liked on the way home, and it only seemed a few minutes before we drove into the yard. Adèle came out to meet us. "Where's uncle?" asked Miss Laura.

"Gone to de big meadow," said Adèle.

"And auntie?"

"She had de colds and chills, and entered into de bed to keep warm. She lose herself in sleep now. You not go near her."

"Are there none of the men about?" asked Miss Laura.

"No, mademoiselle. Dey all occupied way off."

"Then you help me, Adèle, like a good girl," said Miss Laura, hurrying into the house. "We've found a sick horse and cow. What shall I take them?"

"Nearly all animals like de bran mash," said Adèle.

"Good!" cried Miss Laura. "That is the very thing. Put in the things to make it, will you please, and I would like some vegetables for the cow. Carrots, turnips, anything you have, take some of those you have prepared for dinner to-morrow, and please run up to the barn, Adèle, and get some hay, and corn, and oats, not much, for we'll be going back again; but hurry, for the poor things are starving, and have you any milk for the pig? Put it in one of those tin kettles with covers."

For a few minutes, Miss Laura and Adèle flew about the kitchen, then we set off again. Miss Laura took me in the buggy, for I was out of breath and wheezing greatly. I had to sit on the seat beside her, for the bottom of the buggy and the back were full of eatables for the poor sick animals. Just as we drove into the road, we met Mr. Wood. "Are you running away with the farm?" he said with a laugh, pointing to the carrot tops that were gaily waving over the dashboard.

Miss Laura said a few words to him, and with a very grave face he got in beside her. In a short time, we were back on the lonely road. Mr. Harry was waiting at the gate for us, and when he saw Miss Laura, he said, "Why did you come back again? You'll be tired out. This isn't a place for a sensitive girl like you."

"I thought I might be of some use," said she, gently.

"So you can," said Mr. Wood. "You go into the house and sit down, and Harry and I will come to you when we want cheering up. What have you been doing, Harry?"

"I've watered them a little, and got a good fire going. I scarcely think the cow will pull through. I think we'll save the horse. I tried to get the cow out-doors, but she can't move."

"Let her alone," said Mr. Wood. "Give her some food and her strength will come to her. What have you got here?" and he began to take the things out of the buggy. "Bless the child, she's thought of everything, even the salt. Bring those things into the house, Harry, and we'll make a bran mash."

For more than an hour they were fussing over the animals. Then they came in and sat down. The inside of the Englishman's house was as untidy as the outside. There was no upstairs to it—only one large room with a dirty curtain stretched across it. On one side was a low bed with a heap of clothes on it, a chair and a washstand. On the other was a stove, a table, a shaky rocking-chair that Miss Laura was sitting in, a few hanging shelves with some dishes and books on them, and two or three small boxes that had evidently been used for seats.

On the walls were tacked some pictures of grand houses and ladies and gentlemen in fine clothes, and Miss Laura said that some of them were noble people. "Well, I'm glad this particular nobleman has left us," said Mr. Wood, seating himself on one of the boxes, "if nobleman he is. I should call him in plain English, a scoundrel. Did Harry show you his note?"

"No, uncle," said Miss Laura.

"Read it aloud," said Mr. Wood. "I'd like to hear it again."

Miss Laura read:

J. WOOD, Esq., Dear Sir:—It is a matter of great regret to me that I am suddenly called away from my place at Penhollow, and will, therefore not be able to do myself the pleasure of calling on you and settling my little account. I sincerely hope that the possession of my live stock, which I make entirely over to you, will more than reimburse you for any trifling expense which you may have incurred on my account. If it is any gratification to you to know that you have rendered a slight assistance to the son of one of England's noblest noblemen, you have it. With expressions of the deepest respect, and hoping that my stock may be in good condition when you take possession,

I am, dear sir, ever devotedly yours,
HOWARD ALGERNON LEDUC BARRON.

Miss Laura dropped the paper. "Uncle, did he leave those animals to starve?"

"Didn't you notice," said Mr. Wood, grimly, "that there wasn't a wisp of hay inside that shanty, and that where the poor beasts were tied up the wood was gnawed and bitten by them in their torture for food? Wouldn't he have sent me that note, instead of leaving it here on the table, if he'd wanted me to know? The note isn't dated, but I judge he's been gone five or six days. He has had a spite against me ever since I lent him that hundred dollars. I don't know why, for I've stood up for him when others would have run him out of the place. He intended me to come here and find every animal lying dead. He even had a rope around the pig's neck. Harry, my boy, let us go and look after them again. I love a dumb brute too well to let it suffer, but in this case I'd give two hundred dollars more if I could make them live and have Barron know it."

They left the room, and Miss Laura sat turning the sheet of paper over and over, with a kind of horror in her face. It was a very dirty piece of paper, but by-and-by she made a discovery. She took it in her hand and went out-doors. I am sure that the poor horse lying on the grass knew her. He lifted his head, and what a different expression he had now that his hunger had been partly satisfied. Miss Laura stroked and patted him, then she called to her cousin, "Harry, will you look at this?"

He took the paper from her, and said: "That is a crest shining through the different strata of dust and grime, probably that of his own family. We'll have it cleaned, and it will enable us to track the villain. You want him punished, don't you?" he said, with a little, sly laugh at Miss Laura.

She made a gesture in the direction of the suffering horse, and said, frankly, "Yes, I do."

"Well, my dear girl," he said, "father and I are with you. If we can hunt Barron down, we'll do it." Then he muttered to himself as she turned away, "She is a real Puritan, gentle, and sweet, and good, and yet severe. Rewards for the virtuous, punishments for the vicious," and he repeated some poetry:

"She was so charitable and so piteous,
She would weep if that she saw a mouse
Caught in a trap, if it were dead or bled."[1]

Miss Laura saw that Mr. Wood and Mr. Harry were doing all that could be done for the cow and horse, so she wandered down to a hollow at the back of the house, where the Englishman had kept his pig. Just now, he looked more like a greyhound than a pig. His legs were so long, his nose so sharp, and hunger, instead of making him stupid like the horse and cow, had made him more lively. I think he had probably not suffered so much as they had, or perhaps he had had a greater store of fat to nourish him. Mr. Harry said that if he had been a girl, he would have laughed and cried at the same time when he discovered that pig. He must have been asleep or exhausted when we arrived, for there was not a sound out of him, but shortly afterward he had set up a yelling that attracted Mr. Harry's attention, and made him run down to him. Mr. Harry said he was raging around his pen, digging the ground with his snout, falling down and getting up again, and by a miracle, escaping death by choking from the rope that was tied around his neck.

Now that his hunger had been satisfied, he was gazing contentedly at his little trough that was half full of good, sweet milk. Mr. Harry said that a starving animal, like a starving person, should only be fed a little at a time; but the Englishman's animals had always been fed poorly, and their stomachs had contracted so that they could not eat much at one time.

Miss Laura got a stick and scratched poor piggy's back a little, and then she went back to the house. In a short time we went home with Mr. Wood. Mr. Harry was going to stay all night with the sick animals, and his mother would send him things to make him comfortable. She was better by the time we got home, and was horrified to hear the tale of Mr. Barron's neglect. Later in the evening, she sent one of the men over with a whole box full of things for her darling boy, and nice, hot tea, done up for him in a covered dish. When the man came home, he said that Mr. Harry would not sleep in the Englishman's dirty house, but had

---

1   These lines are from the Prologue to Geoffrey Chaucer's *The Canterbury Tales*, written in the fourteenth century, one of the most significant works of English literature.

slung a hammock out under the trees. However, he would not be able to sleep much, for he had his lantern by his side, all ready to jump up and attend to the horse and cow. It was a very lonely place for him out there in the woods, and his mother said that she would be glad when the sick animals could be driven to their own farm.

CHAPTER 28

THE END OF THE ENGLISHMAN

IN a few days, thanks to Mr. Harry's constant care, the horse and cow were able to walk. It was a mournful procession that came into the yard at Dingley Farm. The hollow-eyed horse, and lean cow, and funny, little thin pig, staggering along in such a shaky fashion. Their hoofs were diseased, and had partly rotted away, so that they could not walk straight. Though it was only a mile or two from Penhollow to Dingley Farm, they were tired out, and dropped down exhausted on their comfortable beds.

Miss Laura was so delighted to think that they had all lived, that she did not know what to do. Her eyes were bright and shining, and she went from one to another with such a happy face. The queer little pig that Mr. Harry had christened "Daddy Longlegs," had been washed, and he lay on his heap of straw in the corner of his neat little pen, and surveyed his clean trough and abundance of food with the air of a prince. Why, he would be clean and dry here, and all his life he had been used to dirty, damp Penhollow, with the trees hanging over him, and his little feet in a mass of filth and dead leaves. Happy little pig! His ugly eyes seemed to blink and gleam with gratitude, and he knew Miss Laura and Mr. Harry as well as I did.

His tiny tail was curled so tight that it was almost in a knot. Mr. Wood said that was a sign that he was healthy and happy, and that when poor Daddy was at Penhollow he had noticed that his tail hung as limp and as loose as the tail of a rat. He came and leaned over the pen with Miss Laura, and had a little talk with her about pigs. He said they were by no means the stupid animals that some people considered them. He had had pigs that were as clever as dogs. One little black pig that he had once sold to a man away back in the country had found his way home, through the woods, across the river, up hill and down dale, and he'd been taken to the place with a bag over his head. Mr. Wood said that he kept that pig, because he knew so much.

He said the most knowing pigs he ever saw were Canadian pigs. One time he was having a trip on a sailing vessel, and it anchored in a long, narrow harbor in Canada, where the tide came in with a front four or five feet high called the "bore." There was a village opposite the place where the ship was anchored, and every day at low tide, a number of pigs came down to look for shell-fish. Sometimes they went out for half a mile over the mud flats, but always a few minutes before the tide came rushing in they turned and hurried to the shore. Their instincts warned them that if they stayed any longer they would be drowned.

Mr. Wood had a number of pigs, and after a while Daddy was put in with them, and a fine time he had of it making friends with the other little grunters. They were often let out in the pasture or orchard, and when they were there, I could always single out Daddy from among them, because he was the smartest. Though he had been brought up in such a miserable way, he soon learned to take very good care of himself at Dingley Farm, and it was amusing to see him when a storm was coming on, running about in a state of great excitement carrying little bundles of straw in his mouth to make himself a bed. He was a white pig, and was always kept very clean. Mr. Wood said that it is wrong to keep pigs dirty. They like to be clean as well as other animals, and if they were kept so, human beings would not get so many diseases from eating their flesh.

The cow, poor unhappy creature, never as long as she lived on Dingley Farm, lost a strange melancholy look from her eyes. I have heard it said that animals forget past unhappiness, and perhaps some of them do. I know that I have never forgotten my one miserable year with Jenkins, and I have been a sober, thoughtful dog in consequence of it, and not playful like some dogs who have never known what it is to be really unhappy.

It always seemed to me that the Englishman's cow was thinking of her poor dead calf, starved to death by her cruel master. She got well herself, and came and went with the other cows, seemingly as happy as they, but often when I watched her standing chewing her cud, and looking away in the distance. I could see a difference between her face and the faces of the cows that had always been happy on Dingley Farm. Even the farm hands called her "Old Melancholy," and soon she got to be known by that name, or Mel, for short. Until she got well, she was put into the cow stable, where Mr. Wood's cows all stood at night upon raised platforms of earth covered over with straw litter, and she was tied with a Dutch halter, so that she could lie down and go to sleep when she wanted to. When she got well, she was put out to pasture with the other cows.

The horse they named "Scrub," because he could never be, under any circumstance, anything but a broken-down, plain-looking animal. He was put into the horse stable in a stall next to Fleetfoot, and as the partition was low, they could look over at each other. In time, by dint of much doctoring, Scrub's hoofs became clean and sound, and he was able to do some work. Miss Laura petted him a great deal. She often took out apples to the stable, and Fleetfoot would throw up his beautiful head and look reproachfully over the partition at her, for she always stayed longer with Scrub than with him, and Scrub always got the larger share of whatever good thing was going.

Poor old Scrub! I think he loved Miss Laura. He was a stupid sort of a horse, and always acted as if he was blind. He would run his nose up and down the front of her dress, nip at the buttons, and be very happy if he could get a bit of her watch-chain between his strong teeth. If he was in the field he never seemed to know her till she was right under his pale-colored eyes. Then he would be delighted to see her. He was not blind, though, for Mr. Wood said he was not. He said he had probably not been an over-bright horse to start with, and had been made more dull by cruel usage.

As for the Englishman, the master of these animals, a very strange thing happened to him. He came to a terrible end, but for a long time no one knew anything about it. Mr. Wood and Mr. Harry were so very angry with him, that they said they would leave no stone unturned to have him punished, or at least to have it known what a villain he was. They sent the paper with the crest on it to Boston. Some people there wrote to England, and found out that it was the crest of a noble and highly esteemed family, and some earl was at the head of it. They were all honorable people in this family except one man, a nephew, not a son of the late earl. He was the black sheep of them all. As a young man, he had led a wild and wicked life, and had ended by forging the name of one of his friends, so that he was obliged to leave England and take refuge in America. By the description of this man, Mr. Wood knew that he must be Mr. Barron, so he wrote to these English people, and told them what a wicked thing their relative had done in leaving his animals to starve. In a short time, he got an answer from them, which was, at the same time, very proud and very touching. It came from Mr. Barron's cousin, and he said quite frankly that he knew his relative was a man of evil habits, but it seemed as if nothing could be done to reform him. His family was accustomed to send a quarterly allowance to him, on condition that he led a quiet life in some retired place, but their last remittance to him was lying unclaimed in Boston, and they thought he must be dead. Could Mr. Wood tell them anything about him?

Mr. Wood looked very thoughtful when he got this letter, then he said, "Harry, how long is it since Barron ran away?"

"About eight weeks," said Mr. Harry.

"That's strange," said Mr. Wood. "The money these English people sent him would get to Boston just a few days after he left here. He is not the man to leave it long unclaimed. Something must have happened to him. Where do you suppose he would go from Penhollow?"

"I have no idea, sir," said Mr. Harry.

"And how would he go?" said Mr. Wood. "He did not leave Riverdale Station, because he would have been spotted by some of his creditors."

"Perhaps he would cut through the woods to the Junction," said Mr. Harry.

"Just what he would do," said Mr. Wood, slapping his knee. "I'll be driving over there to-morrow to see Thompson, and I'll make inquiries."

Mr. Harry spoke to his father the next night when he came home, and asked him if he had found out anything. "Only this," said Mr. Wood. "There's no one answering to Barron's description who has left Riverdale Junction within a twelvemonth. He must have struck some other station. We'll let him go. The Lord looks out for fellows like that."

"We will look out for him if he ever comes back to Riverdale," said Mr. Harry, quietly. All through the village, and in the country it was known what a dastardly trick the Englishman had played, and he would have been roughly handled, if he had dared return.

Months passed away, and nothing was heard of him. Late in the autumn, after Miss Laura and I had gone back to Fairport, Mrs. Wood wrote her about the end of the Englishman. Some Riverdale lads were beating about the woods, looking for lost cattle, and in their wanderings came to an old stone quarry that had been disused for years. On one side there was a smooth wall of rock, many feet deep. On the other the ground and rock were broken away, and it was quite easy to get into it. They found that by some means or other, one of their cows had fallen into this deep pit, over the steep side of the quarry. Of course the poor creature was dead, but the boys, out of curiosity, resolved to go down and look at her. They clambered down, found the cow, and, to their horror and amazement, discovered near-by the skeleton of a man. There was a heavy walking-stick by his side, which they recognized as one that the Englishman had carried.

He was a drinking man, and perhaps he had taken something that he thought would strengthen him for his morning's walk, but which had, on the contrary, bewildered him, and made him lose his way and fall into the quarry. Or he might have started before daybreak, and in the darkness have slipped and fallen down this steep wall of rock. One leg was doubled under him, and if he had not been instantly killed by the fall, he must have been so disabled that he could not move. In that lonely place, he would call for help in vain, so he may have perished by the terrible death of starvation—the death he had thought to mete out to his suffering animals.

Mrs. Wood said that there was never a sermon preached in Riverdale that had the effect that the death of this wicked man had, and it reminded her of a verse in the Bible: "He made a pit and he digged it, and is fallen into the ditch which he made."[1] Mrs. Wood said that her husband had written about the finding of Mr. Barron's body to his English relatives, and had received a letter from them in which they seemed relieved to hear that he was dead. They thanked Mr. Wood for his plain speaking in telling them of their relative's misdeeds, and said that from all they knew of Mr. Barron's past conduct, his influence would be for evil and not for good, in any place that he choose to live in. They were having their money sent from Boston to Mr. Wood, and they wished him to expend it in the way he thought best fitted to counteract the evil effects of their namesake's doings in Riverdale.

When this money came, it amounted to some hundreds of dollars. Mr. Wood would have nothing to do with it. He handed it over to the Band of Mercy, and they formed what they called the "Barron Fund," which they drew upon when they wanted money for buying and circulating humane literature. Mrs. Wood said that the fund was being added to, and the children were sending all over the State leaflets and little books which preached the gospel of kindness to God's lower creation. A stranger picking one of them up, and seeing the name of the wicked Englishman printed on the title page, would think that he was a friend and benefactor to the Riverdale people—the very opposite of what he gloried in being.

---

1 Psalms 7:15.

CHAPTER 29

A TALK ABOUT SHEEP

MISS LAURA was very much interested in the sheep on Dingley Farm. There was a flock in the orchard near the house that she often went to see. She always carried roots and vegetables to them, turnips particularly, for they were very fond of them; but they would not come to her to get them, for they did not know her voice. They only lifted their heads and stared at her when she called them. But when they heard Mr. Wood's voice, they ran to the fence bleating with pleasure, and trying to push their noses through to get the carrot or turnip, or whatever he was handing to them. He called them his little Southdowns, and he said he loved his sheep, for they were the most gentle and inoffensive creature that he had on his farm.[1]

One day when he came into the kitchen inquiring for salt, Miss Laura said, "Is it for the sheep?"

"Yes," he replied; "I am going up to the woods pasture to examine my Shropshires."

"You would like to go too, Laura," said Mrs. Wood. "Take your hands right away from that cake. I'll finish frosting it for you. Run along and get your broad-brimmed hat. It's very hot."

Miss Laura danced out into the hall and back again, and soon we were walking up, back of the house, along a path that led us through the fields to the pasture. "What are you going to do, uncle?" she said; "and what are those funny things in your hands?"

"Toe-clippers," he replied; "and I am going to examine the sheep's hoofs. You know we've had warm, moist weather all through July, and I'm afraid of foot rot. Then they're sometimes troubled with over-grown hoofs."

"What do you do if they get foot rot?" asked Miss Laura.

"I've various cures," he said. "Paring and clipping, and dipping the hoof in blue vitriol and vinegar, or rubbing it on, as the English shepherds do. It destroys the diseased part, but doesn't affect the sound."

"Do sheep have many diseases?" asked Miss Laura. "I know one of them myself—that is the scab."

---

1 Southdowns are a breed of sheep. Like the Shropshires, see p. 143, note 1, Southdowns originated in England.

"A nasty thing that," said Mr. Wood, vigorously; "and a man that builds up a flock from a stockyard often finds it out to his cost."

"What is it like?" asked Miss Laura.

"The sheep get scabby from a microbe under the skin, which causes them to itch fearfully, and they lose their wool."

"And can't it be cured?"

"Oh, yes! with time and attention. There are different remedies. I believe petroleum is the best."

By this time we had got to a wide gate that opened into the pasture. As Mr. Wood let Miss Laura go through and then closed it behind her, he said, "You are looking at that gate. You want to know why it is so long, don't you?"

"Yes, uncle," she said; "but I can't bear to ask so many questions."

"Ask as many as you like," he said, good-naturedly. "I don't mind answering them. Have you ever seen sheep pass through a gate or door?"

"Oh, yes, often."

"And how do they act?"

"Oh, so silly, uncle. They hang back, and one waits for another; and, finally, they all try to go at once."

"Precisely; when one goes they all want to go, if it was to jump into a bottomless pit. Many sheep are injured by overcrowding, so I have my gates and doors very wide. Now let us call them up." There wasn't one in sight, but when Mr. Wood lifted up his voice and cried: "Ca nan, nan, nan!" black faces began to peer out from among the bushes; and little black legs, carrying white bodies, came hurrying up the stony paths from the cooler parts of the pasture. Oh how glad they were to get the salt! Mr. Wood let Miss Laura spread it on some flat rocks, then they sat down on a log under a tree and watched them eating it and licking the rocks when it was all gone. Miss Laura sat fanning herself with her hat and smiling at them. "You funny, woolly things," she said "You're not so stupid as some people think you are. Lie still, Joe. If you show yourself, they may run away."

I crouched behind the log, and only lifted my head occasionally to see what the sheep were doing. Some of them went back into the woods, for it was very hot in this bare part of the pasture, but the most of them would not leave Mr. Wood, and stood staring at him. "That's a fine sheep, isn't it?" said Miss Laura, pointing to one with the blackest face, and the blackest legs, and largest body of those near us.

"Yes, that's old Jessica. Do you notice how she's holding her head close to the ground?"

"Yes, is there any reason for it?"

"There is. She's afraid of the grub fly. You often see sheep holding their noses in that way in the summer time. It is to prevent the fly from going into their nostrils, and depositing an egg, which will turn into a grub and annoy and worry them. When the fly comes near, they give a sniff and run as if they were crazy, still holding their noses close to the ground. When I was a boy, and the sheep did that, we thought that they had colds in their heads, and used to rub tar on their noses. We knew nothing about the fly then, but the tar cured them, and is just what I use now. Two or three times a month during hot weather, we put a few drops of it on the nose of every sheep in the flock."

"I suppose farmers are like other people, and are always finding out better ways of doing their work, aren't they, uncle?" said Miss Laura.

"Yes, my child. The older I grow, the more I find out, and the better care I take of my stock. My grandfather would open his eyes in amazement, and ask me if I was an old woman petting her cats, if he were alive, and could know the care I give my sheep. He used to let his flock run till the fields were covered with snow, and bite as close as they liked, till there wasn't a scrap of feed left. Then he would give them an open shed to run under, and throw down their hay outside. Grain they scarcely knew the taste of. That they would fall off in flesh, and half of them lose their lambs in the spring, was an expected thing. He would say I had them kenneled, if he could see my big, closed sheds, with the sunny windows that my flock spend the winter in. I even house them during the bad fall storms. They can run out again. Indeed, I like to get them in, and have a snack of dry food, to break them in to it. They are in and out of those sheds all winter. You must go in, Laura, and see the self-feeding racks. On bright, winter days they get a run in the cornfields. Cold doesn't hurt sheep. It's the heavy rain that soaks their fleeces.

"With my way I seldom lose a sheep, and they're the most profitable stock I have. If I could not keep them, I think I'd give up farming. Last year my lambs netted me eight dollars each. The fleeces of the ewes average eight pounds, and sell for two dollars each. That's something to brag of in these days, when so many are giving up the sheep industry."

"How many sheep have you, uncle?" asked Miss Laura.

"Only fifty, now. Twenty-five here and twenty-five down below in the orchard. I've been selling a good many this spring."

"These sheep are larger than those in the orchard, aren't they?" said Miss Laura.

"Yes; I keep those few Southdowns for their fine quality. I don't make as much on them as I do on these Shropshires. For an all-around sheep I like the Shropshire. It's good for mutton, for wool, and for rearing lambs. There's a great demand for mutton nowadays, all through our eastern cities. People want more and more of it. And it has to be tender, and juicy, and finely flavored, so a person has to be particular about the feed the sheep get."[1]

"Don't you hate to have these creatures killed that you have raised and tended so carefully?" said Miss Laura with a little shudder.

"I do," said her uncle; "but never an animal goes off my place that I don't know just how it's going to be put to death. None of your sending sheep to market with their legs tied together, and jammed in a cart, and sweating and suffering, for me. They've got to go standing comfortably on their legs, or go not at all. And I'm going to know the butcher that kills my animals, that have been petted like children. I said to Davidson, over there in Hoytville, 'If I thought you would herd my sheep and lambs and calves

---

1 In the first decades of the twentieth century, the US invested heavily in developing ways of streamlining the systematic feeding of animal by-products to increasing numbers of animals. At agriculture experiment stations and state colleges across the country, scientists gathered information on the most efficient use of "digester's tankage"—"the cooked meat, bone, and sinew remaining after the expression of fat" from all sorts of slaughtered animals—for feed animals (E.W. Allen 4, Zapoleon 59). A 1910 report by the US Department of Agriculture described "[b]reeders and feeders [as] artists who work with living plastic materials" (E.W. Allen 4). The President of the American Society of Animal Nutrition, a society founded in 1908, accurately prophesied that "[t]he feeder of the future" will "husband" by-product feeds "to an extent as yet unrealized" (E.W. Allen 5). Saunders's almost bucolic rendering of farm life intimates at these upcoming changes in its accounting of how the Woods paid meticulous attention to every aspect of farm life in order to maximize the productivity of the animals.

together, and take them one by one in sight of the rest, and stick your knife into them, or stun them, and have the others lowing, and bleating, and crying in their misery, this is the last consignment you would ever get from me.'

"He said, 'Wood, I don't like my business, but on the word of an honest man, my butchering is done as well as it can be. Come and see for yourself.'

"He took me to his slaughter-house, and though I didn't stay long, I saw enough to convince me that he spoke the truth. He has different pens and sheds, and the killing is done as quietly as possible; the animals are taken in one by one, and though the others suspect what is going on, they can't see it."

"These sheep are a long way from the house," said Miss Laura; "don't the dogs that you were telling me about attack them?"

"No; for since I had that brush with Windham's dog, I've trained them to go and come with the cows. It's a queer thing, but cows that will run from a dog when they are alone will fight him if he meddles with their calves or the sheep. There's not a dog around that would dare to come into this pasture, for he knows the cows would be after him with lowered horns, and a business look in their eyes. The sheep in the orchard are safe enough, for they're near the house, and if a strange dog came around, Joe would settle him, wouldn't you, Joe?" and Mr. Wood looked behind the log at me.

I got up and put my head on his arm, and he went on: "By and by, the Southdowns will be changed up here, and the Shropshires will go down to the orchard. I like to keep one flock under my fruit trees. You know there is an old proverb, 'The sheep has a golden hoof.' They save me the trouble of ploughing. I haven't ploughed my orchard for ten years, and don't expect to plough it for ten years more. Then your Aunt Hattie's hens are so obliging that they keep me from the worry of finding ticks at shearing time. All the year round, I let them run among the sheep, and they nab every tick they see."

"How closely sheep bite," exclaimed Miss Laura, pointing to one that was nibbling almost at his master's feet.

"Very close, and they eat a good many things that cows don't relish—bitter weeds, and briars and shrubs, and the young ferns that come up in the spring."

"I wish I could get hold of one of those dear little lambs," said Miss Laura. "See that sweet little blackie back in the alders. Could you not coax him up?"

"He wouldn't come here," said her uncle kindly, "but I'll try and get him for you."

222   MARGARET MARSHALL SAUNDERS

He rose, and after several efforts succeeded in capturing the black-faced creature, and bringing him up to the log. He was very shy of Miss Laura, but Mr. Wood held him firmly, and let her stroke his head as much as she liked. "You call him little," said Mr. Wood; "if you put your arm around him, you'll find he's a pretty substantial lamb. He was born in March. This is the last of July; he'll be shorn the middle of next month, and think he's quite grown up. Poor little animal! he had quite a struggle for life. The sheep were turned out to pasture in April. They can't bear confinement as well as the cows, and as they bite closer they can be turned out earlier, and get on well by having good rations of corn in addition to the grass, which is thin and poor so early in the spring. This young creature was running by his mother's side, rather a weak-legged, poor specimen of a lamb. Every night the flock was put under shelter, for the ground was cold, and though the sheep might not suffer from lying out-doors, the lambs would get chilled. One night this fellow's mother got astray, and as Ben neglected to make the count, she wasn't missed. I'm always anxious about my lambs in the spring, and often get up in the night to look after them. That night I went out about two o'clock. I took it into my head for some reason or other, to count them. I found a sheep and lamb missing, took my lantern and Bruno, who was some good at tracking sheep, and started out. Bruno barked and I called, and the foolish creature came to me, the little lamb staggering after her. I wrapped the lamb in my coat, took it to the house, made a fire, and heated some milk. Your Aunt Hattie heard me and got up. She won't let me give brandy even to a dumb beast, so I put some ground sugar, which is just as good, in the milk, and forced it down the lamb's throat. Then we wrapped an old blanket round him, and put him near the stove, and the next evening he was ready to go back to his mother. I petted him all through April, and gave him extras—different kinds of meal, till I found what suited him best; now he does me credit."

"Dear little lamb," said Miss Laura, patting him. "How can you tell him from the others, uncle?"

"I know all their faces, Laura. A flock of sheep is just like a crowd of people. They all have different expressions, and have different dispositions."

"They all look alike to me," said Miss Laura.

"I dare say. You are not accustomed to them. Do you know how to tell a sheep's age?"

"No, uncle."

"Here, open your mouth, Cosset," he said to the lamb that he still held. "At one year they have two teeth in the centre of the jaw. They get two teeth more every year up to five years. Then we say they have 'a full mouth.' After that you can't tell their age exactly by the teeth. Now run back to your mother," and he let the lamb go.

"Do they always know their own mothers?" asked Miss Laura.

"Usually. Sometimes a ewe will not own her lamb. In that case we tie them up in a separate stall till she recognizes it. Do you see that sheep over there by the blueberry bushes—the one with the very pointed ears?"

"Yes, uncle," said Miss Laura.

"That lamb by her side is not her own. Hers died and we took its fleece and wrapped it around a twin lamb that we took from another ewe, and gave to her. She soon adopted it. Now, come this way, and I'll show you our movable feeding troughs."

He got up from the log, and Miss Laura followed him to the fence. "These big troughs are for the sheep," said Mr. Wood; "and these shallow ones in the enclosure, are for the lambs. See there is just room enough for them to get under the fence. You should see the small creatures rush to them whenever we appear with their oats, and wheat, or bran, or whatever we are going to give them. If they are going to the butcher, they get corn meal and oil meal. Whatever it is, they eat it up clean. I don't believe in cramming animals. I feed them as much as is good for them, and not any more. Now, you go sit down over there behind those bushes with Joe, and I'll attend to business."

Miss Laura found a shady place, and I curled myself up beside her. We sat there a long time, but we did not get tired, for it was amusing to watch the sheep and lambs. After a while, Mr. Wood came and sat down beside us. He talked some more about sheep-raising; then he said, "You may stay here longer if you like, but I must get down to the house. The work must be done if the weather is hot."

"What are you going to do now?" asked Miss Laura, jumping up.

"Oh! more sheep business. I've set out some young trees in the orchard, and unless I get chicken wire around them, my sheep will be barking them for me."

"I've seen them," said Miss Laura, "standing up on their hind legs and nibbling at the trees, taking off every shoot they can reach."

"They don't hurt the old trees," said Mr. Wood; "but the young ones have to be protected. It pays me to take care of my fruit trees, for I get a splendid crop from them, thanks to the sheep."

"Good-bye, little lambs and dear old sheep," said Miss Laura, as her uncle opened the gate for her to leave the pasture. "I'll come and see you again some time. Now, you had better go down to the brook in the dingle and have a drink. You look hot in your warm coats."

"You've mastered one detail of sheep-keeping," said Mr. Wood, as he slowly walked along beside his niece. "To raise healthy sheep one must have pure water where they can get to it whenever they like. Give them good water, good food, and a variety of it, good quarters—cool in summer, comfortable in winter, and keep them quiet, and you'll make them happy and make money on them."

"I think I'd like sheep-raising," said Miss Laura; "won't you have me for your flock mistress, uncle?"

He laughed, and said he thought not, for she would cry every time any of her charge were sent to the butcher.

After this Miss Laura and I often went up to the pasture to see the sheep and the lambs. We used to get into a shady place where they could not see us, and watch them. One day I got a great surprise about the sheep. I had heard so much about their meekness that I never dreamed that they would fight; but it turned out that they did, and they went about it in such a business-like way, that I could not help smiling at them. I suppose that like most other animals they had a spice of wickedness in them. On this day a quarrel arose between two sheep; but instead of running at each other like two dogs they went a long distance apart, and then came rushing at each other with lowered heads. Their object seemed to be to break each other's skull; but Miss Laura soon stopped them by calling out and frightening them apart. I thought that the lambs were more interesting than the sheep. Sometimes they fed quietly by their mothers' sides, and at other times they all huddled together on the top of some flat rock or in a bare place, and seemed to be talking to each other with their heads close together. Suddenly one would jump down, and start for the bushes or the other side of the pasture. They would all follow pell-mell; then in a few minutes they would come rushing back again. It was pretty to see them playing together and having a good time before the sorrowful day of their death came.[1]

---

1 Along with Joe's momentary sympathy for Bruno in Chapter 17, this
key line is one of a few instances in which the novel suggests that there
is also cruelty in ending an animal life, humanely or not.

CHAPTER 30

A JEALOUS OX

MR. WOOD had a dozen calves that he was raising, and Miss Laura sometimes went up to the stable to see them. Each calf was in a crib, and it was fed with milk. They had gentle, patient faces, and beautiful eyes, and looked very meek, as they stood quietly gazing about them, or sucking away at their milk. They reminded me of big, gentle dogs.

I never got a very good look at them in their cribs, but one day when they were old enough to be let out, I went up with Miss Laura to the yard where they were kept. Such queer, ungainly, large-boned creatures they were, and such a good time they were having, running and jumping and throwing up their heels.

Mrs. Wood was with us, and she said that it was not good for calves to be closely penned after they got to be a few weeks old. They were better for getting out and having a frolic. She stood beside Miss Laura for a long time, watching the calves, and laughing a great deal at their awkward gambols. They wanted to play, but they did not seem to know how to use their limbs.

They were lean calves, and Miss Laura asked her aunt why all the nice milk they had taken had not made them fat. "The fat will come all in good time," said Mrs. Wood. "A fat calf makes a poor cow, and a fat, small calf isn't profitable or fit for sending to the butcher. It's better to have a bony one and fatten it. If you come here next summer, you'll see a fine show of young cattle, with fat sides, and big, open horns, and a good coat of hair. Can you imagine," she went on, indignantly, "that any one could be cruel enough to torture such a harmless creature as a calf?"

"No, indeed," replied Miss Laura. "Who has been doing it?"

"Who has been doing it?" repeated Mrs. Wood, bitterly; "they are doing it all the time. Do you know what makes the nice, white veal one gets in big cities? The calves are bled to death. They linger for hours, and moan their lives away. The first time I heard it, I was so angry that I cried for a day, and made John promise that he'd never send another animal of his to a big city to be killed. That's why all of our stock goes to Hoytville, and small country places. Oh, those big cities are awful places, Laura. It seems to me that it makes people wicked to huddle them together. I'd rather live in a desert than a city. There's Ch—o. Every night since I've been there I pray to the Lord either to change the hearts of some of the wicked people in it, or to destroy them off the face of the earth. You know three years ago I got run down, and your uncle said I'd got to have a change, so he sent me off to my brother's in Ch—o. I stayed and enjoyed myself pretty well, for it is a wonderful city, till one day some Western men came in, who had been visiting the slaughter houses outside the city. I sat and listened to their talk, and it seemed to me that I was hearing the description of a great battle. These men were cattle dealers, and had been sending stock to Ch—o, and they were furious that men, in their rage for wealth, would so utterly ignore and trample on all decent and humane feelings as to torture animals as the Ch—o men were doing.[1]

"It is too dreadful to repeat the sights they saw. I listened till they were describing Texan steers kicking in agony under the torture that was practised, and then I gave a loud scream, and fainted dead away. They had to send for your uncle, and he brought me home, and for days and days I heard nothing but shouting and swearing, and saw animals dripping with blood, and crying and moaning in their anguish, and now, Laura, if you'd lay down a bit of Ch—o meat, and cover it with gold, I'd spurn it from me. But what am I saying? you're as white as a sheet. Come and see the cow stable. John's just had it whitewashed."

Miss Laura took her aunt's arm, and I walked slowly behind them. The cow stable was a long building, well-built, and with no chinks in the walls, as Jenkins's stable had. There were large windows where the afternoon sun came streaming in, and a number of ventilators, and a great many stalls. A pipe of water ran through the stalls from one end of the stable to the other. The floor was covered with sawdust and leaves, and the ceiling and tops of the walls were whitewashed. Mrs. Wood said that her husband would not have the walls a glare of white right down to the floor, because he thought it injured the animals' eyes. So the lower parts of the walls were stained a dark, brown color.

---

1   In 1865, the Union Stock Yard centralized the livestock markets in Chicago to process the cattle from the west for consumption in the east (Pacyga 153). The largest livestock market in the world, during its first year, 1.5 million animals were processed in Chicago, ushering in what would become the era of mass animal production. By 1900, the number surged to 14.6 million animals (Pacyga 154). A group of Chicago women, unable to work with the male-led Illinois Humane Society in 1899, established the Anti-Cruelty Society—with a woman as its president—and directed much of their efforts to address Chicago's infamous slaughtering methods (Beers 56, Hubbard 17).

There were doors at each end of the stable, and just now they stood open, and a gentle breeze was blowing through, but Mrs. Wood said that when the cattle stood in the stalls, both doors were never allowed to be open at the same time. Mr. Wood was most particular to have no drafts blowing upon his cattle. He would not have them chilled, and he would not have them over-heated. One thing was as bad as the other. And during the winter, they were never allowed to drink icy water. He took the chill off the water for his cows, just as Mrs. Wood did for her hens.

"You know, Laura," Mrs. Wood went on, "that when cows are kept dry and warm, they eat less than when they are cold and wet. They are so warm-blooded that if they are cold, they have to eat a great deal to keep up the heat of their bodies, so it pays better to house and feed them well. They like quiet too. I never knew that till I married your uncle. On our farm, the boys always shouted and screamed at the cows when they were driving them, and sometimes they made them run. They're never allowed to do that here."

"I have noticed how quiet this farm seems," said Miss Laura. "You have so many men about, and yet there is so little noise."

"Your uncle whistles a great deal," said Mrs. Wood. "Have you noticed that? He whistles when he's about his work, and then he has a calling whistle that nearly all of the animals know, and the men run when they hear it. You'd see every cow in this stable turn its head, if he whistled in a certain way outside. He says that he got into the way of doing it when he was a boy and went for his father's cows. He trained them so that he'd just stand in the pasture and whistle, and they'd come to him. I believe the first thing that inclined me to him, was his clear, happy whistle. I'd hear him from our house away down on the road, jogging along with his cart, or driving in his buggy. He says there is no need of screaming at any animal. It only frightens and angers them. They will mind much better if you speak clearly and distinctly. He says there is only one thing an animal hates more than to be shouted at, and that's to be crept on—to have a person sneak up to it and startle it. John says many a man is kicked, because he comes up to his horse like a thief. A startled animal's first instinct is to defend itself. A dog will spring at you, and a horse will let his heels fly. John always speaks or whistles to let the stock know when he's approaching."

"Where is uncle this afternoon?" asked Miss Laura.

"Oh, up to his eyes in hay. He's even got one of the oxen harnessed to a hay cart."

"I wonder whether it's Duke?" said Miss Laura.

"Yes, it is. I saw the star on his forehead," replied Mrs. Wood.

"I don't know when I have laughed at anything as much as I did at him the other day," said Miss Laura. "Uncle asked me if I had ever heard of such a thing as a jealous ox, and I said no. He said, 'Come to the barnyard, and I'll show you one.' The oxen were both there, Duke with his broad face, and Bright so much sharper and more intelligent looking. Duke was drinking at the trough there, and uncle said: 'Just look at him. Isn't he a great, fat, self-satisfied creature, and doesn't he look as if he thought the world owed him a living, and he ought to get it?' Then he got the card and went up to Bright, and began scratching him. Duke lifted his head from the trough, and stared at uncle, who paid no attention to him but went on carding Bright, and stroking and petting him. Duke looked so angry. He left the trough, and with the water dripping from his lips, went up to uncle, and gave him a push with his horns. Still uncle took no notice, and Duke almost pushed him over. Then uncle left off petting Bright, and turned to him. He said Duke would have treated him roughly, if he hadn't. I never saw a creature look as satisfied as Duke did, when uncle began to card him. Bright didn't seem to care, and only gazed calmly at them."

"I've seen Duke do that again and again," said Mrs. Wood. "He's the most jealous animal that we have, and it makes him perfectly miserable to have your uncle pay attention to any animal but him. What queer creatures these dumb brutes are. They're pretty much like us in most ways. They're jealous and resentful, and they can love or hate equally well—and forgive, too, for that matter; and suffer—how they can suffer, and so patiently, too. Where is the human being that would put up with the tortures that animals endure and yet come out so patient?"

"Nowhere," said Miss Laura, in a low voice; "we couldn't do it."

"And there doesn't seem to be an animal," Mrs. Wood went on, "no matter how ugly and repulsive it is, but what has some lovable qualities. I have just been reading about some sewer rats, Louise Michel's rats—"

"Who is she?" asked Miss Laura.

"A celebrated Frenchwoman, my dear child, 'the priestess of pity and vengeance,' Mr. Stead calls her. You are too young to know about her but I remember reading of her in 1872, during the Commune troubles in France. She is an anarchist, and she used to wear a uniform, and shoulder a rifle, and help to build barricades. She was arrested and sent as a convict to one of the French penal colonies. She has a most wonderful love for animals in her heart, and when she went home she took four cats with her. She was put into prison again in France and took the cats with her. Rats came about her cell and she petted them and taught her cats to be kind to them. Before she got the cats thoroughly drilled one of them bit a rat's paw. Louise nursed the rat till it got well, then let it down by a string from her window. It went back to its sewer, and, I suppose, told the other rats how kind Louise had been to it, for after that they came to her cell without fear. Mother rats brought their young ones and placed them at her feet, as if to ask her protection for them. The most remarkable thing about them was their affection for each other. Young rats would chew the crusts thrown to old toothless rats, so that they might more easily eat them, and if a young rat dared help itself before an old one, the others punished it."

"That sounds very interesting, auntie," said Miss Laura. "Where did you read it?"

"I have just got the magazine," said Mrs. Wood; "you shall have it as soon as you come into the house."

"I love to be with you, dear auntie," said Miss Laura, putting her arm affectionately around her, as they stood in the doorway; "because you understand me when I talk about animals. I can't explain it," went on my dear young mistress, laying her hand on her heart, "the feeling I have here for them. I just love a dumb creature, and I want to stop and talk to every one I see. Sometimes I worry poor Bessie Drury, and I'm so sorry, but I can't help it. She says, 'What makes you so silly, Laura?'"

Miss Laura was standing just where the sunlight shone through her light-brown hair, and made her face all in a glow. I thought she looked more beautiful than I had ever seen her before, and I think Mrs. Wood thought the same. She turned around and put both hands on Miss Laura's shoulders. "Laura," she said, earnestly, "there are enough cold hearts in the world. Don't you ever stifle a warm or tender feeling toward a dumb creature. That is your chief attraction, my child: your love for everything that breathes and moves. Tear out the selfishness from your heart, if there is any there, but let the love and pity stay. And now let me talk a little more to you about the cows. I want to interest you in dairy matters. This stable is new since you were here, and we've made a number of improvements. Do you see those bits of rock salt in each stall? They are for the cows to lick whenever they want to. Now, come here, and I'll show you what we call 'The Black Hole.'"

It was a tiny stable off the main one, and it was very dark and cool. "Is this a place of punishment?" asked Miss Laura, in surprise.

Mrs. Wood laughed heartily. "No, no; a place of pleasure. Sometimes when the flies are very bad and the cows are brought into the yard to be milked and a fresh swarm settles on them, they are nearly frantic; and though they are the best cows in New Hampshire, they will kick a little. When they do, those that are the worst are brought in here to be milked where there are no flies. The others have big strips of cotton laid over their backs and tied under them, and the men brush their legs with tansy tea, or water with a little carbolic acid in it. That keeps the flies away, and the cows know just as well that it is done for their comfort, and stand quietly till the milking is over. I must ask John to have their nightdresses put on sometime for you to see. Harry calls them 'sheeted ghosts,' and they do look queer enough standing all round the barnyard robed in white."

CHAPTER 31

IN THE COW STABLE

"ISN'T it a strange thing," said Miss Laura, "that a little thing like a fly, can cause so much annoyance to animals as well to people? Sometimes when I am trying to get more sleep in the morning, their little feet tickle me so that I am nearly frantic and have to fly out of bed."

"You shall have some netting to put over your bed," said Mrs. Wood; "but suppose, Laura, you had no hands to brush away the flies. Suppose your whole body was covered with them, and you were tied up somewhere and could not get loose. I can't imagine more exquisite torture myself. Last summer, the flies here were dreadful. It seems to me that they are getting worse and worse every year, and worry the animals more. I believe it is because the birds are getting thinned out all over the country. There are not enough of them to catch the flies. John says that the next improvements we make on the farm are to be wire gauze at all the stable windows and screen doors to keep the little pests from the horses and cattle.

"One afternoon last summer, Mr. Maxwell's mother came for me to go for a drive with her. The heat was intense, and when we got down by the river, she proposed getting out of the phaeton and sitting under the trees, to see if it would be any cooler. She was driving a horse that she had got from the hotel in the village, a roan horse that was clipped, and check-reined, and had his tail docked. I wouldn't drive behind a tailless horse now. Then, I wasn't so particular. However, I made her unfasten the check-rein before I'd set foot in the carriage. Well, I thought that horse would go mad. He'd tremble and shiver, and look so pitifully at us. The flies were nearly eating him up. Then he'd start a little. Mrs. Maxwell had a weight at his head to hold him, but he could easily have dragged that. He was a good dispositioned horse, and he didn't want to run away, but he could not stand still. I soon jumped up and slapped him, and rubbed him till my hands were dripping wet. The poor brute was so grateful, and would keep touching my arm with his nose. Mrs. Maxwell sat under the trees fanning herself and laughing at me, but I didn't care. How could I enjoy myself with a dumb creature writhing in pain before me? "A docked horse can neither eat nor sleep comfortably in the fly season. In one of our New England villages they have a sign up, 'Horses taken in to grass. Long tails, one dollar and fifty cents.

Short tails, one dollar.' And it just means that the short-tailed ones are taken on cheaper, because they are so bothered by the flies that they can't eat much, while the long-tailed ones are able to brush them away and eat in peace. I read the other day of a Buffalo coal dealer's horse that was in such an agony through flies, that he committed suicide. You know animals will do that. I've read of horses and dogs drowning themselves. This horse had been clipped and his tail was docked, and he was turned out to graze. The flies stung him till he was nearly crazy. He ran up to a picket fence, and sprang up on the sharp spikes. There he hung, making no effort to get down. Some men saw him, and they said it was a clear case of suicide.

"I would like to have the power to take every man who cuts off a horse's tail, and tie his hands, and turn him out in a field in the hot sun, with little clothing on, and plenty of flies about. Then we would see if he wouldn't sympathize with the poor dumb beast. It's the most senseless thing in the world, this docking fashion. They've a few flimsy arguments about a horse with a docked tail being stronger-backed, like a short-tailed sheep, but I don't believe a word of it. The horse was made strong enough to do the work he's got to do, and man can't improve on him. Docking is a cruel, wicked thing. Now, there's a ghost of an argument in favor of check-reins, on certain occasions. A fiery, young horse can't run away, with an overdrawn check, and in speeding horses a tight check-rein will make them hold their heads up, and keep them from choking. But I don't believe in raising colts in a way to make them fiery, and I wish there wasn't a race horse on the face of the earth, so if it depended on me, every kind of check-rein would go. It's pity we women can't vote, Laura. We'd do away with a good many abuses."[1]

Miss Laura smiled, but it was a very faint, almost an unhappy smile, and Mrs. Wood said hastily, "Let us talk about something else. Did you ever hear that cows will give less milk on a dark day than on a bright one?"

---

1   Along with other progressive movements of the period—temperance, labor, child welfare—the humane movement provided opportunities for white, middle-class women to exert increasing amounts of influence. Women were considered more fit than men for "moral" and pedagogical work, and with that license they took on powers that went beyond the traditional feminine sphere of their own homes. Suffrage seemed the next logical step in extending that moral influence, but women in the US could not vote until the Nineteenth Amendment (1920).

"No, I never did," said Miss Laura.

"Well, they do. They are most sensitive animals. One finds out all manner of things about animals if he makes a study of them. Cows are wonderful creatures, I think, and so grateful for good usage that they return every scrap of care given them, with interest. Have you ever heard anything about dehorning, Laura?"

"Not much, auntie. Does uncle approve?"

"No, indeed. He'd just as soon think of cutting their tails off, as of dehorning them. He says he guesses the Creator knew how to make a cow better than he does. Sometimes I tell John that his argument doesn't hold good, for a man in some ways can improve on nature. In the natural course of things, a cow would be feeding her calf for half a year, but we take it away from her, raise it as well as she could and get an extra quantity of milk from her in addition. I don't know what to think myself about dehorning. Mr. Windham's cattle are all polled, and he has an open space in his barn for them, instead of keeping them in stalls, and he says they're more comfortable and not so confined. I suppose in sending cattle to sea, it's necessary to take their horns off, but when they're going to be turned out to grass, it seems like mutilating them. Our cows couldn't keep the dogs away from the sheep if they didn't have their horns. Their horns are their means of defense."

"Do your cattle stand in these stalls all winter?" asked Miss Laura.

"Oh, yes, except when they're turned out in the barnyard, and then John usually has to send a man to keep them moving or they'd take cold. Sometimes on very fine days they get out all day. You know cows aren't like horses. John says they're like great milk machines.[1] You've got to keep them quiet, only exercising enough to keep them in health. If a cow is hurried or worried, or chilled

---

1   The Woods's micromanagement reflects the evolving mentality of using science to maximize farmers' efficiency and productivity. By the 1920s, Purina, a major producer of animal feed, developed a "Calf Chow" that contained 27.7% digestible protein, most of which came from "blood flour." Also known as "blood meal," this key ingredient was, in short, the dried blood of slaughtered animals, producing a feed that Purina proclaimed was "a perfect whole milk *equivalent* in every way" ("Purina Calf Chow. Advertisement."). The mother cow, in the meantime, was conceived of as the *equivalent* of a "Milk Factory," in need of "a steady stream of the proper raw materials ... to manufacture into finished products" (*Purina Cow Book: The A-B-C of Milk Making* 24).

or heated, it stops her milk yield. And bad usage poisons it. John says you can't take a stick and strike a cow across the back, without her milk being that much worse, and as for drinking the milk that comes from a cow that isn't kept clean, you'd better throw it away and drink water. When I was in Chicago, my sister-in-law kept complaining to her milkman about what she called the 'cowy' smell to her milk. 'It's the animal odor, ma'am,' he said, 'and it can't be helped. All milk smells like that.' 'It's dirt,' I said, when she asked my opinion about it. 'I'll wager my best bonnet that that man's cows are kept dirty. Their skins are plastered up with filth and as the poison in them can't escape that way, it's coming out through the milk, and you're helping to dispose of it.' She was astonished to hear this, and she got her milkman's address, and one day dropped in upon him. She said that these cows were standing in a stable that was comparatively clean, but that their bodies were in just the state that I described them as living in. She advised the man to card and brush his cows every day, and said that he need bring her no more milk.

"That shows how you city people are imposed upon with regard to your milk. I should think you'd be poisoned with the treatment your cows receive; and even when your milk is examined you can't tell whether it is pure or not. In New York the law only requires thirteen per cent. of solids in milk. That's absurd, for you can feed a cow on swill and still get fourteen per cent. of solids in it. Oh! you city people are queer."

Miss Laura laughed heartily. "What a prejudice you have against large towns, auntie."

"Yes, I have," said Mrs. Wood, honestly. "I often wish we could break up a few of our cities, and scatter the people through the country. Look at the lovely farms all about here, some of them with only an old man and woman on them. The boys are off to the cities, slaving in stores and offices, and growing pale and sickly. It would have broken my heart if Harry had taken to city ways. I had a plain talk with your uncle when I married him, and said, 'Now my boy's only a baby and I want him to be brought up so that he will love country life. How are we going to manage it?'

"Your uncle looked at me with a sly twinkle in his eye, and said I was a pretty fair specimen of a country girl, suppose we brought up Harry the way I'd been brought up. I knew he was only joking, yet I got quite excited. 'Yes,' I said, 'Do as my father and mother did. Have a farm about twice as large as you can manage. Don't keep a hired man. Get up at daylight and slave till dark. Never take a holiday. Have the girls do the housework, and take care of the hens, and help pick the fruit, and make the boys tend the colts and the calves, and put all the money they make in the bank. Don't take any papers, or they would waste their time reading them, and it's too far to go to the post office oftener than once a week; and'—but I don't remember the rest of what I said. Anyway your uncle burst into a roar of laughter. 'Hattie,' he said, 'my farm's too big. I'm going to sell some of it, and enjoy myself a little more.' That very week he sold fifty acres, and he hired an extra man, and got me a good girl, and twice a week he left his work in the afternoon, and took me for a drive. Harry held the reins in his tiny fingers, and John told him that Dolly, the old mare we were driving, should be called his, and the very next horse he bought should be called his, too, and he should name it and have it for his own; and he would give him five sheep, and he should have his own bank book, and keep his accounts; and Harry understood, mere baby though he was, and from that day he loved John as his own father. If my father had had the wisdom that John has, his boys wouldn't be the one a poor lawyer and the other a poor doctor in two different cities; and our farm wouldn't be in the hands of strangers. It makes me sick to go there. I think of my poor mother lying with her red hands crossed out in the churchyard, and the boys so far away, and my father always hurrying and driving us—I can tell you, Laura, the thing cuts both ways. It isn't all the fault of the boys that they leave the country."

Mrs. Wood was silent for a little while after she made this long speech, and Miss Laura said nothing. I took a turn or two up and down the stable, thinking of many things. No matter how happy human beings seem to be, they always have something to worry them. I was sorry for Mrs. Wood for her face had lost the happy look it usually wore. However, she soon forgot her trouble, and said:

"Now, I must go and get the tea. This is Adèle's afternoon out."

"I'll come, too," said Miss Laura, "for I promised her I'd make the biscuits for tea this evening and let you rest." They both sauntered slowly down the plank walk to the house, and I followed them.

CHAPTER 32

OUR RETURN HOME

IN October, the most beautiful of all the months, we were obliged to go back to Fairport. Miss Laura could not bear to leave the farm, and her face got very sorrowful when any one spoke of her going away. Still, she had gotten well and strong, and was as brown as a berry, and she said that she knew she ought to go home, and get back to her lessons.

Mr. Wood called October the golden month. Everything was quiet and still, and at night and in the morning the sun had a yellow, misty look. The trees in the orchard were loaded with fruit, and some of the leaves were floating down, making a soft covering on the ground.

In the garden there were a great many flowers in bloom, in flaming red and yellow colors. Miss Laura gathered bunches of them every day to put in the parlor. One day when she was arranging them, she said, regretfully, "They will soon be gone. I wish it could always be summer."

"You would get tired of it," said Mr. Harry, who had come up softly behind her. "There's only one place where we could stand perpetual summer, and that's in heaven."

"Do you suppose that it will always be summer there?" said Miss Laura, turning around, and looking at him.

"I don't know. I imagine it will be, but I don't think anybody knows much about it. We've got to wait."

Miss Laura's eyes fell on me. "Harry," she said, "do you think that dumb animals will go to heaven?"

"I shall have to say again, I don't know," he replied. "Some people hold that they do. In a Michigan paper, the other day, I came across one writer's opinion on the subject. He says that among the best people of all ages have been some who believed in the future life of animals. Homer and the later Greeks, some of the Romans and early Christians held this view—the last believing that God sent angels in the shape of birds to comfort sufferers for the faith. St. Francis called the birds and beasts his brothers. Dr. Johnson believed in a future life for animals, as also did Wordsworth, Shelley, Coleridge, Jeremy Taylor, Agassiz, Lamartine, and many Christian scholars.[1] It seems as if they ought to

---

1 In the Catholic tradition, St. Francis is the patron saint of animals.
Saunders names an impressive list of writers (William Words- *(continued)*

Animal religion?

have some compensation for their terrible sufferings in this world. Then to go to heaven, animals would only have to take up the thread of their lives here. Man is a god to the lower creation. Joe worships you, much as you worship your Maker. Dumb animals live in and for their masters. They hang on our words and looks, and are dependent on us in almost every way. For my own part, and looking at it from an earthly point of view, I wish with all my heart that we may find our dumb friends in paradise."

"And in the Bible," said Miss Laura, "animals are often spoken of. The dove and the raven, the wolf and the lamb, and the leopard, and the cattle that God says are his, and the little sparrow that can't fall to the ground without our Father's knowing it."

"Still, there's nothing definite about their immortality," said Mr. Harry. "However, we've got nothing to do with that. If it's right for them to be in heaven, we'll find them there. All we have to do now is to deal with the present, and the Bible plainly tells us that 'a righteous man regardeth the life of his beast.'"

"I think I would be happier in heaven if dear old Joe were there," said Miss Laura, looking wistfully at me. "He has been such a good dog. Just think how he has loved and protected me. I think I should be lonely without him."

"That reminds me of some poetry, or rather doggerel," said Mr. Harry, "that I cut out of a newspaper for you yesterday," and he drew from his pocket a little slip of paper, and read this:

> "Do doggies gang to heaven, Dad?
>   Will oor auld Donald gang?
> For noo to tak' him, faither wi' us,
>   Wad be maist awfu' wrang."

There was a number of other verses, telling how many kind things old Donald the dog had done for his master's family, and then it closed with these lines:

> "Withoot are dogs. Eh, faither, man,
>   'Twould be an awfu' sin
> To leave oor faithfu' doggie *there*,
>   He's *certain* to win in.

worth, Percy Bysshe Shelley, Alphonse de Lamartine), clergymen (Jeremy Taylor), and scientists (Louis Agassiz) who expressed sentiments favorable to animals, though none of the named men would have considered themselves a part of the animal protection movement.

"Oor Donald's no like ither dogs,
    He'll *no* be lockit oot,
If Donald's no let into heaven,
    I'll no gang there one foot."[1]

"My sentiments exactly," said a merry voice behind Miss Laura and Mr. Harry, and looking up they saw Mr. Maxwell. He was holding out one hand to them, and in the other kept back a basket of large pears that Mr. Harry promptly took from him, and offered to Miss Laura. "I've been dependent upon animals for the most part of my comfort in this life," said Mr. Maxwell, "and I sha'n't be happy without them in heaven. I don't see how you would get on without Joe, Miss Morris, and I want my birds, and my snake, and my horse—how can I live without them? They're almost all my life here."

"If some animals go to heaven and not others, I think that the dog has the first claim," said Miss Laura. "He's the friend of man—the oldest and best. Have you ever heard the legend about him and Adam?"

"No," said Mr. Maxwell.

"Well, when Adam was turned out of paradise, all the animals shunned him, and he sat bitterly weeping with his head between his hands, when he felt the soft tongue of some creature gently touching him. He took his hands from his face, and there was a dog that had separated himself from all the other animals, and was trying to comfort him. He became the chosen friend and companion of Adam, afterward of all men."

"There is another legend," said Mr. Harry, "about our Saviour and a dog. Have you ever heard it?"

"We'll tell you that later," said Mr. Maxwell, "when we know what it is."

---

1 The question of whether animals had souls and were capable of going to Heaven was earnestly debated by clergymen and philosophers alike. See, for example, Joseph Hamilton, *Animal Futurity: A Plea for the Immortality of the Brutes* (Belfast: C. Aitchison, 1877), J. Frewen Moor, *The Future State of Animals* (Winchester: Warren & Son, 1889), and Thomas G. Gentry, *Life and Immortality, or, Soul of Animals Mortal or Immortal?* (Philadelphia: Burk & McFetridge, 1897). Saunders's own view is evident from the 1902 sequel to this novel, *Beautiful Joe's Paradise* (see Appendix E1, p. 297, for excerpt), which she wrote shortly after a favorite dog died. While she does not claim that animals have souls, she does suggest that they have some sort of afterlife, and that they are reunited with their human masters when they follow in death.

Mr. Harry showed his white teeth in an amused smile, and began: "Once upon a time our Lord was going through a town with his disciples. A dead dog lay by the wayside, and every one that passed along flung some offensive epithet at him. Eastern dogs are not like our dogs, and seemingly there was nothing good about this loathsome creature, but as our Saviour went by, he said, gently, 'Pearls cannot equal the whiteness of his teeth.'"

"What was the name of that old fellow," said Mr. Maxwell, abruptly, "who had a beautiful swan that came every day for fifteen years, to bury its head in his bosom and feed from his hand, and would go near no other human being?"

"Saint Hugh, of Lincoln. We heard about him at the Band of Mercy the other day," said Miss Laura.

"I should think that he would have wanted to have that swan in heaven with him," said Mr. Maxwell. "What a beautiful creature it must have been. Speaking about animals going to heaven, I dare say some of them would object to going, on account of the company that they would meet there. Think of the dog kicked to death by his master, the horse driven into his grave, the thousands of cattle starved to death on the plains—will they want to meet their owners in heaven?"

"According to my reckoning, their owners won't be there," said Mr. Harry. "I firmly believe that the Lord will punish every man or woman who ill-treats a dumb creature just as surely as he will punish those who ill-treat their fellow-creatures. If a man's life has been a long series of cruelty to dumb animals, do you suppose that he would enjoy himself in heaven, which will be full of kindness to every one? Not he, he'd rather be in the other place, and there he'll go, I fully believe."

"When you've quite disposed of all your fellow-creatures and the dumb creation, Harry, perhaps you will condescend to go out into the orchard and see how your father is getting on with picking the apples," said Mrs. Wood, joining Miss Laura and the two young men, her eyes twinkling and sparkling with amusement.

"The apples will keep, mother," said Mr. Harry, putting his arm around her. "I just came in for a moment to get Laura. Come, Maxwell, we'll all go."

"And not another word about animals," Mrs. Wood called after them. "Laura will go crazy some day, through thinking of their sufferings, if some one doesn't do something to stop her."

Miss Laura turned around suddenly. "Dear Aunt Hattie," she said, "you must not say that. I am a coward, I know, about hearing of animals' pains, but I must get over it. I want to know how they suffer. I *ought* to know, for when I get to be a woman, I am going to do all I can to help them."

"And I'll join you," said Mr. Maxwell, stretching out his hand to Miss Laura. She did not smile, but looking very earnestly at him, she held it clasped in her own. "You will help me to care for them, will you?" she said.

"Yes, I promise," he said, gravely. "I'll give myself to the service of dumb animals, if you will."

"And I too," said Mr. Harry, in his deep voice, laying his hand across theirs. Mrs. Wood stood looking at their three fresh, eager, young faces, with tears in her eyes. Just as they all stood silently for an instant, the old village clergyman came into the room from the hall. He must have heard what they said, for before they could move he had laid his hands on their three brown heads. "Bless you, my children," he said, "God will lift up the light of his countenance upon you, for you have given yourselves to a noble work. In serving dumb creatures, you are ennobling the human race."

Then he sat down in a chair and looked at them. He was a venerable old man, and had long, white hair, and the Woods thought a great deal of him. He had come to get Mrs. Wood to make some nourishing dishes for a sick woman in the village, and while he was talking to her, Miss Laura and the two young men went out of the house. They hurried across the veranda and over the lawn, talking and laughing, and enjoying themselves as only happy young people can, and with not a trace of their seriousness of a few moments before on their faces.

They were going so fast that they ran right into a flock of geese that were coming up the lane. They were driven by a little boy called Tommy, the son of one of Mr. Wood's farm laborers, and they were chattering and gabbling, and seemed very angry. "What's all this about?" said Mr. Harry, stopping and looking at the boy. "What's the matter with your feathered charges, Tommy, my lad?"

"If it's the geese you mean," said the boy, half crying and looking very much put out, "it's all them nasty potatoes. They won't keep away from them."

"So the potatoes chase the geese, do they?" said Mr. Maxwell, teasingly.

"No, no," said the child, pettishly; "Mr. Wood he sets me to watch the geese, and they runs in among the buckwheat and the potatoes, and I tries to drive them out, and they doesn't want to come, and," shamefacedly, "I has to switch their feet, and I hates to do it, 'cause I'm a Band of Mercy boy."

"Tommy, my son," said Mr. Maxwell, solemnly "you will go right to heaven when you die, and your geese will go with you."

"Hush, hush," said Miss Laura; "don't tease him," and putting her arm on the child's shoulder, she said, "You are a good boy, Tommy, not to want to hurt the geese. Let me see your switch, dear."

He showed her a little stick he had in his hand, and she said, "I don't think you could hurt them much with that, and if they will be naughty and steal the potatoes, you have to drive them out. Take some of my pears and eat them, and you will forget your trouble." The child took the fruit, and Miss Laura and the two young men went on their way, smiling, and looking over their shoulders at Tommy, who stood in the lane, devouring his pears and keeping one eye on the geese that had gathered a little in front of him, and were gabbling noisily and having a kind of indignation meeting, because they had been driven out of the potato field.

Tommy's father and mother lived in a little house down near the road. Mr. Wood never had his hired men live in his own house. He had two small houses for them to live in, and they were required to keep them as neat as Mr. Wood's own house was kept. He said that he didn't see why he should keep a boarding house, if he was a farmer, nor why his wife should wear herself out waiting on strong, hearty men, that had just as soon take care of themselves. He wished to have his own family about him, and it was better for his men to have some kind of family life for themselves. If one of his men was unmarried, he boarded with the married one, but slept in his own house.

On this October day we found Mr. Wood hard at work under the fruit trees. He had a good many different kind of apples. Enormous red ones, and long, yellow ones that they called pippins, and little brown ones, and smooth-coated sweet ones, and bright red ones, and others, more than I could mention. Miss Laura often pared one and cut off little bits for me, for I always wanted to eat whatever I saw her eating.

Just a few days after this, Miss Laura and I returned to Fairport, and some of Mr. Wood's apples traveled along with us, for he sent a good many to the Boston market. Mr. and Mrs. Wood came to the station to see us off. Mr. Harry could not come, for he had left Riverdale the day before to go back to his college. Mrs. Wood said that she would be very lonely without her two young people, and she kissed Miss Laura over and over again, and made her promise to come back again the next summer.

I was put in a box in the express car, and Mr. Wood told the agent that if he knew what was good for him he would speak to me occasionally, for I was a very knowing dog, and if he didn't treat me well, I'd be apt to write him up in the newspapers. The agent laughed, and quite often on the way to Fairport, he came to my box and spoke kindly to me. So I did not get so lonely and frightened as I did on my way to Riverdale.

How glad the Morrises were to see us coming back. The boys had all gotten home before us, and such a fuss as they did make over their sister. They loved her dearly, and never wanted her to be long away from them. I was rubbed and stroked, and had to run about offering my paw to every one. Jim and little Billy licked my face, and Bella croaked out, "Glad to see you, Joe. Had a good time? How's your health?"

We soon settled down for the winter. Miss Laura began going to school, and came home every day with a pile of books under her arm. The summer in the country had done her so much good that her mother often looked at her fondly, and said the white-faced child she sent away had come home a nut-brown maid.

CHAPTER 33

PERFORMING ANIMALS

A WEEK or two after we got home, I heard the Morris boys talking about an Italian who was coming to Fairport with a troupe of trained animals, and I could see for myself, whenever I went to town, great flaming pictures on the fences, of monkeys sitting at tables, dogs and ponies, and goats climbing ladders, and rolling balls, and doing various tricks. I wondered very much whether they would be able to do all those extraordinary things, but it turned out that they did.

The Italian's name was Bellini, and one afternoon the whole Morris family went to see him and his animals, and when they came home, I heard them talking about it.[1] "I wish you could have been there, Joe," said Jack, pulling up my paws to rest on his knees. "Now listen, old fellow, and I'll tell you all about it. First of all, there was a perfect jam in the town hall. I sat up in front, with a lot of fellows, and had a splendid view. The old Italian came out dressed in his best suit of clothes—black broadcloth, flower in his buttonhole, and so on. He made a fine bow, and he said he was 'pleased too see ze fine audience, and he was going to show zem ze fine animals, ze finest animals in ze world.' Then he shook a little whip that he carried in his hand, and he said 'zat zat whip didn't mean zat he was cruel. He cracked it to show his animals when to begin, end, or change their tricks.' Some boy yelled, 'Rats! you do whip them sometimes,' and the old man made another bow, and said, 'Sairteenly, he whipped zem just as ze mammas whip ze naughty boys, to make zem keep still when zey was noisy or stubborn.'

"Then everybody laughed at the boy, and the Italian said the performance would begin by a grand procession of all the animals, if some lady would kindly step up to the piano and play

---

1 While Saunders seems to approve of using animals for entertainment, Henry Bergh—the founder of the first animal protection society in the US—repeatedly attacked P.T. Barnum for the way he handled animals in his circus. Both men appreciated the value of publicity, defending their positions via the popular periodicals of the day. In his autobiography, Barnum eventually expressed his "admiration" of Bergh's work, and quotes a published 1885 letter from Bergh wherein Bergh describes Barnum as "one of the most humane and kind-hearted men living" (Barnum 323, 351).

a march. Nina Smith—you know Nina, Joe, the girl that has black eyes and wears blue ribbons, and lives around the corner—stepped up to the piano, and banged out a fine loud march. The doors at the side of the platform opened, and out came the animals, two by two, just like Noah's ark. There was a pony with a monkey walking beside it and holding on to its mane, another monkey on a pony's back, two monkeys hand in hand, a dog with a parrot on his back, a goat harnessed to a little carriage, another goat carrying a birdcage in its mouth with two canaries inside, different kinds of cats, some doves and pigeons, half a dozen white rats with red harness, and dragging a little chariot with a monkey in it, and a common white gander that came in last of all, and did nothing but follow one of the ponies about.

"The Italian spoke of the gander, and said it was a stupid creature, and could learn no tricks and he only kept it on account of its affection for the pony. He had got them both on a Vermont farm, when he was looking for show animals. The pony's master had made a pet of him, and had taught him to come whenever he whistled for him. Though the pony was only a scrub of a creature, he had a gentle disposition, and every other animal on the farm liked him. A gander, in particular, had such an admiration for him, that he followed him wherever he went, and if he lost him for an instant, he would mount one of the knolls on the farm and stretch out his neck looking for him. When he caught sight of him, he gabbled with delight, and running to him, waddled up and down beside him. Every little while the pony put his nose down, and seemed to be having a conversation with the goose. If the farmer whistled for the pony and he started to run to him, the gander, knowing he could not keep up, would seize the pony's tail in his beak, and flapping his wings, would get along as fast as the pony did. And the pony never kicked him. The Italian saw that this pony would be a good one to train for the stage, so he offered the farmer a large price for him, and took him away.

"Oh, Joe, I forgot to say, that by this time all the animals had been sent off the stage except the pony and the gander, and they stood looking at the Italian while he talked. I never saw anything as human in dumb animals as that pony's face. He looked as if he understood every word that his master was saying. After this story was over, the Italian made another bow, and then told the pony to bow. He nodded his head at the people, and they all laughed. Then the Italian asked him to favor us with a waltz, and the pony got up on his hind legs and danced. You should have seen that gander skirmishing around, so as to be near the pony and yet keep out of the way of his heels. We fellows just roared, and we would have kept him dancing all the afternoon if the Italian hadn't begged 'ze young gentlemen not to make ze noise, but let ze pony do ze rest of his tricks.' Pony number two came on the stage, and it was too queer for anything to see the things the two of them did. They helped the Italian on with his coat, they pulled off his rubbers, they took his coat away and brought him a chair, and dragged a table up to it. They brought him letters and papers, and rang bells, and rolled barrels, and swung the Italian in a big swing, and jumped a rope, and walked up and down steps—they just went around that stage as handy with their teeth as two boys would be with their hands, and they seemed to understand every word their master said to them.

"The best trick of all was telling the time and doing questions in arithmetic. The Italian pulled his watch out of his pocket and showed it to the first pony, whose name was Diamond, and said, 'What time is it?' The pony looked at it, then scratched four times with his forefoot on the platform. The Italian said, 'Zat's good— four o'clock. But it's a few minutes after four—how many?' The pony scratched again five times. The Italian showed his watch to the audience, and said that it was just five minutes past four. Then he asked the pony how old he was. He scratched four times. That meant four years. He asked him how many days in a week there were; how many months in a year; and he gave him some questions in addition and subtraction, and the pony answered them all correctly. Of course, the Italian was giving him some sign; but, though we watched him closely, we couldn't make out what it was. At last, he told the pony that he had been very good, and had done his lessons well; if it would rest him, he might be naughty a little while. All of a sudden a wicked look came into the creature's eyes. He turned around, and kicked up his heels at his master, he pushed over the table and chairs, and knocked down a blackboard where he had been rubbing out figures with a sponge held in his mouth. The Italian pretended to be cross, and said, 'Come, come; this won't do,' and he called the other pony to him, and told him to take that troublesome fellow off the stage. The second one nosed Diamond, and pushed him about, finally bit him by the ear, and led him squealing off the stage. The gander followed, gabbling as fast as he could, and there was a regular roar of applause.

"After that, there were ladders brought in, Joe, and dogs came on, not thoroughbreds, but curs something like you. The Italian says he can't teach tricks to pedigree animals as well as to scrubs.

Those dogs jumped the ladders, and climbed them, and went through them, and did all kinds of things. The man cracked his whip once, and they began; twice, and they did backward what they had done forward; three times, and they stopped, and every animal, dogs, goats, ponies, and monkeys, after they had finished their tricks, ran up to their master, and he gave them a lump of sugar. They seemed fond of him, and often when they weren't performing went up to him, and licked his hands or his sleeve. There was one boss dog, Joe, with a head like yours. Bob, they called him, and he did all his tricks alone. The Italian went off the stage, and the dog came on and made his bow, and climbed his ladders, and jumped his hurdles, and went off again. The audience howled for an encore, and didn't he come out alone, make another bow, and retire. I saw old Judge Brown wiping the tears from his eyes, he'd laughed so much. One of the last tricks was with a goat, and the Italian said it was the best of all, because the goat is such a hard animal to teach. He had a big ball, and the goat got on it and rolled it across the stage without getting off. He looked as nervous as a cat, shaking his old beard, and trying to keep his four hoofs close enough together to keep him on the ball.

"We had a funny little play at the end of the performance. A monkey dressed as a lady, in a white satin suit and a bonnet with a white veil, came on the stage. She was Miss Green and the dog Bob was going to elope with her. He was all rigged out as Mr. Smith, and had on a light suit of clothes, and a tall hat on the side of his head, high collar, long cuffs, and he carried a cane. He was a regular dude. He stepped up to Miss Green on his hind legs, and helped her on to a pony's back. The pony galloped off the stage; then a crowd of monkeys, chattering and wringing their hands, came on. Mr. Smith had run away with their child. They were all dressed up too. There were the father and mother, with gray wigs and black clothes, and the young Greens in bibs and tuckers. They were a queer-looking crowd. While they were going on in this way, the pony trotted back on the stage; and they all flew at him and pulled off their daughter from his back, and laughed and chattered, and boxed her ears, and took off her white veil and her satin dress, and put on an old brown thing, and some of them seized the dog, and kicked his hat, and broke his cane, and stripped his clothes off, and threw them in a corner, and bound his legs with cords. A goat came on, harnessed to a little cart, and they threw the dog in it, and wheeled him around the stage a few times. Then they took him out and tied him to a hook in the wall, and the goat ran off the stage, and the monkeys ran to one side, and one of them pulled out a little revolver, pointed it at the dog, fired, and he dropped down as if he was dead.

"The monkeys stood looking at him, and then there was the most awful hullabaloo you ever heard. Such a barking and yelping, and half a dozen dogs rushed on the stage, and didn't they trundle those monkeys about. They nosed them, and pushed them, and shook them, till they all ran away, all but Miss Green, who sat shivering in a corner. After a while, she crept up to the dead dog, pawed him a little, and didn't he jump up as much alive as any of them? Everybody in the room clapped and shouted, and then the curtain dropped, and the thing was over. I wish he'd give another performance. Early in the morning he has to go to Boston."

Jack pushed my paws from his knees and went outdoors, and I began to think that I would very much like to see those performing animals. It was not yet tea time, and I would have plenty of time to take a run down to the hotel where they were staying; so I set out. It was a lovely autumn evening. The sun was going down in a haze, and it was quite warm. Earlier in the day I had heard Mr. Morris say that this was our Indian summer, and that we should soon have cold weather.

Fairport was a pretty little town, and from the principal street one could look out upon the blue water of the bay and see the island opposite, which was quite deserted now, for all the summer visitors had gone home, and the Island House was shut up.

I was running down one of the steep side streets that led to the water when I met a heavily-laden cart coming up. It must have been coming from one of the vessels, for it was full of strange-looking boxes and packages. A fine-looking nervous horse was drawing it, and he was straining every nerve to get it up the steep hill. His driver was a burly, hard-faced man, and instead of letting his horse stop a minute to rest he kept urging him forward. The poor horse kept looking at his master, his eyes almost starting from his head in terror. He knew that the whip was about to descend on his quivering body. And so it did, and there was no one by to interfere. No one but a woman in a ragged shawl who would have no influence with the driver. There was a very good humane society in Fairport, and none of the teamsters dared ill use their horses if any of the members were near. This was a quiet out-of-the-way street, with only poor houses on it, and the man probably knew that none of the members of the society would be likely to be living in them. He whipped his horse, and whipped him, till every lash made my heart ache, and if I had dared I would have bitten him severely. Suddenly, there was a dull thud in the street. The horse had fallen down. The driver ran to his head, but he was quite dead. "Thank God!" said the poorly-dressed woman, bitterly; "one more out of this world of misery." Then she turned and went down the street. I was glad for the horse. He would never be frightened or miserable again, and I went slowly on, thinking that death is the best thing that can happen to tortured animals.

The Fairport hotel was built right in the centre of the town, and the shops and houses crowded quite close about it. It was a high, brick building, and it was called the Fairport House. As I was running along the sidewalk, I heard some one speak to me, and looking up I saw Charlie Montague. I had heard the Morrises say that his parents were staying at the hotel for a few weeks, while their house was being repaired. He had his Irish setter, Brisk, with him, and a handsome dog he was, as he stood waving his silky tail in the sunlight. Charlie patted me, and then he and his dog went into the hotel. I turned into the stable yard. It was a small, choked-up place, and as I picked my way under the cabs and wagons standing in the yard, I wondered why the hotel people didn't buy some of the old houses near by, and tear them down, and make a stable yard worthy of such a nice hotel. The hotel horses were just getting rubbed down after their day's work, and others were coming in. The men were talking and laughing, and there was no sign of strange animals, so I went around to the back of the yard. Here they were, in an empty cow stable, under a hay loft. There were two little ponies tied up in a stall, two goats beyond them, and dogs and monkeys in strong traveling cages. I stood in the doorway and stared at them. I was sorry for the dogs to be shut up on such a lovely evening, but I suppose their master was afraid of their getting lost, or being stolen, if he let them loose.

They all seemed very friendly. The ponies turned around and looked at me with their gentle eyes, and then went on munching their hay. I wondered very much where the gander was, and went a little farther into the stable. Something white raised itself up out of the brownest pony's crib, and there was the gander close up beside the open mouth of his friend. The monkeys make a jabbering noise, and held on to the bars of their cage with their little black hands, while they looked out at me. The dogs sniffed the air, and wagged their tails, and tried to put their muzzles through the bars of their cage. I liked the dogs best, and I wanted to see the one they called Bob, so I went up quite close to them. There were two little white dogs, something like Billy, two mongrel spaniels, an Irish terrier, and a brown dog asleep in the corner, that I knew must be Bob. He did look a little like me, but he was not quite so ugly for he had his ears and his tail.

While I was peering through the bars at him, a man came in the stable. He noticed me the first thing, but instead of driving me out, he spoke kindly to me, in a language that I did not understand. So I knew that he was the Italian. How glad the animals were to see him! The gander fluttered out of his nest, the ponies pulled at their halters, the dogs whined and tried to reach his hands to lick them, and the monkeys chattered with delight. He laughed and talked back to them in queer, soft-sounding words. Then he took out of a bag on his arm, bones for the dogs, nuts and cakes for the monkeys, nice, juicy carrots for the ponies, some green stuff for the goats, and corn for the gander.

It was a pretty sight to see the old man feeding his pets, and it made me feel quite hungry, so I trotted home. I had a run down town again that evening with Mr. Morris, who went to get something from a shop for his wife. He never let his boys go to town after tea, so if there were errands to be done, he or Mrs. Morris went. The town was bright and lively that evening, and a great many people were walking about and looking into the shop windows.

When we came home, I went into the kennel with Jim, and there I slept till the middle of the night. Then I started up and ran outside. There was a distant bell ringing, which we often heard in Fairport, and which always meant fire.

CHAPTER 34

A FIRE IN FAIRPORT

I HAD several times run to a fire with the boys, and knew that there was always great noise and excitement. There was a light in the house, so I knew that somebody was getting up. I don't think—indeed I know, for they were good boys—that they ever wanted anybody to lose property, but they did enjoy seeing a blaze, and one of their greatest delights, when there hadn't been a fire for some time, was to build a bonfire in the garden.

Jim and I ran around to the front of the house and waited. In a few minutes, some one came rattling at the front door, and I was sure it was Jack. But it was Mr. Morris, and without a word to us, he set off almost running toward the town. We followed after him, and as we hurried along, other men ran out from the houses along the streets, and either joined him; or dashed ahead. They seemed to have dressed in a hurry, and were thrusting their arms in their coats, and buttoning themselves up as they went. Some of them had hats and some of them had none, and they all had their faces toward the great red light that got brighter and brighter ahead of us. "Where's the fire?" they shouted to each other. "Don't know—afraid it's the hotel, or the town hall. It's such a blaze. Hope not. How's the water supply now? Bad time for a fire."

It was the hotel. We saw that as soon as we got on to the main street. There were people all about, and a great noise and confusion, and smoke and blackness, and up above, bright tongues of flame were leaping against the sky. Jim and I kept close to Mr. Morris's heels, as he pushed his way among the crowd. When we got nearer the burning building, we saw men carrying ladders and axes, and others were shouting directions, and rushing out of the hotel, carrying boxes and bundles and furniture in their arms. From the windows above came a steady stream of articles, thrown among the crowd. A mirror struck Mr. Morris on the arm, and a whole package of clothes fell on his head and almost smothered him; but he brushed them aside and scarcely noticed them. There was something the matter with Mr. Morris—I knew by the worried sound of his voice when he spoke to any one. I could not see his face, though it was as light as day about us, for we had got jammed in the crowd, and if I had not kept between his feet, I should have been trodden to death. Jim, being larger than I was, had got separated from us.

Presently Mr. Morris raised his voice above the uproar, and called, "Is every one out of the hotel?" A voice shouted back, "I'm going up to see."

"It's Jim Watson, the fireman," cried some one near. "He's risking his life to go into that pit of flame. Don't go, Watson." I don't think that the brave fireman paid any attention to this warning, for an instant later the same voice said, "He's planting his ladder against the third story. He's bound to go. He'll not get any farther than the second, anyway."

"Where are the Montagues?" shouted Mr. Morris. "Has any one seen the Montagues?"

"Mr. Morris! Mr. Morris!" said a frightened voice, and young Charlie Montague pressed through the people to us. "Where's papa?"

"I don't know. Where did you leave him?" said Mr. Morris, taking his hand and drawing him closer to him. "I was sleeping in his room," said the boy, "and a man knocked at the door and said, 'Hotel on fire. Five minutes to dress and get out,' and papa told me to put on my clothes and go downstairs, and he ran up to mamma."

"Where was she?" asked Mr. Morris, quickly.

"On the fourth flat. She and her maid Blanche were up there. You know, mamma hasn't been well and couldn't sleep, and our room was so noisy that she moved upstairs where it was quiet." Mr. Morris gave a kind of groan. "Oh I'm so hot, and there's such a dreadful noise," said the little boy, bursting into tears, "and I want mamma." Mr. Morris soothed him as best he could, and drew him a little to the edge of the crowd.

While he was doing this, there was a piercing cry. I could not see the person making it, but I knew it was the Italian's voice. He was screaming, in broken English that the fire was spreading to the stables, and his animals would be burned. Would no one help him to get his animals out? There was a great deal of confused language. Some voices shouted, "Look after the people first. Let the animals go." And others said, "For shame. Get the horses out." But no one seemed to do anything, for the Italian went on crying for help. I heard a number of people who were standing near us say that it had just been found out that several persons who had been sleeping in the top of the hotel had not got out. They said that at one of the top windows a poor housemaid was shrieking for help. Here in the street we could see no one at the upper windows, for smoke was pouring from them.

The air was very hot and heavy, and I didn't wonder that Charlie Montague felt ill. He would have fallen on the ground if Mr. Morris hadn't taken him in his arms, and carried him out of the crowd. He put him down on the brick sidewalk, and unfastened his little shirt, and left me to watch him, while he held his hands under a leak in a hose that was fastened to a hydrant near us. He got enough water to dash on Charlie's face and breast, and then seeing that the boy was reviving, he sat down on the curbstone and took him on his knee. Charlie lay in his arms and moaned. He was a delicate boy, and he could not stand rough usage as the Morris boys could.

Mr. Morris was terribly uneasy. His face was deathly white, and he shuddered whenever there was a cry from the burning building. "Poor souls—God help them. Oh, this is awful," he said; and then he turned his eyes from the great sheets of flame and strained the little boy to his breast. At last there were wild shrieks that I knew came from no human throats. The fire must have reached the horses. Mr. Morris sprang up, then sank back again. He wanted to go, yet he could be of no use. There were hundreds of men standing about, but the fire had spread so rapidly, and they had so little water to put on it that there was very little they could do. I wondered whether I could do anything for the poor animals. I was not afraid of fire, as most dogs, for one of the tricks that the Morris boys had taught me was to put out a fire with my paws. They would throw a piece of lighted paper on the floor, and I would crush it with my forepaws; and if the blaze was too large for that, I would drag a bit of old carpet over it and jump on it. I left Mr. Morris, and ran around the corner of the street to the back of the hotel. It was not burned as much here as in the front, and in the houses all around, people were out on their roofs with wet blankets, and some were standing at the window watching the fire, or packing up their belongings ready to move if it should spread to them. There was a narrow lane running up a short distance toward the hotel, and I started to go up this, when in front of me I heard such a wailing, piercing noise, that it made me shudder and stand still. The Italian's animals were going to be burned up, and they were calling to their master to come and let them out. Their voices sounded like the voices of children in mortal pain. I could not stand it. I was seized with such an awful horror of the fire that I turned and ran, feeling so thankful that I was not in it. As I got into the street, I stumbled over something. It was a large bird—a parrot, and at first I thought it was Bella. Then I remembered hearing Jack say that the Italian had a parrot. It was not dead, but seemed stupid with the smoke. I seized it in my mouth, and ran and laid it at Mr. Morris's feet. He wrapped it in his handkerchief, and laid it beside him.

I sat, and trembled, and did not leave him again. I shall never forget that dreadful night. It seemed as if we were there for hours, but in reality it was only a short time. The hotel soon got to be all red flames, and there was very little smoke. The inside of the building had burned away, and nothing more could be gotten out. The firemen and all the people drew back, and there was no noise. Everybody stood gazing silently at the flames. A man stepped quietly up to Mr. Morris, and looking at him, I saw that it was Mr. Montague. He was usually a well-dressed man, with a kind face, and a head of thick, grayish brown hair. Now his face was black and grimy, his hair was burnt from the front of his head, and his clothes were half torn from his back. Mr. Morris sprang up when he saw him, and said, "Where is your wife?"

The gentleman did not say a word, but pointed to the burning building. "Impossible!" cried Mr. Morris. "Is there no mistake? Your beautiful young wife, Montague. Can it be so?" Mr. Morris was trembling from head to foot.

"It is true," said Mr. Montague, quietly. "Give me the boy." Charlie had fainted again, and his father took him in his arms, and turned away.

"Montague!" cried Mr. Morris, "my heart is sore for you. Can I do nothing?"

"No, thank you," said the gentleman, without turning around; but there was more anguish in his voice than in Mr. Morris's, and though I am only a dog, I knew that his heart was breaking.

CHAPTER 35

BILLY AND THE ITALIAN

MR. MORRIS stayed no longer. He followed Mr. Montague along the sidewalk a little way, and then exchanged a few hurried words with some men who were standing near, and hastened home through streets that seemed dark and dull after the splendor of the fire. Though it was still the middle of the night, Mrs. Morris was up and dressed and waiting for him. She opened the hall door with one hand and held a candle in the other. I felt frightened and miserable, and didn't want to leave Mr. Morris, so I crept in after him.

"Don't make a noise," said Mrs. Morris. "Laura and the boys are sleeping, and I thought it better not to wake them. It has been a terrible fire, hasn't it? Was it the hotel?" Mr. Morris threw himself into a chair and covered his face with his hands.

"Speak to me, William!" said Mrs. Morris, in a startled tone. "You are not hurt, are you?" and she put her candle on the table and came and sat down beside him.

He dropped his hands from his face, and tears were running down his cheeks. "Ten lives lost," he said; "among them Mrs. Montague."

Mrs. Morris looked horrified, and gave a little cry, "William, it can't be so!"

It seemed as if Mr. Morris could not sit still. He got up and walked to and fro on the floor. "It was an awful scene, Margaret. I never wish to look upon the like again. Do you remember how I protested against the building of that death-trap? Look at the wide, open streets around it, and yet they persisted in running it up to the sky. God will require an account of those deaths at the hands of the men who put up that building. It is terrible—this disregard of human lives. To think of that delicate woman and her death agony." He threw himself in a chair and buried his face in his hands.

"Where was she? How did it happen? Was her husband saved, and Charlie?" said Mrs. Morris, in a broken voice.

"Yes; Charlie and Mr. Montague are safe. Charlie will recover from it. Montague's life is done. You know his love for his wife. Oh, Margaret! when will men cease to be fools? What does the Lord think of them when they say, 'Am I my brother's keeper?' And the other poor creatures burned to death—their lives are as precious in his sight as Mrs. Montague's."

Mr. Morris looked so weak and ill that Mrs. Morris, like a sensible woman, questioned him no further, but made a fire and got him some hot tea. Then she made him lie down on the sofa, and she sat by him till day-break, when she persuaded him to go to bed. I followed her about, and kept touching her dress with my nose. It seemed so good to me to have this pleasant home after all the misery I had seen that night. Once she stopped and took my head between her hands, "Dear old Joe," she said, tearfully, "this a suffering world. It's well there's a better one beyond it."

In the morning the boys went down town before breakfast and learned all about the fire. It started in the top story of the hotel, in the room of some fast young men, who were sitting up late playing cards. They had smuggled wine into their room and had been drinking till they were stupid. One of them upset the lamp, and when the flames began to spread so that they could not extinguish them, instead of rousing some one near them, they rushed downstairs to get some one there to come up and help them put out the fire. When they returned with some of the hotel people, they found that the flames had spread from their room, which was in an "L" at the back of the house, to the front part, where Mrs. Montague's room was, and where the housemaids belonging to the hotel slept. By this time Mr. Montague had gotten upstairs; but he found the passageway to his wife's room so full of flames and smoke, that, though he tried again and again to force his way through, he could not. He disappeared for a time, then he came to Mr. Morris and got his boy, and took him to some rooms over his bank, and shut himself up with him. For some days he would let no one in; then he came out with the look of an old man on his face, and his hair as white as snow, and went out to his beautiful house in the outskirts of the town.

Nearly all the horses belonging to the hotel were burned. A few were gotten out by having blankets put over their heads, but the most of them were so terrified that they would not stir.

The Morris boys said that they found the old Italian sitting on an empty box, looking at the smoking ruins of the hotel. His head was hanging on his breast, and his eyes were full of tears. His ponies were burned up, he said, and the gander, and the monkeys, and the goat, and his wonderful performing dogs. He had only his birds left, and he was a ruined man. He had toiled all his life to get this troupe of trained animals together, and now they were swept from him. It was cruel and wicked, and he wished he could die. The canaries, and pigeons, and doves, the hotel people had allowed him to take to his room, and they were safe. The parrot was lost—an educated parrot that could answer forty questions, and, among other things, could take a watch and tell the time of day.

Jack Morris told him that they had it safe at home, and that it was very much alive, quarrelling furiously with his parrot Bella. The old man's face brightened at this, and then Jack and Carl, finding that he had had no breakfast, went off to a restaurant near by, and got him some steak and coffee. The Italian was very grateful, and as he ate, Jack said the tears ran into his coffee cup. He told them how much he loved his animals, and how it "made ze heart bitter to hear zem crying him to deliver zem from ze raging fire."

The boys came home, and got their breakfast and went to school. Miss Laura did not go out. She sat all day with a very quiet, pained face. She could neither read nor sew, and Mr. and Mrs. Morris were just as unsettled. They talked about the fire in low tones, and I could see that they felt more sad about Mrs. Montague's death than if she had died in an ordinary way. Her dear little canary Barry, died with her. She would never be separated from him, and his cage had been taken up to the top of the hotel with her. He probably died an easier death than his poor mistress. Charlie's dog escaped, but was so frightened that he ran out to their house, outside the town.

At tea time, Mr. Morris went down town to see that the Italian got a comfortable place for the night. When he came back, he said that he had found out that the Italian was by no means so old a man as he looked, and that he had talked to him about raising a sum of money for him among the Fairport people, till he had become quite cheerful, and said that if Mr. Morris would do that, he would try to gather another troupe of animals together and train them.

"Now, what can we do for the Italian?" asked Mrs. Morris. "We can't give him much money, but we might let him have one or two of our pets. There's Billy, he's a bright, little dog, and not two years old yet. He could teach him anything."

There was a blank silence among the Morris children. Billy was such a gentle, lovable, little dog, that he was a favorite with every one in the house. "I suppose we ought to do it," said Miss Laura, at last, "but how can we give him up?"

There was a good deal of discussion, but the end of it was that Billy was given to the Italian. He came up to get him, and was very grateful, and made a great many bows, holding his hat in his hand. Billy took to him at once, and the Italian spoke so kindly to him, that we knew he would have a good master. Mr. Morris got quite a large sum of money for him, and when he handed it to him, the poor man was so pleased that he kissed his hand, and promised to send frequent word as to Billy's progress and welfare.

CHAPTER 36

DANDY THE TRAMP

ABOUT a week after Billy left us, the Morris family, much to its surprise, became the owner of a new dog.

He walked into the house one cold, wintry afternoon and lay calmly down by the fire. He was a brindled bull-terrier, and he had on a silver-plated collar, with "Dandy" engraved on it. He lay all the evening by the fire, and when any of the family spoke to him, he wagged his tail, and looked pleased. I growled a little at him at first, but he never cared a bit, and just dozed off to sleep, so I soon stopped.

He was such a well-bred dog, that the Morrises were afraid that some one had lost him. They made some inquiries the next day, and found that he belonged to a New York gentleman who had come to Fairport in the summer in a yacht. This dog did not like the yacht. He came ashore in a boat whenever he got a chance, and if he could not come in a boat, he would swim. He was a tramp, his master said, and he wouldn't stay long in any place. The Morrises were so amused with his impudence, that they did not send him away, but said every day, "Surely he will be gone to-morrow."

However, Mr. Dandy had gotten into comfortable quarters, and he had no intention of changing them, for a while at least. Then he was very handsome, and had such a pleasant way with him, that the family could not help liking him. I never cared for him. He fawned on the Morrises, and pretended he loved them, and afterward turned around and laughed and sneered at them in a way that made me very angry. I used to lecture him sometimes, and growl about him to Jim, but Jim always said, "Let him alone. You can't do him any good. He was born bad. His mother wasn't good. He tells me that she had a bad name among all the dogs in her neighborhood. She was a thief and a runaway." Though he provoked me so often, yet I could not help laughing at some of his stories, they were so funny.

We were lying out in the sun, on the platform at the back of the house one day, and he had been more than usually provoking, so I got up to leave him. He put himself in my way, however, and said, coaxingly, "Don't be cross, old fellow. I'll tell you some stories to amuse you, old boy. What shall they be about?"

"I think the story of your life would be about as interesting as anything you could make up," I said, dryly.

"All right, fact or fiction, whichever you like. Here's a fact, plain and unvarnished. Born and bred in New York. Swell stable. Swell coachman. Swell master. Jewelled fingers of ladies poking at me, first thing I remember. First painful experience—being sent to vet. to have ears cut."

"What's a vet.?" I said.

"A veterinary—animal doctor. Vet. didn't cut ears enough. Master sent me back. Cut ears again. Summer time, and flies bad. Ears got sore and festered, flies very attentive. Coachman set little boy to brush flies off, but he'd run out in yard and leave me. Flies awful. Thought they'd eat me up, or else I'd shake out brains trying to get rid of them. Mother should have stayed home and licked my ears, but was cruising about neighborhood. Finally coachman put me in dark place, powdered ears, and they got well."

"Why didn't they cut your tail, too?" I said, looking at his long, slim tail, which was like a sewer rat's.

"'Twasn't the fashion, Mr. Wayback, a bull-terrier's ears are clipped to keep them from getting torn while fighting."

"You're not a fighting dog," I said.

"Not I. Too much trouble. I believe in taking things easy."

"I should think you did," I said, scornfully. "You never put yourself out for any one, I notice; but, speaking of cropping ears. What do you think of it?"

"Well," he said, with a sly glance at my head, "it isn't a pleasant operation; but one might well be out of the world as out of the fashion. I don't care, now my ears are done."

"But," I said, "think of the poor dogs that will come after you."

"What difference does that make to me?" he said. "I'll be dead and out of the way. Men can cut off their ears, and tails, and legs, too, if they want to."

"Dandy," I said, angrily, "you're the most selfish dog that I ever saw."

"Don't excite yourself," he said, coolly. "Let me get on with my story. When I was a few months old, I began to find the stable yard narrow, and wondered what there was outside of it. I discovered a hole in the garden wall, and used to sneak out nights. Oh, what fun it was. I got to know a lot of street dogs, and we had gay times, barking under people's windows and making them mad, and getting into back yards and chasing cats. We used to kill a cat nearly every night. Policeman would chase us, and we would run and run till the water just ran off our tongues, and we hadn't a bit of breath left. Then I'd go home and sleep all day, and go out again the next night. When I was about a year old, I began to stay out days as well as nights. They couldn't keep me home. Then I ran away for three months. I got with an old lady on Fifth Avenue, who was very fond of dogs. She had four white poodles, and her servants used to wash them, and tie up their hair with blue ribbons, and she used to take them for drives in her phaeton in the park, and they wore gold and silver collars. The biggest poodle wore a ruby in his collar worth five hundred dollars. I went driving, too, and sometimes we met my master. He often smiled, and shook his head at me. I heard him tell the coachman one day that I was a little blackguard, and he was to let me come and go as I liked."

"If they had whipped you soundly," I said, "it might have made a good dog of you."

"I'm good enough now," said Dandy, airily. "The young ladies who drove with my master used to say that it was priggish and tiresome to be too good. To go on with my story: I stayed with Mrs. Judge Tibbett till I got sick of her fussy ways. She made a simpleton of herself over those poodles. Each one had a high chair at the table, and a plate, and they always sat in these chairs and had meals with her, and the servants all called them Master Bijou, and Master Tot, and Miss Tiny, and Miss Fluff. One day they tried to make me sit in a chair, and I got cross and bit Mrs. Tibbett, and she beat me cruelly, and her servants stoned me away from the house."

"Speaking about fools, Dandy," I said, "if it is polite to call a lady one, I should say that that lady was one. Dogs shouldn't be put out of their place. Why didn't she have some poor children at her table, and in her carriage, and let the dogs run behind?"

"Easy to see you don't know New York," said Dandy, with a laugh. "Poor children don't live with rich, old ladies. Mrs. Tibbett hated children, anyway. Then dogs like poodles would get lost in the mud, or killed in the crowd if they ran behind a carriage. Only knowing dogs like me can make their way about." I rather doubted this speech; but I said nothing, and he went on, patronizingly: "However, Joe, thou hast reason, as the French say. Mrs. Judge Tibbett *didn't* give her dogs exercise enough. Their claws were as long as Chinamen's nails, and the hair grew over their pads, and they had red eyes and were always sick, and she had to dose them with medicine, and call them her poor, little, 'weeny-teeny, sicky-wicky doggies.' Bah! I got disgusted with her.[1] When

---

1   Upper-class women were linked to lapdogs—small, weak, undesirable canines that reflected their owners' uselessness. These women and dogs had shared misogynist, anti-aristocratic, and anti-foreigner characterizations since at least the eighteenth century (Wyett 278, 281).

I left her, I ran away to her niece's, Miss Ball's. She was a sensible young lady, and she used to scold her aunt for the way in which she brought up her dogs. She was almost too sensible, for her pug and I were rubbed and scrubbed within an inch of our lives, and had to go for such long walks that I got thoroughly sick of them. A woman, whom the servants called Trotsey, came every morning, and took the pug and me by our chains, and sometimes another dog or two, and took us for long tramps in quiet streets. That was Trotsey's business, to walk dogs, and Miss Ball got a great many fashionable young ladies who could not exercise their dogs, to let Trotsey have them, and they said that it made a great difference in the health and appearance of their pets. Trotsey got fifteen cents an hour for a dog. Goodness, what appetites those walks gave us, and didn't we make the dog biscuits disappear? But it was a slow life at Miss Ball's. We only saw her for a little while every day. She slept till noon. After lunch she played with us for a little while in the greenhouse, then she was off driving or visiting, and in the evening she always had company, or went to a dance, or to the theatre. I soon made up my mind that I'd run away. I jumped out of a window one fine morning, and ran home. I stayed there for a long time. My mother had been run over by a cart and killed, and I wasn't sorry. My master never bothered his head about me, and I could do as I liked. One day when I was having a walk, and meeting a lot of dogs that I knew, a little boy came behind me, and before I could tell what he was doing, he had snatched me up, and was running off with me. I couldn't bite him, for he had stuffed some of his rags in my mouth. He took me to a tenement house, in a part of the city that I had never been in before. He belonged to a very poor family. My faith, weren't they badly off—six children, and a mother, and father, all living in two tiny rooms. Scarcely a bit of meat did I smell while I was there. I hated their bread and molasses, and the place smelled so badly that I thought I should choke.

"They kept me shut up in their dirty rooms for several days; and the brat of a boy that caught me slept with his arm around me at night. The weather was hot and sometimes we couldn't sleep, and they had to go up on the roof. After a while, they chained me up in a filthy yard at the back of the house, and there I thought I should go mad. I would have liked to bite them all to death, if I had dared. It's awful to be chained, especially for a dog like me that loves his freedom. The flies worried me, and the noises distracted me, and my flesh would fairly creep from getting no exercise. I was there nearly a month, while they were waiting for a reward to be offered. But none came; and one day, the boy's father, who was a street peddler, took me by my chain and led me about the streets till he sold me. A gentleman got me for his little boy, but I didn't like the look of him, so I sprang up and bit his hand, and he dropped the chain, and I dodged boys and policemen, and finally got home more dead than alive, and looking like a skeleton. I had a good time for several weeks, and then I began to get restless and was off again. But I'm getting tired; I want to go to sleep."

"You're not very polite," I said, "to offer to tell a story, and then go to sleep before you finish it."

"Look out for number one, my boy," said Dandy, with a yawn; "for if you don't, no one else will," and he shut his eyes and was fast asleep in a few minutes.

I sat and looked at him. What a handsome, good-natured, worthless dog he was. A few days later, he told me the rest of his history. After a great many wanderings, he happened home one day just as his master's yacht was going to sail, and they chained him up till they went on board, so that he could be an amusement on the passage to Fairport.

It was in November that Dandy came to us, and he stayed all winter. He made fun of the Morrises all the time, and said they had a dull, poky, old house, and he only stayed because Miss Laura was nursing him. He had a little sore on his back that she soon found out was mange. Her father said it was a bad disease for dogs to have, and Dandy had better be shot; but she begged so hard for his life, and said she would cure him in a few weeks that she was allowed to keep him. Dandy wasn't capable of getting really angry, but he was as disturbed about having this disease as he could be about anything. He said that he had got it from a little, mangy dog, that he had played with a few weeks before. He was only with the dog a little while, and didn't think he would take it, but it seemed he knew what an easy thing it was to get.

Until he got well he was separated from us. Miss Laura kept him up in the loft with the rabbits, where we could not go; and the boys ran him around the garden for exercise. She tried all kinds of cures for him, and I heard her say that although it was a skin disease, his blood must be purified. She gave him some of the pills that she made out of sulphur and butter for Jim, and Billy, and me, to keep our coats silky and smooth. When they didn't cure him, she gave him a few drops of arsenic every day, and washed the sore, and, indeed his whole body, with tobacco water or carbolic soap. It was the tobacco water that cured him.

Miss Laura always put on gloves when she went near him, and used a brush to wash him, for if a person takes mange from a dog, they may lose their hair and their eyelashes. But if they are careful, no harm comes from nursing a mangy dog, and I have never known of any one taking the disease.

After a time, Dandy's sore healed, and he was set free. He was right glad, he said, for he had got heartily sick of the rabbits. He used to bark at them and make them angry, and they would run around the loft, stamping their hind feet at him, in the funny way that rabbits do. I think they disliked him as much as he disliked them. Jim and I did not get the mange. Dandy was not a strong dog, and I think his irregular way of living made him take diseases readily. He would stuff himself when he was hungry, and he always wanted rich food. If he couldn't get what he wanted at the Morrises', he went out and stole, or visited the dumps at the back of the town.

When he did get ill, he was more stupid about doctoring himself than any dog that I have ever seen. He never seemed to know when to eat grass or herbs, or a little earth, that would have kept him in good condition. A dog should never be without grass. When Dandy got ill he just suffered till he got well again, and never tried to cure himself of his small troubles. Some dogs even know enough to amputate their limbs. Jim told me a very interesting story of a dog the Morrises once had, called Gyp, whose leg became paralyzed by a kick from a horse. He knew the leg was dead, and gnawed it off nearly to the shoulder, and though he was very sick for a time, yet in the end he got well.

To return to Dandy. I knew he was only waiting for the spring to leave us, and I was not sorry. The first fine day he was off, and during the rest of the spring and summer we occasionally met him running about the town with a set of fast dogs. One day I stopped, and asked him how he contented himself in such a quiet place as Fairport, and he said he was dying to get back to New York, and was hoping that his master's yacht would come and take him away.

Poor Dandy never left Fairport. After all, he was not such a bad dog. There was nothing really vicious about him, and I hate to speak of his end. His master's yacht did not come, and soon the summer was over, and the winter was coming, and no one wanted Dandy, for he had such a bad name. He got hungry and cold, and one day sprang upon a little girl, to take away a piece of bread and butter that she was eating. He did not see the large house-dog on the door sill, and before he could get away, the dog had seized him, and bitten and shaken him till he was nearly dead. When the dog threw him aside, he crawled to the Morrises', and Miss Laura bandaged his wounds, and made him a bed in the stable.

One Sunday morning she washed and fed him very tenderly, for she knew he could not live much longer. He was so weak that he could scarcely eat the food that she put in his mouth, so she let him lick some milk from her finger. As she was going to church, I could not go with her, but I ran down the lane and watched her out of sight. When I came back, Dandy was gone. I looked till I found him. He had crawled into the darkest corner of the stable to die, and though he was suffering very much, he never uttered a sound. I sat by him, and thought of his master in New York. If he had brought Dandy up properly he might not now be here in his silent death agony. A young pup should be trained just as a child is, and punished when he goes wrong. Dandy began badly, and not being checked in his evil ways, had come to this. Poor Dandy! Poor, handsome dog of a rich master! He opened his dull eyes, gave me one last glance, then, with a convulsive shudder, his torn limbs were still. He would never suffer any more.

When Miss Laura came home, she cried bitterly to know that he was dead. The boys took him away from her, and made him a grave in the corner of the garden.

CHAPTER 37

THE END OF MY STORY

I HAVE come now to the last chapter of my story. I thought when I began to write, that I would put down the events of each year of my life, but I fear that would make my story too long, and neither Miss Laura nor any boys and girls would care to read it. So I will stop just here, though I would gladly go on, for I have enjoyed so much talking over old times, that I am very sorry to leave off.

Every year that I have been at the Morrises', something pleasant has happened to me, but I cannot put all these things down, nor can I tell how Miss Laura and the boys grew and changed, year by year, till now they are quite grown up. I will just bring my tale down to the present time, and then I will stop talking, and go lie down in my basket, for I am an old dog now, and get tired very easily.

I was a year old when I went to the Morrises, and I have been with them for twelve years. I am not living in the same house with Mr. and Mrs. Morris now, but I am with my dear Miss Laura, who is Miss Laura no longer, but Mrs. Gray. She married Mr. Harry four years ago, and lives with him and Mr. and Mrs. Wood, on Dingley Farm. Mr. and Mrs. Morris live in a cottage near by. Mr. Morris is not very strong, and can preach no longer. The boys are all scattered. Jack married pretty Miss Bessie Drury, and lives on a large farm near here. Miss Bessie says that she hates to be a farmer's wife, but she always looks very happy and contented, so I think that she must be mistaken. Carl is a merchant in New York, Ned is a clerk in a bank, and Willie is studying at a place called Harvard. He says that after he finishes his studies, he is going to live with his father and mother.

The Morrises' old friends often come to see them. Mrs. Drury comes every summer on her way to Newport, and Mr. Montague and Charlie come every other summer. Charlie always brings with him his old dog Brisk, who is getting feeble, like myself. We lie on the veranda in the sunshine, and listen to the Morrises talking about old days, and sometimes it makes us feel quite young again. In addition to Brisk we have a Scotch collie. He is very handsome, and is a constant attendant of Miss Laura's. We are great friends, he and I, but he can get about much better than I can. One day a friend of Miss Laura's came with a little boy and girl, and "Collie" sat between the two children, and their father took their picture with a "kodak."[1] I like him so much that I told him I would get them to put his picture in my book.

When the Morris boys are all here in the summer we have gay times. All through the winter we look forward to their coming, for they make the old farmhouse so lively. Mr. Maxwell never misses a summer in coming to Riverdale. He has such a following of dumb animals now, that he says he can't move them any farther away from Boston than this, and he doesn't know what he will do with them, unless he sets up a menagerie. He asked Miss Laura the other day, if she thought that the old Italian would take him into partnership. He did not know what had happened to poor Bellini, so Miss Laura told him.

A few years ago the Italian came to Riverdale, to exhibit his new stock of performing animals. They were almost as good as the old ones, but he had not quite so many as he had before. The Morrises and a great many of their friends went to his perform-ance, and Miss Laura said afterward, that when cunning little Billy came on the stage, and made his bow, and went through his antics of jumping through hoops, and catching balls, that she almost had hysterics. The Italian had made a special pet of him for the Morrises' sake, and treated him more like a human being than a dog. Billy rather put on airs when he came up to the farm to see us, but he was such a dear, little dog, in spite of being almost spoiled by his master, that Jim and I could not get angry with him. In a few days they went away, and we heard nothing but good news from them, till last winter. Then a letter came to Miss Laura from a nurse in a New York hospital. She said that the Italian was very near his end, and he wanted her to write to Mrs. Gray to tell her that he had sold all his animals but the little dog that she had so kindly given him. He was sending him back to her, and with his latest breath he would pray for heaven's bless-ing on the kind lady and her family that had befriended him when he was in trouble.

The next day Billy arrived, a thin, white scarecrow of a dog. He was sick and unhappy, and would eat nothing, and started up at the slightest sound. He was listening for the Italian's footsteps, but he never came, and one day Mr. Harry looked up from his

---

1 After Kodak's dissemination of the hand-held in 1888, cameras made their way into homes of the middle classes (Tagg 81). Saunders would typically provide the images that she wished to include in her books. In this case, she included a Kodak photograph of a Collie with two children.

newspaper and said, "Laura, Bellini is dead." Miss Laura's eyes filled with tears, and Billy, who had jumped up when he heard his master's name, fell back again. He knew what they meant, and from that instant he ceased listening for footsteps, and lay quite still till he died. Miss Laura had him put in a little, wooden box, and buried him in a corner of the garden, and when she is working among her flowers, she often speaks regretfully of him, and of poor Dandy, who lies in the garden at Fairport.

Bella, the parrot, lives with Mrs. Morris, and is as smart as ever. I have heard that parrots live to a very great age. Some of them even get to be a hundred years old. If that is the case, Bella will outlive all of us. She notices that I am getting blind and feeble, and when I go down to call on Mrs. Morris, she calls out to me, "Keep a stiff upper lip, Beautiful Joe. Never say die, Beautiful Joe. Keep the game a-going, Beautiful Joe."

Mrs. Morris says that she doesn't know where Bella picks up her slang words. I think it is Mr. Ned who teaches her, for when he comes home in the summer he often says, with a sly twinkle in his eye, "Come out into the garden, Bella," and he lies in a hammock under the trees, and Bella perches on a branch near him, and he talks to her by the hour. Anyway, it is in the autumn after he leaves Riverdale that Bella always shocks Mrs. Morris with her slang talk.

I am glad that I am to end my days in Riverdale. Fairport was a very nice place, but it was not open and free like this farm. I take a walk every morning that the sun shines. I go out among the horses and cows, and stop to watch the hens pecking at their food. This is a happy place, and I hope my dear Miss Laura will live to enjoy it many years after I am gone.

I have very few worries. The pigs bother me a little in the spring, by rooting up the bones that I bury in the fields in the fall, but that is a small matter, and I try not to mind it. I get a great many bones here, and I should be glad if I had some poor, city dogs to help me eat them. I don't think bones are good for pigs.

Then there is Mr. Harry's tame squirrel out in one of the barns that teases me considerably. He knows that I can't chase him, now that my legs are so stiff with rheumatism, and he takes delight in showing me how spry he can be, darting around me and whisking his tail almost in my face, and trying to get me to run after him, so that he can laugh at me. I don't think that he is a very thoughtful squirrel, but I try not to notice him.

The sailor boy who gave Bella to the Morrises has got to be a large, stout man, and is the first mate of a vessel. He sometimes comes here, and when he does, he always brings the Morrises presents of foreign fruits and curiosities of different kinds.

Malta, the cat, is still living, and is with Mrs. Morris. Davy, the rat, is gone, so is poor old Jim. He went away one day last summer, and no one ever knew what became of him. The Morrises searched everywhere for him, and offered a large reward to any one who would find him but he never turned up again. I think that he felt he was going to die, and went into some out-of-the-way place. He remembered how badly Miss Laura felt when Dandy died, and he wanted to spare her the greater sorrow of his death. He was always such a thoughtful dog, and so anxious not to give trouble. I am more selfish. I could not go away from Miss Laura, even to die. When my last hour comes, I want to see her gentle face bending over me, and then I shall not mind how much I suffer.

She is just as tender-hearted as ever, but she tries not to feel too badly about the sorrow and suffering in the world, because she says that would weaken her, and she wants all her strength to try to put a stop to some of it. She does a great deal of good in Riverdale, and I do not think that there is any one in all the country around who is as much beloved as she is.

She has never forgotten the resolve that she made some years ago, that she would do all that she could to protect dumb creatures. Mr. Harry and Mr. Maxwell have helped her nobly. Mr. Maxwell's work is largely done in Boston, and Miss Laura and Mr. Harry have to do the most of theirs by writing, for Riverdale has got to be a model village in respect of the treatment of all kinds of animals. It is a model village not only in that respect, but in others. It has seemed as if all other improvements went hand in hand with the humane treatment of animals. Thoughtfulness toward lower creatures has made the people more and more thoughtful toward themselves, and this little town is getting to have quite a name through the State for its good schools, good society, and good business and religious standing. Many people are moving into it, to educate their children. The Riverdale people are very particular about what sort of strangers come to live among them.

A man who came here two years ago and opened a shop, was seen kicking a small kitten out of his house. The next day a committee of Riverdale citizens waited on him, and said they had had a great deal of trouble to root out cruelty from their village, and they didn't want any one to come there and introduce it again, and they thought he had better move on to some other place. The man was utterly astonished, and said he'd never heard of such particular people. He had had no thought of being cruel. He didn't think that the kitten cared; but now when he turned the thing over in his mind, he didn't suppose cats liked being kicked about any more than he would like it himself, and he would promise to be kind to them in future. He said, too, that if they had no objection, he would just stay on, for if the people there treated dumb animals with such consideration, they would certainly treat human beings better, and he thought it would be a good place to bring up his children in. Of course they let him stay, and he is now a man who is celebrated for his kindness to every living thing; and he never refuses to help Miss Laura when she goes to him for money to carry out any of her humane schemes.

There is one most important saying of Miss Laura's that comes out of her years of service for dumb animals that I must put in before I close, and it is this. She says that cruel and vicious owners of animals should be punished; but to merely thoughtless people, don't say "Don't" so much. Don't go to them and say, "Don't overfeed your animals, and don't starve them, and don't overwork them, and don't beat them," and so on through the long list of hardships that can be put upon suffering animals, but say simply to them, "Be kind. Make a study of your animals' wants, and see that they are satisfied. No one can tell you how to treat your animal as well as you should know yourself, for you are with it all the time, and know its disposition, and just how much work it can stand, and how much rest and food it needs, and just how it is different from every other animal. If it is sick or unhappy, you are the one to take care of it; for nearly every animal loves its own master better than a stranger, and will get well quicker under his care."

Miss Laura says that if men and women are kind in every respect to their dumb servants, they will be astonished to find how much happiness they will bring into their lives, and how faithful and grateful their dumb animals will be to them.

Now I must really close my story. Good-bye to the boys and girls who may read it; and if it is not wrong for a dog to say it, I should like to add, "God bless you all." If in my feeble way I have been able to impress you with the fact that dogs and many other animals love their masters and mistresses, and live only to please them, my little story will not be written in vain. My last words are, "Boys and girls, be kind to dumb animals, not only because you will lose nothing by it, but because you ought to; for they were placed on the earth by the same Kind Hand that made all living creatures."

Appendix A: Selected Reviews of Beautiful Joe

[Widely adopted in schools and consistently heading the lists of children's favorite books, *Beautiful Joe* was heralded as a vital piece of humane education. A few critics found, however, that the quality of the writing suffered for the sake of the pedagogical message.]

1. From "Books for Young Folks," *Books* (December 1894)

"Beautiful Joe" has been compared to "Black Beauty" the horse. It is a volume most proper for young folks, since it teaches kindness to animals, the true relation they bear to human beings in this world of ours, and dwells most sympathetically upon the kindly treatment they should receive at human hands. Were there more of such books placed in the hands of our boys at a tender age, there would be less need for humane societies and penal codes for those who abuse dumb creatures.

2. From "Editorial Notes," *McMaster University Monthly* (February 1894)

[T]he varied incidents of the home life afford Joe many good opportunities of giving us, in the most charming style, his views of the claims upon our sympathies of the lower animals generally, and of household pets more particularly. That these have greater capabilities and endowments more closely allied to our own faculties of reason and moral perception than is commonly supposed, the authoress takes for granted throughout the book, and justly so. Moreover, that the habit of treating our domestic animals, not as mere unfeeling brutes, but as intelligent creatures, keenly sensitive to pain and suffering, and gratefully responsive to care and kindness, cannot fail to exert a most elevating influence upon our own moral natures, is a fact that Joe's narrative proves beyond all doubt.

3. From "Beautiful Joe," *Sunday School Times* (7 April 1894)

Beautiful Joe does for the dog what Black Beauty did for the horse. [...] The book is intelligent, clean, and not over emotional. While it would be better and more popular if condensed to half its length, it presents, on the whole, a strong plea for a complete change in our treatment of animals.

4. From "Books and Authors," *Record of Christian Work* (June 1894)

The story is in the form of an autobiography, and while most of the characters are introduced simply to express certain views of humane people as to the treatment of brute creation, they are rather more life-like than is usual in purpose stories.

5. From "Fiction," *Literature* (June 1898)

Beautiful Joe is a dog, and in his own way he is quite as fascinating as Black Beauty, but the chronicle of his life and adventures is somewhat longer and more elaborate than the story of the horse. The purpose is more obvious, the style often didactic. The book is an excellent one, but we doubt whether it will be quite as popular with English children as "Black Beauty."

6. From "Our Book Table," *Chinese Recorder and Missionary Journal* (1908)

[*Beautiful Joe* was translated for the use of Christian missionaries abroad. This review is of the edition translated into Chinese by Mrs. MacGillivray, the wife of Reverend Donald MacGillivray. The tenor of the review reflects the period's investment in the discourse of humane-ness as a tool to distinguish some peoples as more "civilized" than others.[1]]

The Chinese need instruction on no subject more than on that of kindness to dumb creatures, and this is *the only book* of its kind in the Chinese language. There are *millions* of children in China who would prize the book if it were put into their hands and even the grown-up population would read it with pleasure, and, let us hope, with profit.

---

1   In 1894, a Japanese translation was also prepared. The American Baptist Pub-
    lication Society hoped that "[i]n war times it may have a pacific effect on the
    Japs" (qtd. in Langille 18). Copies of the Chinese, Swedish, Esperanto and
    other translations are housed at Acadia University's Esther Clark Wright
    Archives.

Appendix B: Readings on Animal Protectionism

1. Prosecutions

[In 1866, shortly after founding the American Society for the Prevention of Cruelty to Animals (ASPCA), Henry Bergh pushed through a law in New York banning the overloading or overworking of horses, bull-baiting, dog- and cockfighting, neglect, and abandonment. The ASPCA was also empowered to enforce the new law, and Bergh did so zealously, often purposefully making a spectacle in order to advertise the ASPCA's work. *Our Dumb Animals*, the organ of the Massachusetts SPCA under George T. Angell, was similarly used to spread humane ideas. The following reports highlight how representations of victims and rescuers often propagated race and gender stereotypes.]

a. From "Cruelty to Animals—First Case of Punishment under the New Law," *New York Times* (13 April 1866)

The first arrest, since the passage by the Legislature of the act incorporating the "American Society for the Prevention of Cruelty to Animals," was effected on Wednesday, by a member thereof. The offender is a German butcher named Manz, living in Brooklyn, and the offence carrying a load of calves in his cart, piled up like wood, their legs tightly bound by cords, and one of them so disposed of as to bring his eye in contact with a sharp stick, thereby destroying the sight, and threatening, at each motion of the vehicle, to tear it out of its socket. Taken before Justice Dowling at the Tombs; he was promptly fined $10 and discharged.[1] The gentleman in question had a warm chase after the offender, from Broadway to the Williamsburgh ferry, but persevered until his arrest and punishment were effected. Who will next imitate this example, and thereby testify to these torturers of the brute creation, that their long carnival of cruelty is drawing to a close.

---

1 "The Tombs" has been the popular name of one of New York City's principal jails since it was first established in 1838.

b. From "Mr. Bergh's Good Work," *New York Times* (18 July 1874)

Washington Williams was held in $300 bail by Justice Murray, at Jefferson Market,[1] yesterday, on complaint of Mr. Henry Bergh, of the Society for the Prevention of Cruelty to Animals. Williams is a colored man in the employment of a firm on Broadway, near Bleecker street, owning a cider factory, who employ a large Newfoundland dog as the motive power in an apple-grinding machine. The tread mill—for it is nothing else—in which the unfortunate animal is daily placed and compelled to work is conspicuously placed in a front window to attract the attention of passers-by.

c. "Cruel Cases," *Our Dumb Animals* (May 1874)[2]

It has not been our custom to report cases of severe cruelty in our paper, as the community are, or ought to be, convinced of it already, and the perusal of these cases is painful to many of our readers. But the following are a few of the cases we have prosecuted, and are submitted only as specimens:—Tying cord tightly around a horse's tongue, keeping it on all night, from which it became so swollen that he could not get it back into his mouth for two or three days. Torturing a cat, by pouring spirits of turpentine into her body. Beating horse with a crowbar. Driving a horse to death. Stabbing horses with a bayonet and knife. Throwing a dog from a third-story window. Beating a horse with a cart-stake. Drawing horse's tongue out by the roots. Scalding a dog. Chopping off the tail of a horse. Thrusting a fork into a horse's body. Dragging a horse by a chain around his neck. Pouring kerosene oil on a cow, and igniting it; this last case, we are sorry to say, by a woman!

2. Humane Destruction

[In cities like Philadelphia and New York, when stray dogs were impounded, the usual policy was to keep alive for a couple of days those dogs that appeared to be of worth, giving their owners a chance to claim them or for interested parties to buy them. As the humani-

---

1   Justice Henry Murray was presiding justice at Jefferson Market, which served as a New York City courthouse from 1877 to 1945. Located on Sixth Avenue and Tenth Street, the ornate building stood out like "a jewel in a swine's snout" (qtd. in Harris 92), its exterior concealing the prison within.
2   *Our Dumb Animals*, the first magazine devoted to the humane treatment of animals, was established in 1868 by George T. Angell of the American Humane Education Society (Beers 88).

KILLING ANIMALS HUMANELY.

HUMANITY requires that animals be killed in the quickest and least painful manner. The following circular has been sent by our AMERICAN HUMANE EDUCATION SOCIETY very widely through the country.

THE HORSE.

THE DOG.

SHOOTING. — Place the pistol muzzle within a few inches of the head, and shoot at the dot, aiming toward the centre of the head.

BLOWS. — Blindfold, and with a heavy axe or hammer strike just below the foretop, at the point indicated in the present cut. Two vigorous, well-directed blows will make death sure.

Be careful not to shoot or strike too low.

SHOOTING. — Place the pistol muzzle near the head, aiming a little one side of the centre of the top of the skull, and shoot downward at the dot, so that the bullet shall go through the brain into or toward the neck.

Do not shoot too low or directly in the middle, because of thick bones.

After much consultation with veterinary surgeons and experts, no better or more merciful method of killing cats has been found than to put, with a long-handled wooden spoon, about half a teaspoonful of *pure* cyanide of potassium on the cat's tongue, *as near the throat as possible.* The suffering is only for a few seconds. Great care must be used to get *pure* cyanide of potassium, and to keep it tightly corked.

For further information, when needed, write

GEO. T. ANGELL,
President [*of the American Humane Education Society, the Massachusetts Society for the Prevention of Cruelty to Animals, and the Parent American Band of Mercy*],
19 Milk Street, Boston.

To minimize animal suffering, the American Humane Education Society distributed pamphlets to teach the public how to kill their animals quickly and effectively. This pamphlet was included in the back matter of Anna Sewell's *Black Beauty* (Boston: Youth's Companion, 1895).

tarians felt that a miserable life was worse than death, the mongrel thousands—described by *Harper's New Monthly* as "the 'zero multiplied by infinity' of worthlessness" (Carroll 191)—were killed.]

a. From "Drowning the Dogs," *New York Times* (8 July 1877)

The drowning of unlicensed dogs began at 5 A.M. yesterday, and lasted until 1 P.M., during which time 738 full-grown dogs and about 20 puppies were disposed of. At 1:30 o'clock the pound was ready for the reception of the canines caught during the day. The place was closed at 5 P.M., and at that time 524 dogs had been received. It was decided at first to drown these at 5 A.M. to-morrow, but Officer George H. Lambert, of Bergh's force, insisted that the dogs were of too good a class generally to be so quickly destroyed, and got the drowning postponed until Tuesday morning, in order that ample opportunity may be had by those who have lost dogs to redeem them if in the pound, and by those who wish good dogs to buy them there.

Thirteen catchers and their assistants, and one newsboy, were bitten yesterday. [...] The total number of full-grown dogs received at the pound during the week was 2,059; number drowned, 1,500; number redeemed, 31; number sold, 2; number released on account of previous license, 2; payment to the catchers, $617.70. The largest number of dogs captured in one day by any one catcher was 108.

b. From William K. Horton, "The Humane Destruction of Small Animals," *Our Dumb Animals* (November 1911)[1]

It must be plain that the destruction of animal life is a highly distasteful duty, and that there is no pleasure to be derived from it other than the knowledge that a public duty on behalf of mankind and to the animals themselves is being well performed. [...]

Homeless animals multiply with astonishing rapidity: they lead wretched lives when left to themselves, suffering the tortures of hunger, thirst, and disease; and it seems evident that if they can be destroyed without pain, it is best for the animals themselves, as well as for humanity at large. To put these forsaken and suffering creatures into a sleep from which they do not awake is not cruelty to them, since it causes them no pain. It would be cruelty to allow their suffering to continue [...].

---

1   Horton was general manager of the ASPCA from 1907 to 1929 (Lane 148).

c. From W.F. Morse, "The Humane and Sanitary Disposal of Superfluous Animal Life," *American Journal of Public Health* (July
1913)[1]

The domestic animals are a necessary factor as food for sustaining
human life or as beasts of burden to bear a part of the heavy labor, or
as our companions or associates in many intimate relations, they con-
tribute in no small degree to our happiness and amusements.

But their span of life is short, and presently they become old and
decrepit and finally an incumbrance to be mercifully disposed of.

[...] One very noteworthy feature of death by the automatic electric
cage[2] is the fact that there is absolutely nothing repulsive about it. The
bodies come from the cages, relaxed and warm, and so perfectly
peaceful in appearance that, if it were not for the widely opened eyes,
they would seem asleep. The effect on the operator is very noticeable,
especially if he has been used to other and less beneficent methods of
slaughter.

3. The Vivisection Controversy

[In the last few decades of the nineteenth century, doctors and scientists institutionalized the practice of experimenting on living animals.
Women and the working class were more likely to propose its abolition. Their enemies were usually white professional men protected by
their social position, yet the virulence with which they defended the
practice suggests how threatened they felt by anti-vivisectionists. The
ensuing controversy contributed to the fragmentation of the humanitarian movement, distinguishing the moderates from the radicals.]

a. From Caroline Earle White, *An Answer to Dr. Keen's Address
Entitled "Our Recent Debts to Vivisection"* (1886)

[On March 11, 1885, Dr. William Keen defended vivisection to the
graduating class of the Women's Medical College of Pennsylvania.
After citing the medical advancements that he attributed to the practice, Keen argued that the costs of the use of animals in medical
research were comparatively low. Each side of the controversy accused
the other of misrepresenting facts—how many animals, how much

---

1 W.F. Morse was a consulting sanitary engineer in New York City.
2 By 1919, these electric cages had been adopted in the UK by the RSPCA,
and in Rome, Italy, by the Rome Society for the Protection of Animals
("Electric Cages for Animals" 37).

pain, how much anesthetic. In this excerpt, the Vice-President of the American Society for the Restriction of Vivisection, Caroline Earle White disputes the vivisectionists' claim that only a "few" animals were subjected to painful experiments.]

It is a favorite euphemism with vivisectors and the advocates of vivisection to say a "few" animals. Is it not better, they almost invariably ask, that a *few* animals should suffer, than that the human race should be deprived of any advantage that it is possible to obtain? Allow me to give you some idea of what is implied in the term "a *few* animals."

Dr. Schiff, the eminent Vivisector, during his residence in Florence, of ten years, is generally stated to have killed in his experiments fourteen thousand dogs. The Vivisector, Flourens, in his own writings, says: "Magendie sacrificed 4000 dogs to prove the correctness of Sir Charles Bell's views with regard to the distinction of the sensitive and motor nerves; he then sacrificed 4000 more to prove these views erroneous. I took up the experiments in my turn, and demonstrated the first opinion to be the right one; in order to arrive at my results I also vivisected a great number of dogs."[1]

If four vivisectors alone can thus be shown to have put to death about twenty-five thousand animals, some ten thousand of which were in one single series of experiments, and those some of the most terrible that can be imagined, since they were made on the nerves, is it too much to say that all that have been offered up on what are called by physiologists the "bloodless altars" of Science, since these experiments first began may correctly be represented by the term millions?

b. From Lena Palmer, "Vivisection," *New York Medical Times* (March 1889)

Two main objections are urged against this system of cutting into the living body; first, what is the good of it, and secondly, that it is need-

---

1 White's source for these numbers is Frances Power Cobbe, the Anglo-Irish social reformer and leading suffragist and anti-vivisectionist. In "Vivisection and its Two-Faced Advocates" (1882), Cobbe cites the vivisectors' own writings, outlining in graphic detail the experiments conducted on living, and usually conscious, animals (612). The four vivisectors named here are J. Moritz Schiff, Marie-Jean-Pierre Flourens, François Magendie, and Sir Charles Bell. Apparently Flourens felt the need to re-test Bell's theory because the latter had been constrained by British anti-vivisectionists from using anything but stunned animals (Otis 558). Defenders of vivisection contended that Cobbe misread or fabricated her information (Brunton 897, Yeo 898). For more on the movement, see French and Lansbury.

less cruelty, giving fearful agony to animals and rendering the operators hard-hearted and callous. [...]

The second objection is that it gives fearful agony to animals, and
causes operators to become callous and hard-hearted. It is to be feared
that this objection comes chiefly from a clan who have allowed a rather
sickly and ignorant sentimentalism to usurp the place of reason and
inquiry. [...] In your own experiences are the surgeons[,] all of whom
must have witnessed distressing cases, and some of whom have taken
part in experiments on the living animals, callous and brutalized men?
Who will dare to insult a noble profession by saying so? Is it not the
motive and not the actual deed which hardens and renders cruel?

c. From Dr. George Fleming, *Vivisection: A Prize Essay* (1871)

[The medical profession typically dismissed anti-vivisectionist arguments by claiming that the latter had no medical knowledge with
which to understand the nature, validity, or value of the procedures.
Anti-vivisectionists responded by soliciting expert opinions such as
Dr. George Fleming's. A respected English veterinary surgeon,
Fleming's essay won an RSPCA prize and was published in London
in 1866, then republished in the US by the Women's Branch of the
Pennsylvania SPCA. Doubtless the medical profession took umbrage
at the unfavorable comparison to inquisitors and butchers.]

At first the physiologist or experimentalist may not be very cruel, his
experiments may be few, conducted with as great a regard as possible
to the avoiding of pain, and having the elucidation of the most profitable researches in view; but to him, as to other men, habit may
render that which was at first, perhaps, sickening and repulsive, an
affair of but little moment; and the ready infliction of pain to any
degree, and in any amount, will not, in all probability, appear in the
same disgusting light, that it will do to the uninitiated, and less hardened individual. There are but few men who are capable of performing the parts of executioners, even when stern justice demands the
taking away of life, or those of butchers, when animals must be sacrificed as food for man; and the dissector of live animals who has
imbibed a taste, or fancies he sees some necessity for the practice, does
not often exalt his labor to a more enviable degree in the estimation of
the feeling and thinking world. [...] The vivisectionist may be aptly
compared to a remorseless inquisitor, who attempts to wring the
secrets of nature from his victims by the most harrowing and pro-
tracted tortures; whereas the hangman, the headsman, and the
butcher, are mercifully prompted to obviate suffering by instantaneous
death.

d. From Dr. George Murray Humphry, *Vivisection: What Good Has It Done?* (1882)

[Professor of Anatomy and Physiology at the University of Cambridge, Dr. Humphry delivered this speech at the 1881 meeting of the British Medical Association. It was later published by the newly formed Association for the Advancement of Medicine by Research, a group of physicians organized in 1882 to resist restrictions proposed by anti-vivisectionists.]

[...] Vivisection must not be viewed from the side of sentiment only. It must be regarded as a matter upon which the welfare of mankind is eminently dependent—so much so, that we must not allow our feelings for the lower animals to sway our judgment, and must no longer allow the exaggerated statements which are made respecting it to pass unchallenged. Disease is increasing with civilization; and, unless we meet disease—the disease which civilization causes—by the powers which civilization gives us, our people will degenerate; and bear in mind, and let the world bear in mind, that there is no physical degeneration without a moral degeneration.

e. From Dr. Michael Foster, "Vivisection," *Popular Science Monthly* (April 1874)

[In *On the Origin of Species* (1859), Charles Darwin employed the metaphor of a "struggle for existence" to describe natural relationships. Darwin's theory of natural selection—the intergenerational process by which certain traits are passed on and others not, depending on which traits allow an organism to successfully reproduce in the context of its particular environment—was influenced by Robert Malthus's 1798 theory of population explosion. Malthus had argued that as human populations increased, the increasing scarcity of resources would inevitably lead to competition and misery. Darwin specified that his use of the term "struggle for existence" was metaphorical—intended to capture both interdependent as well as competitive relationships—but his writings focused on competition between species (65-66). Readers initially responded heatedly to *Origin*, particularly for how it conflicted with Christian thought, but in the course of a few decades Darwin's theory of evolution was generally accepted. Foster's argument here takes the idea of "struggle for existence" literally to justify human dominion over animals.]

[...] Unless man destroys animals, animals would soon destroy man. [...] The very conditions of his existence lay upon him the burden, and in so doing give him the right, to use the world around him, the lives of animals included, to aid him in his strife. [...]

If we believe that man is to govern the world, and he must either govern or succumb, then we must be prepared to use animals selfishly, if you please to call it so—to use animals for our advantage—to kill them when we have need of their deaths—to kill them with pain when the pain is for our benefit; and, inasmuch as the greater includes the less, to inflict pain without death where their pain does us good. Our good is, in fact, the rule of our conduct toward animals. Whenever an animal is killed by man, or suffers pain at the hand of man, without benefit to man, or where the same benefit could be gained without the death or without the pain, then the death or the pain can no longer be justified. The man who inflicts them is a cruel man; he no longer does good, but harm, to humanity, and humanity ought to stop his hand.

Appendix C: Teachers' Lesson Plans for Humane Education

[Humane teachings shaped child education across the US, and *Beautiful Joe* was popular in and out of the classroom. The following were suggested lesson plans for teachers.]

1. From Oliver Angell, *The Child's Fourth Book* (1888)[1]

LESSON XXVIII. CRUELTY TO ANIMALS DESERVES PUNISHMENT.

1. "What is the matter now, Charles?" said Mr. Vincent to his son; "why do you look so sorrowful?" "Because," replied Charles, "a boy who was going by has been beating Mungo, and made him cry; I am sure he has hurt him very much, and I do not like to have my dog hurt, do you, papa?" "Certainly not," said his father; "that must have been a very wicked boy. I have a great mind to run after him and punish him as he has deserved. All who wantonly beat animals, deserve to be beat in their turn, or to be punished."

QUESTIONS.

What was the occasion of Charles Vincent's sorrow? What did his father tell him? How ought those boys to be used, who wantonly beat dumb animals? ˷

LESSON XXIX. HONEST OLD TRAY.

    1. O! don't hurt the dog, poor honest old Tray;
    What good will it do thee, to drive him away?
        Kind usage is justly his right;
    Remember how faithful he is to his charge,
    And barks at the rogues when we set him at large,
        And guards us by day and by night.

    2. Though thou, by and by, will grow up to a man,
    And Tray is a dog, let him grow as he can,
        Remember, my good little lad,
    A dog that is honest, and faithful and mild,
    Is not only better than is a bad child,
        But better than men who are bad.

---

1   Angell was principal of Franklin High School in Providence, RI.

3. If thou art a boy, and Tray is but a beast,
I think it should teach thee one lesson at least;
     Thou ought to act better than he!
And if, without reason or judgment or sense,
Tray does as we bid him, and gives no offence,
     How diligent Richard should be.

4. If I do but just whistle, as oft thou hast seen,
He seems to say, "Master what is it you mean?
     My courage and duty are tried."
And see, when I throw my hat over the pale,
He fetches it back, and comes wagging his tail,
     And lays it down close by my side.

5. Then honest old Tray, let him sleep at his ease,
While you from him learn to endeavor to please,
     And obey me with spirit and joy:
Or else we shall find (what would grieve me to say,)
That Richard's no better than honest Old Tray,
     And a brute has more sense than a boy.

2. From John S. Clark, Mary Dana Hicks, and Walter S. Perry, "Love of Animals," *Teacher's Manual Part I for the Prang Elementary Course in Art Instruction* (1898)[1]

Beautiful and truthful anecdotes of the intelligence and affection of animals, particularly of dogs, abound in all juvenile literature of the day. The children might be permitted to reproduce some of these stories as a language lesson and to illustrate them by drawing. [...] The highest result of the lesson is not obtained if it does not lead to gentle thoughts and tender treatment of all dumb animals.

3. From J.W. Searson and George E. Martin, *Studies in Reading* (1913)

[Martin was superintendent of city schools of Nebraska City, NE. These study questions follow an excerpt of Chapters 1 and 2 of *Beautiful Joe*.]

---

1 Louis Prang (1842-1909) was a Boston chromolithographer who is credited as the first to mass-produce Christmas cards in 1874. He also published widely used publications for art instruction. For more on Prang, see Meggs. Archival materials can be found in the Louis Prang Papers, 1848-1932, in the Archives of American Art, Washington, DC.

NOTES

1. Read Saunders' "Beautiful Joe."
2. Learn what is done in your community to protect horses, cattle, and dogs from cruelty.
3. What laws protect the lower animals?
4. Give instances you have observed in which older people and children have been kind to the lower animals.
5. Look up the meanings of the following words and expressions: thoroughbred, cur, illtreated [sic], savage, patient, anxiously, disposition, pleadingly, gaunt, scarred creature, agony, moaning, bandaged, rescuing, punished, maimed, immediately, hideous, trooped.

EXERCISES

1. Why is the speaker called "Beautiful Joe" when he is so ugly?
2. When and why does the dog tell this story?
3. What good word had he heard his mistress say concerning cruelty to animals?
4. In what surroundings was Beautiful Joe born?
5. Explain "I don't think there can be a worse man in the world than that milkman."
6. Why did Beautiful Joe's mother love her master?
7. Just what kind of man was her master? Give proof.
8. What does "He aimed a kick at us as we passed" show?
9. What is shown of the master in his killing the brothers and sisters of Beautiful Joe?
10. Give passages to show whether or not dumb animals have grief.
11. What spirit did Beautiful Joe show toward the master? Was he justified in this?
12. What is shown of the master in his treatment of Beautiful Joe?
13. What friend appeared at this time?
14. What tells us the nature of the new friends of Beautiful Joe?
15. Just what kind of girl is Laura? Give proofs.
16. What is shown of the children in that they named this poor, maimed dog Beautiful Joe?

4. From Paul Whitfield Horn and Edwin DuBois Shurter, *New American Readers Book 4* (1919)

[Horn was superintendent of city schools in Houston, TX. These study questions precede an excerpt of Chapters 1 and 2 of *Beautiful Joe*.]

STUDY SUGGESTIONS. 1. Who tells this story? 2. How does he describe himself? 3. What is said of Joe's early life? 4. How does his new home differ from his old one? 5. What kind of man was his old master? 6. Read the passages that tell you of Joe's sorrows. 7. How did "Beautiful Joe" get his name? 8. What do *you* do to help in the prevention of cruelty to animals? 9. Is there a society for that purpose in your town? What could you do to organize a branch society in your school? 10. In reading the story remember the dog is telling the story himself. You must therefore imagine how he felt, and repeat his story just as naturally and sympathetically as you can.

5. From Emma Miller Bolenius, *Advanced Lessons in Everyday English* (1921)

[A successful textbook writer, Bolenius linked language instruction with cultural assimilation (Enoch 135). In this reader, she asks students to pledge allegiance to both the US and to the English language as part of her larger mission to Americanize African Americans, Native Americans, and Chicano/a students (Enoch 135). This composition assignment accompanies a condensed version of the first four paragraphs of Chapter 1 of *Beautiful Joe* and an excerpt from Helen Keller's "The Story of My Life." Helen Keller was celebrated for overcoming her handicaps as a deaf-blind person, pursuing a Bachelor's degree at Radcliffe College and later becoming a lecturer and advocate. At the age of 22 she wrote her memoir, "The Story of My Life" (New York: Doubleday, Page & Co., 1903), which was held up to children as an example of what could be achieved with hard work and determination (Rankin 16).]

Project 22. Composing Autobiographies.

12. Writing an Autobiographical Letter. Imagine yourself to be a dog, telling his own story.

Copy the first paragraph about Beautiful Joe [...] as the beginning of a letter. Then tell what happened to the dog in his first year.

Appendix D: Readings on Pet-Keeping Culture

1. The Dangers and Benefits of Pet-Keeping

[As pet-keeping for companionship became widespread, a loud minority discouraged the practice. Both sides had scientific experts on their side. On one hand, proponents believed that pet-keeping was essential to child development, particularly of boys; on the other, detractors argued that the practice was symptomatic of excess sentimentality.]

a. From Dr. Charles L. Dana, "The Zoophil-Psychosis: A Modern Malady," *Medical Record* (6 March 1909)

[Far from being a quack scientist, Dana was a leading figure in neurology for over five decades, serving variously as president and trustee of organizations such as the New York Academy of Medicine and the American Neurological Association ("Dana, Charles Loomis" 538). He also published prolifically, including his 1893 *Text-Book of Nervous Diseases*, which went into several printings (538).]

Case II.—*Zoophil-Obsession.* A lady about 40 years old, married but childless and not desirous of children, lived with her husband and sister in a quiet suburb of a large city. Her interest in life lay, to some extent, in her sister and husband and house, but it was mostly in sick cats. She could not bear to have a cat suffer. She made her home a hospital for stray sick cats; and the house was always full of them. If she heard a "meowing" at night she was unhappy and would wake her husband and make him go out and catch the animal, if he could and bring it home. The man's life was made utterly wretched by this condition of affairs, and I was consulted.

The patient herself was a woman in good general health, fairly intelligent, but unsocial, unsexual, and interested only in her domestic and animal affairs, and the conduct of her husband, for she was of a very jealous and exacting disposition, ruling the situation by her selfish querulence. The cat obsession was only one phase, though the most disturbing one, of an unstable constitution; it dominated the situation. Her views on animal suffering were in the abstract, on a high ethical plane, while her conduct was on the lowest possible. She did not [...] have any "insight" or appreciation of her lack of consideration for the human side of her household, or of the real folly of her point of view. [...] She naturally belonged to some kind of zoophilic society, and even organized a little society of her own.

This condition had gradually developed during a period of about five years; until she had become the chronic victim of the cat obsession. She was advised treatment by a gynecologist, for there was some absence or perversion of instinct in her case.

[...] The attitude of the civilized communities to animals has undergone great change in the last century.

[...] But when new things are added to our civilization we do not always assimilate them properly, for there is a large class of the unstable, and of the uneducated or over-educated who eagerly seize on what most appeals to their sensibilities, which are developed in excess of judgment.

[...] Now, it is much easier to pet a dog or nurse a kitten, than to tell the exact truth, or speaking more concretely, to nurse the sick; provide thoughtfully for the poor; or keep watch over the temper and make a household comfortable. Thus the kindly feelings of the indolent and unintelligent often take this line of least resistance; and then the feelings and interests grow, until the care for the pets vastly exceeds that in any other unselfish work. The dog is plump and over-cared for; and the cat is more happy than the husband. [...]

There will come next tears over the suffering of a fading flower, and sorrow over the unquenched thirst of the withering plant.

b. From Reverend Eli Hartness, "Pets and Their Long Life," *Old and New* (September 1872)

[Reverend Eli Hartness was pastor of the First Congregational Church at Huddersfield, West Yorkshire. *Old and New* was founded and later edited by the influential Unitarian clergyman and author Edward Everett Hale.]

[I]t is a very simple affair to keep a horse or a cow, a cat or a dog. They never will grow up drunkards, nor take to the street, nor in any way make home a scene of disgust and misery. If they prove what we do not take a fancy to, we can easily dispose of them, and forget them; and what becomes of them we think no affair of ours. If any pleasure can be had from them, we think it is our own; and, if they inflict any pain, we are not obliged to endure it. Their faults are no essential trouble to us; and we never lie awake at night thinking what possibly may become of them. They are of short life too: we shall not meet them twenty or thirty years hence; and, if were unexpectedly to come across them, they would not be bearing our name, nor known as ours, and to us they would bring no disgrace. As to the next world too: who thinks himself responsible there for his horse or dog? Who expects to meet his cow or his sheep in heaven,—brutes that perish? [...]

[Pets] have succeeded in bringing in a new moral element. It isn't a beast; it isn't a brute: it doesn't make the members of the family unhappy nor cross, nor set them a bad example, nor in any way lower their moral tone. It often calls out moral principle, even from those who seem to be destitute of it.

c. From Alvin George Eberhart, "Children's Pets," *Everything About Dogs* (1902)

[Eberhart was a prominent breeder and well known for his pedigree pugs (Raymond-Mallock 41).]

Nothing in the world is more natural than the child's desire for pets. There are few children who do not early manifest a strong inclination for something to love, and this imperative desire, if fostered, becomes a powerful agency for the child's growth of character. Every little girl loves her doll, but often she becomes dissatisfied and longs for something alive, something which will return her caresses. [...] Perhaps the mother is very busy, or if she gives the matter any thought, she may dislike animals and consider cats a nuisance, dogs noisy, birds a great care, rabbits destructive, and white rats dirty. She may wonder why the children do not love their home and how it is that they are always teasing to visit that home where the children have pets of various kinds, "a perfect menagerie," as she scornfully calls it. Alas! How many mothers and fathers cherish their selfish ease and consult their convenience, without a thought of finding their highest enjoyment in the true development of their children.

Our first plea in favor of children owning pets is the desire for personal possession which every child has. The wish for something that shall belong exclusively to himself and be cared for by him. This care, this responsibility, can not fail to make a boy more manly and a girl more womanly. [...] Show us a boy or a girl that is cruel or brutal to animals and we will show you a child sure to come to some bad end; but the child who early learns kindness and gentleness to the brute creation will also manifest the same spirit toward his fellow creatures.

d. From Eva C.E. Lückes, "Children and Pets," *Babyhood* 3.25 (December 1886)

[For nearly four decades, Lückes served as Matron of the London Hospital. Celebrated as the "matron of matrons" (Tooley 154) and the "head of the nursing world" ("Death of Miss Eva Lückes" 495),

Lückes managed the operations and training of nurses of this large East End institution from 1880 to 1919.]

"I cannot put up with dogs and cats about besides the children!" is the exclamation of a well-meaning but overworked mother sometimes; and with many children playing around, perhaps in small quarters, such a statement at first sight does not appear unreasonable. But if the said mother realized that association with these animals was likely to have a beneficial effect upon the children she would not usually be slow to submit to the additional inconvenience. [...] As children grow more observant and thoughtful the care of living pets is a most useful means of developing their sympathies.

[In the next issue, the editor issued the following note ("No title").]

[...] The positions taken by the writer of the article were generally sound, but some cautions from a sanitary point of view are not out of place. Children should be taught, if possible, just how and how far to be friendly with their pets. Not only should they be taught that the dog or cat has sensibility, and may be hurt by their energetic and careless caressing, but they should be also taught—and here is the sanitary point—that certain familiarities cannot be permitted. The habit of kissing dogs and cats is, so far as we have noticed, less common among children than among adult keepers of lap-dogs and cats; but the child should be made to understand that it must not kiss the animal, nor allow the latter to lick its hands or face, particularly the latter. [...] It is no hardship to the animals to be taught "to keep their place."

e. From "Household Pets," *Good Housekeeping* (10 December 1887)

Human affections demand something to pet. Parental instinct delights in having a pet, preferably a child of its own, but it may be another's child, and even a cat, or a dog, or a horse. This instinct requires that the object of its petting shall be small, usually, and at any rate it must be more or less helpless. The larger pet the smaller, and the stronger pet the weaker.

[...] It is said that as the human race advances in civilization, the workings of the mind will appear more and more in facial expression. The Indian and all the lower races have but slight facial expression, compared with that of more advanced races.

How worthy of kinship with man, then, is the dog! Watch him as he approaches his master, tail motionless, and with sober demeanor, perhaps not in doubt as to what his reception will be, but respectfully waiting for the first advances to come from his owner. The first slight token of kind notice is reflected in the movement of the eye and the slight motion of the tail, and when there can be no further doubt of the nature of the reception, the dog's natural language of feeling makes up for his poverty of vocal language, and man's faithful friend and servant responds with abundant demonstrations to his master's confidence and regard.

f. From Dr. Granville Stanley Hall, *Adolescence* (1905)

[The first President of the American Psychological Association, Dr. Granville Stanley Hall is considered the father of child study. Earlier in the century, German zoologist Ernst Haeckel had proposed that each individual relives every stage of its species' evolutionary history (this theory is known as, "ontogeny recapitulates phylogeny"). Exaggerating the gill-like arches on the neck of the human embryo, Haeckel argued that the embryo recapitulated all human evolutionary stages during gestation.[1] This dangerously erroneous theory would serve as justification for racism, as all the human races were sorted into an evolutionary ladder where the "lower races" gradually recapitulated all the evolutionary stages that Caucasian races had already achieved. In this excerpt from the two-volume *Adolescence*, Hall begins with the premise that children are closer to humanity's animal ancestors.]

To the young child, there is no gap between his soul and that of animals. They feel, think, act, much as he does. They love, hate, fear, learn, sleep, make toilets, sympathize, and have nearly all the basal psychic qualities that the child has. Indeed, we might almost define the animal world as consisting of human qualities broken up and widely scattered throughout nature and as having their highest utility in teaching psychology to the young by a true pedagogical method. [...]

[T]he dog teaches loyalty, reverence, and fidelity, which illustrate the very ideal of man's relation to God, as well as patience, sympathy, good-will, companionship, occupation that keeps from mischief, and the sense of responsibility that ownership can teach. To this end also the dog should be studied more systematically and scientifically. In respect to this animal the average child should repeat somewhat more fully the history of the race. [...]

I can almost believe that, if pedagogy is ever to become adequate to the needs of the soul, the time will come when animals will play a far larger educational role than has yet been conceived, that they will be cur-

---

1 For a critique of recapitulation theory, see Stephen Jay Gould's *Ontogeny and Philogeny* (Cambridge: Belknap, 1985).

riculized, will acquire a new and higher humanistic or culture value in the future comparable with their utility in the past, and that there will be a new poignancy of regret over the loss by extermination of many species akin to that now felt at the barbaric iconoclasm that has deprived the world of so many of the priceless monuments of antiquity. [...]

g. From Dr. W. Fowler Bucke, "Cyno-Psychoses: Children's Thoughts, Reactions, and Feelings Toward Pet Dogs," *Pedagogical Seminary* (1903)[1]

There is a relation between the number of domesticated animals and the grade of civilization. The use of any new thing by man has been an uplift to him. Environment has materially developed him if he has been interested. No one can recount what the dog has done in the life of the race nor the child, to give the type of mind we see to-day.

h. From Mabel A. Marsh, "Children and Animals," *Studies in Education* (1902)

[Along with Stanford University professor of education Earl Barnes and the British educator Thomas G. Tibbey, Marsh promoted the idea that animals were essential to children's emotional development (Barnes 163, Tibbey 103). For more on the turn-of-the-century belief in the value of children's study of nature, see Myers.]

The greatest difficulty of adult life lies in the adjusting of our relations to the human part of our environment and it is only fair to the child to give him, as far as possible, a training that may be of use to him in this direction; the social instincts need to be encouraged and the unsocial to be repressed, if the man is to grow up adequately prepared for his life-work.

[The child's] relations with other people are too complex, too little under his own control, too liable to sudden and unexpected developments to be quite satisfactory. It is well to begin with something simpler and easier, and this is often to be found in the relation between the child and his pet. An animal has sufficient individuality to make a charming companion and friend, without either the weakness that another child usually shows for wanting the same things at the same time, and appealing to the ordeal of combat if he is not given

---

1 As superintendent of the Training School at State Normal School at Geneseo, NY (now the State University of New York at Geneseo), Bucke also published a lengthy educational text called *The School and Its Problems: A Syllabus and Bibliography* (self-published, 1914).

them, or the exasperating respect of the grown-up person for such trivial and tiresome unessentials as clean hands and untorn clothes.

[...] The pet thus becomes a most important factor in the child's development, a factor that we can not afford to leave out of account.

Any one setting out to deliberately use the pet as a means of developing the social instincts of the child, would naturally wish for information on three points: First, what kind of animal should be chosen as a pet? Secondly, what reasons should determine this choice? Thirdly, what is the appropriate reaction of the child upon the pet?

i. From K.G. Cash, "Children's Pets: A Side Study," *Studies in Education* (1902)[1]

[While proponing pet-keeping and humane treatment of animals in general, this researcher also implicitly argues for moderation, expressing approval of children whose sympathies for animal suffering are well-developed yet who temper this sympathy with a realistic acceptance of the status quo.]

The papers on which the study is based were written by London Board School children, 650 by girls and 600 by boys. The children wrote in response to the test:

Tom bought a bird and kept it in a cage and took good care of it. His sister Mary wanted him to set it free, but Tom wished to keep it. What would you have done with the bird? Why?

[I]t would seem that the boys are either more selfish or more practical than the girls between the ages of 10 and 13. It would also seem that the boys feel an increasing interest in the control and care of the bird, which apparently arises from a love of power and active doing, while the girls say less about what they could do with the bird, because of their increasing interest in its welfare.

[...] In the study the children fall into three groups:

In the first, are those with whom the satisfaction of personal desire is the strongest motive for action; and action follows immediately on the desire. There is no considerable power of sustained thought, nor of altruistic feeling.

---

1 Cash's study follows Marsh's in the same issue of *Study in Education*, and followed up on the latter's suggestion that as children grow older they become more likely to think of others (Cash 100).

In the second group, there is evidence of an increase both in imaginative feeling and in intellectual capacity. The children have begun to consider the matter from the bird's point of view, and often they recognize some responsibility other than that of merely "being kind" to living creatures. Like most reformers, when possessed with one idea they act accordingly, and not necessarily with worldly wisdom. There is a freshness and spontaneity about them which is often lost when it becomes tempered with worldly wisdom.

In the third group are the children who have reached that stage when they are capable of seeing both sides of the matter. They can inhibit action in order to weigh evidence, and can look forward to the possible consequence of their action. These children are not less sympathetic than those of the second group; but they are becoming wordly wise. They are learning to adapt themselves to things as they are.

2. Training Manuals

a. From James E. Le Rossignol, "The Training of Animals," *American Journal of Psychology* (November 1892)

[Le Rossignol was a Quebecois writer and teacher who published several critiques of socialism and communism as well as folk stories of Quebec. At G. Stanley Hall's suggestion, Le Rossignol took notes from a collection of books on dogs for the benefit of students of animal psychology. Dog training manuals that went beyond "breaking" hunting dogs spread alongside pet-keeping, dictating care as well as behavior. These excerpts summarize the prevailing attitude regarding the proper power dynamic between master and pet.]

Praktische Abhandlung von dem Leithund, Carl von Heppe. Angsburg, 1751, pp. 499. [The dog] must be taught to love his master and always to obey his commands.

Ansfürliche Geschichte der Hunde, Anon. Leipzig, 1781, pp. 374. Dogs are trained by means of a judicious use of rewards and punishments, by the association of pleasant feelings with certain actions and painful feelings with others. The dog's own impulse towards self-preservation leads him to obedience, and when habits are formed rewards and punishments are no longer necessary.

Kunopaedia; a Practical Essay on Breaking or Training the English Spaniel or Pointer, William Dobson. London, 1814, pp. 235. Obedience is rewarded by caressing, while the contrary is punished with the whip. After whipping, the master must make friends with the dog before letting him go, and he must never be chased, that he may not learn he is swifter than his master. [...] The great principle to be followed is that of complete obedience.

The Dog, William Youatt. Philadelphia[,] 1857, pp. 392. The practitioner must understand the nature of the dog. He must be firm and courageous as well as kind and gentle in order to make the dog sensible of his power and of his good intentions.

Vollständige Unterricht, alle Arten Hunde abzurichten, Christian Friedr. Gottl. Thon. Ilmenau, 1832, pp. 296. The trainer must be careful to select a dog of the proper race, size and temperament for the particular kind of hunting he is to learn. Still, the natural temperament of the dog may be greatly modified by careful training. The trainer must not only know the nature of the dog, but must exercise great care and patience. The dog must learn to know and love his master and the master must treat him kindly and never punish him too severely.

House Dogs and Sporting Dogs, John Meyrick, Lond.[,] 1861, pp. 250. Some dogs are rendered vicious by whipping, while others require it to subdue their obstinacy.

Breeding, Training, Management, Diseases, etc., of Dogs, Francis Butler. Brooklyn, 1879, pp. 391. The dog should learn to obey from a desire to please his master rather than from a fear of punishment.

Dog-Breaking, General W.N. Hutchinson, Lond.[,] 1876, 6th Ed., pp. 348. The breaker should possess a thorough knowledge of dog natures. He should have perfect command of his temper and should use no severity.

Histoire du Chien chez tous les Peuples du Monde, Elzéar Blaze. Paris, 1843, pp. 460. The dogs of civilized nations show much higher development of character than those of savages. The disposition of the male is also very different from that of the female. The character of a dog depends on the education he has received, on the kind of people about him and especially on the conformation of his skull. Education can do much to change the natural disposition of a dog.

b. From Dorothy Canfield, "Pets," *What Shall We Do Now?: A Book of Suggestions for Children's Games and Employments* (1907)

[Canfield, later Canfield Fisher, was the first woman appointed to the Vermont state board of education and is credited for introducing the Montessori method of early childhood education in the US ("Fisher, Dorothy Canfield" 236).]

Tricks for Dogs

Always begin by training him to "trust," for it is the foundation of his training, and he will learn it before he is two months old. Do not keep him "on trust" for more than a second or two at first, but gradually make the time longer, until he will let you leave the room and not touch the biscuit until you return. [...] Treat him always with patience and firmness; be quick to reward but never give in to him. [...]

What is Due to Dogs

Do not overdo your mastership. Remember that a dog needs much liberty and independence to develop his individuality, and an enterprising puppy learns more by observation and experience in a week than a pampered lap-dog does in his whole life; he learns self-reliance, but he will always run to his master or mistress in any real difficulty, and you who are his master or mistress must be wary not to misunderstand or disregard him, for he needs sympathy and love, and if he does not get them he either becomes cowed and stupid or a n'er-do-weel.

Appendix E: Selections from Other Animal Literature

1. From Marshall Saunders, *Beautiful Joe's Paradise* (Boston: L.C. Page, 1902)

[This sequel to *Beautiful Joe* differs significantly in setting, structure and tone. The first-person narrator is a boy named Sam Emerson, and at the opening of the novel his dog Rag-time is killed by a neighboring boy. Seeing his distress, the animals who come to shepherd Rag-time to the island paradise for dead animals decide to take Sam along. There he meets with Joe, who is president of the island, as well as Rag-time, characters from *Beautiful Joe*, and many new creatures. On this island, all the animals speak English and are in complete health— except for being dead, that is. Here they await their masters' passing so they might spend eternity together. The excerpt below captures a scene where a wise old monkey explains to Sam what happens to the animals on the island.

The Christian belief that non-human animals lacked immortal souls was commonly used to justify the ill-treatment of animals. The rise of animal protectionism ignited open debate on the question, with laypersons and clergy arguing both sides. Although careful to avoid the word "souls," Saunders's sequel argues the case for animal afterlife. Reviewers remarked on the novel's similarity to Elizabeth Stuart Phelps's spiritualist novel, *The Gates Ajar* (1868). While *Paradise* elevates the animal by granting it a form of immortality, it also reaffirms the stark inequality of their subject positions: all the animals are beholden to the one human boy. *Paradise* is also Saunders's experiment with the genre of utopianism that was very popular at the turn of the century. As with many utopias of the period, Saunders's paradise was racially segregated.]

[From Chapter 3, "The Beautiful Island"]

"I feel queer," I said. "What makes all these animals look at me so?"

[The monkey] smiled a kind of grave smile. "The animals on this part of the Island have nearly all been used to the companionship of man. He is a divinity to them, and they will never be perfectly happy till they meet their former masters."

"And when will that be?" I asked, eagerly.

He gave a strange far-away look out over the sea. "No one knows.

Away off there is the World of the Blessed. Every little while a beautiful white air-ship comes gliding along, and takes away some of our best animals. That world is also full of islands, and they are said to be a thousand times more beautiful than this little paradise."

"Then every animal finds his owner there?"

"Yes, if the owner has already arrived. There are some very happy meetings there."

"But how is there room for everybody?" I said. "People have been dying for thousands of years."

"Don't you remember I told you that there are other worlds besides this one and yours?" he said, calmly.

I kept quiet a minute, trying to take it in, then I said, "Worlds upon worlds?"

"Yes, systems of worlds."

"And all with people on them?"

"No, not every one," said my new friend. "Not all are habitable."

"Why, it is enormous to think of," I said; "it gives a fellow a kind of back-handed blow on his imagination."

The old monkey looked at me pityingly. "So you have been supposing that the great Maker of the universe had only your little sphere to command. You are—oh, what are you, and we?" he said, choking all up, and looking at the sea and land.

"Our worlds," he went on, when he got his breath, "are only two drops of water in an ocean, two little stars in the field of the sky. We go on after death. People and animals, too, are transferred from one world to another. This satisfies the love of travel implanted in every breast."

"But when I die, I wish to be with my mother, my friends," I said, sharply.

"Your wish will be gratified, boy. Do you suppose your Creator would be cruel enough to set you down in the midst of a savage African tribe where my forefathers lived? No, families, communities, races, will be kept together if they wish, and yet there will be freedom for all [...]."

2. From Louise S. Patteson, *Pussy Meow: The Autobiography of a Cat* (Philadelphia: George W. Jacobs, 1901)

[Patteson was one of the many American writers who, in the wake of *Beautiful Joe*, took up pens to write animal autobiographies. Cat autobiographies were much less common than those of dogs. As the American Baptist Publication Society explained to Saunders, in rejecting her proposal for a companion novel to *Beautiful Joe* featuring a cat's narrative, "[i]t is difficult to understand why this should be the case but the dog and the horse excite very much more interest than the cat" (Rowland, letter dated 15 March 1905). Yet the publisher need not have looked too deeply for a reason: for centuries, the cat had been vilified on both sides of the Atlantic as a hypocritical, unfaithful ingrate who would pretend an attachment to a human master only for food and shelter. The cat, in short, was as evil as the dog was saintly, and thus, was of less interest as a protagonist. (The cat, predictably, was associated with women and girls.) In 1913, Saunders did eventually publish a cat autobiography, *Pussy Black-Face: The Story of a Kitten and Her Friends.*]

[From Chapter 3, "My Reasons for Writing This Story"]

After Guy had finished reading the story of Black Beauty, he read one written by a dog, "Beautiful Joe." I saw his picture in the book, but I did not think him half as beautiful as my friend Dennis that visits me every day. But Joe had a beautiful spirit, and that counts far more than a beautiful body. Who could read of the cruel blows and kicks and all the other insults which he suffered so patiently at the hands and feet of old Jenkins, without feeling in his inmost soul that henceforth he would defend and protect all helpless and harmless creatures? In this way Joe conferred a lasting benefit upon his fellow-dogs, and even I, who am only a cat, with no natural fondness for dogs, must say that I learned many things from Joe that made me have more respect for dogs. I also became filled with a desire to be as good and useful a cat as Joe was a dog, and it was during those long, lonesome days when I was without any companions that the thought came to me about writing this story. May be you think a cat does not even have thoughts. How dreadful! Well, I thought if dogs and horses can write stories, why can't I? And so I concluded to try.

I had often heard mistress read stories about cats, cat shows and cat clubs, but it was always about Persian cats and Angoras, and I made up my mind that my story should be about tigers and Maltese and black cats, because they are considered to be of so very little importance. [...]

Oh, if with this story I start all the world to think for awhile about cats—Maltese and tigers and black cats, that are so much exposed to suffering because within the reach of everybody, I shall feel that I have done some real good. And even if I do not write as good a story as did Black Beauty, or Beautiful Joe, you will at least know that I tried to do what I could to help my fellow-cats. And who knows but some cats, older and wiser than myself, may be encouraged by my effort to do more?

3. From Walter Emanuel, *A Dog Day, or The Angel in the House* (New York: E.P. Dutton, 1919)

[Emanuel was also known as "Charivaria," the "pungent paragraphist of *Punch*," a British humor and satire magazine. *A Dog Day* was very popular both in England and America (*Reform Advocate* 88). The quirky story, written as a diary rather than an autobiography, features a dog who is selfish, ungrateful, and emotionally unattached—and yet is thoroughly charming. The diary opens with a parody of the trope of a faithful dog that, like Beautiful Joe, saves his family by catching a burglar.]

A.M.

7   Woke up feeling rather below par, owing to disturbed rest. Hardly enough energy to stretch myself. In the middle of the night a strange man came in by the kitchen window, very quietly, with a bag. I chummed up to him at once. He was nice to me, and I was nice to him. He got me down a piece of meat that I could not reach myself. While I was engaged on this, he took a whole lot of silver things and put them into the bag. Then, as he was leaving, the brute—I believe, now, it was an accident—trod on my toe, making me yelp with pain. I bit him heartily, and he dropped his bag, and scurried off through the window again. My yelping soon woke up the whole house, and, in a very short time, old Mr. Brown and young Mr. Brown appear. They at once spot the bag of silver. They then declare I have saved the house, and make no end of fuss with me. I am a hero. Later on Miss Brown came down and fondled me lots, and kissed me, and tied a piece of pink ribbon round my neck, and made me look a fool. What's the good of ribbon, I should like to know? It's the most beastly tasting stuff there ever was.

8.30. Ate breakfast with difficulty. Have no appetite.

8.35. Ate kittens' breakfast.

8.36. An affair with the cat (the kittens' mother). But I soon leave her, as the coward does not fight fair, using claws.

9.0. Washed by Mary. A hateful business. Put into a tub, and rubbed all over—mouth, tail, and everywhere—with filthy soapy water, that loathsome cat looking on all the while, and sneering in her dashed superior way. I don't know, I am sure, why the hussy should be so conceited. She has to clean herself. I keep a servant to clean me. At the same time I often wish I was a black dog. They keep clean so much longer. Every finger-mark shows up so frightfully on the white part of me. I am a sight after Cook has been stroking me.

9.30. Showed myself in my washed state to the family. All very nice to me. Quite a triumphal entry, in fact. It is simply wonderful the amount of kudos I've got from that incident with the man. Miss Brown (whom I rather like) particularly enthusiastic. Kissed me again and again, and called me "a dear, clean, brave, sweet-smelling little doggie."

9.40. While a visitor was being let in at the front-door I rushed out, and had the most glorious roll in the mud. Felt more like my old self then.

4. **From Charles G.D. Roberts, "The Animal Story,"** *The Kindred of the Wild: A Book of Animal Life* **(Boston: L.C. Page & Co., 1903)**

[Roberts, a preeminent Canadian author, is considered one of the creators of the first Canadian literary genre, the realistic wild animal story, a genre that became very popular in the US in the early twentieth century as Americans sought out the "wilderness" to recharge frayed nerves. In 1903, one of the key American nature writers and conservationists of the nineteenth century, John Burroughs, famously accused Roberts, his fellow Canadian author Ernest Thompson Seton, and the American author William Long of falsely representing nature, a charge that Burroughs's friend, the hunter-conservationist president Theodore Roosevelt, later levied against the popular fiction writer Jack London. (See Appendix E6, p. 304). The "nature-fakers" controversy raged for years across the pages of prominent periodicals such as *Science*. In this excerpt, Roberts records the history of the animal story genre, classifying the humanized animals of *Beautiful Joe* and *Black Beauty* as predecessors to a more realistic animal fiction.]

Whether avowedly or not, it is with the psychology of animal life that the representative animal stories of to-day are first of all concerned. Looking deep into the eyes of certain of the four-footed kindred, we have been startled to see therein a something, before unrecognised, that answered to our inner and intellectual, if not spiritual selves. We have suddenly attained a new and clearer vision, where we were blindly wont to predicate mere instinct and automatism. It is as if one should step carelessly out of one's back door, and marvel to see unrolling before his new-awakened eyes the peaks and seas and misty valleys of an unknown world. Our chief writers of animal stories at the present day may be regarded as explorers of this unknown world, absorbed in charting its topography. They work, indeed, upon a substantial foundation of known facts. They are minutely scrupulous as to their natural history, and assiduous contributors to that science. But above all are they diligent in their search for the motive beneath the action. [...] The animal story at its highest point of development is a psychological romance constructed on a framework of natural science.

The real psychology of the animals, so far as we are able to grope our way toward it by deduction and induction combined, is a very different thing from the psychology of certain stories of animals which paved the way for the present vogue. Of these, such books as "Beautiful Joe" and "Black Beauty" are deservedly conspicuous examples. It is no detraction from the merit of these books, which have done great service in awakening a sympathetic understanding of the animals and sharpening our sense of kinship with all that breathe, to say that their psychology is human. Their animal characters think and feel as human beings would think and feel under like conditions. [...]

The next stage must be regarded as, in literature, a climax indeed, but not the climax in this genre. I refer to the "Mowgli" stories of Mr. Kipling.[1] In these tales the animals are frankly humanised. Their individualisation is distinctly human, as are also their mental and emotional processes, and their highly elaborate powers of expression. Their motives are complex; whereas the motives of real animals, so far as we have hitherto been able to judge them, seem to be essentially simple, in the sense that the motive dominant at a given moment quite obliterates, for the time, all secondary motives. Their reasoning powers and their constructive imagination are far beyond anything which present knowledge justifies us in ascribing to the inarticulate kindreds. [...]

The animal story, as we now have it, is a potent emancipator. It frees us for a little from the world of shop-worn utilities, and from the mean tenement of self of which we do well to grow weary. It helps us return to nature, without requiring that we at the same time return to barbarism. It leads us back to the old kinship of earth, without asking us to relinquish by way of toll any part of the wisdom of the ages, any fine essential of the "large result of time."

5. From Ernest Thompson Seton, *Krag, the Kootenay Ram* (New York: Charles Scribner's Sons, 1897)

[Seton, an English-born Canadian author, is credited along with Charles G.D. Roberts for developing the genre of the animal story. He was also one of the founders of the Boy Scouts of America, which pro-

---

1 In 1902, Rudyard Kipling published *Just So Stories*, a popular volume of stories about a boy named Mowgli and his jungle animal companions.

moted more intimate contact with the "wilderness"—an imagined space of the "natural" where no "culture" exists. Young boys' exposure to the trials of nature, the Boy Scouts believed, would help them develop a "virile" masculinity. (G. Stanley Hall also promoted this idea.) Seton was also embroiled in the "nature faker" controversy. (See headnote in Appendix E4, p. 301.) This excerpt is from the opening of *Krag*, which Roberts upheld as an example of the pinnacle of the realistic wild animal story.]

Up went his rifle, and in a moment one or both would have fallen, had not Scotty's eye, before he pulled, rested on two tiny new-born Lambs that got up on their long wobbly legs, in doubt, for a moment, whether to go to the new-comer, or to follow their mothers.

The old Sheep bleated a shrill alarm to their young and circled back. The Lambs' moment of indecision was over, they felt that their duties lay with the creatures that looked and smelt like themselves, and coolly turned their uncertain steps to follow their mothers.

Of course Scotty could have shot any or all of the Sheep, as he was within twenty yards of the farthest, but there is in man an unreasoning impulse, a wild hankering to catch alive; and without thinking of what he could do with them afterward, Scotty, seeing them so easily in his power; leaned his gun in a safe place and ran after the Lambs. But the distressed mothers had by now communicated a good deal of their alarm to their young, the little things were no longer in doubt that they should avoid the stranger, and when he rushed forward, his onset added the necessary final touch and for the first time in their brief lives they knew danger and instinctively sought to escape it. They were not yet an hour old, but nature had equipped them with a set of valuable instincts. And though the Lambs were slow of foot compared with the man, they showed at once a singular aptitude at dodging, and Scotty failed to secure them at once as he had expected.

Meanwhile the mothers circled about, bleating piteously and urging the little ones to escape. Scotty, plunging around in his attempt, alarmed them more and more, and they put forth all the strength of their feeble limbs in the effort to go to their mothers. The man slipping and scrambling after them was unable to catch either, although more than once he touched one with his hand. But very soon this serious game of tag was adroitly steered by the timid mothers away from the lupin bed, and once on the smooth, firmer ground, the Lambs got an advantage that quite offset the weariness they began to feel, and Scotty, dashing and chasing first this way and then that, did not realize that the whole thing was being managed by the old ones, till they reached the lowest spur of the Gunder Peak, a ragged, broken, rocky cliff, up which the mothers bounded. Then the little ones felt a new sense, just as a young duck must when first he drops in the water. Their little black rubber hoofs gripped the slippery rocks as no man's foot can do it, and they soared on their new-found mountain wings, up and away, till led by their mothers out of sight.

6. From Jack London, *The Call of the Wild* (New York: Grosset & Dunlap, 1903)

[London was, along with other authors, as described above, publicly charged with "nature-faking." He defended his novels as attempts to "protest against the 'humanizing' of animals" of which other writers were guilty and argued that his portrayal of dogs as capable of rudimentary reason was well founded in fact (London, "Other Animals" 200). Reminding his attackers to humbly remember that "[w]e who are so very human are very animal," London accused Burroughs of "stiff-necked pride" in refusing to recognize his "relatives" ("Other Animals" 210).

Aligning himself with writers such as Roberts and Seton, London— an American whose work was well received in England—set his dogs in the wilderness. In *The Call of the Wild*, a domesticated dog named Buck is stolen and sold to haul sleds in the Canadian Northlands, and that frontier experience causes him to revert back to his "wild," wolf-like origins. In this excerpt from Chapter 2, he is introduced to "the law of club and fang" that dictates the violent ethics of the wilderness. Another newcomer, Curly, is set upon by a gang of huskies and torn to pieces. This incident, which reads like a gang rape, affirms the novel's message that only men belong in the "wild." In this male-dominated novel, all the female characters die horrible deaths and the central focus of the story is on the intimate relationship between a man and his male dog.]

Buck's first day on the Dyea beach was like a nightmare. Every hour was filled with shock and surprise. He had been suddenly jerked from the heart of civilization and flung into the heart of things primordial. No lazy, sun-kissed life was this, with nothing to do but loaf and be bored. Here was neither peace, nor rest, nor a moment's safety. All was confusion and action, and every moment life and limb were in peril. There was imperative need to be constantly alert; for these dogs and men were not town dogs and men. They were savages, all of them, who knew no law but the law of club and fang.

He had never seen dogs fight as these wolfish creatures fought, and his first experience taught him an unforgettable lesson. It is true, it was a vicarious experience, else he would not have lived to profit by it. Curly was the victim. They were camped near the log store, where she, in her friendly way, made advances to a husky dog the size of a full-grown wolf, though not half so large as she. There was no warning, only a leap in like a flash, a metallic clip of teeth, a leap out equally swift, and Curly's face was ripped open from eye to jaw.

It was the wolf manner of fighting, to strike and leap away; but there was more to it than this. Thirty or forty huskies ran to the spot and surrounded the combatants in an intent and silent circle. Buck did not comprehend that silent intentness, nor the eager way with which they were licking their chops. Curly rushed her antagonist, who struck again and leaped aside. He met her next rush with his chest, in a peculiar fashion that tumbled her off her feet. She never regained them. This was what the on-looking huskies had waited for. They closed in upon her, snarling and yelping, and she was buried, screaming with agony, beneath the bristling mass of bodies.

Appendix F: Substantive Variants

1. "Black Jim" Chapter (1907 edition)

[In the 1920, 1925, and 1934 editions, this chapter has only small variations.]

A few months after Dandy died we had a new pet—this one, the most amusing and provoking creature that had entered the family.

The Morris boys were walking in the pinewood near Fairport one day, and I was trotting ahead of them, when I smelt something alive.

I sniffed about, and there crouching on a heap of pine needles was a featherless young crow.

I barked, and the boys hurried to pick up the poor creature. There were no old crows near-by, so they took it home with them.

It became Jack's pet, and soon it got old enough to follow him about. Jack fed him frogs, mice, worms, beef, and bread and milk, and soon the ugly young bird became a glossy creature with strong wings, a heavy beak, and a voice that used to make me jump when he stole up behind me as I lay sleeping in the sun.

"Our painful pleasure," Miss Laura used to call him, for though she loved him almost as much as her brothers did, he was a great worry to her.

He began by teasing the creatures about the place, especially with regard to their food, until most of them got to understand him so well that they would run if they saw him coming.

The guinea-pig, Jeff, and the rabbits would stick their heads out of the stable door, and if Black Jim—we had to call him this to distinguish him from Jim the dog—was in the garden, they would go back again. The tame rat always ran to his friend Bella the parrot, for Black Jim was afraid of her saucy tongue.

The pigeons and Willie's bantams hated him, for when they were all out in the garden feeding, he would swoop down among them, and send the pigeons flying and the bantams running with their legs sticking straight out behind them.

Then, with solemn crow satisfaction, he would eat their grain, taking on a hypocritical air of penitence when Miss Laura scolded him.

One day he played a shabby trick on Mary the cook. She had bought a fine steak, and it lay on a plate in the pantry window.

I saw Jim eyeing it from a tree, but before I really knew what was passing through his crow mind, he had swooped down, and had borne it up to the top of the stable.

Mary came into the pantry just in time to see it going, and her gestures and cries were so comical, as she ran out and looked up at Black Jim tearing the family dinner to pieces, that Miss Laura and the boys who had rushed to the windows, just shrieked with laughter.

Sometimes they did not laugh at his tricks. I saw him one day sneak up to Malta as she sat over her dinner out in the yard. You know cats eat slowly, and the way she mouthed her food, turning her head first on one side and then on the other, seemed to prove to the crow that she had something especially nice.

He made a quick run, nipped her by the tail, bracing himself on his sturdy legs, the way I had seen the Morrises' sailor-boy friend, Henry Smith, brace himself on his ship when he was hauling in a rope.

Malta began spitting and growling, and just as I was rushing to her rescue, she foolishly did what Black Jim wanted her to do—turned on him. He sprang forward, gobbled up a lot of food from the plate and flew off with it.

He got a severe scolding for this from Miss Laura, but he did not care. He flew away from her, and went into the house to Mr. Morris' study. He loved that room—there were so many pencils and pens about, and it was such fun to scatter the ink in the big ink-bottle.

I heard Mr. Morris say one day to Miss Laura, "That crow is out of his sphere. Could you not persuade him to join his wild kindred in the woods?"

"He is Jack's pet," she replied, "and though he has taken him to the woods, he always comes back."

"If Jack loves him we must put up with him," said Mr. Morris, and he patiently put all the small articles about the room into drawers.

About the best fun Black Jim had was with the table when it was laid for a meal. He carried away spoons, knives, forks, and napkin rings, and hid them under a piece of old carpet in the garden, where Jim the dog and I found them and carried them back to the house.

One day he got a great fright. He was carrying the table-bell in his beak when it rang.

He dropped it as if it had been red-hot, and flying to the top of the table, said "Caw! Caw!" a great many times.

He not only persecuted Mr. Morris in his study, but in his pulpit. He had a very sociable disposition, and when Sunday came, he wanted to go to church.

As soon as he could fly, he started down the street after the family. I barked warningly, but a crow is wilful, and won't mind any one. He was cunning enough to follow the Morrises at some distance, and when they came home, I heard them talking about his actions.

Just after they were all nicely seated in church, and Mr. Morris was giving out a hymn, the family, to their dismay, heard a friendly "Caw!" and looking up saw Black Jim in one of the open windows.

As soon as he discovered their pew he flew to it, as if to say, "How glad you must be to see me!"

They were not glad, and made frantic efforts to catch him, whereupon he scolded them in his harsh voice, flew to Mr. Morris in the pulpit, and perched on his shoulder with an air of "Here, at least, I shall be welcome."

Mr. Morris seeing his congregation in fits of suppressed laughter, had hard work to keep his composure, but he did so, and putting his hand in his pocket, offered Black Jim his gold pencil-case.

Thrown off his guard, the mischievous bird seized it with a grateful "Caw!" and Mr. Morris quickly put his hands over his wings and beckoned to Jack to come and get him.

After that Black Jim was locked up every Sunday morning for a time, but he got so cunning that he would not allow himself to be caught. Then Jack used to capture him Saturday evening, until finally, Black Jim became so knowing that he would not let Jack come near him any day toward the last of the week.

Mr. Morris had to put screens in the church windows at his own expense, but when the congregation heard of it, they refunded the money.

Black Jim by this time—we had had him nearly a year—had begun to plague the whole town, but he was so clever that everybody but a few cranky persons forgave him. He did such funny things that he became a celebrity, and it is wonderful what human beings will put up with from celebrities.

The housekeepers got to dread Mondays, for he visited the clotheslines far and near, and stealing the pins for his secret hoard, he let the different washes fly to the four winds of heaven.

One morning he did a very naughty thing, and yet great good came of it. Near the Morrises lived an old gentleman called Daniels who was a passionate lover of flowers. Black Jim often visited him, and would walk around his flower-beds and snip off blossoms here and there.

One would think that Mr. Daniels would hate him, but he did not. He said that birds do good service to man in destroying insect pests, and if Black Jim wished to break off a few flowers he might. He had plenty, and it would not hurt the plants to be pruned.

I used to call on the old man too, for most dogs love to visit their neighbors, but he never talked to me about his flowers, as he did to Black Jim. Perhaps he thought dogs did not care for them, but I could have assured him that dogs love strong-smelling things.

Well, one day he pointed to a large, beautiful flower in his conservatory, and said that it was a night-blooming cereus, and had come out a few hours earlier. This was early in the morning. He seemed very proud of it, and when he left us to speak to a man, I watched Black Jim anxiously.

He had his head on one side, and he was looking at this large beautiful flower. Unfortunately, the conservatory door was open, and before I could utter one bark, he had flown in, broken off the flower, and was carrying it off in his big beak.

I could have bitten him, I was so angry and disturbed about the honor of the family. However, I was powerless. I can keep cats, and dogs, and chickens in order, but birds are beyond me.

When Mr. Daniels came back, he did not perceive the theft of his lovely blossom, and I lay down on a heap of weeds and mourned about the sad conduct of Black Jim.

Then a very strange thing happened. While I lay on the weeds, and Mr. Daniels hoed about some plants, the garden gate opened, and another old man came hurrying up to Mr. Daniels.

Both his hands were stretched out. One held the flower that Black Jim had stolen, the other grasped Mr. Daniels' arm.

"Edward," he said in a choked voice, "will you forgive me?"

Mr. Daniels dropped his hoe, and stared at him in amazement.

The other old man extended the flower. "I know how you prize this, Edward—how you have waited for its blossoming—and to bestow on me your choicest bloom—it was noble, considering how I have used you."

Mr. Daniels stared in through the open conservatory door. His flower certainly was missing, but I could see that he could not imagine how it had got into the other old man's hand. However, he was pretty wise, and said nothing, but just shook hands in silence. Then they both acted as if they were ashamed of their emotion, and fell to talking of gardening matters.

I watched them for a while, then I ran home. There was a mystery there I could not fathom, but the explanation came. Before night, a pretty story was flying around town to the effect that a long-drawn-out quarrel between Mr. Daniels and his next door neighbor, Mr. Juniper, had been settled in a delightful way by Mr. Daniels, who had quietly stolen in, and laid on his friend's table the most highly prized flower in his possession.

Mr. Daniels said nothing, and I said nothing, and the rascal Black Jim said nothing, but after a time the true version of the story leaked out. I think some one had seen the crow on his way through the window of Mr. Juniper's house with the flower in his beak.

Anyway it was a great feather in Black Jim's cap, and after that no matter what mischief he did, every one forgave him, for had he not reconciled these two old enemies?

I saw him do a funny thing one day at a baseball game. A man who had some pears in his pocket reached one up to a chubby urchin who sat on a fence above him.

The boy was so young that he could not talk plainly, but he knew what was good to eat, for after one bite he half shut his eyes and said, "It am small, but it am 'lishus."

Black Jim, who attended all the ball games, heard him, and in one swoop he took that "'lishus" pear from the poor child.

The little urchin's astonishment was so ludicrous, that everybody near burst into roars of laughter, and the man gave him another pear.

Everybody knew Black Jim, and nearly everybody petted him. If Mrs. Morris or Miss Laura went downtown, he often followed them, and when they went into a store he perched near-by, cawing for them to come out.

He never allowed any one to touch him but members of the family. He would let them catch him, and shake him, or tickle him. Often when they were playing with him he would turn on his back, defending himself with his claws and beak, having as many tricks as a kitten.

He used to go to Mrs. Morris' grocer and catch mice for him, always getting some dainty in return. The butcher gave him choice morsels of meat, but the dressmaker never liked to see him, for he stole her thimbles and spools.

Nothing frightened him. Once he saw a big dog gnawing a bone. He flew right in his face. I ran up to distract the dog's attention, but there was no need of my interference, for the dog stood, muzzle in air, gazing foolishly at his bone sailing off over the housetops.

We got Black Jim in the spring, and before we had had him a year he became restless. After taking his daily bath that he fairly yelled for, if Jack did not give it to him, he would fly up to the stable roof, dress his feathers, and stare up into the sky.

One day he espied some wild crows passing overhead, and with a glad "Caw!" he flew up and joined them.

When night came he did not return, and I felt badly, for Jack was seeking his pet all over the neighborhood.

Animals and birds understand each other, but Jack was a human being, and I could not tell him that every drop of wild blood in Jim was calling out for his brother and sister crows.

Jack went to bed in great anxiety, for he feared that some mishap had befallen his pet.

We did not see him for a whole week. Then one day as Jack was standing in the garden, there was a rush of wings and Jim was on his shoulder, pinching his ear and thrusting his black face into his young master's, and talking about the joys of wild life.

I never saw Jack so pleased. He could not bear to part from his pet, and all day long he kept him with him, caressing him, and giving him choice bits of food.

Black Jim had a regular carnival of mischief on that visit. I remember for one thing, he called at all his downtown haunts, and court being in session, even got into the judge's private office through an open window.

He upset the judge's inkstand over some valuable legal documents, and flew off with his gold eyeglasses that were never seen again.

He soon disappeared. The first crow soaring overhead attracted him, and we did not see him for weeks.

On his second return he was more shy, and would not allow Jack to catch him. On his third, he sat on the stable roof and talked crow talk very earnestly.

There were several other returns, but he never again came down into the yard, and finally he became weaned away from us and never came back.

Sometimes the Morrises used to think he was dead, but I knew better. Jim was alive and well, and had a family of his own in the pinewood. He remembered the Morrises, and if any of the family went into the wood, he cawed affectionately, though he did not go near them.

2. Variant to the Introduction (1920 edition)

[In the 1920 edition, the original introduction was omitted. The following was added on the left flap of the book jacket.]

This is the story of a real dog which has become an animal classic that never grows old.

Beautiful Joe wasn't handsome when he started life, and the ill treatment of his first master did not improve his appearance. But he had a beautiful character and when he was taken into another home where there were other animals he had an adventurous and happy life.

The author became acquainted with Beautiful Joe when she was visiting friends and she admired and loved his sterling qualities. Upon her return to her home in Nova Scotia she wrote his own story as he might have told it himself, weaving into it the pets and the people of her own family.

There is a human quality running through all its descriptions of animal life that makes it intensely interesting, while with the story is combined much practical information on the care of household pets.

Beautiful Joe has brought pleasure to millions of readers, and you will enjoy it, too.

3. Bruno's Alternative Fate (1965 edition)

"Let me look at Bruno, Uncle John," said a soft voice from behind. It was my dear Miss Laura. Mr. Wood looked surprised. Then he shrugged.

"I warn you, Bruno is a vicious dog," said Mr. Wood as he led us to the large brown dog chained behind one of the sheds. "Be careful," he admonished as Miss Laura knelt beside the dog. He must have seen the love for all animals that showed in her eyes. He made no move to snap at her.

Slowly, ever so slowly, her hand crept near him; then she was stroking her coat; then she was running her fingers through his fur, touching his skin. The big dog flinched, but he kept looking steadily and somehow trustfully up into her kind face. Suddenly her fingers stopped. Bruno gave a howl of pain, a savage howl. Hastily Miss Laura got up.

"Have you looked over his coat recently, Uncle John?" she asked.

"Not since three weeks ago when he almost bit me."

Miss Laura looked down at the dog at her feet. "That must have been about the time when that wood tick started burrowing into his flesh. He has a nasty sore there now."

Mr. Wood shook his head. He scratched his nose. Then he said, "And to think I was about to kill that poor creature! I, who pride myself on my care and kindness to animals. You have proved to me, Miss Laura, something I have known all along yet needed to be reminded of, the wisdom of the old saying, 'One can never be too careful.' I shall tie up Bruno and remove the tick this morning."

The wood tick was removed later that morning, and for the rest of my stay there Bruno was a good-natured, well-behaved dog, and we became good friends.

Works Cited and Recommended Reading

Archival Sources

[The largest archival collection on Margaret Marshall Saunders—including the 1893 manuscript of *Beautiful Joe*—is in the Esther Clark Wright Archives of Acadia University (Wolfville, Nova Scotia). Other archives are available at the Marshall Saunders Sous-Fonds, Mount Allison University (Sackville, New Brunswick); the Edward Manning Saunders and Marshall Saunders Archive in the William Ready Division of Archives and Research Collections, McMaster University Library (Hamilton, Ontario); the Lorne and Edith Pierce Collection, Queen's University Archives (Kingston, Ontario); and the William Arthur Deacon Papers, Thomas Fisher Rare Book Library, University of Toronto (Toronto, Ontario).]

Margaret Marshall Saunders Fonds, Esther Clark Wright Archives, Acadia University, Wolfville, Nova Scotia, "Correspondence (1883-1896)" 1943.001-SAU/3

Banes, Charles H. Letter to Marshall Saunders. 9 April 1894.
Blaikie, John. Letter to Marshall Saunders. 17 February 1894.
——. Letter to Marshall Saunders. 28 February 1894.
Saunders, Margaret Marshall. Letter to Mary F. Lovell. 14 February 1894.
——. Letter to Charles H. Banes. 20 March 1894.

"Correspondence (1894-1925)" 1943.001-SAU/4

Coleman, Sydney H. Letter to Marshall Saunders. 15 March 1918.
Hubman, H.A. Letter to Marshall Saunders. 14 December 1922.
——. 21 February 1923.
Rice, Frank H. Letter to Marshall Saunders. 31 July 1923.
Rowland, A.J. Letter to Marshall Saunders. 15 March 1905.
——. Letter to T.F. Jarrold. 2 April 1898.
——. Letter to Mr. Lemen. 14 March 1904.
——. Letter to H.A. Hubman. 24 January 1923.

Other Archival Sources

Saunders, Margaret Marshall. "How I Began to Write." "Manuscript
    [19—?] Entitled How I Began to Write." 1943.001-SAU/24. Mar-
    garet Marshall Saunders Fonds, Esther Clark Wright Archives,
    Acadia University, Wolfville, Nova Scotia.
Saunders, Margaret Marshall. Letter to William A. Deacon. 19 Sep-
    tember 1936. William Arthur Deacon Papers, Box 22 (1893-
    1977), courtesy of the Thomas Fisher Rare Book Library, Univer-
    sity of Toronto, Toronto, Ontario.
——. Letter to [J.H. Ferguson]. 14 October 1938. Edward Manning
    Saunders and Marshall Saunders archive, William Ready Division
    of Archives and Research Collections, McMaster University
    Library, Hamilton, Ontario.

Editions of *Beautiful Joe*

Saunders, Margaret Marshall. *Beautiful Joe: An Autobiography*.
    Philadelphia: American Baptist Publication Society, 1894.
——. *Beautiful Joe: The Autobiography of a Dog*. London: Jarrold &
    Sons, 1895.
——. *Beautiful Joe's Paradise, or, the Island of Brotherly Love*. Boston:
    L.C. Page, 1902.
——. *Beautiful Joe*. Philadelphia: Griffith & Rowland, 1907.
——. *Beautiful Joe: A Dog's Own Story*. New York: Grosset & Dunlap,
    1920.
——. *Beautiful Joe*. New York: A.L. Burt, 1922.
——. *Beautiful Joe*. London: Jarrolds Pubs., 1925.
——. *Beautiful Joe: A Dog's Own Story*. Toronto: McClelland &
    Stewart, 1934.
——. *Beautiful Joe*. Racine: Whitman, 1965.
Currie, Quinn. *Beautiful Joe: The True Story of a Brave Dog by
    Marshall Saunders*. Seattle: Storytellers Ink, 1990.

Primary and Secondary Sources

Allen, E.W. *Experiment Record Station* 22. Washington, DC:
    Government Printing Office, 1910.
Allen, Elizabeth Akers. "A Hero in a Good Cause." *The Triangular
    Society: Leaves from the Life of a Portland Family*. Portland: Hoyt,
    Fogg & Donham, 1886. 162-68.
Amory, Cleveland. "Introduction." *Beautiful Joe: The True Story of a
    Brave Dog by Marshall Saunders*. Ed. Quinn Currie. Seattle:
    Storytellers Ink, 1990.

Angell, George T. *Autobiographical Sketches and Personal Recollections.* Boston: American Humane Education Society, 1884.

Angell, Oliver. *The Child's Fourth Book.* Philadelphia: E.H. Butler, 1888.

Avila, Jim. "USDA to Let Industry Self-Inspect Chicken." *ABCNews.com.* 18 April 2012.

Barclay, Eliza. "2013 Was the Year Bills to Criminalize Animal Cruelty Videos Failed." *NPR.org.* 27 December 2013.

Barnes, Earl. "Relation of Children to Animals." *Pennsylvania School Journal* 52 (1903): 161-64.

Barnum, P.T. *The Life of P.T. Barnum Written by Himself.* Buffalo: Courier, 1888.

Beard, DeAnna M. Toten. "'The Power of Woman's Influence': Nineteenth-Century Temperance Theatricality and the Drama of Nellie H. Bradley." *Theatre History Studies* (January 2006): 52-70.

"Beautiful Joe." *Sunday School Times* 36.14 (April 1894): 221.

Bederman, Gail. *Manliness and Civilization: A Cultural History of Gender and Race in the United States, 1880-1917.* Chicago: Chicago UP, 1995.

Beers, Diane L. *For the Prevention of Cruelty: The History and Legacy of Animal Rights Activism in the United States.* Athens: Swallow/Ohio UP, 2006.

Bender, Thomas. "Urbanization." *The Reader's Companion to American History.* Ed. Eric Foner and John A. Garraty. Boston: Houghton Mifflin, 1991. 1001-04.

Berdoe, Edward. "The Dog Hell of Paris." *Animals' Friend.* Ed. Sidney G. Trist. London: Offices of the Animals' Friend, 1897. 74-76.

"Bergh on Pasteur." *Maryland Medical Journal.* Ed. Thomas A. Ashby and Eugene F. Cordell. Baltimore: Journal Pub. Co., 1884.

Binderup, Barbara Lynn. "Letters of Margaret Marshall Saunders from 1893 to 1894." BA thesis, Acadia University, 1992.

Blakeley, Phyllis R. "Margaret Marshall Saunders: The Author of *Beautiful Joe.*" *Nova Scotia Historical Quarterly* 1.3 (September 1971): 225-39.

Bolenius, Emma Miller. *Advanced Lessons in Everyday English.* New York: American Book, 1921.

"Books and Authors." *Record of Christian Work* 13.3 (June 1894): 447.

"Books for Young Folks." *Books* 9.10 (December 1894): 164-72.

Browne, Junius Henri. *The Great Metropolis; a Mirror of New York.* Hartford: American Pub. Co., 1869.

Brunton, T. Lauder. Letter. *Contemporary Review* 41 (January-June 1882): 897-98.

Bucke, W. Fowler. "Cyno-Psychoses: Children's Thoughts, Reactions, and Feelings Toward Pet Dogs." *Pedagogical Seminary* 10 (1903): 459-512.

Canfield, Dorothy. "Pets." *What Shall We Do Now?: A Book of Suggestions for Children's Games and Employments.* New York: Frederick A. Stokes, 1907.

Carlson, Cody. "The Ag-Gag Laws: Hiding Factory Farm Abuses from Public Scrutiny." *Atlantic.com.* 20 March 2012.

Carroll, A.L. "An Apology for Dogs." *Harper's New Monthly* 35 (June-November 1867): 191-92.

Carswell, Lilian P. "Telling the Truth about Animals: Epistemology, Ethics, and Animal Minds in Melville, Darwin, Saunders, and London." PhD dissertation, Columbia University, 2004.

Cash, K.G. "Children's Pets: A Side Study." *Studies in Education* 2. Ed. Earl Barnes. Philadelphia: n.p., 1902. 100-07.

Cavallo, Dominick. *Muscles and Morals: Organized Playgrounds and Urban Reform, 1880-1920.* Philadelphia: U Pennsylvania P, 1981.

Clark, John S., Mary Dana Hicks, and Walter S. Perry. "Love of Animals." *Teacher's Manual Part I for The Prang Elementary Course in Art Instruction.* Boston: Prang Educational, 1898. 133.

Cobbe, Frances Power. "Vivisection and Its Two-Faced Advocates." *Contemporary Review* 41 (January-June 1882): 610-26.

—— and Benjamin Bryan. *Vivisection in America: How It Is Taught, How It Is Practiced.* London: Swan, Sonnenschein, 1890.

Cordell, Ryan C. "'Enslaving You, Body and Soul': The Uses of Temperance in Uncle Tom's Cabin and 'Anti-Tom' Fiction." *Studies in American Fiction* 36.1 (Spring 2008): 3-26.

Cosslett, Tess. *Talking Animals in British Children's Fiction, 1786-1914.* London: Ashgate, 2006.

Cox, Samuel. "How to Take a Bird's Nest." *The Bird's Nest and Other Sermons for Children of All Ages.* New York: Thomas Whittaker, 1888. 1-15.

"Crank." *Slang and Its Analogues Past and Present.* Ed. John S. and William Ernest Henley Farmer. n.p.: Printed for subscribers only, 1891.

"Cruel Cases." *Our Dumb Animals* 6.12 (May 1874): 108.

"Cruelty to Animals—First Case of Punishment under the New Law." *New York Times.* 13 April 1866.

Dana, Charles L. "The Zoophil-Psychosis: A Modern Malady." *Medical Record* 75 (January-June 1909): 381-83.

"Dana, Charles Loomis." *National Cyclopedia of American Biography.* XIII. New York: James T. White, 1906.

Darwin, Charles. *On the Origin of Species by Means of Natural Selection.* London: John Murray, 1859.

Davies, Gwendolyn. "Margaret Marshall Saunders: Making Regionalism International." *Literature of Region and Nation.* Vol. 2. Ed. Winnifred Bogaards. Saint John: U of New Brunswick, 1998.

———. *Margaret Marshall Saunders: Education through Fiction.* Truro: Nova Scotia Teachers College, 1995.

———. "Marshall Saunders and the Urbanization of the Animal." *Other Selves: Animals in the Canadian Literary Imagination.* Ottawa: U Ottawa P, 2007. 170-83.

"Death of Miss Eva Lückes." *Medical Record* 95 (4 January to 18 June 1919): 495-96.

DeMello, Margo. *Speaking for Animals: Animal Autobiographical Writing.* New York: Routledge, 2013.

Dickens, Charles. *Pictures from Italy and American Notes for General Circulation.* London: Chapman and Hall, 1866.

Dolan, Elizabeth A. *Seeing Suffering in Women's Literature of the Romantic Era.* Aldershot: Ashgate, 2008.

"Drowning the Dogs." *New York Times.* 8 July 1877.

Eberhart, Alvin George. "Children's Pets." *Everything about Dogs.* Camp Dennison, Ohio: Eberhart Kennels, 1902. 192-93.

Eddy, Sarah J. *Songs of Happy Life: For Schools, Homes and Bands of Mercy.* Providence, RI: Art and Nature Study, 1897.

"Editorial Notes." *McMaster University Monthly* 3 (June 1893 to May 1894): 224-26.

"Electric Cages for Animals." *National Humane Review* 7.2 (February 1919): 37.

Elias, Edith L. *Abraham Lincoln.* New York: Frederick A. Stokes, 1920.

Emanuel, Walter. *A Dog Day, or The Angel in the House.* New York: E.P. Dutton, 1919.

"Encore." *OED Online.* Oxford UP. March 2014.

Enoch, Jessica. *Refiguring Rhetorical Education: Women Teaching African American, Native American, and Chicano/a Students.* Carbondale: Southern Illinois P, 2008.

Fennell, C.A.M. *Stanford Dictionary of Anglicised Words and Phrases.* Cambridge: Cambridge UP, 1892.

Ferguson, Moira. "Breaking in Englishness: Black Beauty and the Politics of Gender, Race and Class." *Women* 5.1 (1994): 34-52.

"Fiction." *Literature, The American Edition.* New York: Harper & Bros., 1898. 675-76.

"Fisher, Dorothy Canfield." *Notable American Women: The Modern Period.* Ed. Barbara and Carol Hurd Green Sicherman. Cambridge, MA: Radcliffe College, 1980. 235-37.

Fleming, George. *Vivisection: A Prize Essay.* Philadelphia: Women's Branch of the Pennsylvania Society for the Prevention of Cruelty to Animals, 1871.

Foster, Michael. "Vivisection." *Popular Science Monthly* (April 1874): 672-85.

Francione, Gary. *Introduction to Animal Rights: Your Child or the Dog?* New York: Little, Brown, 2009.

French, Richard D. *Antivivisection and Medical Science in Victorian Society*. Princeton: Princeton UP, 1975.

Fudge, Erica. *Pets*. Stocksfield, UK: Acumen, 2008.

Gerson, Carole. "Canadian Women Writers and American Markets, 1880-1940." *Context North America: Canadian/U.S. Literary Relations*. Ottawa: U Ottawa P, 1994. 107-18.

Glover, H. Clay. *Diseases of the Dog and How to Feed*. New York: Westminster Kennel Club, 1897.

Gordon, Elizabeth Putnam. *Women Torch-Bearers: The Story of the Women's Christian Temperance Union*. Evanston, IL: National Women's Christian Temperance Union, 1924.

Gottlieb, Richard. *Forcing the Spring: The Transformation of the American Environmental Movement*. Washington, DC: Island P, 2005.

Graham, J.C. "Animal Stories Best Suited for Children." *Wisconsin Journal of Education* 40.1 (January 1908): 100.

Grier, Katherine C. *Pets in America: A History*. New York: Harvest, 2006.

Hall, Granville Stanley. *Adolescence: Its Psychology and Its Relations to Physiology, Anthropology, Sociology, Sex, Crime, Religion and Education*. New York: D. Appleton, 1905.

Haralson, Eric L. "Mars in Petticoats: Longfellow and Sentimental Masculinity." *Nineteenth-Century Literature* 51.3 (1996): 327-55.

Harde, Roxanne. "'Better Friends': Marshall Saunders Writing Humane Education and Envisioning Animal Rights." *Jeunesse* 1.2 (Winter 2009): 85-108.

Harkins, Edward F. and C.H.L. Johnston. "Marshall Saunders." *Little Pilgrimages Among the Women Who Have Written Famous Books*. Boston: L.C. Page, 1902. 173-89.

Harris, Luther S. *Around Washington Square: An Illustrated History of Greenwich Village*. Baltimore: Johns Hopkins UP, 2003.

Hartness, Eli. "Pets and Their Long Life." *Old and New* 6 (July 1872 to January 1873): 297-304.

Heider, Carmen. "Suffrage, Self-Determination, and the Women's Christian Temperance Union in Nebraska, 1879-1882." *Rhetoric & Public Affairs* 8 (Spring 2005): 85-107.

"Henry Bergh as Don Quixote." *Capital Stories About Famous Americans: A Budget of Tales of Love, Heroism, and Adventure on Land and Sea*. Ed. Rev. Louis Albert Banks. New York: Christian Herald, 1905. 66-77.

Hinkle, Lynda L. "'Where No Human Aid Is Possible,' Or Is It? How the Temperance Movement and Suffrage Movement Changed the Family." *MP Journal* 2.6 (February 2010): 116-34.

"The Home Angel." *American Home Magazine*. Chicago: American Fashion Co., 1897. 17.

Horn, Paul Whitfield and Edwin DuBois Shurter. *New American Readers Book 4*. Boston: Ginn, 1919.

Horton, W.K. "The Humane Destruction of Small Animals." *Our Dumb Animals* 44.6 (November 1911): 85.

"Household Pets." *Good Housekeeping* 6 (12 November 1887 to 28 April 1888): 82.

Howard, Dorothy. "Marshall Saunders: A Tribute to Canada's Most Revered Author." *Saturday Night* 82.26 (March 1947): 21.

Hubbard, F. Morse. *Prevention of Cruelty to Animals in the States of Illinois, Colorado, and California*. New York: Columbia UP, 1916.

"Humane." *OED Online*. Oxford University Press, March 2014.

Humphry, G.M. *Vivisection: What Good Has It Done?* London: J.W. Kolckmann, 1882.

Hurren, Elizabeth T. *Dying for Victorian Medicine: English Anatomy and Its Trade in the Dead Poor, 1834-1929*. Houndmills: Palgrave Macmillan, 2012.

Hutcheson, Philo A. "Eliot, Charles William." *American National Biography Online*.

Jalonick, Mary Clare. "USDA Poultry Inspections Could Get Streamlined, Saving $95 Million." *Huffington Post*. 20 January 2012.

Johnston, Robert M. "'The Least of the Commandments': Deuteronomy 22:6-7 in Rabbinic Judaism and Early Christianity." *Andrews University Seminary Studies* 20.3 (Autumn 1982): 205-15.

Kean, Hilda. *Animal Rights: Political and Social Change in Britain Since 1800*. London: Reaktion, 1998.

Keller, Helen. *The Story of My Life*. New York: Doubleday, Page & Co., 1903.

Lane, Marion and Stephen Zawistowski. *Heritage of Care: The American Society for the Prevention of Cruelty to Animals*. Santa Barbara, California: Praeger, 2007.

Langille, Jacqueline Dawn. "Letters From 1894 to 1906 from the Marshall Saunders Collection of the Acadia University Esther Clark Wright Archives." MA thesis, Acadia University, 1993.

Lansbury, Coral. *The Old Brown Dog: Women, Workers, and Vivisection in Edwardian England*. Madison: U Wisconsin P, 1985.

Le Rossignol, James E. "The Training of Animals." *American Journal of Psychology* 5 (1892): 205-13.

Lederer, Susan E. *Subjected to Science: Human Experimentation in*

America before the Second World War. Baltimore: Johns Hopkins UP, 1997.

Ledger, Sally and Alison C. Ledger. *The New Woman: Fiction and Feminism at the Fin de Siècle.* Manchester: Manchester UP, 1997.

Lee, Rawdon. *A History and Description of the Collie or Sheep Dog in His British Varieties.* London: Horace Cox, 1890.

Levenstein, Harvey. *Revolution at the Table: The Transformation of the American Diet.* New York: Oxford UP, 1988.

Lloyd, Richard. "Urbanization and the Southern United States." *Annual Review of Sociology* 38 (August 2012): 483-506.

London, Jack. *The Call of the Wild.* New York: Grosset & Dunlap, 1903.

——. "The Other Animals." *The Wild Animal Story.* Ed. Ralph H. Lutts. Philadelphia: Temple UP, 1998. 199-210.

Lossing, Benson J. *History of New York City.* Vol. 2. New York: Perine Engraving, 1884.

Lückes, Eva C.E. "Children and Pets." *Babyhood* 3.25 (December 1886): 4-7.

Mangum, Teresa. "Narrative Dominion or The Animals Write Back? Animal Genres in Literature and the Arts." *A Cultural History of Animals in the Age of Empire.* Ed. Kathleen Kete. New York: Berg, 2007. 153-74.

Marsh, Mabel A. "Children and Animals." *Studies in Education* 2 (1902): 83-99.

McCabe, James D. *Lights and Shadows of New York Life; or, the Sights and Sensations of the Great City.* Philadelphia: National Pub. Co., 1875.

McHugh, Susan. *Dog.* London: Reaktion, 2004.

McSpadden, J. Walker. *The Story of Abraham Lincoln.* New York: Barse & Hopkins, 1922.

Meggs, Phillip B. and Alston W. Purvis. *History of Graphic Design.* Hoboken, NJ: John Wiley, 2012.

Melvill, Henry. "Sermon VIII. The Bird's Nest." *Sermons on Certain of the Less Prominent Facts and References.* New York: Stanford and Swords, 1845. 65-72.

Miller, Hugh [Mrs.]. *Stories of the Dog and His Cousins.* London: T. Nelson & Sons, 1876.

Morse, Deborah Denenholz. "Unforgiven: Drunken Mothers in Hesba Stretton's Religious Tract Society and Scottish Temperance League Fiction." *Other Mothers: Beyond the Maternal Ideal.* Ed. Ellen Bayuk Rosenman and Claudia C. Klaver. Columbus: Ohio State UP, 2008. 101-24.

Morse, W.F. "The Humane and Sanitary Disposal of Superfluous Animal Life." *American Journal of Public Health* 3.7 (July 1913): 1226-34.

Mount, Nick. *When Canadian Literature Moved to New York*. Toronto: Toronto UP, 2005.

"Mr. Bergh's Good Work." *New York Times*. 18 July 1874.

Myers, O. Gene. *The Significance of Children and Animals: Social Development and Our Connections to Other Species*. West Lafayette, IN: Purdue UP, 2007.

Nielsen, Kim E. *The Radical Lives of Helen Keller*. New York: NYUP, 2004.

Niven, Charles D. *History of the Humane Movement*. New York: Transatlantic Arts, 1967.

"No title." *Babyhood* 3.26 (January 1887): 43.

Norman, Jessica. "Transcriptions of the Documents Dated 1906-1914 in the Margaret Marshall Saunders Fonds." Research project, Acadia University, June 2008.

O'Connor, Stephen. *Orphan Trains: The Story of Charles Loring Brace and the Children He Saved and Failed*. Chicago: U Chicago UP, 2004.

Oppel, Jr., Richard A. "Taping of Farm Cruelty is Becoming the Crime." *New York Times*. 6 April 2013.

"Orange, the ASPCA's Official Color." *ASPCA.org*. 2014.

Oshinsky, David. "Temperance to Excess." *New York Times*. 21 May 2010.

Otis, Laura, ed. *Literature and Science in the Nineteenth Century: An Anthology*. Oxford: Oxford UP, 2002.

"Our Book Table." *Chinese Recorder and Missionary Journal* 39 (1908): 44-51.

Pacyga, Dominic A. "Chicago: Slaughterhouse to the World." *Meat, Modernity, and the Rise of the Slaughterhouse*. Ed. Paula Young Lee. Durham: U New Hampshire P, 2008. 153-97.

Palmer, Lena. "Vivisection." *New York Medical Times* 16 (1889): 375-76.

Patteson, S. Louise. *Pussy Meow: The Autobiography of a Cat*. Philadelphia: George W. Jacobs & Co., 1901.

Perkins, David. "Human Mouseness: Burns and Compassion for Animals." *Texas Studies in Literature and Language* 42.1 (Spring 2000): 1-15.

———. *Romanticism and Animal Rights*. Cambridge: Cambridge UP, 2003.

Philpott, Tom. "USDA Ruffles Feathers with New Poultry Inspection Policy." *MotherJones.com*. 24 April 2013.

Pomeroy, Elsie. "Memories of Marshall Saunders." *Maritime Advocate and Busy East* (April 1955): 15-18.

Potter, Mary Sweet. "Our Domestic Animals." *Good Housekeeping* 9.13 (October 1889): 38.

"Purina Calf Chow. Advertisement." *The Country Gentleman* 84 (1919).

Purina Cow Book: The A-B-C of Milk Making. Columbus, Ohio: W.A. Rice, 1921.

"Questions for Anti-Vivisectionists." *Medical World* 15 (1897): 310.

Rankin, Jean Sherwood. *Everyday English Book One: Language Lessons for Intermediate Grades.* Boston: Educational Pub. Co, 1902.

Raymond-Mallock, Lillian C. *Toy Dogs.* Battlecreek, MI: Dogdom Pub. Co., 1907.

Reform Advocate (28 August 1915): 88.

Regin, Ernest Sol. "A Word About Dog-Collars." *Outing* 12.1 (1888): 261-65.

Reinalda, Bob. *Routledge History of International Organizations, from 1815 to the Present Day.* New York: Routledge, 2009.

Richardson, Angelique and Chris Willis, eds. *The New Woman in Fiction and in Fact: Fin-de-siècle Feminisms.* London: Palgrave Macmillan, 2001.

Riis, Jacob A. *How the Other Half Lives.* New York: Charles Scribner's Sons, 1890.

Ritvo, Harriet. *The Animal Estate: The English and Other Creatures in the Victorian Age.* Cambridge: Harvard UP, 1987.

Roberts, Charles G.D. "The Animal Story." *The Kindred of the Wild: A Book of Animal Life.* Boston: L.C. Page & Co., 1903. 15-29.

Rydge, John. *A Complete Guide to the Cure of All Diseases Incident to Horses, Cattle, Sheep, and Dogs.* London: Clerc Smith, 1827.

Sanders, Karen E. "Margaret Marshall Saunders: Children's Literature as an Expression of Early Twentieth Century Social Reform." Master's thesis, Dalhousie University, 1978.

Saunders, Margaret Marshall. "The Story of My Life." *Ontario Library Review* 2.2 (1927): 42.

Searson, J.W. and George E. Martin. *Studies in Reading.* Chicago: University Pub. Co., 1913.

Seton, Ernest Thompson. *Krag, the Kootenay Ram.* New York: Charles Scribner's Sons, 1897.

———. *Krag and Johnny Bear.* New York: Charles Scribner's Sons, 1906.

Sewell, Anna. *Black Beauty: His Grooms and Companions.* London: Jarrold & Sons, 1877.

Shepard, Charles H. "Hydrophobia." *JAMA* 29.17 (23 October 1897): 824-28.

Shevelow, Kathryn. *For the Love of Animals: The Rise of the Animal Protection Movement.* New York: Henry Holt, 2008.

Showalter, Elaine. *Daughters of Decadence: Women Writers of the Fin-de-Siècle*. New Brunswick: Rutgers UP, 1993.

"Special Meeting." *Annual Reports of the President and Treasurer of Harvard College, 1892–93*. Cambridge: Harvard UP, 1894.

Stables, William Gordon. *Sable & White: The Autobiography of a Show Dog*. London: Jarrold & Sons, 1893.

Stoneley, Peter. "Sentimental Emasculations: *Uncle Tom's Cabin* and *Black Beauty*." *Nineteenth-Century Literature* 54.1 (January 1999): 53-72.

Stowe, Harriet Beecher. *My Wife and I*. Cambridge: Riverside, 1871.

Tagg, John. *The Burden of Representation: Essays on Photographies and Histories*. Minneapolis: U Minnesota P, 1988.

Tahmincioglu, Eve. "Remember the Milkman? In Some Places, He's Back." *New York Times*. 16 December 2007.

Thomas, Keith. *Man and the Natural World: A History of the Modern Sensibility*. New York: Pantheon Books, 1983.

Tibbey, Thomas G. "Branch Reports." *The Paidologist* 2.2 (July 1900): 103-05.

Tooley, Sarah A. *The History of Nursing in the British Empire*. London: S.H. Bousfield, 1906.

Tuan, Yi-Fu. *Dominance and Affection: The Making of Pets*. New Haven: Yale UP, 1984.

Turner, James. *Reckoning with the Beast: Animals, Pain, and Humanity in the Victorian Mind*. Baltimore: Johns Hopkins UP, 1984.

"Urbanization." *The American Economy: A Historical Encyclopedia*. Ed. Cynthia L. Clarke. Santa Barbara: ABC-CLIO, 2011.

Washington, Harriet A. *Medical Apartheid: The Dark History of Medical Experimentation on Black Americans from Colonial Times to the Present*. New York: Harlem Moon, 2006.

Waterston, Elizabeth. "Margaret Marshall Saunders: A Voice for the Silent." *Silenced Sextet: Six Nineteenth-Century Canadian Women Novelists*. Ed. Lorraine McMullen, Carrie MacMillan, and Elizabeth Waterston. Montreal: McGill-Queen's UP, 1993. 137-68.

Wheeler, Daniel E. *Abraham Lincoln*. New York: Macmillan, 1921.

Whipple, Wayne. *The Story-Life of Lincoln: A Biography Composed of Five Hundred True Stories*. Philadelphia: John C. Winston Co., 1908.

White, Caroline E. *An Answer to Dr. Keen's Address Entitled "Our Recent Debts to Vivisection."* Philadelphia: American Society for the Restriction of Vivisection, 1886.

Whitlock, Brand. *Abraham Lincoln*. Boston: Small, Maynard & Co., 1916.

Williams, Samuel. "Reporting the Great Murder Trial." *Pearson's Magazine* 7.4 (April 1907): 625-27.

Wolfe, Cary. "In the Shadow of Wittgenstein's Lion." *Zoontologies: The Question of the Animal Minneapolis.* Ed. Cary Wolfe. Minneapolis: U Minnesota P, 2003. 1-57.

Wyett, Jody L. "The Lap of Luxury: Lapdogs, Literature, and Social Meaning in the 'Long' Eighteenth Century." *LIT* 10.4 (March 2000): 275-301.

Yeo, Gerald F. Letter. *Contemporary Review* 41 (January to June 1882): 898.

Zapoleon, L.B. *Inedible Animal Fats in the United States.* Stanford: Stanford UP, 1929.

from the publisher

A name never says it all, but the word "broadview" expresses a good deal of the philosophy behind our company. We are open to a broad range of academic approaches and political viewpoints. We pay attention to the broad impact book publishing and book printing has in the wider world; we began using recycled stock more than a decade ago, and for some years now we have used 100% recycled paper for most titles. As a Canadian-based company we naturally publish a number of titles with a Canadian emphasis, but our publishing program overall is internationally oriented and broad-ranging. Our individual titles often appeal to a broad readership too; many are of interest as much to general readers as to academics and students.

Founded in 1985, Broadview remains a fully independent company owned by its shareholders—not an imprint or subsidiary of a larger multinational.

If you would like to find out more about Broadview and about the books we publish, please visit us at **www.broadviewpress.com**. And if you'd like to place an order through the site, we'd like to show our appreciation by extending a special discount to you: by entering the code below you will receive a 20% discount on purchases made through the Broadview website.

Discount code: **broadview20%**

Thank you for choosing Broadview.

Please note: this offer applies only to sales of bound books within the United States or Canada.